MACMILLAN MASTER GUIDES

GENERAL EDITOR: JAMES GIBSON

MACMILLAN MASTER GUIDES

WILLIAM SHAKESPEARE	*cont.*	*A Midsummer Night's Dream* Kenneth Pickering
		Henry IV Part I Helen Morris
		Romeo and Juliet Helen Morris
		The Tempest Kenneth Pickering
GEORGE BERNARD SHAW		*St Joan* Leonée Ormond
RICHARD SHERIDAN		*The School for Scandal* Paul Ranger
		The Rivals Jeremy Rowe
JOHN WEBSTER		*The White Devil* and *The Duchess of Malfi* David A. Male

Forthcoming

JANE AUSTEN	*Sense and Sensibility* Judy Simons
SAMUEL BECKETT	*Waiting for Godot* Jennifer Birkett
WILLIAM BLAKE	*Songs of Innocence* and *Songs of Experience* Alan Tomlinson
GEOFFREY CHAUCER	*The Pardoner's Tale* Geoff Lester
	The Wife of Bath's Tale Nicholas Marsh
	The Knight's Tale Anne Samson
T.S. ELIOT	*Murder in the Cathedral* Paul Lapworth
HENRY FIELDING	*Joseph Andrews* Trevor Johnson
E.M. FORSTER	*Howards End* Ian Milligan
THOMAS HARDY	*The Mayor of Casterbridge* Ray Evans
GERARD MANLEY HOPKINS	*Selected Poems* R. Watt
BEN JONSON	*Volpone* Michael Stout
JOHN KEATS	*Selected Poems* John Garrett
HARPER LEE	*To Kill a Mockingbird* Jean Armstrong
ARTHUR MILLER	*Death of a Salesman* Peter Spalding
WILLIAM SHAKESPEARE	*Richard II* Charles Barber
	Henry V Peter Davison
	Twelfth Night Edward Leeson
	As You Like It Kiernan Ryan
ALFRED TENNYSON	*In Memoriam* Richard Gill

Further titles are in preparation

MACMILLAN MASTER GUIDES

SONS AND LOVERS

BY D.H. LAWRENCE

R. P. DRAPER

MACMILLAN
EDUCATION

First edition 1986

Published by
MACMILLAN EDUCATION LTD
Houndmills, Basingstoke, Hampshire RG21 2XS
and London
Companies and representatives
throughout the world

Printed in Hong Kong

British Library Cataloguing in Publication Data
Draper, R. P.
Sons and lovers by D.H. Lawrence. —
(Macmillan master guides)
1. Lawrence, D. H. Sons and lovers
I. Title   II. Lawrence, D. H. Sons and
lovers
823′.912   PR6023.A9356
ISBN 0-333-41673-2 Pbk
ISBN 0-333-41674-0 Pbk/export

CONTENTS

GENERAL EDITOR'S PREFACE

The aim of the Macmillan Master Guides is to help you to appreciate the book you are studying by providing information about it and by suggesting ways of reading and thinking about it which will lead to a fuller understanding. The section on the writer's life and background has been designed to illustrate those aspects of the writer's life which have influenced the work, and to place it in its personal and literary context. The summaries and critical commentary are of special importance in that each brief summary of the action is followed by an examination of the significant critical points. The space which might have been given to repetitive explanatory notes has been devoted to a detailed analysis of the kind of passage which might confront you in an examination. Literary criticism is concerned with both the broader aspects of the work being studied and with its detail. The ideas which meet us in reading a great work of literature, and their relevance to us today, are an essential part of our study, and our Guides look at the thought of their subject in some detail. But just as essential is the craft with which the writer has constructed his work of art, and this may be considered under several technical headings – characterisation, language, style and stagecraft, for example.

The authors of these Guides are all teachers and writers of wide experience, and they have chosen to write about books they admire and know well in the belief that they can communicate their admiration to you. But you yourself must read and know intimately the book you are studying. No one can do that for you. You should see this book as a lamp-post. Use it to shed light, not to lean against. If you know your text and know what it is saying about life, and how it says it, then you will enjoy it, and there is no better way of passing an examination in literature.

JAMES GIBSON

ACKNOWLEDGEMENTS

Cover illustration: *Ennui* by Walter Sickert. Courtesy of the Bridgeman
Art Gallery.

1 D.H. LAWRENCE : LIFE AND BACKGROUND

David Herbert Lawrence was born on 11 September 1885, at Eastwood, a mining village seven miles north-west of Nottingham, on the borders of Nottinghamshire and Derbyshire. The area is now more built up than it was in Lawrence's day; at the end of the nineteenth century it was still very much a mixture of industrial and rural England. In his essay, 'Nottingham and the Mining Countryside' – which was written towards the end of Lawrence's life, and remains the best introduction to him and his background – he says of this area: 'To me it seemed, and still seems, an extremely beautiful countryside . . . To me, as a child and a young man, it was still the old England of the forest and agricultural past; there were no motor-cars, the mines were, in a sense, an accident in the landscape, and Robin Hood and his merry men were not very far away.'

His father, Arthur Lawrence, was a coal-miner at the near-by Brinsley pit, and his mother, Lydia (her maiden name was Beardsall), had been a school-teacher at Sheerness, in Essex, before she came to Nottingham and met her future husband. They were strongly contrasted characters, like Mr and Mrs Morel in *Sons and Lovers*, who are closely based on Lawrence's own parents. Arthur was a handsome, black-bearded man, an excellent dancer and a lively, attractive talker, though uneducated and throughout his life virtually illiterate. Like his fellow-colliers he drank a lot, as he needed to do in order to replace the fluid that was sweated out of him by his heavy manual labour at the pit face. On his marriage he 'took the pledge', that is, he swore an oath to give up alcohol, but it was not long before he returned to his former drinking habits, which became a source of frequent quarrelling between him and his wife. Lydia came from very different stock. Her father, George Beardsall, was 'fiercely religious' and 'a noted preacher who often took over the Wesleyan pulpit' (Harry T. Moore: *The Priest of Love*), and she inherited something of his disposition. Though married to a collier, she never blended with the mining community. As Lawrence wrote in his 'Autobiographical Sketch', she was 'superior' and a member really of 'the lower bourgeoisie'. The father's natural language was the Nottinghamshire and Derbyshire dialect with its archaic 'thee' and 'tha' (thou), but the mother 'spoke King's English, without an accent, and never in her life could even imitate a sentence of the dialect which my father spoke, and which we children spoke out of doors.' (*Phoenix II*)

The Lawrences had five children (three boys and two girls), but Mrs Lawrence was determined that they should not lead ordinary working-class lives. The eldest one, Earnest, was clever, athletic and got on exceptionally well in his business career, but, like the William of *Sons and Lovers*, fell in love with an unsuitably shallow girl and died at the age of twenty-three. All Mrs Lawrence's devotion and ambition were then focused on David Herbert. He won a scholarship to the leading boys' school in Nottingham, the High School, and on leaving school at the age of 16 obtained a job as a clerk in the Nottingham firm of Haywood's, manufacturers of surgical goods. His health was never very good, however, and after only a few months he succumbed to an attack of pneumonia which, he later declared, damaged his health for life. On recovering he did not return to Haywood's but became an uncertificated teacher, first at the local school in Eastwood and then in the town of Ilkeston, just across the border in Derbyshire.

Before he fell ill Lawrence had already made the acquaintance of the Chambers family who ran a small holding called 'The Haggs' in the country-side just to the north of Eastwood. This provided the inspiration for Willey Farm in the novel. During his convalescence he was taken there on a number of occasions to help him to get better, and his relationship with Mr and Mrs Chambers and their children deepened into a love of the whole family and the farm and all the countryside round about. The Haggs became one of the most important and formative experiences of his life, as he fully recognised in a letter written when he had been living abroad for a decade or more, to the youngest member of the family, David Chambers (who later became a professor at Nottingham University):

> Whatever I forget, I shall never forget the Haggs – I loved it so. I loved to come to you all, it really was a new life began in me there . . . Oh, I'd love to be nineteen again, and coming up through the Warren and catching the first glimpse of the buildings . . . If there is anything I can ever do for you, do tell me. – Because whatever else I am, I am somewhere still the same Bert who rushed with such joy to the Haggs (14 November 1982).

He was very fond of the sons and had a particularly close friendship with the eldest, Alan, but it was one of the daughters, Jessie (the fictional 'Miriam'), who in due course meant the most to him. Their youthful love-affair is one of the major themes of *Sons and Lovers*, though one should be wary of regarding the Paul–Miriam story as an accurate reflection of what took place between David Herbert and Jessie. One should read Jessie's own version in her fascinating memoir, *D. H. Lawrence, A Personal*

Record, which she published in 1935 under the initials 'ET'. Of course, that, too, should not be read uncritically; it needs to be yet further balanced by the memoirs of other people who knew both her and Lawrence, some of which are published in the *Composite Biography* edited by Edward Nehls, and in the second edition of Jessie's book, edited by her brother, David, in 1965.

Lawrence now seemed to be developing a career in education. At first his status was that of a 'pupil-teacher', i.e. he taught classes of younger pupils, while himself receiving more advanced instruction – from 1903–4 at the newly opened Pupil-Teacher Centre in Ilkeston. There he proved to be a brilliant scholar, and at the end of 1904 he came first in a nationwide examination which enabled him, subsequently, to enter what was then the University College of Nottingham to undertake full-time study for the teaching profession. On gaining his certificate in 1908 he was appointed as a schoolmaster at a boys' school in Croydon, in the suburbs of south London.

It was while studying at University College that Lawrence began his career as a writer. Some time in 1907 he started work on his first novel, *The White Peacock*, which, like *Sons and Lovers*, is set in his home background and draws especially on his knowledge of the countryside around the Haggs. He also began writing poetry. Jessie was deeply interested in all his work, and it was she above all who encouraged him and urged him to exercise his talent. In 1909 she sent some of his poems to one of the London literary journals, *The English Review*, whose editor, Ford Madox Ford, was sufficiently impressed to accept them for publication and to wish to meet Lawrence, who later commented: 'The girl had launched me, so easily, on my literary career, like a princess cutting a thread, launching a ship.'

However, Lawrence's affair with Jessie was not going well. A terse note in the first of the two 'autobiographical sketches' in *Phoenix II* reads: 'Already the intense physical dissatisfaction with Miriam'. He had always enjoyed a wide variety of friendships with girls, and he flirted with many of them even while regarding Jessie as his true sweetheart. In 1909–10 he began to form a relationship with Louie Burrows, a fellow-student at Ilkeston and University College, which led to his proposing marriage to her, suddenly and without premeditation, as he claimed, in a railway train. The engagement lasted for a little over one year; but the same sexual tensions which had beset the affair with Jessie influenced this one, too, and were made worse by financial and prudential considerations which Lawrence found it hard to bear. While teaching at Croydon he was also involved in an affair with Helen Corke, who had herself been caught up in an affair with a married man who committed suicide. This story provided Lawrence with the material for his second novel, *The Trespasser* (1912), in which the heroine, like the figure who appears in the 'Helen' poems, is a 'dreaming woman', consuming her lover's spirit, but leaving his body unsatisfied.

But Lawrence's most serious psychological problem was that posed by his relationship with his mother. She was the woman 'whom he loved best on earth', and he could not form a bond with anyone else which compared in passion and commitment with what he felt for her. In August 1910 she became ill with cancer, and she dragged through a painful period of suffering till her death on 9 December. This was the time when he proposed to Louie, and his sudden, unpredictable behaviour perhaps reflected his disturbed state of mind. Some indication of how he was feeling is to be found in a letter he wrote on 3 December 1910, to Rachel Annand Taylor, a minor poet whom he made his confidante for a while. After describing the opposition between his mother and father, in terms which inevitably suggest the conflict between Mr and Mrs Morel, he comments: 'This has been a kind of bond between me and my mother. We have loved each other, almost with a husband and wife love, as well as filial and maternal . . . We have been like one, so sensitive to each other that we never needed words. It has been rather terrible and has made me, in some respects, abnormal.'

By the end of 1911, then, Lawrence was in an emotional impasse, deeply distressed by the death of his mother and faced with the failure of both his affair with Jessie and his engagement to Louie. In November he became seriously ill again and had to give up teaching. He was, however, making progress as an author, and he resolved now to try to make his living by his writing. He took up work again on a novel which he had begun in 1910, *Paul Morel* - the earlier title of what was to become *Sons and Lovers*, and sent portions of the manuscript to Jessie for her comments.

In her memoir Jessie recalls that in October, 1911 she received about two-thirds of the story. It was autobiographical, but it seemed to her evasive; the writing was 'extremely tired', in places it struck 'a curious, half-apologetic note, bordering on the sentimental', and some of the material was 'story-bookish'. Her advice was that 'he should write the whole story again, and keep it true to life'. This, apparently, Lawrence did, and when she began to receive the revised version Jessie was delighted. It was now fresh and real: 'His descriptions of family life were so vivid, so exact, and so concerned with everyday things we had never even noticed before,' and yet these commonplace details were 'full of mystery'. And she was impressed by the veracity of his working-class scenes, which he was uniquely able to portray from within. Altogether she felt that 'Lawrence was coming into his true kingdom as a creative artist, and an interpreter of the people to whom he belonged'. The work continued into the early months of 1912, but as Jessie began to see what Lawrence was now making of their relationship she was bitterly disappointed. She had thought that by encouraging him to face the problem of his mother and herself he would work it out 'with integrity' - by which she seems to have meant that he would recognise the injustice done to her. Instead the mother was still being made supreme; 'and for the sake of that supremacy every disloyalty was permissible'. In her view he had, after all, failed in his task and capitulated to the psychological domination of the mother even after her death. 'His mother conquered indeed,' she concluded, 'but the vanquished one was her son. In *Sons and Lovers* Lawrence handed his mother the laurels of victory.'

This was not, however, the final stage of *Sons and Lovers*. There was yet a third phase of revision, prompted, according to Keith Sagar, by the criticisms of the publisher's readers, Walter de la Mare and Edward Garnett, and, above all, by Frieda Weekley (see *D. H. Lawrence: A Calendar of his Works* and the Introduction to the Penguin edition of *Sons and Lovers*). Frieda was the wife of Ernest Weekley, the professor of modern languages at University College, Nottingham, and she first met Lawrence when he came to lunch one day in April, 1912. She was immediately arrested by his appearance – 'What kind of a bird was this?' she thought; and they were soon caught up in intense discussion: 'We talked about Oedipus and understanding leaped through our words' (from Frieda's own memoir, *'Not I But the Wind . . .'*). Frieda was a totally different kind of woman from any that Lawrence had met before. Her maiden name was Richtofen, and her father was a German baron; she was full of vivacity and intelligence, extraordinarily liberated, especially for 1912, in her attitude towards sex, and fearlessly frank and outspoken. She was also fifteen years younger than her husband. Within a few days Lawrence and she were in love, and she invited him to spend the night with her. But Lawrence insisted that they must go away and live together permanently, even though this meant deserting her three children as well as her husband. They eloped in May, going first to her family in Metz, and then walking over the Alps to Italy. At first Professor Weekley would not hear of a divorce, but eventually he agreed – though at the cost to Frieda of separation from her children whom she loved dearly – and she and Lawrence were married in July, 1914.

The death of his mother and the elopement with Frieda were the two most momentous events in Lawrence's life. They were also significantly connected; for the second arose, in a sense, out of the impasse which was brought to a head by the first. Lawrence was in need of a woman who could give him the impetus to escape from the emotional prison of his past, and Frieda, with her unconventional outlook, and a cosmopolitan background which admirably complemented the English provincial culture that had been Lawrence's until he moved to Croydon, was perfectly cast for this role. With her help Lawrence was able to tap his true, spontaneous self, which his affairs with Jessie and Louie had bottled up, but at the same time she had the courage and independence to stand up to him, and battle with him, and act as his severest critic.

Referring to the time just after their elopement, Frieda writes: 'He was then rewriting his *Sons and Lovers*, the first book he wrote with me . . .' The claim is somewhat exaggerated; but it is probably true that it was now, as Lawrence tackled the manuscript for the third time, that her very different kind of intelligence and emotional response were brought to bear on the composition of the novel. Frieda also knew something about the latest psychological theories emanating from Vienna (she described herself as 'a great Freud admirer'), and it is quite likely that her heated arguments with Lawrence on these matters had their influence on him. She certainly felt that his love for his mother was 'overpowerful' and that it harmed him, and it may well be that the 'Oedipal' strain in *Sons and Lovers*, which presents Paul as a victim of his excessive love for his mother and unable thereby to form satisfactory relations with other women, became a more prominent theme at this stage of revision. It is with this in mind that we should read the famous letter explaining the meaning of the novel, written to Edward Garnett on 14 November 1912, when Lawrence finally sent the text off to his publisher:

. . . a woman of character and refinement goes into the lower class, and has no satisfaction in her own life. She has had a passion for her husband, so the children are borne of passion, and have heaps of vitality. But as her sons grow up she selects them as lovers – first the eldest, then the second. These sons are *urged* into life by their reciprocal love of their mother – urged on and on. But when they come to manhood, they can't love, because their mother is the strongest power in their lives, and holds them . . . As soon as the young men come into contact with women, there's a split. William gives his sex to a fribble, and his mother holds his soul. But the split kills him, because he doesn't know where he is. The next son gets a woman who fights for his soul – fights his mother. The son loves the mother – all the sons hate and are jealous of the father. The battle goes on between the mother and the girl, with the son as object. The mother gradually proves stronger, because of the tie of blood. The son decides to leave his soul in his mother's hands, and, like his elder brother go for passion. He gets passion. The split begins to tell again. But, almost unconsciously, the mother realises what is the matter, and begins to die. The son casts off his mistress, attends to his mother dying. He is left in the end naked of everything, with the drift towards death.

This is a very important document for the interpretation of *Sons and Lovers*, though it stresses only one aspect of a novel which is an altogether more richly complex creation, with different layers of meaning reflecting its different stages of composition. Properly understood, the letter merely states the view that was uppermost in Lawrence's mind after his last, and Frieda-orientated, revision.

Sons and Lovers was published in 1913. By then Lawrence was at work on other books, including poetry, short stories, travel sketches and his next major novel, *The Rainbow*. This was originally called *The Sisters*, in accordance with its concern with the love-affairs of a pair of sisters, Ursula and Gudrun Brangwen; but as the material developed in Lawrence's mind it was split into two novels – *The Rainbow*, published in 1915 (and rapidly banned because certain scenes in it were too explicitly sexual for the climate of the day), and *Women in Love*, completed in 1916, but not published till 1921 (though a private edition appeared in America in 1920).

Lawrence and Frieda returned to England in 1914, just before the First World War broke out. Lawrence made no secret of his anti-war sentiments. For a while he hoped to co-operate with the philosopher, Bertrand Russell, in writing and delivering a series of lectures advocating positive life-values rather than the acceptance of mechanistic destruction which it seemed to him that the war represented; and he planned to emigrate with a few friends to establish a new community, which he called 'Rananim', based on those values. He was prevented, however, from leaving the country; and – partly because of his ideas, partly because of the German nationality of his wife – he was suspected of spying and, in 1917, expelled from Cornwall where he was living at the time. On two or three occasions he was called up for medical examination for compulsory military service, but found unfit because of his weak chest. This whole experience filled him with loathing and disgust, as can be seen from his thinly disguised fictional account of it in the 'Nightmare' chapter of *Kangaroo* (1923). It confirmed his growing disillusionment with England.

In 1919 Lawrence was seriously ill once more, with influenza. On recovering he and Frieda left for the continent, and, except for brief visits to relatives and friends, he was not to return to his native land again. Till 1922 he spent most of his time in Italy and Sicily, where he wrote many of the highly original poems ('Snake', 'Fish', 'Man and Bat', etc.) which were published in the collection, *Birds, Beasts and Flowers* (1923); and he continued his novel writing with *The Lost Girl* (begun in 1912, though not completed till 1920) and *Aaron's Rod*, the latter part of which is based on Lawrence's experiences in post-war Italy. In 1922 the psychological study, *Fantasia of the Unconscious*, and the volume of short stories, *England, My England*, were both published in New York. It now seemed to Lawrence that his major audience lay in America rather than England, and, accordingly, his thoughts turned more and more to the establishment of a transatlantic 'Rananim'. None the less, when he decided to leave Europe he made his initial move eastwards, visiting first Ceylon and then Australia. At Perth, in Western Australia, he met Molly Skinner, who showed him the manuscript of a novel which he rewrote and published (jointly with her) as *The Boy in the Bush*. Later he and Frieda rented a seaside bungalow in New South Wales, where *Kangaroo* was written. From there, via New Zealand and the Pacific Ocean, Lawrence at last reached the west coast of America, and in September 1922 he settled at a ranch in New Mexico. (The building and its surrounding desert area are brilliantly evoked in the long short-story, *St. Mawr*.)

Lawrence now became deeply interested in the American Indians. In 1923 he moved south to Mexico, where he wrote a series of poems, short stories and travel sketches, all of which explore the primitive consciousness embodied in the animistic religion of the Indians; and in his novel,

The Plumed Serpent (1926), he imagined the creation of a modern political movement based on revival of the worship of the ancient Aztec gods.

After completing this exhausting task Lawrence succumbed to yet another, almost fatal attack of illness. On recovering he decided to return to Europe. The period 1925-8 was spent mainly in Italy once more where, at the Villa Mirenda, near Florence, he worked on *Lady Chatterley's Lover* (1928). This is the most frankly sexual of all his novels, but also, significantly, one in which his imagination turns once again to his native Nottinghamshire and Derbyshire area, and in which tenderness, expressed in dialect, rather than the savage, alien culture of the Indians, becomes his major theme. He now also took up again his earlier, youthful interest in painting, and in July 1929 an exhibition of his work at the Warren Gallery in London was raided by the police, who took away thirteen supposedly obscene paintings. The episode was farcical, and it provoked one of Lawrence's more amusingly satirical poems, 'Innocent England': 'Oh what a pity, Oh! don't you agree/that figs aren't found in the land of the free!'

During the last months of his life, although he was a very sick man, Lawrence still continued to write, and in the poems which were post-humously published as *Last Poems* (1932) he expressed some of his most beautiful and moving thoughts on the subject of death, including 'Bavarian Gentians' and 'The Ship of Death'. In February 1930 he was persuaded to enter a sanatorium at Vence, in the south of France, but the régime was intolerable to one of his temperament. On 1 March he moved into the nearby Villa Robermond, and on 2 March he died. His body was cremated; and in 1935 his ashes were transported to the ranch in New Mexico.

2 SUMMARIES AND CRITICAL COMMENTARY

2.1 PART ONE: CHAPTER SUMMARIES AND COMMENTARY

Chapter 1

Summary

The novel opens with a brief historical survey of the development of the Nottinghamshire and Derbyshire coalfield and the building of the miners' houses called 'the Bottoms'. The first 'scene' shows the children's excitement at the Bestwood wakes and Mr Morel's return with a coconut. A retrospective view sketches in Mrs Morel's girlhood, her meeting with her future husband and the first few months of their married life. Disillusionment follows as Mrs Morel discovers the lies he has told her about his financial position. The first child, William, is born, and conflict between the mother and father reaches a climax in Mr Morel's cutting off of the boy's curls. Mr Morel, who had become a teetotaller on marrying, reverts to his old drinking habits, and the chapter concludes with an extended episode narrating his day's excursion to Nottingham and, on his return, the quarrel between him and the pregnant Mrs Morel, which ends with her being locked out of the house for several hours.

Commentary

This initial chapter concentrates particularly on the contrast between Mr and Mrs Morel. It shows both what has brought them together – the mutual fascination of personalities that are so different as to cast a temporary spell of glamorous strangeness on each other, and the inevitable process of disenchantment, seen more especially, however, from Mrs Morel's point of view, as reality breaks in upon them after the honeymoon period. The physical setting of the mining area is also sketched in, and through such vividly presented scenes as the wakes and the walk to Nottingham the reader is made to feel the pulse of actual living in a working-class environment. The chapter builds up to, and culminates in, the remarkably evocative passage describing Mrs Morel's sensations when she is left in the garden in the moonlight – the first full-scale example of Lawrence's ability to transform commonplace material into powerfully resonant symbolism.

Chapter 2

Summary
Mrs Morel's third child, Paul, is born; the Congregational minister, Mr Heaton, comes to tea; in another quarrel between husband and wife Mr Morel flings a drawer at Mrs Morel, which catches her on the forehead and draws blood; Mr Morel retreats more and more from family life, taking refuge in the public house. In a culminating episode he threatens to leave home, wrapping his things up in a large bundle, which Mrs Morel finds in the coalplace. He slinks back at night.

Commentary
This chapter is a series of domestic vignettes illustrating the deterioration in the relationship between Mr and Mrs Morel. It begins with an attractive portrayal of Mr Morel as he gets his breakfast, the vividly sharp details communicating a sense of intimate, private pleasure. But it is a lonely happiness: 'With his family about, meals were never so pleasant'. When Paul is born the neighbours, Mrs Kirk and Mrs Anthony, rally round to help the woman in labour, but on coming home from the pit Mr Morel resents their intrusion and is too tired to summon up any real feeling for the baby. When Mr Heaton makes his visits Mrs Morel turns to him for the intellectual satisfaction she cannot get from her husband, though she is inwardly sceptical of his spiritual idealism ('. . . his young wife is dead; that is why he makes his love into the Holy Ghost'). Morel resents his wife's fuss and show of respectability, and in retaliation he deliberately exaggerates his own coarseness and vulgarity in what his wife regards as a self-indulgent manner. It is a short, effectively dramatised episode which adds to the growing sense of the husband's isolation, but it is also done with a comic gusto which is a relief from some of the more heavily charged scenes of domestic conflict. On a more imaginatively suggestive level the immediately following episode in which Mrs Morel takes the baby Paul out to see the sunset gives another dimension to her growing estrangement from her husband, and the drawer-flinging episode clinches this by showing Morel's inability to face up responsibly to his own bad behaviour. There is a touch of authorial condemnation here: we are told that as Morel watched the blood soak through to the baby's head 'finally, his manhood broke', and that by failing to admit his fault 'he broke himself . . . There was this deadlock of passion between them, and she was stronger.' Consequently, 'The family life withdrew, shrank away.' Morel seeks consolation in the Palmerston public house where the other drinkers take him in 'warmly', so that 'In a minute or two they had thawed all responsibility out of him . . .' His stealing of petty sums of money from his wife's purse marks a further decline of trust between them, and leads

to his pretence of leaving home. This, however, is again given humorous treatment. Mrs Morel's language when replying to William's query about his father: 'He says he's run away', suggests that it is a little boy's trick; and the discovery of the bundle in the coal-place is treated mockingly: 'Every time she saw it, so fat and yet so ignominious, slunk into its corner in the dark, with its ends flopping like dejected ears from the knots, she laughed again.' The bundle in its 'blue handkerchief' thus becomes a comic emblem of Morel's emotional defeat.

Chapter 3

Summary

Morel is ill; but as he recovers his wife becomes less close to him. A fourth child, Arthur, is born. Mrs Morel's feelings become increasingly focused on William. She stands between him and his father, and she responds to him almost as a lover – even to the extent of feeling jealous of his going out dancing and meeting girls. He gets a job in London, and though she is pleased by his promotion, she is distressed at the prospect of losing him.

Commentary

The title of this chapter is a clear indication of its theme; 'The Casting off of Morel – the Taking on of William.' The return to something like intimacy between husband and wife during Morel's illness is only a temporary lull in the process of alienation which is now gathering momentum. It is a poignant reminder of what is in fact decaying. The episode in which Morel threatens to punish William for having torn Alfred Anthony's collar, simply because Mrs Anthony has complained to him, shows the lack of understanding between him and his wife, and Mrs Morel's defence of William shows both her greater strength of personality and where her real emotional allegiance now lies. The quarrel culminates in the succinct statement: 'He [Morel] was afraid of her.' Their division is heightened by her determination that William shall not go down the pit; and though William starts as a clerk earning less than he would as a miner, he is clever, wins promotion, and is soon, by Bestwood standards, 'rich'. His triumphs are a tribute to his mother (for example, she takes his running prize 'like a queen'). There is, however, a touch of his father in him in that he is very fond of dancing, which fills his mother with misgivings – as do his adolescent flirtations. The incident of the girl who comes asking for him shows Mrs Morel's rather puritanical disapproval and, though she seems not to realise this, the extent to which she fears sexual displacement by a rival. The chapter ends appropriately with a scene in which William goes through the love-letters he has received from his various girls, before burning them preparatory to his departure for London, while his mother bakes a rice cake for him to take away with him. The triviality of the letters is symbolised by Paul's being given the 'pretty tickets from the corner of the notepaper – swallows and forget-me-nots and ivy sprays'; but Mrs Morel has a lover's anxiety that William's vanity will eventually be flattered by some such girl.

Chapter 4

Summary

Paul now becomes the centre of attention, though the period covered by this chapter also includes the time before and after William's departure for London. The material consists of a series of vignettes: the ritual burning of Annie's doll, Arabella; William nearly coming to blows with his father over the latter's treatment of the mother; Morel doing odd jobs about the house and telling stories of the pit; Paul ill, then convalescent; Paul collecting pay for his father; Mrs Morel at Eastwood market; children's games by the lamplight; miners returning early from the pit; William coming home for Christmas.

Commentary

Lawrence is effecting another transition in this chapter. He is still concerned with the transfer of Mrs Morel's love from her husband to William – a theme which is furthered by the quarrel between father and son and the brilliant evocation of the Christmastime excitement when William comes home for five days; but Paul is now brought to the fore, and his slightly less passionate, but more subtle, relationship with his mother is developed. His illness attracts more anxious care from his mother, and Lawrence risks a passage which is both beautiful and psychologically ambiguous when he describes the singularly restful nature of the sleep he shares with his mother during his convalescence: 'Sleep is still most perfect, in spite of hygienists, when it is shared with a beloved.' The exclusion of the father is again emphasised; he is called 'an outsider', and in an authorial comment which strikes an embarrassingly portentous note it is said that 'He had denied the God in him.' But this is followed immediately by such delightfully vivid and convincing scenes of the better times when he does odd jobs about the house, involving all his children with him, that it is impossible to dismiss him as merely a blight on the family life. There is a significant degree of imaginative continuity between such moments and the energy and zest which the Scargill Street children display in 'the wild, intense games' which go on 'under the lamp-post, surrounded by so much darkness', and likewise the vitality and excitement associated with the preparations for Christmas. Nonetheless, the most remarkable features in the chapter are those which give a vivid and touching reality to the growing sense of experiences *shared* by Paul and his mother. The outstanding example is Mrs Morel's visit to the market and her subsequent communion with Paul over her 'extravagant' purchase of the little dish and the roots of pansies and daisies. It is the immediate, intuitive awareness of each other's feelings which makes this relationship so peculiarly intense and establishes it as something unique.

Chapter 5

Summary

The chapter begins with news of Morel's serious injury down the mine and Mrs Morel's visit to him in hospital; but its main substance is Paul's starting work at Jordan's surgical factory. He finds an advertisement in the Co-operative reading room at Bestwood, is summoned for interview in Nottingham, and begins as a clerk in the 'Spiral' department, under Mr Pappleworth. He gets to know some of the workers in the other departments, including Polly, overseer of the factory girls, and Fanny, in the finishing-off room. William's story is also furthered as we learn about his growing affair with 'Gipsy'.

Commentary

For the first time one has the feeling that the novel is being padded out with a certain amount of superfluous material. The news of the accident is given dramatically in dialogue form, though not so succinctly and effectively as in the closely related dialect poem, 'A Collier's Wife'; and the account of Paul's first experience of factory life is interesting as a piece of fictional sociology, but unduly extended for what it reveals of his development. Thematically, the most important parts are those which touch on Paul's feelings that he is becoming 'a prisoner of industrialism', and which describe the visit made by Paul and his mother to Nottingham, on the day of his interview at Jordan's. The sensitive, feminine (but not effeminate) side of Paul and the artistic aspect of his temperament (for example, in his appreciation of Fanny's hair as a painterly subject) are also significant features of his character which are brought out by his contact with the factory girls.

Chapter 6

Summary

After a brief sketch of the youngest son, Arthur, including reference to his winning of a scholarship to the Grammar School, this chapter concentrates on William. When he brings his fiancée home for Christmas she behaves in a fashion of queenly superiority to his family. On later visits it becomes increasingly clear that William not only resents this, but also finds her vain and trivial – to such an extent that he becomes painfully outspoken in his criticism of her. The story of Paul and his mother continues with their first visit to Willey Farm; and new characters – Mrs Leivers, Edgar, Maurice, and, above all, Miriam – are introduced. William falls ill. His mother goes to London to nurse him, but he dies. A telegram is sent summoning Mr Morel. The young man's body is brought home, and the coffin is placed in the Morels' front room. Mrs Morel is entirely pre-occupied with the death of William, and not until Paul also becomes seriously ill does she wake to the realisation that she is in danger of losing her second son as well. But she now gives him her undivided attention, and over a seven-week period she devotedly nurses him back to health.

Commentary
The split caused in William's love-life by his devotion to his mother becomes increasingly apparent in this chapter: he is attracted physically by 'Gipsy', but despises her for the lack of intelligence and moral fibre that he so admires in his mother. It is as if he has been drawn to her precisely because her appeal is sexual and non-intellectual since that means she does not challenge his feeling for his mother, while at the same time he wilfully keeps up what he knows to be an inadequate relationship as a kind of self-punishment. His rash and subsequent brain fever seem like the revenge his body takes for being thus divorced from his mind. However, Lawrence does not theorise in this way; he leaves the reader to draw his own conclusion. The devastating emotional effect of William's death on his mother is translated into the graphic scene of the coffin being carried into the house. Her keening repetition of 'Oh, my son – my son!' takes on the stylised quality of a scene from classical tragedy. The intervening episode of her first visit to Willey Farm with Paul, besides looking forward to Part Two of the novel, counterpoints this tragedy of mother-love with a sense of more vital and creative contact with the natural world. It is because of her instinctive awareness that Paul's work at Jordan's is undermining his health that she suggests the visit to the Haggs, but, ironically, with the death of William she becomes oblivious of her second son's needs until she is threatened with a repetition of catastrophe in the form of *his* serious illness. The withdrawal of the mother's attention is nearly fatal. And the recovery, when it comes, is not only recovery for Paul, but for his mother, too: ' "For some things," said his aunt, "it was a good thing Paul was ill that Christmas. I believe it saved his mother." ' This underlines what a perilously necessary kind of love has developed between the mother and her sons.

2.2 PART TWO: CHAPTER SUMMARIES AND COMMENTARY

Chapter 7

Summary

In his convalescence Paul starts making regular visits to Willey Farm, and a love-affair – not, however, acknowledged as such – develops between him and Miriam. It is impeded and sometimes baffled by the inhibitions of the two young people and the jealous suspicion of Mrs Morel and Paul's family, but nonetheless grows, if unsteadily, into an absorbing relationship. Its progress is marked by a series of emotional episodes such as those of the swing, Paul's teaching Miriam algebra and their mutual

episode – Paul's own immaturity, Miriam's unbalanced seriousness, and Mrs Morel's possessiveness; and no simple judgement can be made for or against any of these characters. Even Mr Morel's drunkenness, and his coarse resentment of the tenderness between mother and son (" 'At your mischief again?'' he said venomously'), has some justification. Mrs Morel may retort that she at least is 'sober', but she and Paul are suffering from an emotional intoxication which is arguably more harmful than Morel's 'bellyful of beer'. And perhaps the quite unintellectual husband instinctively realises this. The scene is set for a conflict which might really bring things out into the open; but Mrs Morel's illness prevents this. The crisis is deflected, and next morning, 'Everybody tried to forget the scene'.

Chapter 9

Summary

The conflict within Paul causes him to be increasingly hostile to Miriam, as in his cutting remarks about her attitude towards the daffodils. He suggests that they should stop seeing each other, and later, because of what people are saying, that they should either get engaged or break off altogether; but their meetings continue all the same. Miriam feels that she represents the 'higher' aspects of Paul's love, but that there is also a 'lower' aspect, which she will test by seeing how he reacts to Clara. Despite her feminist brittleness Paul is attracted to Clara; and when he, Clara and Miriam encounter Miss Lamb, with the stallion on which she lavishes her emotion, it becomes clear that there is an unsatisfied sexual urge in Clara, too. To Miriam it now seems that Paul can indeed 'choose the lesser in place of the higher', and the final sign of her 'defeat' (as alluded to in the chapter-title, 'Defeat of Miriam') is the letter which he writes to her saying that he can only give her 'a spirit love', not 'embodied passion'. Other passages in this chapter include an account of Paul's visit to Lincoln with his mother and his anguish that she shows signs of sickness and age; a sketch of the relationship between Annie and her boyfriend Leonard, leading to their marriage; and a scene of courtship between Arthur and Beatrice which is characterised by the teasing playfulness and frank enjoyment of sexual contact which are so notably missing from Paul's relations with Miriam.

Commentary

The imbalance in the relationship between Paul and Miriam has already been made apparent in previous chapters, and this one shows its further exacerbation until some kind of show-down becomes inevitable. Paul is irritable with her and criticises her for what he feels to be an excess of emotion in her response even to such natural manifestations of spring-time as daffodils growing under a hedge. He accuses her of lacking restraint or reserve, though the narrative, in such a sentence as 'One after another she turned up to him the faces of the yellow, bursten flowers appealingly, fondling them lavishly all the while', suggests that what he resents is a sensuousness in her response which he longs to have directed towards himself. There is undoubtedly frustration in Miriam's attitude, and it is her misfortune that Paul is too much the victim of his own unfathomed emotions to appreciate what she herself needs and to find a tactful and loving way of offering it. Lawrence's own artistic detachment seems to be at fault in this chapter. Paul's experience is very close to his own, and he tends to make authorial comments that criticize Miriam from Paul's point of view instead of holding the balance between them. Thus, when Miriam sees that he is attracted to Clara and decides to 'test' his preference for 'higher' or 'lower' things, the relevant paragraph ends with a sentence – 'She forgot that her "higher" and "lower" were arbitrary' – which jars on the reader by making over-explicit judgement of her limitations. Paul, however, is given statements which seem to ask for the reader's endorsement. For example, in reaction against Miriam's soulfulness, he comments that 'It's not religious to be religious . . . a crow is religious when it sails across the sky. But it only does it because it feels itself carried to where it's going, not because it thinks it is being eternal.' This implies a revaluation of the concept of religion which is not merely an expression of Paul's character, but a radical criticism of the nature of religious feeling which the reader is expected to respond to sympathetically. The letter which Paul sends to Miriam is perhaps not quite in this same category – its language is too pretentiously adolescent, and this serves to make us at least sceptical of its contents. But its theme of body v. spirit is obviously in tune with the way the Paul–Miriam affair is being presented, and so, once more, it tends to invite the reader to side with Paul and against Miriam. (And when we realise that it is, in fact, very like a letter which Lawrence actually wrote to Jessie Chambers we have the slightly uneasy feeling that the larger, imaginative awareness of Lawrence, the artist, is being subordinated to the narrower understanding of Lawrence, the man.) Miriam's way of thinking and feeling does, of course, warrant criticism; and it is a legitimate function of the novel to make its readers more discriminating in such matters. But this task is more effectively done when, for example, we are shown, rather than told, how easily and naturally Arthur and Beatrice can flirt with each other, while the implications of the contrast with the deeper, yet more inhibited, relationship of Paul and Miriam are left to the reader's own judgement. Both the finer potentiality of Paul and Miriam's love and its abnormal seriousness can then be recognised; and the 'defeat' of Miriam can be perceived as a consequence of something tragically disabling in the quality of her affair with Paul – something which transcends authorial interference or prejudice.

Chapter 10

Summary

Paul wins a prize of twenty guineas for one of his paintings, and he begins to get invitations to dinners, at which he wears William's dress suit. His mother feels he is getting on socially and that the family is going up in the world. Arthur leaves the army, marries Beatrice, and at last accepts the need to settle down. Paul is thus the only one left at home. He starts to develop an affair with Clara: first, he visits her in her home at Sneinton, where she makes lace with her mother, and then, after he has helped her to get back to her previous employment at Jordan's, they gradually get to know each other. On Paul's twenty-third birthday Fanny and the other factory girls give him some paints as a present. Clara is excluded, though she is aware that something is going on. When Paul lets her know what it is, she gives him a volume of verse. They have tea together at the village of Lambley, and Paul questions her about her broken marriage with Baxter. In another conversation, about Miriam, Clara tells him that he is mistaken in thinking that Miriam wants only 'soul communion' with him: 'She wants you.' He expresses doubt, but Clara says, 'You've never tried.'

Commentary

The episode of Paul's visit to Sneinton is an arresting one. The portrait of Mrs Radford (Clara's mother), a vigorous character who has 'the strength and sang-froid of a woman in the prime of life', provides a very effective foil to Clara herself, who in this context seems a less proud and self-contained person than hitherto; and the details of the kitchen and the lace-making exemplify Lawrence's great gift of making something imaginatively striking out of superficially drab and uninteresting material. The use of contrast is particularly effective. Paul is first admitted to the little-used front parlour, 'a small, stuffy, *defunct* room' (my italics), the lifelessness of which is emphasised by its adornment with 'deathly enlargements of photographs of departed people done in carbon'. But he is then invited into the kitchen, which is also 'a little, darkish room', but quite transformed because 'smothered in white lace'. The work makes for untidiness, but it is an active and living untidiness. Mrs Radford, though blunt, is hospitable, and even Clara, despite her sense of shame, catches Paul's attention with her arms 'creamy and full of life beside the white lace'. There is nonetheless something missing, and the frank Mrs Radford provides the clue to what this is: 'A house o' women is as dead as a house wi' no fire, to my thinkin' . . . I like a man about, if he's only something to snap at.' This tacitly gives Paul the clue to what is wrong with Clara – that, for all her aggressive feminism, she needs the fulfilment which only connection with one of the other sex can bring; and it provides a basis on which an affair between them can be built up. This is not done with a rush, however. At Jordan's Clara continues to be stiff and 'superior'; she wants attention from Paul, but is too proud to let him see it. The incident of the birthday present shows him that she is vulnerable in her isolation, and their relationship proceeds at a slow, but plausible, pace after that. It is clearly moving towards the kind of physical contact that is so markedly absent from Paul's previous experience of love; but, interestingly, it is this aspect of their developing intimacy which precipitates again the issue of the spiritual versus the physical in the Miriam affair, and, accordingly, it is with a challenge to Paul's understanding of Miriam's real needs that the treatment of his relationship with Clara, in this chapter, ends. However, as so often in this novel, the theme of sexual relations is not pursued in a narrowly exclusive way. Not only does this chapter give us glimpses of the jobs that people do (for example, the lace-making and the factory work at Jordan's) as a complement to their emotional lives, so that we get a far more realistic impression of the interaction between work and private feeling, but we also have a sense that there are wider social implications in the developments taking place in Paul's life. Thus, his mother rejoices that he is being given an entrée into middle-class society by his success as a painter, and Paul delights in this for her sake. It is, indeed, almost symbolic that she allows him to have William's evening dress altered and to wear it when he is invited out to dinner: Paul now represents that extension into a more sophisticated world (though Lawrence keeps us aware that it is still only a rather bourgeois, provincial world) which gave her such vicarious satisfaction when all her hopes were settled on her first son. Paul, on the other hand, feels that his roots – the deep, vital connections that really matter – still belong to the working-class. As he expresses it in discussion with his mother: ' . . . from the middle classes one gets ideas, and from the common people – life itself, warmth'. The distinction, of course, comes altogether too neat and pat. His mother is quick to point out that he doesn't care to talk to his father's pals, and that the working-class people he chooses to mix with are those who, like himself, enjoy the exchange of ideas in a middle-class way. This contradiction is not resolved – and there is no need that it should be in a novel. But it helps to give a sense of different levels of interaction between intelligence and instinct, sophistication and communal involvement, which adds satisfying complexity to the presentation of Paul as a young man caught up in emotional and social changes which have a universal human significance.

Chapter 11

Summary

Paul returns to Miriam once more and visits her frequently. His physical frustration becomes so great that he begs her to sleep with him (though, given the mores of the time, it is not, of course, expressed as explicitly as that). At first she says, 'Not now'; but then she forces herself to promise that she will accept him. One evening after picking cherries at Willey Farm there is a beautiful sunset which rouses his desire to a particularly high pitch; but it is not until he visits her at her grandmother's cottage, which she has to herself for a few days, that he actually does make love to her. She gives herself, however, not spontaneously, but as a sacrifice. She takes him again on a number of occasions afterwards; but she never manages to overcome her inhibition and their attempt at a physical relationship is at last recognised, by Paul at least, as a failure. He eventually decides to break off the affair yet again, and this he does in a difficult and painful scene between them. Meanwhile he has begun to see Clara again.

Commentary

This is one of the most powerful, but also uncomfortable chapters in the novel. Its title, 'The Test on Miriam', is a slightly odd one, as it suggests a deliberate submitting of Miriam to a trial – a trial, presumably, of her ability to meet Paul in a free, spontaneous experience of physical love. The actual narration does not, however, suggest anything as cruelly and coldly calculated as that. Paul's 'test' is as much a test of himself as of Miriam; it is an attempt to find out whether the two of them can come together in a complete and mutually satisfying relationship which is consummated in the sexual act. (Though if a modern, feminist critic were to protest that the focus seems to be all on Paul's satisfaction rather than Miriam's, one would have to admit that there is some truth in that.) The process is one of imaginative exploration; Lawrence does not know all the answers in advance (even though, of course, he knows what the outcome will be), but is groping his way through difficult, uncharted terrain. The analytical method, which has become more marked since the beginning of Part Two, becomes even more prominent here. The opening paragraphs give a brilliant rendering of Paul's tortured consciousness as he puzzles over, and questions himself about, the 'obstacle' that seems to prevent him from feeling 'a joyous desire to marry [Miriam] and to have her'. Two explanations are offered: that 'desire' is unable to battle successfully with 'virginity' – which seems to mean that they are both, but Miriam more particularly, conditioned by Victorian Puritanism about sex which treats it as shameful; and that Paul belongs to the class of 'the sons of mothers whose husbands had blundered rather brutally through their feminine sanctities' so that they are hypersensitive about doing the same to any woman, hurting the woman being like hurting the mother. The latter explanation seems to be a form of the mother-fixation theory which pervades the novel. Impatience, however, rather than tenderness seems to be characteristic of Paul's attitude towards Miriam, as it had been earlier in their relationship. When he sees her singing at the piano, 'her mouth seemed hopeless. She sang like a nun singing to heaven.' This implies a third explanation – reflected elsewhere in the presentation of Miriam – that she has a romantic-religiose temperament which prevents her from responding on anything but the 'spiritual' level; that she is, in fact, humanly inadequate, and (as Mrs Morel insists) an inevitable blight on Paul's hopes of fulfilment. It is this last 'explanation' which tends to dominate in the narration of Miriam's failure to rise to the 'test'; and it is coupled with a new emphasis on the significance of the unconscious in the act of love, as can be seen, for example, in the crucial cherry-tree episode and its aftermath. Paul is roused by the dark, warm evening, the rocking motion of the tree in the wind and the splendour of the glowing sunset to a state of intense excitement which has sexual overtones: the movement of the tree 'stirred the blood' and the cherries touched Paul's ears and neck, as if they were a woman's fingers, 'sending a flash down his blood'. He invites Miriam to share in this mood, which she does to a certain extent, even picking up some of the cherries he throws at her and hanging them over her ears; but there is also an undertone of cruelty and violence (symbolised by the crows which had been shot and the cherry-stones 'hanging quite bleached, like skeletons, picked clear of flesh') which frightens her. The ruthless demand of mindless instinct is perhaps what is hinted at here, and it is something that Miriam cannot come to terms with. In this mood Paul becomes a strange, starkly impersonal creature; he speaks of liking the darkness and wishing it were thicker, and we are told that 'He seemed to be almost unaware of her as a person: she was only to him then a woman.' Ordinary values are changed – life and day, i.e. the world of conscious awareness, become mere shadows, and death and night the desirable reality: 'The highest of all was to melt out into the darkness and sway there, identified with the great Being.' In other words, he seeks release from the strain of self-consciousness and the effort of the will (features which are painfully characteristic of his intercourse with Miriam) by identifying himself with the universal, unconscious state of existence, and aspiring to be like the fir-trees, simply a 'presence' in the darkness. Miriam cannot really share this state with him. Her replies are monosyllabic, and she is afraid. When, at the cottage, she finally yields to him, it is in a mood of resignation, and, again, it is the sense of 'sacrifice' which predominates in her. She is fatally unable to reciprocate Paul's emotion; and though the physical relationship between them continues for nearly a year there is no improvement. Indeed, this sense that Miriam is not with him in the instinctual enjoyment of their love-making ultimately leads Paul to revulsion from her. Instead of enjoying an experience with her of unselfconscious sharing he feels that he is being constantly assessed, and he begins to hate her for this. And he then becomes blatantly unfair: 'She took all and gave nothing, he said. At least, she gave no living warmth. She was never alive, and giving off life . . . She was only his conscience, not his mate.' The end is preluded by another natural scene, complementary to the cherry-tree episode, when Paul goes out of doors on a moonlit night and catches the coarse, sharp scent of some flowers. Without its being deliberately spelt out, this is again an experience of immediate, instinctual life which by-passes the taut, conscious condition that he has come to associate with Miriam, and it finally decides him to break off their relationship. It is precisely this capacity for sympathy with raw, unconscious life – now an overriding psychological necessity for Paul – which he feels Miriam is incapable of achieving; and his relationship with her is one that seems to undermine his own capacity for achieving it, too. Cruel as his treatment of her may seem, it does, therefore, have its justification in terms of emotional honesty. The same cannot be said, however, for his behaviour in the actual scene of the breaking-off. It is not surprising that Miriam, who has yielded so much to him, should be angry and regard him as showing child-like irresponsibility; and his claim that he wants them to separate so that she can be independent is blatantly inadequate. The analysis of Miriam's response which is then given by the narrator looks unconvincingly rigged: she could not help recognising, we are told, that there was some truth in what Paul said; she hated her feeling of bondage to him because it was something she could not control; and their relationship was a struggle for dominance which she resented because she could not be the dominant partner. Such an interpretation is, however, altogether too convenient for Paul; it lets him too easily off the hook. There seems more genuine truth in Miriam's bitter exclamation that 'It has been one long battle between us – you fighting away from me,' the implication here being that Paul has never been able to make a properly mature response to the emotional demands involved in love. Paul, however, chooses to take her statement as meaning that 'There had never been anything really between them,' that she had known this all along, and that therefore 'She had really played with him, not he with her.' He is thus able to put the blame on her, instead of acknowledging his own inadequacy. In this way he protects himself from the deeply disturbing knowledge of his own immaturity; and it is of a piece with this self-deception that after leaving her he enters a public house to drink and flirt with a group of girls as 'a reaction towards restoring his self-esteem'. Although this does not mean that he is callously indifferent, it does suggest that in his immaturity he cannot face the implications of his behaviour with the frankness and humility it requires. Moreover, one cannot help questioning whether Lawrence himself realises quite what has been revealed. The scene of the breaking-off reads too much as if it were offered not merely as an account, but a justification, of Paul's conduct. The elements which point to a different meaning are there (as I have tried to suggest in the above commentary); but authorial endorsement seems to be given to Paul's view of things, and even Miriam's 'thoughts' seem to provide a rather too convenient apology for him. Is Lawrence here exemplifying the principle which he later enunciated in *Studies in Classic American Literature* – that it is the 'tale' which is to be trusted, not the 'artist'? Almost *because* we feel that our sympathies are being influenced in favour of Paul, and against Miriam, we end up by having more compassion for her. The attempt to put her emotionally in the wrong is counter-productive, and at the end of this chapter it is she who excites the true, tragic pity: 'Very few people cared for her, and she for very few people. She remained alone with herself, waiting.'

Chapter 12

Summary

Paul acquires growing confidence in himself as a painter. He and his mother take a holiday in the Isle of Wight, but Mrs Morel becomes overstrained with walking. (There are other little hints throughout this chapter that her health is not good.) Having broken off with Miriam, he returns immediately to Clara. One afternoon he invites her to go to Clifton Grove with him, and on the way he buys her some carnations, which he pins on her coat. The path is wet and muddy after heavy rain, and the River Trent is in full spate. They clamber along the steep cliff side of the Grove, find a secluded place, and make love. Afterwards they have tea at a cottage. On another occasion he brings her home to tea with his mother; Miriam calls in and all three meet in the garden; he walks Clara to the railway station at night and almost makes her miss her train. Later he and Clara, wearing evening dress, go to the theatre in Nottingham. He is too late to catch the last train home, and so Clara invites him to spend the night at her home in Sneinton. After supper and a long delay playing cards he goes up to his room, waits till Mrs Radford has gone to bed, and then comes down and makes love to Clara.

Commentary

The main focus of this chapter is Paul's affair with Clara and its sexual consummation. Their mutual delight in the satisfaction of the body is a positive contrast to the one-sided, sacrificial sexual union of Paul and Miriam. It is in harmony with natural forces, as suggested by the symbolic details accompanying their love-making in Clifton Grove. The repeated references to the effects of the rain, and especially its swelling of the waters of the Trent, carry associations of fertility and fulfilment; and the animate and the inanimate come together in such images as those of the river 'travelling in a soft body' and sliding by 'in a body, utterly silent and swift, intertwining among itself like some subtle, complex creature'. The carnations given by Paul to Clara also play their part. After the love-making they lie smashed on the ground, mingled with the pervasive wetness and looking 'like splashed drops of blood', while 'red, small splashes fell from her bosom, streaming down her dress to her feet'. These are strong, positive marks of the vitality of the experience. It is also noteworthy that immediately afterwards Paul speaks to Clara in dialect, using, in particular, the dialect form of the second person pronoun (i.e. 'tha' [= thou] and 'thee', instead of 'you') with its much greater sense of tenderness and intimacy. Even the patiently realistic account of the difficulty the two lovers have in following the path, which is so muddy and at various points flooded by the river, contributes to the expression of the special quality of their love. Instead of being spiritualised and religiously exalted above things earthy and physical – the characteristics, again, associated with the Miriam affair – this love is close to the solid realities of the earth. And though the actual love-making, unlike what we find in the later Lawrence, especially in *Lady Chatterley's Lover*, is left to the reader's imagination, that is an advantage rather than a disadvantage, for it suggests that a level of immediate, physical contact is reached which is beyond conscious articulation. The symbolic details help us to feel this; but it is as if conscious awareness is blotted out at the high-point of sexual union, which takes place, as it were, in an unconscious, non-verbal space between the words of the novel. (But see below p. 27, where this question is raised again in the slightly different context of Chapter 13.) Afterwards the lovers come back to a more ordinary level of consciousness, as Paul carefully cleans Clara's boots for her, restores her 'respectability' and makes her look 'as irreproachable as Britannia herself!' In the everyday world such appearances have to be kept up; but an afterglow of passion still surrounds the lovers and their words, making the scene which follows – the tea at the little old lady's cottage – relaxed and warm. There is some talk of what the old lady would say if she knew Clara was a married woman who had just made love with someone not her husband, but this only serves to throw into relief how free the lovers are from the furtiveness and guilt which, especially at the date when *Sons and Lovers* was written, they might be expected to feel. The truth, indeed, is probably grasped intuitively by the old lady, but she, too, shares the pleasure which radiates from the lovers, helping to confirm the sense that this is an experience which, at least for the moment, transcends the usual kind of moral judgement. It is, moreover, highly appropriate that she expresses her sympathy in the form of a gift, once more, of flowers: 'three tiny dahlias in full blow [i.e. in full bloom], neat as bees, and speckled scarlet and white'. Mrs Morel is rather more concerned about the propriety of Paul's new affair, and sceptical of its capacity to last, but she, too, condones it, even to the extent of allowing Paul to bring Clara home to tea and to go with her to chapel. This, it must be admitted, strains credulity somewhat; as does the continuation, despite all that has happened, of Paul's willingness to go on seeing Miriam from time to time and to have such discussions as the one in which he compares the marriage of Clara and Baxter Dawes with that of his own mother and father. The purpose of this may well be to underline the theme that full physical satisfaction constitutes a necessary stage in the fulfilment of the human being – hence Paul's assertion that because his mother has known 'the real, real flame of feeling through another person', if only briefly, she is left with 'not a tiny bit of feeling of sterility about her'. Nevertheless, the time and place chosen for such remarks seem peculiarly inept, and, if taken realistically, they make Paul sound almost callow. It is a welcome relief to turn from such improbable conversations to the more convincingly realised details of Paul and Clara's visit to the theatre and their subsequent love-making at Clara's house. Here again Lawrence successfully validates his description of passionate experience by connecting it with ordinary, commonplace details, such as the 'nice crozzly [crispy] bit' of bacon that Mrs Radford puts on Paul's plate. Like the wet muddiness of Clifton Grove, this enables us to feel the love of Clara and Paul as a living, sensuous reality. Slightly comic though it may be, because of the bacon we can accept the passion on the hearthrug as we cannot accept the would-be profundities that Paul utters to Miriam.

26

Chapter 13

Summary
In the previous chapter Paul, on leaving the theatre with Clara, had noticed an anonymous 'pair of brown eyes which hated him'. It now becomes evident that they belonged to Baxter Dawes, who picks a quarrel with Paul in a public house. Paul throws a glass of beer in Baxter's face, and in the upshot Baxter is ejected from the pub. He bears a deep grudge, however, and at the factory he threatens Paul again, knocking down Mr Jordan when the latter tries to intervene. As a result he is sacked, and later prosecuted; but he gets off when Paul admits that the quarrel arose over Clara. The love-affair continues, and Paul goes on holiday with Clara to Mablethorpe. The relationship becomes less close, however, and it is apparent that they are starting to drift apart. After seeing her home one night Paul is waylaid by Baxter Dawes and attacked. He fights back, and seems at one point to be on the verge of strangling Dawes; but he gives way and is knocked unconscious. Subsequently, Paul falls ill and is nursed back to health by his mother; though she herself now shows signs of more serious illness and begins seeing a doctor in Nottingham. On his recovery Paul goes with a friend for a few days to Blackpool, while his mother stays with Annie – now living with her husband in Sheffield. Paul joins them in Sheffield, to find that his mother has collapsed and is in bed. Her illness is diagnosed as cancer. After two months at Annie's she is little better, and she is brought back to Bestwood in a hired car.

Commentary
Paul's relationship with Clara shows marked signs of deterioration in this chapter. They still find great satisfaction in their love-making; and for Paul in particular it is a marvellous experience in which he feels himself fused unconsciously with the vital forces that surge through him, Clara and the whole of the natural world. 'It was as if he, and the stars, and the dark herbage, and Clara were licked up in an immense tongue of flame which tore onwards and upwards.' (This might be compared with those paintings of cypresses and corn-fields in which Van Gogh gives a similar impression of a powerful, unifying energy surging through natural phenomena.) But Clara resents the way in which Paul seems to withdraw his conscious self and take no cognisance of her personally. The experience 'was something that happened because of her, but it was not her . . . It was as if they had been blind agents of a great force.' Thus, although she is still 'mad with desire of him', she feels increasingly insecure. Marriage between them seems out of the question, not only because she is already married to another man, but also because Paul is unwilling to commit

himself to her in a relationship of companionship as well as passion. Their love belongs to the darkness only. It is, says Clara, as if Paul didn't love her in the daytime, and he tacitly agrees: 'Love-making stifles me in the daytime.' Nor does Clara really want a divorce from Baxter. She may prefer Paul as a lover, but she feels that Baxter is less egotistically locked within his own self than Paul. This part of the discussion, like the corresponding discussion between Paul and Miriam in Chapter 11, sounds somewhat strained and unnatural; it may well have been Lawrence's rather clumsy way of preparing the ground for the reunion of Clara and Baxter to come later. But it does at least serve to give a much-needed critical perspective to Paul's conduct towards Clara. The prominence which Lawrence accords to Paul's point of view on almost all matters, and the way in particular that his emphasis on the impersonality of the sexual experience is backed up by the immensely persuasive force of Lawrence's poetic imagination, tend to set the tone both for analysis and evaluation of his affair with Clara. Her objections, however, remind us that it also has another dimension – one which shows up his immaturity, his inability to achieve an adult standard of commitment in the most intimate and exacting of personal relations, and, quite simply, his egotism. A properly balanced relationship would fully involve the day-time as well as the night-time self, and we need Clara's criticism of Paul to remind us that the imaginatively compelling quality of his sense of fusion with the natural world is only one side of a coin, the reverse side of which is a dangerous tendency to compartmentalise the 'day' and 'night' experiences, and so split his own personality in two. The rest of the chapter does, in fact, lend some valuable support to this other perspective, in that it shows the beginning of a process of disintegration in Paul. The marvellous love-making itself begins to take on a more 'mechanical' quality; and after the fight with Baxter, even though he recovers physically, he is left with 'a constant sickness and gnawing at his heart', and we are told that 'his life seemed unbalanced, as if it were going to smash to pieces.' Indeed, the defeat by Dawes, when at one stage in the fight it had seemed as if Paul was getting the upper hand, might well be interpreted as an expression of Paul's losing his will to live, or as an unconscious acceptance that he is guilty and deserves punishment – not merely for stealing another man's wife, but for failing to meet the psychological demands of love. The illness of Mrs Morel might also be seen as some kind of retribution. Paul's sister, Annie, says that if she had been at home she would have seen for herself what was happening, implicitly criticising her brother for being so wrapped up in himself that he ignored the signs of his mother's condition. This does not, of course, mean that Mrs Morel's illness would not have occurred, or even that its fatal effect could have been avoided, if Paul had taken proper notice; but it does suggest that there has been some failure in Paul's attention even to his cherished mother, and that his grief over her illness is the result not only of love (though it is certainly in the main that), but also, in some degree, of remorse.

Chapter 14

Summary
Paul hears that Baxter Dawes is in hospital recovering, but only slowly, from typhoid. He goes to visit him, and some kind of relationship starts to form between them. He tells Clara, who also pays a visit, but without much success – though, in her reaction away from Paul, she now declares that Baxter loved her better than Paul. The main theme of the chapter is the prolonged dying of Mrs Morel. She resists death with all the force of her will, and her suffering torments Paul till he is in a desperate state. Eventually, in conspiracy with Annie, he gives his mother an overdose of morphia, and she at last dies. The contact with Baxter is kept up intermittently, while the affair with Clara becomes more hopeless. Finally, Paul and Baxter meet in Skegness, where the latter is convalescing, and Paul contrives a reunion between Baxter and Clara.

Commentary
The death of Mrs Morel is the emotional climax of the novel, even more disastrous for Paul than the collapse of his affairs with Miriam and Clara. Lawrence entitles the chapter, 'The Release', which has a double meaning. In the more obvious sense it means that Mrs Morel is given 'release' from her suffering from cancer, which is so agonisingly drawn out that Paul commits what is, in effect, an act of euthanasia. In another sense, however, it is Paul who is released from the crippling emotional burden of his love for his mother, and also of her love for him, which both now tacitly realise is preventing him from forming a profound and stabilising bond with any other woman. The overdose of morphia presents Lawrence with a very difficult narrative problem. He must show that it is done consciously and deliberately, and even convey the impression that there is a part of Paul's mind that now wants to be rid of his mother, without, however, suggesting any criminal intent in what Paul does, or in any way impairing the tenderness, and compassion and, above all, love, which he feels for his mother. This is done supremely well.

Lawrence is not afraid of the sentimentality which the scenes between the bed-ridden dying woman and her devoted son might easily communicate. Their simple, almost laconic exchanges carry a wealth of emotional significance, which more gushing expression might make suspect; and touches of seeming contradiction – as when the words, 'And she sniffed in her old scornful way. As she lay she looked like a girl', are followed immediately by 'But there were the dark pain-circles beneath that made him ache again' – only serve to emphasise Mrs Morel's courageous determination not to make a fuss, and the still deeper emotional effect which this has on Paul.

At the same time Lawrence makes it clear to the reader that there is a certain fragile keeping up of appearances between mother and son which they intuitively realise is necessary as a defence against complete emotional collapse: 'For they had both come to the condition when they had to make much of the trifles, lest they should give in to the big thing, and their human independence would go smash.' Nor does Lawrence hide the less admirable aspects of Mrs Morel's dying; she holds herself rigid with such a hard intensity of will and stubborn resistance to the inevitable that Paul is forced to exclaim, almost cruelly, 'Mother, if I had to die, I'd die, I'd *will* to die.'

Likewise, in spite of her conventional religious conformity Mrs Morel is indifferent to the after-life (she tells the minister 'It is the living I want, not the dead'), and she is totally unforgiving to her husband on her death-bed. There is thus an honesty and openness about the counter-currents of feeling involved in this painfully prolonged dying which leaves the reader assured that the complexities of a difficult problem have not been ignored for the sake of an overwhelming effect of pathos.

Yet genuine pathos is certainly there, and Lawrence does not shirk the high tone of tragedy when he senses that it is appropriate. This is especially true of the paragraph which describes the body of Mrs Morel lying in her bedroom when all the 'sick-room litter' has been taken away. This is a scene of stark, yet lyric, beauty; as Keith Sagar points out, it has marked similarities to Lawrence's poem on the death of his mother, 'The Bride'. The remarkable image which presents 'the sweep of the sheet from the raised feet' as being 'like a clean curve of snow' seems to convert the dead woman's shroud into a solemnly beautiful natural phenomenon; and her plaited hair, with its strands of grey, acquires a moving quality of poetic resonance when transformed into 'filigree of silver and brown'. Like one of the great nineteenth-century operatic composers – Verdi, for example – Lawrence brings his scene of tragic pathos to its climax with a ritual gesture, which, however, is also one of familiar intimacy, as Paul strokes the hair from her temples, and then crouches on the floor whispering, 'Mother, mother!'

If the modern reader is embarrassed by this, it may be because the twentieth century has lost touch with the tradition of mourning which allows grief its rhetorically appropriate and emotionally necessary outlet. In this death-scene Lawrence shows that for him the tradition is still available, and that it is one within which he can work with natural tact and accomplishment. It should be noted, however, that what Paul enacts is a private rather than a public ritual. By contrast the funeral is treated almost perfunctorily. Its most notable feature is 'the drenching cold rain;' and Mr Morel's sanctimonious remarks to his wife's relatives about 'what a good lass she'd been', and how 'he'd done his best for her' and had 'nothing to reproach himself for', have only a hollow ring. The explanation for this difference of treatment may be that for Lawrence serious and sincere emotion belongs essentially to the private and personal life. The public formalities are suspect. Thus the funeral becomes a mere interlude, after which the novel continues with its focus on Paul's emotional life.

The remainder of the chapter completes the effect of his mother's death by showing how it colours his feelings and invades even his love-making with Clara. This ceases to be vital and becomes another form of death: 'He wanted her – he had her – and it made her feel as if death itself had her in its grip.' There is perhaps a more positive note in the tentative friendship which develops between Paul and Baxter. This looks forward to the man-to-man relationships which have greater significance in later novels such as *Women in Love*, *Aaron's Rod* and *Kangaroo*; but here it remains subordinate to the theme of Paul's relations with women. By restoring Clara to Baxter Lawrence seems to suggest that there is a potentiality for renewal in this all but broken relationship which throws into relief the complete blockage in Paul's emotional life after his mother's death. 'His mother had really supported his life,' and now there is no one to take her place. Certainly Clara cannot fill the gap. She increasingly looks for someone who is willing to make a commitment to *her*; she is radically dissatisfied with a man who seems to 'waft about with any wind' as the 'evanescent' Paul does. It becomes a telling criticism of Paul that even Baxter Dawes seems more capable of this commitment than he.

Chapter 15

Summary
Clara joins Baxter in Sheffield; Morel goes to live with a Bestwood family; and Paul, taking lodgings in Nottingham, is virtually alone. Life for him seems 'to have gone smash'; he cannot paint, and he takes to drinking in public houses. One Sunday evening he sees Miriam again at chapel and invites her back to his lodgings. There she says that they ought to get married. He half-heartedly agrees, but so half-heartedly that she knows it is useless. They part, and Paul seems to want to abandon himself to the emptiness of the night. Finally, however, he turns and walks towards the lights of the city.

Commentary
Having failed in each of his relationships with women and, as the climax of all, having lost his mother, Paul finds life devoid of meaning. He seems 'derelict'. All creative vitality has gone out of him, including, apparently, even his ability to paint – the picture he did on the day of his mother's death was his last. Lacking the inner, subjective response which would make it seem purposeful, the external world, for Paul, becomes a mere simulacrum of reality. In a remarkable anticipation of the later twentieth-century sense of the 'absurd' (the feeling that life is irrationally pointless), Paul moves about Nottingham in a state of despair:

> There seemed no reason why people should go along the street, and houses pile up in the daylight. There seemed no reason why these

things should occupy the space, instead of leaving it empty. His friends talked to him: he heard the sounds, and he answered. But why there should be the noise of speech he could not understand.

His mother had been his essential bond with the universe, and without her he has lost, as it were, his umbilical link with the life-giving principle and the creative principle that enables him to give shape and coherence to the sensations which register on his consciousness. A piece of paper blown along at his feet brings the death of his mother back to his mind again. Why it should do this is left to the reader's imagination to construct, but it is possibly because he feels himself as passive and pointless without his mother as the blown scrap of paper. In any case it is a brilliant image for the desolate state of mind to which he is reduced. Lawrence, as always, makes an obscure and difficult experience intelligible to us by fixing it with a commonplace, yet memorable, image. In the same way he describes Paul sitting up late at night while 'two mice, careering wildly, scampered cheekily over his slippers'. Paul, by contrast, 'had not moved a muscle. He did not want to move. He was not thinking of anything.' This state of complete passiveness is in sharp contrast to the lively activity of the mice, and it is thus given a more chilling sense of emptiness and desolation. At this point in the novel Paul does seem, as Lawrence expresses it in the letter to Edward Garnett, to be left 'naked of everything, with the drift towards death'. The encounter with Miriam also seems to confirm this. We learn that she has begun to train as a teacher and is thus, unlike Paul, on the way to achieving a sense of purpose in life (an impression not to be easily eradicated by Paul's doctrinaire assertion that work cannot mean the same to a woman as it does to a man). She shows the possibility of being able to stand on her own feet, while Paul seems hopelessly dangling because there is no one to support him. When Miriam yet again brings up the question of marriage, he neither answers firmly yes or no, but merely admits that he does not want it much. Somewhat repetitively, he thinks of her again as being only capable of 'sacrificing' herself to him.

Marriage is impossible because 'She could not take him and relieve him of the responsibility of himself'. The active role, it seems, is somehow transferred to her; he himself is only to be passively relieved of responsibility. In such a condition it is, indeed, 'the end then between them'. And, finally, in the remarkably paragraph evoking his feelings after he has seen her home we are given an overwhelming sense of his tragically wasted life and his readiness, now that the living connection with his mother has been severed, to let himself 'drift' into the annihilating darkness of death: 'On every side the immense dark silence seemed pressing him, so tiny a spark, into extinction . . .' To break off the quotation at this point, however, with a series of dots is to risk a distortion of Lawrence's meaning. The sentence continues, after 'extinction', with the words: 'and yet, almost nothing, he could not be extinct'. This must also be joined with the last sentence of the paragraph: 'So much, and himself, infinitesimal, at the

core a nothingness, and yet not nothing.' The final contradiction, 'and yet
not nothing', though expressed in so tentatively negative a form, implies
that there is still a chance that Paul's self, described earlier as 'one tiny
upright speck of flesh, less than an ear of wheat lost in the field,' might
yet somehow live and grow, and that the diminutive 'so tiny a spark'
might be fanned into flame again. And once we are made aware of this
possibility we remember other hints dropped earlier in the chapter: for
example, the use of phrases which suggest dogged determination in spite
of all ('. . . . his soul oscillated, first on the side of death, then on the side
of life, doggedly'; 'The despairing doggedness in his tone . . .'); and the
subtle reference to the flowers – always so significant in this novel – which
Paul has in his room ('the freesias so sweet and spring-like, the scarlet
anemones flaunting over the table'), and which in a rare positive gesture,
inconsistent with his otherwise negative behaviour, he thrusts into Miriam's
hands. These are, of course, no more than delicately muted hints, slightly
modifying the pervasive atmosphere of desolation and despair, but they at
least provide a springboard for what comes at the very end of the chapter,
when Paul, tempted to capitulate to his longing for his mother, nevertheless determines not to give in: 'He would not take that direction, to the
darkness, to follow her. He walked towards the faintly humming, glowing
town, quickly.' He turns from night and annihilation towards light and
life. Moreover, the absolutely final word is 'quickly' – which can mean
both 'speedily' and 'with life in him' (as, for example, in the phrase, 'the
quick and the dead,' where 'quick' = 'living').

The likelihood that Lawrence deliberately chose the word 'quickly'
(and intended its ambivalence) as the note on which to end this chapter
is increased if we recall the use he made of the word 'broken' at the end
of Chapter 14. There the 'broken' Baxter Dawes contrasted with Paul by
showing some ability to reconstruct from defeat. Here the word 'quickly'
gathers up the tacit meaning which 'broken' had for Paul, and converts it,
if not into a sign of renewal, at least into a refusal of defeat. It modifies
the bleak finality of 'the drift towards death' by hinting that somewhere
inside him Paul still retains enough pluck and determination to carry on
his fight for individuality and wholeness. In doing so it also provides some
justification for his ultimate rejection of Miriam. However his treatment of
her is viewed, there is truth in his conviction that he cannot 'hope to give
life to her by denying his own'. It is only through affirmation of life that
life can be sustained, and the implication is that Paul cannot renew his
creativity by passive submission – only by the protection and cultivation
of his own essential 'quickness'. Thus the final note of *Sons and Lovers* is
one of qualified hope. It does not assert that Paul has won through at
last to a final resolution of his problems, nor even that he is sure of success
in the future. All it does is to leave that possibility open. Notwithstanding
the title of this last chapter, all is not quite 'derelict'; the spark of life
remains.

3 THEMES AND ISSUES

3.1 SETTING

The setting of *Sons and Lovers* is the late nineteenth-century mining community of Bestwood which belongs to a phase of development prior to the mechanisation and urbanisation of the twentieth century. Consequently, the picture of industrial life presented in this novel is very different from what it would be today. In Lawrence's own lifetime changes were taking place which made him feel that the world he had known in his youth was becoming a thing of the past. He comments on this in his essay, 'Nottingham and the Mining Countryside', written in 1929; and, although there is undoubtedly an element of retrospective idealisation in that essay, it is a useful indication of Lawrence's attitude and values.

'Nottingham and the Mining Countryside' sketches the growth of Eastwood (the original of Lawrence's fictional 'Bestwood') from a place which was merely a tiny hamlet at the beginning of the century to a much larger settlement, with a population of about 3000, when Lawrence was born in 1885. Its expansion followed in the wake of the developing mining industry. New dwellings were erected to house the miners and their families; and these, says Lawrence, were 'planked down' on the slope of a hill, creating something of an eyesore in their harsh regimentation. The site was splendid and the surrounding countryside beautiful, but, instead of taking advantage of these opportunities to build townships which '*might* have been like the lovely hill-towns of Italy', the developers spawned 'nasty red-brick, flat-faced dwellings with dark slate roofs'. On the other hand, unspoilt nature was still close by: there was a sheep dipping-hole, for example, where children could swim, and Lawrence relates how his father, walking across the field to his work, would hunt for mushrooms, 'or perhaps pick up a skulking rabbit, which he would bring home at evening inside the lining of his pit-coat'. Life was thus 'a curious cross between industrialism and the old agricultural England'; and the miners, who spoke the dialect of 'broad Derbyshire', lived 'almost entirely by instinct'. Above all, 'the pit did not mechanize men'.

The underground workers 'formed a sort of intimate community', with a uniquely 'physical awareness and intimate *togetherness*'. So that, says Lawrence, 'if I think of my childhood, it is always as if there was a lustrous sort of inner darkness, like the gloss of coal, in which we moved and had our real being'.

In novels like *The Rainbow* and *Women in Love* Lawrence portrays mining districts which are in the process of being dehumanised by industrialism, and in *Lady Chatterley's Lover* he paints a picture of Tevershall (the equivalent of 'Bestwood', and again derived from his own Eastwood) which presents it as the ultimate end-product of that process: 'The utter negation of natural beauty, the utter negation of the gladness of life, the utter absence of the instinct for shapely beauty which every bird and beast has, the utter death of the human intuitive faculty . . .' (Chapter 11). This kind of diagnosis of the evils of industrialisation is now so strongly associated with Lawrence that it is easy to overlook the fact that he did not always take this view. *Sons and Lovers* was written earlier than any of the works just mentioned and, in particular, some sixteen years before *Lady Chatterley*. Accordingly, it reflects a less hardened attitude. We can detect the seeds of his later criticism in it; but the assumptions about industrialism are by no means the same, and the implied attitude is rather more complex.

We can sense this from the very beginning, in the historical sketch with which *Sons and Lovers* opens. This is not a merely pessimistic account of industrial development. It is true that there is a marked difference between the mines described in the first paragraph, some of which went back to 'the time of Charles II', and the new developments which took place 'some sixty years ago'. The first belonged to a pre-industrial phase which 'scarcely soiled' the waters of the brook, and which gave rise to a kind of mining that was little more than an extension of natural activity: 'the few colliers and the donkeys burrowing down like ants into the earth, making queer mounds and little black places among the corn-fields and the meadows'. The second was more abrupt and on a larger, corporate scale, involving the backing of 'financiers'; with its accompanying railway development, it spread rapidly till it had effectively manacled the countryside: 'six mines like black studs on the countryside, linked by a loop of fine chain, the railway'. The effect of this image is, however, ambiguous; the 'black studs' and the 'chain' may seem inimical, but they also suggest adornments to a dress, as if they in some way enhance the countryside. Similarly, there is gain as well as loss in the transition from one phase to the other. The 'notorious Hell Row', old and decrepit, was burned down, 'and much dirt was cleansed away'. The buildings which replaced them, 'the Bottoms', were, by contrast, 'substantial and very decent', 'neat' in appearance and possessing flower-filled front gardens. This is again offset by the fact that the inhabitants do their real living not at the front, but in the kitchens at the back, which open on to a 'nasty alley of ash-pits', so that the quality of life is not enhanced to the extent that it might be. The progress made is therefore seen as limited, but it is not entirely discounted. Lawrence suggests that it has both advantages and disadvantages.

In the views attributed to Paul Morel there is an even more marked tendency to avoid a pessimistic interpretation of industrialisation. For example, when Paul and Clara discuss the mining countryside near Bestwood, Clara expresses a somewhat conventional opinion that the pit is an ugly intrusion on the beauties of nature: 'What a pity there is a coal-pit here where it is so pretty!' But Paul does not agree. It is something he is used to, and which he positively likes:

I like the rows of trucks, and the headstocks, and the steam in the daytime, and the lights at night. When I was a boy, I always thought a pillar of cloud by day and a pillar of fire by night was a pit, with its steam, and its lights, and the burning bank, – and I thought the Lord was always at the pit-top.

Paul alludes here to the Bible, Exodus 13:21–2, which narrates how the Israelites were led out of Egypt by divine guidance: 'And the Lord went before them by day in a pillar of a cloud, to lead them the way; and by night in a pillar of fire, to give them light; to go by day and night:/He took not away the pillar of cloud by day, nor the pillar of fire by night, from before the people.' That he sees the pit in these terms is an interesting commentary on his imaginative engagement with his surroundings. The chapel-going Paul is fed with romantic associations from the Bible which might be compared with those which Lawrence himself attributes to the Nonconformist hymns of his childhood in the essay, 'Hymns in a Man's Life'. However, these associations are not isolated from the world around him, but overflow the commonplaces of his industrial environment. His mind works to synthesise rather than divide; it brings together the seemingly remote glamour of the biblical story and the ordinary, down-to-earth business of men going to work to earn a living, and out of the two it creates a fresh and original union.

In apparent contradiction to this view there is the rather different reaction earlier in the novel when Paul goes to the Co-operative Society reading-room to look for job advertisements. He gazes out of the window and already feels himself 'a prisoner of industrialism'. Seeing the old, much-loved landscape of home, he feels that: 'He was being taken into bondage. His freedom in the beloved home valley was going now' (Chapter 5). How seriously we ought to take this comment is not easy to say; it may be, and very likely is, no more than a reflection of a sensitive boy's natural reluctance to face the prospect of change. But what can be said is that it is towards the new, commercial world that his fears are directed rather than the old, familiar mining world. In the landscape which Paul gazes at the pits still seem to have their proper place; and, as suggested by the image in the sentence, 'Two collieries, among the fields, waved their small white plumes of steam', these particular pits are both an integral part of the countryside and capable of seeming gay and attractive.

A similar impression is conveyed in Chapter 6 when Paul describes the pit as being 'like something alive almost – a big creature that you don't know'. There is nothing inimical here. This is an industrial activity which is not dehumanised, but, on the contrary, is redeemed because it has the feel of men on it: 'But I like the feel of *men* on things, while they're alive. There's a feel of men about the trucks, because they've been handled with men's hands, all of them.'

There are, of course, aspects of the mining world which are less congenial. Paul, for example, finds it highly distasteful to have to wait in the office to collect his father's pay – though this may be more a matter of his self-consciousness than anything else; and, more seriously, the harsh, laborious conditions of Mr Morel's work undermine his temper, making him irritable and disagreeable on a number of occasions. The dangers of his job are fully recognised as well. Accidents inevitably occur, and one of them brings Morel near to losing his life; he endures great pain as he is carried in the ambulance to hospital over the jolting cobbled roads, and, though Mrs Morel is inclined to think that her husband plays a bit too much for sympathy, the laconic testimony of the sane and sensible Barker ('But it *wor* bad for him, Mrs Morel, it *wor* that!') convinces her that his suffering is real enough. Such episodes are, however, always seen in more than one light. For example, the sardonic sense of humour characteristic of the mining community puts the pay-collecting scene into proportion when Mr Braithwaite advises the Bower boy to tell his father to keep off the drink, and one of the colliers interjects; 'An' niver mind if he puts his foot through yer.' And the same sense of humour, this time coming from Mrs Morel, relives the would-be tragic self-pity of the injured Morel's 'I s'll niver come out of 'ere but in a wooden box' with the crisp retort: '. . . if you want them to carry you into the garden in a wooden box, when you're better, I've no doubt they will'.

3.2 CLASS

In Chapter 10, as we have already seen (p. 20), Paul associates the middle-class with 'ideas' and the working-class with 'life itself, warmth'. This awareness of different class values is another aspect of the setting within which the novel operates. It is another manifestation of that duality between intellect and sensuousness which is reflected in the contrast between Paul's parents and between Miriam and Clara.

The immediacy with which the texture of working-class life is presented in this novel is one of its major triumphs. Jessie Chambers shows herself to be a worthy appreciator of this element in Lawrence's genius when she writes: 'Born and bred of working people, he had the rare gift of seeing them from within, and revealing them on their own plane'. What she means is beautifully illustrated by the half-dozen paragraphs at the beginning of Chapter 2 which describe how Mr Morel spends the hour that he has to himself in the morning between getting up and going to the pit. They are crammed with vivid detail which communicates to the reader directly, without any need for explanatory comment, the intense pleasure that the miner gets from the practical business of breakfasting and preparing for work. We hear the 'bang, bang of the poker' as he smashes the coal, and we feel his love of sheer physical warmth as he blocks out draughts and piles up 'a big fire'. And his use of a newspaper instead of a table-cloth, and a clasp-knife instead of a fork; his manner of toasting his bacon before the fire, while catching the drips of fat on a thick slice of bread; the way he drinks his tea from the saucer instead of the cup – not only are all these distinctive features of his working-class way of life, but, more importantly, they communicate his delighted satisfaction in enjoying, for the time being at least, a sense of complete freedom from the tyranny of polite convention.

This is a lonely pleasure since Mrs Morel's very different values virtually separate him from the family. When he wants company he has to seek for it in the masculine society of the public house, or down the mine, or in the weekly ritual of sharing out the group's earnings. (It's perhaps worth noting, however, that only the last of these is presented with the same concrete immediacy as the breakfasting, perhaps because the youthful Lawrence would not have been admitted – and under his mother's influence would not have wanted to be admitted – to the public house evenings, and because, as far as we know, he never himself went down the mine.) Nevertheless, there are occasional interludes when Morel can still make contact with the family. These tend to occur when he can involve them in little jobs, such as making fuses, which are part of his work, but which he can do at home, or when he tells the children stories about Taffy, the pit pony, or the mice which steal his lunch from his pocket. After such evenings the children lie in bed, with a sense of security, as the miners due for the night shift tramp by outside – a poignant reminder of the warmth and harmony which becomes an increasingly rare experience for them.

In contrast Mrs Morel is both more closely and more consistently linked with her family. She is in some respects a middle-class figure, but in others still markedly working-class. Her white-collar ambitions for her sons make her seem to be striving through them to enter a higher class, as do her educated interests and her liking for the more intellectual companionship of the Congregational minister. To this extent the scene in Chapter 2 where she entertains Mr Heaton to tea and is interrupted by the return of her husband is a little comedy of conflict between class attitudes. Morel's behaviour is quite deliberately boorish because he resents the superior airs which he feels his wife is putting on for the occasion. When the minister politely offers to shake hands with him he rubs in the dirty nature of his manual work ('Tha niver wants ter shake hands wi' a hand like that, does ter? There's too much pick-haft and shovel-dirt on it'); and he makes the minister feel the sweat on his singlet, simply in order to embarrass his wife. Yet the scene, for all that, is one that still belongs essentially to working-class life. Even before Morel enters it is tinged with mild irony as Mrs Morel listens to the exposition of Christ's miracle in changing the water to wine, but thinks to herself that the minister is only compensating for the death of his young wife by making 'his love into the Holy Ghost'. Moreover, all the time he is speaking the baby has to be held and the batter-pudding and potatoes have to be got ready for supper; and at the height of the interchange between the two men the narrator puts in an effective reminder that 'The room was full of the smell of meat and vegetables and pit-clothes'.

Many of the scenes involving Mrs Morel and the children are also essentially working-class – for example, when she goes to the fair with William and Annie (Chapter 1), or when she shares with Paul the guilty pleasure of her purchases at Eastwood market (Chapter 4). And if she tends to be somewhat aloof from the rest of the mothers and pride herself on the achievements which lift her sons out of their class, she is still very much a participant in the community of the working-class when she talks with Mrs Kirk or Mrs Anthony, and she benefits from its custom of helping out at times of pregnancy and sickness. Even the Women's Guild attached to the local Co-operative Society, where Mrs Morel reads the discussion papers which satisfy her 'superior' intellectual side (and fill her children with 'the deepest respect'), is part of what was, in fact, a genuinely working-class self-help movement. It is resented by some of the husbands as a 'clat-fart shop' because it gives the women 'a new standard of their own, rather disconcerting,' and to that extent it may seem a challenge to innate working-class conservatism; but, like the suffragette interests of Clara later in the novel, it reflects the social and political activities that were actually stirring working-class people in the latter part of the nineteenth century.

Most of the examples mentioned in this section, it will be noticed, come from Part One of the novel. The vivid portrayal of working-class society gives way to other concerns in Part Two; and for this reason some readers find the earlier chapters of *Sons and Lovers* more attractive than the later ones. Thematically, however, there is good reason for the change. The function of Part One is to give a full, and properly complex, sense of the influences that help to shape the life of Paul Morel, whose more individual sensibility becomes the focus of Part Two. The intertwining, and sometimes conflicting, strands of class are an important part of his background. By enabling us to feel the tensions and satisfactions of the working-class environment, and to gauge its worth by the middle-class values which also impinge upon it, Lawrence gives us a better understanding of Paul and a more complex standard by which to judge him.

3.3 MOTHER-DOMINATION

Because of the different layers of composition resulting from Lawrence's three stages of writing *Sons and Lovers* the theme of mother-domination is not as straightforward as it might be. This complication is, however, something which enriches the novel, producing complexity rather than confusion. In the text as we have it today there are both positive and negative aspects to Mrs Morel's influence on Paul. The statement made in the letter to Garnett (see above, p. 6) thus needs modifying; to present the mother's influence as wholly destructive is to distort the subtler truth of the novel itself.

Even in the letter there is some recognition of a vital element in the relation between the mother and her sons. Mrs Morel is said to have had a passion for her husband, and so 'the children are born of passion, and have heaps of vitality'. What this means is not altogether clear; it is hardly likely that Lawrence intends a merely biological meaning, implying that passionate love produces physically healthier children. More probably he wants to suggest that the emotional and sexual satisfaction experienced by the mother, if only for a short time, gave her a degree of fulfilment which released her capacity for enjoyment of life, and that in such a favourable ambience the children could feel free to develop without strain and anxiety. Clearly this does not last. The mother's disappointment in the father leads to the transfer of her deepest feelings from him to her offspring, and particularly the male offspring, whom, unconsciously, she begins to treat as substitutes for her husband. From this develops the inhibitive influence – the excessive emotional demands interfering with the sons' own development – which is outlined in the Garnett letter.

Lawrence is explicit about this transfer of feeling when, in Chapter 1, he sketches the process by which Mrs Morel begins to find that her husband is a rather different man from the one she took him to be. The birth of William is referred to in the following terms: 'His mother loved him passionately. He came just when her own bitterness of disillusion was hardest to bear . . . She made much of the child, and the father was jealous.' To some extent such jealousy is a natural part of the change in a marriage which comes about with the birth of a child, but what is ominous in this case is that the arrival of the baby coincides with intense disappointment in the husband, with the result that: 'She turned to the child; she turned from the father'. This shift of attention is dramatically illustrated by the hair-cutting episode three paragraphs later, when, as a reaction to the charming manner in which his wife dresses up the baby, and especially to her delight in 'the twining wisps of hair clustering round his head', Morel cuts off all the child's curls. The ostensible reason for Morel's action is his disapproval of the effeminacy which he thinks is being foisted on the boy: 'Yer non want ter make a wench on 'im.' But tell-tale comments such as 'Morel laughed uneasily', and 'bending his head to shield his eyes from hers', indicate that this aggressiveness is more bluster than confidence; he knows that what he has done is deeply offensive to his wife, but he hasn't the courage to face up to her. What he does not know – though the scene is so contrived that the reader certainly grasps it – is that he has been driven by resentment of her emotional abandonment of himself in favour of the child to take revenge on the new object of her love, and in a way that particularly strikes at her middle-class pretensions in making the child a projection of the 'superiority' she feels with regard to her husband. In an unfortunately portentous comment – but one that is still highly relevant to the situation – this is later branded as an 'act of masculine clumsiness;' and it is further said to be 'the spear through the side' of Mrs Morel's love for her husband.

If in this incident Mrs Morel seems to be self-righteous, and yet is allowed to remain immune from criticism, she receives rather different treatment in what may be regarded as the corresponding scene in Chapter 2. This is the scene in which Mrs Morel takes the baby Paul out to see the sunset. It does not involve her husband, but it is perhaps to the point that it follows soon after her conflict with him over the minister's visit, and that it is immediately preceded by the sentence: 'Morel had kicked William, and the mother would never forgive him'. As the scene opens Mrs Morel might thus seem to be full of resentment towards her husband. Nonetheless, it is not anger that she feels, but unusual peace: 'With Mrs Morel it was one of those still moments when the small frets vanish, and the beauty of things stands out, and she had the peace and the strength to see herself.' A 'golden glow' floods over everything, creating a sense of plenitude and fertility. In this mood Mrs Morel sees a few stooks of corn in a field which 'stood up as if alive', and her ambitious hopes for Paul take the form of imagining him as a Joseph – the biblical figure who dreamt that his brother's sheaves of corn 'made obeisance' to his sheaf (Genesis 37:7). The baby is attracted towards the light and seems to clamber with his hands towards it; but the mother, noticing 'the peculiar knitting' of its brows and 'the heaviness of its eyes', is disturbed and uneasy. She has an obscure sense that she and her husband have wronged the child: 'And at that moment she felt, in some inner place of her soul, that she and her husband were guilty'. As if to propitiate this feeling, and to 'make up to [the child] for having brought it into the world unloved,' she tells herself that she will love it all the more – she will 'carry it in her love'. Whereupon she has the sudden impulse to thrust the child 'forward to the crimson, throbbing sun, almost with relief'. The child, too, lifts its fist, as if in confirmation. Immediately, however, a contrary wave of feeling makes her pull back the child; though she is, says the narrator, 'ashamed almost of her impulse to give him back whence he came'.

The scene is a symbolic one, and like all good symbolism it does not admit of simple translation into conscious terms. But it does seem to suggest that Mrs Morel, guiltily aware of the harm which might be done to the child, is able for a moment to transcend the frustrations of her marriage and, in tune with the natural vitality suggested by the scene, to let the child make its own unimpeded contact with the source of life, the sun. If this interpretation is correct, it would suggest that there are both creative and destructive elements in the mother's relationship to the child. She wants to give it its fundamental independence, so that it can grow to its own mature manhood; but these feelings are crossed by an obscure sense that her own attitude towards the father is harmful to the child – that the strain and anxiety which she perceives in its face is a sign of the burden which she is unwittingly imposing upon it. The scene is thus an ambiguous pointer to the future of Paul. It suggests that his mother has an instinct which enables her to recognise the true, vital interests of her child, but that this is held in perilous balance with her demand that it should compensate for the unsatisfactoriness of her relationship with her husband.

As William, and more particularly Paul, grow up, this ambiguous quality in their relationship with their mother becomes increasingly manifest. William's eager enjoyment of the fair is incomplete without his mother; he wants to win the egg-cups with the moss-roses on them for her sake, and when he gets her to accompany him he sticks close to her, 'bristling with a small boy's pride of her'. When she leaves, he is torn between her and the wakes, split in his feelings as he will be later. His first prize for running is given to her, and she receives it 'like a queen'. However, when he goes dancing – a pastime which, significantly, he enjoys as much as his father did – it is 'in spite of his mother', and she is ridiculously haughty with the partners who come asking after him: 'I don't approve of the girls my son meets at dances'. In the critical relationship between William and 'Gipsy' she plays no obviously hostile part. On the contrary, it is Mrs Morel who defends the girl against the increasingly cutting remarks that William makes about her; but the source of those remarks is, at least indirectly, the mother. He senses the mother's disapproval even though this is made explicit only to Paul, not William himself, and his fiancée's inability to match his intelligence and serious interests is constantly measured in his mind by comparison with the companionship he has known with his mother: 'He was accustomed to having all his thoughts sifted through his mother's mind; so, when he wanted companionship, and was asked in reply to be the billing and twittering lover, he hated his betrothed.' The very choice of words such as 'billing' and 'twittering' is loaded with the mother's kind of judgement. She has fostered in him the need for satis-factions which go well beyond conventional love-making, but there is no woman who can meet those needs except his mother. We are not told how it is that he has fallen for a girl who is so obviously shallow, but it is easy to guess that her attraction is precisely that she does not offer a real challenge to the sacred ground held by his mother. By the same token, however, she will never make him a real wife, even though he feels honour-bound not to break their engagement. This is the split which proves fatal, and it is to be presumed that the erysipelas, complicated by pneumonia, which kills him is psychosomatic, i.e. a physical manifestation of profound psychological disturbance. He dies because of the imbalance created by his mother's love for him.

Paul's history is an extended parallel to William's and comes perilously near to producing the same result. In him, too, we see the stimulating, yet also devastating effect of an exceptional intimacy between mother and son. Their mutual fondness and sensitivity to each other's feelings can be seen actively realised in some of the most lively scenes in the novel, including Mrs Morel's return from Eastwood market with her purchases, their visit to Nottingham when Paul is interviewed for the job at Jordan's and their later visit to Lincoln. But more even than with William, there is something very like an erotic element in the mother's relationship with Paul. When, for example, as a child he goes picking blackberries he also brings home a spray as a special gift for her, which she receives with more than ordinary motherly affection: ' "Pretty!" she said, in a curious tone, of a woman accepting a love-token.' When he is sick she comforts him, and helps to restore him to health by sleeping with him, prompting the tender, but slightly over-defensive, comment from the narrator that 'Sleep is still most perfect, in spite of hygienists, when it is shared with a beloved'. Still more strikingly, when he is very ill, just after William's death, and his anguished cry for attention brings his mother's mind back to him, there comes the curious sentence: 'He put his head on her breast, and took ease of her for love.' Lawrence is imprecise here, possibly even a little evasive; but it is difficult to escape the conclusion that it is something very like the feeling between sexual lovers which is being evoked.

There is also a corresponding hostility between father and son. When Paul is ill, his father's presence, we are told, 'seemed to aggravate all his sick impatience'. In the battles between father and mother he is uncritically on his mother's side; with childish extravagance he can even pray that his father will die; and when the father is in hospital he takes pleasure in replacing him as 'the man of the house'. There is, in fact, a kind of rivalry between Paul and his father, which, when Paul is a young man, brings them near to blows (as had happened previously with William and his father).

The quarrel which occurs in Chapter 8, and the events leading up to it, again have sexual overtones. There has just been a flare-up of Mrs Morel's jealousy of Miriam, followed by a very emotional scene in which the mother says: 'And I've never – you know, Paul – I've never had a husband – not really'. After this she gives him 'a long, fervent kiss', and the son strokes her face, and kisses her, too. This is the point at which the father returns, somewhat the worse for drink:

> Morel came in, walking unevenly. His hat over one corner of his eye. He balanced in the doorway.
> 'At your mischief again?' he said venomously.

Mrs Morel's emotion turned into sudden hate of the drunkard who had come in thus upon her.

'At any rate, it is sober,' she said.

'H'm – h'm! H'm – h'm!' he sneered.

Morel then goes into the pantry, where he finds a piece of pork-pie – a tit-bit bought for Paul. When his wife objects, he flings it in the fire, and Paul squares up to him ready for a fight. Only the mother's sudden moan and sickness prevent them from hitting each other.

Several elements come to a head in this scene: Mrs Morel's feelings about Paul's relationship with Miriam; the frustration in her marriage and her turning to Paul for compensatory response; Morel's inarticulate sense of being sexually ousted by his son; Paul's devotion to his mother and resentment of his father. Morel's drunkenness produces a surliness to which his wife is very quick to react; but her and Paul's behaviour also has its element of emotional intoxication, which more than justifies the sneer she gets when she claims that it is at least 'sober'. The father has, in fact, stumbled on what is virtually a love-scene between his wife and son, and the resultant near-fight is a dramatic expression of their unnatural sexual situation. The mother's sudden attack of illness (though we have been given hints of its development earlier in the novel) is also significant. It is as if the harm being done by the demands she makes on her son is at last erupting into her consciousness and taking its physical toll. The last sentence of the chapter, however, reads: 'Everybody tried to forget the scene.' It is not a climax in which the whole relationship between mother and son is finally brought out in the open; the novel has not, in fact, run more than approximately half its course at this point. But it is a crucial stage in which the destructive element in the relationship is seen to be tragically outweighing its creative potentiality.

The subsequent development of that relationship is mainly downhill. Mrs Morel continues to have high hopes for Paul; and he, on his part, continues to love his mother, to draw sustenance for his painting from her, and, as in the Lincoln excursion, to share new experiences with her. But the latter, for example, is marred by Paul's greater awareness of his mother's age. 'Why can't a man have a *young* mother?' he blurts out when he notices that she can hardly climb the hill up to the cathedral. Both know this to be an absurdly futile protest; but it is a revealing one. Paul is demanding of her what it would be more natural to demand of a sweetheart, and she, having encouraged such a demand, is becoming increasingly aware of her inability to play such a role. Later still, when not only the affair with Miriam, but also that with Clara is breaking down, Paul's realisation goes further. He acknowledges that he does not want to marry anybody, that he feels as if he wronged his women, and he finally admits to his mother: 'And I never shall meet the right woman while you live.' This is followed by two laconic sentences which nevertheless tell a good deal about Mrs Morel's reactions: 'She was very quiet. Now she began to feel again tired, as if she were done.' The implication here is that she grasps that she is now a barrier to his fulfilment rather than a means towards it, and that her ability to fight for her own health is thereby undermined as well. However, she does not lose her will-power. Her grit and determination – qualities which she has been able to pass on to her son as part of the beneficent aspect of her influence – remain with her, even when the fatal cancer takes hold; but now they serve only to prolong both her and Paul's suffering. What was positive turns into something entirely negative, and, coupled with her rigidly unforgiving attitude to her husband, it makes her death seem an appalling summation of a vitality which has been blocked, perverted and ultimately converted into destruction.

3.4 THE MIRIAM AFFAIR

As we have seen, consideration of the relationship between Mrs Morel and her sons inevitably involves reference to the sons' relations with their girl-friends; and the letter to Garnett puts the blame for the failure of the sons' sexual lives wholly on the mother. In another comment, the so-called 'Foreword to *Sons and Lovers*', sent to Garnett in January 1913, Lawrence broadens his approach to include a theory about the relations between the sexes in which man is represented as the spokesman of the Word and woman as the embodiment of the Flesh. Man must go out into the world, but for inspiration and nourishment he needs to return constantly to the woman, 'like bees in and out of a hive'. If, however, it is his mother who attempts to perform this role, instead of a wife, the result is not renewal of the man, but destruction: 'he carries for her, but is never received into her for his confirmation and renewal, and so wastes himself away in the flesh'. Again the emphasis is on the destructive effect of mother-love.

Although the 'Foreword' is a longer piece than the letter of 14 November 1912, it is actually less detailed in its reference to the novel; in many ways it relates more to *The Rainbow* with which Lawrence was preoccupied at the time. But it does usefully direct attention to the creative activity of man, especially as an artist, and his dependence on the love of a woman. What Lawrence is suggesting is that a fully satisfactory sexual relationship is indispensable to man's creative purpose in the world at large, and he sees mother-domination, though capable of providing a vital initial stimulus, as something which is bound in the end to destroy the man and his work. In *Sons and Lovers* the main emphasis is on Paul as a man, but he is also shown in what is at least the minor role of artist; and, interestingly, his relationship to his sweetheart, Miriam, is one that involves both aspects of his being, as Lawrence's own affair with Jessie Chambers involved him as both man and writer.

For Miriam, and for the Leivers family generally, Paul is the Word, the conscious spokesman who articulates the wonders and excitements of the natural world for them. On one of his early visits to The Haggs (Chapter 7) Mrs Leivers and Miriam take him to see a wren's nest. They already respond to it, but it is his illuminating comment that 'It's almost as if you were feeling inside the live body of the bird' which makes it seem 'to start to life' for them; and likewise when he says of the celandines that he likes them, 'when their petals go flat back with the sunshine. They seem to be pressing themselves at the sun,' Miriam appreciates these flowers as she has never done before.

The excitement is mutual, for Paul himself is urged by this kind of sensitive response into more intense awareness of the natural world and encouraged to express it in his paintings. A curious distinction is made, however, between his mother's interest and that of Miriam and the Leivers:

> It was not his art Mrs Morel cared about; it was himself and his achievement. But Mrs Leivers and her children were almost his disciples. They kindled him and made him glow to his work . . .

Elsewhere he is shown working at home, with his mother sitting in her rocking-chair, and he insists that he does his best work in such circumstances; but it is to Miriam that he needs to bring his work when he has finished it, for:

> Then he was stimulated into knowledge of the work he had produced unconsciously. In contact with Miriam he gained insight; his vision went deeper. From his mother he drew the life-warmth, the strength to produce; Miriam urged this warmth into intensity like a white light.

This may well be intended to suggest that the mother's influence is more vital than Miriam's; but, if so, it is double-dged, for the effect can also be to suggest that Miriam and the Leivers have a more disinterested concern for his art. There is a slight suspicion of special pleading in the way the mother is represented as a source of warmth; Miriam's pleasure in his artistic capacity seems more sincere, and she seems to give as well as take. Nevertheless, there is a quality of religious extravagance in her responses which makes Paul uneasy. In the episode of the wild-rose bush, for example, she is eager for them to share 'a communion . . . something holy'; and though the experience is authenticated by the brilliance of Lawrence's description ('its long streamers trailed thick right down to the grass, splashing the darkness everywhere with great spilt stars, pure white'), her 'ecstasy' and attitude of 'worship' make him feel 'anxious and imprisoned'. We are not told why, but the emphasis on the whiteness of the roses, and the use of a phrase like 'white, virgin scent', in conjunction with the prevalence of religious diction, hint that a natural experience is being inappropriately translated on to a spiritual plane, that the 'communion'

Miriam seeks is a means of evading, or making safe, the sexual feeling aroused by Paul. Her dependence on his capacity to articulate natural experiences for her thus becomes a way of neutralising the dangerously sensuous element in those experiences. Instead of being the woman who, for Paul, can represent the Flesh, and to whom he can therefore return for renewal, she subtly denies that role. 'With Miriam,' we are told, 'he was always on the high plane of abstraction, when his natural fire of love was transmitted into the fine steam of thought.'

Mrs Morel's antipathy to Miriam would appear to be based on her objection to such soulful possessiveness: ' "She is one of those who will want to suck a man's soul out till he has none of his own left," she said to herself; "and he is such a gaby as to let himself be absorbed. She will never let him become a man; she never will." ' But the mother is also obviously jealous, so that her comments cannot be altogether trusted. Paul's intense regard for his mother is itself a factor preventing him from taking the kind of lead in his relationship with Miriam that might help her to overcome her problems. It is he who first tries to insist that their friendship is purely platonic; and, in a perhaps uncharacteristic, but nonetheless revealing passage at the end of Chapter 7, it is said that 'He was afraid of her. The fact that he might want her as a man wants a woman had in him been suppressed into a shame.' This, of course, is the earlier adolescent phase of their affair, but when he is sent back to her by Clara to 'test' her capacity for physical intimacy, he still shows no greater maturity. He is, after all, a poor wooer, ill-equipped to overcome those puritanically induced fears which make Miriam able to approach the sexual act only in a mood of self-sacrifice. In what seems to be a paragraph representing Paul's thoughts (Chapter 11, 'He courted her now like a lover') he complains of not being allowed to forget his responsibility and leave himself 'to the great hunger and impersonality of passion'. What is totally lacking, however, is anything like adequate realisation of what the experience might mean for Miriam. Her wanting him 'to look at her with eyes full of love' is merely set in antithesis to his 'eyes, full of the dark, impersonal fire of desire,' which she rejects. The possibility of a love embracing both personal responsibility and passionate spontaneity is ignored.

But this is not to say that Miriam could ever have been a suitable mate for Paul. She cannot take the lead any more than he; and her failure to do so is convincingly shown in her last interview with Paul in Chapter 15. It is one of the ironies of their relationship that she is too much like his mother in certain respects to be an effective counterbalance to his mother's influence. The possessiveness that Paul resents in her (though it must be said that the evidence for its existence comes mainly from Paul's feelings rather than her actions) is at least equalled by his mother's, and it is his eagerness to share his most serious thoughts with Miriam which particularly arouses Mrs Morel's jealousy. The mother has cultivated the intellectual side of her relationship with her son to compensate for the lack of a finer companionship with her husband, and it is this which Miriam threatens to take away from her. Even the girl's religious attitude, though romanticised and spiritualised in a way that arouses Mrs Morel's contempt, derives from the same Puritan background. For Paul to have married Miriam would, therefore, have been too much like marrying his own mother; it could not have been a creative way forward for him.

3.5 THE CLARA AFFAIR

The swing towards the affair with Clara is already implicit in the impasse of Paul's affair with Miriam. It is likewise implicit in the contrast between his parents, for if Miriam appeals to that side of Paul which has affinities with his mother, Clara attracts the sensuous side which links him to his father.

When first introduced Clara seems to be a feminist, disillusioned with marriage, and ready to take a more independent and hostile line towards men than Miriam. But the episode with Miss Limb and the stallion (Chapter 9) is an early indication that this is only a thin intellectual veneer covering her frustration; when she blurts out that she supposes Miss Limb's crankiness is because 'she wants a man' it is her own subconscious need that she reveals. Similarly, when she is seen in the context of her Sneinton home (Chapter 10) it becomes evident to Paul that she is not quite the 'high and mighty' creature he has previously thought her, but someone who finds it bitter to be 'put aside by life, as if it had no use for her'. The missing normality is indicated by her mother, who says that 'A house o' women is as dead as a house wi' no fire" and she adds that she likes 'a man about, if he's only something to snap at'. At the same time Clara's capacity for enjoyment of life is revealed in little details like the competitive eagerness with which she enters into the game of jumping over the hay and the anger she displays when Paul teases her (Chapter 9). Their combativeness with each other is like the battle of wits between Beatrice and Benedick in Shakespeare's *Much Ado About Nothing*; it shows how much they are drawn by instinct to notice each other.

The scene of Paul and Clara's love-making by the River Trent has already been analysed in the Commentary on Chapter 12 (see above, pp. 24-5). Its important features are its spontaneity and tenderness, contrasting so strongly with the tensions and frustrated harshness generated by the Miriam affair and Paul's dawning sense of the strain in his relationship with his mother. Through the affair with Clara Paul recovers something of what should have been his inheritance from the easy-going sensuousness of his father; and he is able to escape from that sense of responsibility which he found so crushing in his affair with Miriam, just as his father had escaped from Mrs Morel's nagging demands by sinking himself in the unexacting warmth of his mates in the public house.

There is also a difference, however, which makes itself felt in the different emphases accorded to Morel's flight from responsibility and Paul's respectively. Morel's is presented in the context of his moral cowardice; at this stage it is his wife's values which seem to predominate (perhaps because this part of the novel is not radically changed from what it was in the first or second draft), and accordingly the father's wish to escape from the conscious awareness of his duties is coloured with a strong sense of disapproval. In Chapter 13, however, where Lawrence attempts to evoke the quality of Paul's experience of making love to Clara, the underlying values seem to have changed. We are very likely in contact here with the final draft; the language suggests affinities with novels that Lawrence was to write in the years following *Sons and Lovers* (*The Rainbow* and *Women in Love*, for example) in which release from the pressures and anxieties of distinctively human consciousness into the impersonal, instinctual condition of awareness that man shares with all animal creation is presented as a powerful force of renewal. The individual is submerged as seemingly insignificant in the flood-like tide of life, which gives a restorative sense of peace:

> To know their own nothingness, to know the tremendous living flood which carried them always, gave them rest within themselves. If so great a magnificent power could overwhelm them, identify them altogether with itself, so that they knew they were only grains in the tremendous heave that lifted every grass-blade its little height, and every tree, and living thing, then why fret about themselves? They could let themselves be carried by life, and they felt a sort of peace each in the other.

And in another passage this sense of oneness with unconscious being is linked with the symbolism of the River Trent:

> As a rule, when he started love-making, the emotion was strong enough to carry with it everything – reason, soul, blood – in a great sweep, like the Trent carries bodily its back-swirls and intertwinings, noiselessly. Gradually the little criticism, the little sensations, were lost, thought also went, everything borne along in one flood. He became, not a man with a mind, but a great instinct.

The poetic quality of the writing here is itself an indication of how highly such experience is valued by Lawrence. His imagination is fully engaged as he seeks to communicate its uniquely vital nature. But he does not cease to be a novelist as well. In their context these passages demand that we relate them to the characters whose experience they represent; and when we do so, we find that although the first passage refers to 'they' and 'their', implying unanimity between Paul and Clara, the next paragraph separates Clara's response from his: 'But Clara was not satisfied. Something great was there . . . But it did not keep her.' The second passage focuses more exclusively on Paul's feelings; 'he' replaces 'they', and the narrator makes an important qualification: 'And Clara knew this held him to her, so she trusted altogether to the passion. It, however, failed her very often.'

How far this hint of Clara's dissatisfaction is intended to show awareness of a difference between the needs of men and women in general (for example, that the sexual experience is only really satisfactory for women when the impersonal quality which means so much to Paul is also combined with a sense of personal security) it is difficult to say. It is, however, a saving grace, as far as the realistic level of *Sons and Lovers* is concerned, that Lawrence does not allow his celebration of 'Passion' to blind him to other needs, even though these may seem, when consciousness is drowned under the flood of instinct, to be merely part of 'the little criticism, the little sensations'. The return to the ordinary level of consciousness is inevitable, and with it these seemingly petty demands reassert themselves as continuing necessities of everyday existence.

3.6 PAUL AND BAXTER DAWES

It is in accord with the natural ebb and flow which constitutes the rhythm of *Sons and Lovers* that not only should there be a retreat to the ordinary level of reality once more after the extraordinary experience of Paul and Clara's love-making, but that there should also be a return, after so much emphasis on Paul's relations with women, to the masculine world. In Part One the presence of men is felt, for example, in the vivid scenes from Morel's life, the athleticism of William and the glimpses we are given from time to time of such working men as Barker, Purdy and the miners who help to carry William's coffin; and in Part Two Paul's friendship with the Leivers brothers, especially Edgar, is a reminder of the masculine dimension. Mrs Morel, Miriam and Clara, however, dominate Chapters 7-12, and it is not until the appearance of Baxter Dawes that major importance again attaches to a man.

The connection is through Clara, of course, and at first it is Baxter's jealousy as the outraged husband (though it was he who deserted Clara) which brings him into confrontation with Paul. Their fight is also influenced by the dominant female emphasis since it can be regarded as bringing at last into physical reality the threatened, but unaccomplished, conflicts between Morel and his sons, in Chapters 4 and 8 respectively. The fight does more than this, however. It brings Paul and Baxter together. Just as love, in Paul's affairs with women is perpetually shadowed by revulsion and hate, so – as a corollary almost – hatred between the two men carries with it an implicit undertone of comradeship, which is made way for, and enabled to emerge into the open, by the purgative effect of their physical combat.

We have noted how the love-making with Clara anticipates an important theme of Lawrence's later work, and it may be that the treatment of the Baxter relationship also points towards a preoccupation which becomes much more significant in, for example, the friendship of Birkin and Gerald in *Women in Love* and that between Aaron and Lilly in *Aaron's Rod*. It has been suggested that these later male relationships reveal homosexual tendencies in Lawrence, but there is little reason for thinking that the same applies to the Paul–Baxter relationship. Their fight has none of the homoerotic overtones of the 'Gladiatorial' wrestling match in Chapter 20 of *Women in Love*; its main function is to provide a discharge for the violence which has been accumulating between the two men, and to suggest – especially through the otherwise inexplicable relaxing of Paul's will when he is at the point of beating Baxter – a retribution which Paul accepts half-knowingly as his desert.

Once this 'rough justice' (the phrase used by Sir Francis Bacon for revenge) has been accomplished, the way is open for Paul to make amends by visiting the sick Baxter in hospital and eventually bringing him and Clara together again. And this suits Paul's own interests, since he has by now come to recognise the limitations of his own feeling for Clara. But beyond either of these levels of motivation there is also the simple satisfaction of a relationship which is not built on the mutual expectations of intense emotional involvement that Paul has experienced, to excess, in his relations with the women in his life; one which puts him in touch again, if only fleetingly, with the male comradeship known by his father in his working-class world. Their conversations are plain, even laconic, tending to slip back into the dialect, and the relationship is left, almost slackly, to develop at its own pace – to be carried by a tacit community of feeling rather than forced towards expression. It is, furthermore, low key because it is both literally and metaphorically a convalescent relationship, bridging the period of Baxter's recovery from illness and assisting him to finding a basis for renewal of his marriage with Clara.

3.7 THE QUESTION OF TRAGEDY

The letter to Garnett of 14 November 1912 concludes with a reference to Paul's final 'drift towards death' and the claim that *Sons and Lovers* 'is a great tragedy . . . the tragedy of thousands of young men in England . . .'. What Lawrence means here by 'tragedy' is open to debate. In another letter written in the same year he says that 'Tragedy ought really to be a great kick at misery'; and in the Preface to his play, *Touch and Go*, written in 1919, he rejects the idea of tragedy as defeat, substituting a more positive view of tragedy as 'creative crisis'. (See the chapter on 'D. H. Lawrence: Tragedy as Creative Crisis' in R. P. Draper, *Lyric Tragedy*, Macmillan, 1985.) This would seem to fit in well with the affirmative ending of the novel already discussed on p. 32 above. But the coupling of tragedy with 'the drift towards death' is undeniably consistent with a more traditional view implying suffering and waste.

Which meaning, then, provides the right terms for interpreting *Sons and Lovers*? Paul is the tragic hero – though there are subsidiary tragic figures in Mrs Morel and Miriam, and a prelusive tragic hero in William, whose fate foreruns that of Paul. When his career is viewed across the whole history of the novel it seems to show a rise in his fortunes in Part One as his talents and opportunities are unfolded, countered by increasing frustration and despair in Part Two as his attempts to centre his life on a fulfilling relationship with a woman are defeated by the split between Word and Flesh which is his inheritance from his mother and father. This is the classical pattern of tragedy. On the other hand his affairs can be seen as threats to entrap him in relationships which could only, at best, bring him partial fulfilment, and to escape from them is therefore to resist the inevitability which is normally associated with tragedy. Even his mother's death has this ambiguous status; it represents both the nadir of his downward tragic progress and, as we have seen, not only 'release' from suffering for her, but also a 'release' for Paul – which he himself has helped to bring about – from the crippling effects of mother-domination. Both meanings of 'tragedy' are thus incorporated in the structure of the novel. It is built on an apparent contradiction.

The explanation for this contradiction may lie in the remark made by Lawrence in a letter of 26 October 1913, probably with *Sons and Lovers* specifically in mind: 'But one sheds one's sicknesses in books – repeats and presents again one's emotions, to be master of them.' The implication to be wary of here is that the novel is a purely confessional work. It does contain a great deal of Lawrence's personal experience, but it is that material shaped and interpreted by art. One pattern that Lawrence could detect in his own life was the traditional pattern of tragedy; and he was very probably assisted in seeing the relevance of such a pattern by what he managed to learn, during the later stages of the novel's composition, about the psychologically harmful effects of mother-love and, in particular, the notion of the 'Oedipus complex'. From this, perhaps, *Sons and Lovers* derived its destructive meaning. But the process of writing was also a means by which Lawrence could face the damaging influence of his own devotion to his much-loved mother and, by exploring it imaginatively, achieve a kind of emotional therapy. That is to say, he practised Conrad's famous dictum, 'In the destructive element immerse . . .' and by so doing he turned the destructive into something that was also creative.

However, that does not quite do justice to the complexity of *Sons and Lovers*. This process of imaginative exploration further meant the rediscovery of elements in Lawrence's own life and background which were intensely vital and enjoyable – elements which included not only getting behind the mother-induced hostility to the father in order to find his sensuous inheritance from the father, but also re-living the real, positive satisfactions of his relationship with his mother and renewing his pleasure in the Nottinghamshire and Derbyshire environment of his youth. This was not simply therapeutic purgation, but an active, outgoing process of creation. Hence the quite un-depressing effect of his realisation of a seemingly depressing and frustrating theme. Notwithstanding Lawrence's own comments, *Sons and Lovers* is not so much 'tragedy' as 'counter-tragedy'; an answer to tragedy paradoxically found in the process of fashioning it.

4 TECHNIQUES

4.1 PLOT AND STRUCTURE

When *Sons and Lovers* was first published, in 1913, even favourable reviewers considered that it was deficient in plot-construction. The critic of the *Westminster Gazette* said that he would make 'no attempt to summarize the story' since 'Definite plot there is none – the book begins with Paul's mother's marriage and ends with her death – but Paul, the unheroic hero, is left still vacillating before his life, and there is no reason why a later book should not continue the record of his aimless way.' And even Harold Massingham, reviewer for the *Daily Chronicle*, who was generous in his praise (to him *Sons and Lovers* was 'far and away the best book' Lawrence had yet written), said quite bluntly: 'It has little or no pretensions to plot-architecture, its incident is not external, and in the crisis of psychological evolution it bothers hardly at all about continuity, balance or arrangement.'

The reason behind these views must be sought in the ideas about plot which critics had inherited from the nineteenth-century novel. Plot, it was felt, should consist of a connected series of events which were linked together by a chain of cause and effect. It should be rationally explicable and logically coherent. Mystery and seemingly bizarre, unaccountable actions, such as those one finds in Dickens' *Great Expectations* or *Bleak House*, were acceptable – indeed, such startling eruptions were valued as a means of arresting the reader's attention and, at a time when most novels were first printed in magazines in serialised form, of exciting his interest so that he would read on in order to discover how such things came about. But in the end the mystery would have to be dispersed and reason made to prevail, as in a modern 'who-dunnit' detective story. In less sensational novels, like those of George Eliot, for example, the events might seem more humdrum and commonplace, but the demand for an interconnecting web of logic and reason was equally strong. In George Eliot's fictional world one event leads inevitably to another by a process which she analyses with considerable skill, and, in novels like *Adam*

Bede or *Middlemarch*, everything can be seen finally as the outcome of conscious choices made by her characters.

Lawrence, however, was seeking to portray a world which seemed less amenable to reason than it had been in the heyday of the Victorian novel. He wished to explore the emotions of his characters and suggest the often irrational forces which governed their lives in spite of themselves. He was not a fatalist, that is, one who believes that all men's actions are pre-determined, but he was aware of the psychological obscurity in which decisions are often made. Accordingly, a simple cause-and-effect dependence of one event upon another was inappropriate for his purposes; he needed a looser, more fluctuating form which would allow the undercurrents of feeling and the hidden emotional connections to emerge through a process of imaginative suggestion. Like the French Impressionist painters, to whose work the paintings of the young Paul Morel have some resemblance, he wanted to blur the hard, separate outlines of things in the interest of a vision which saw them as more fluently and tentatively related. In the groping words that Paul uses in his attempt to convey the quality of his paintings, the Lawrentian form is 'the shimmering protoplasm in the leaves and everywhere, and not the stiffness of the shape. That seems dead to me. Only this shimmeriness is the real living. The shape is a dead crust. The shimmer is inside really.'

This is not, however, an apology for laziness and structural incoherence. As we have seen, Lawrence worked hard at *Sons and Lovers*, strenuously revising and re-revising it; and as he insists to Garnett, in the letter which gives the 'idea' of the novel (see above, p. 6), 'I wrote it again, pruning and shaping and filling it in. I tell you it has got form – *form*: haven't I made it patiently, out of sweat as well as blood?' In a letter to another friend Ernest Collings, written 24 December 1912, he seems to resent the suggestion that he should try to give his novel more 'form'; but it is conventional, received notions of form that he rejects: 'They want me to have form: that means, they want me to have *their* pernicious ossiferous skin-and-grief form, and I won't.' Lawrence worked to give *Sons and Lovers* its own form, appropriate to its own theme and implicit vision of life; and it is in such terms that it is plotted.

The shaping principle is not unlike that of Wordsworth's great auto biographical poem, *The Prelude*, which is subtitled, 'Growth of a Poet's Mind'. *Sons and Lovers* is about the growth and development of Paul's emotional life; and though it differs markedly from *The Prelude* in concerning itself with family life and sexual relations as formative influences on a young man who is not specifically destined to be a poet, it is an interesting minor variation on that theme that Paul Morel is seen gradually emerging in the novel as a talented painter. The main focus, however, is on Paul as boy and young man, rather than artist, with balance carefully maintained between the conditioning circumstances of his life and the responses which he makes, sometimes negatively, sometimes positively to the crises arising from these circumstances. And the novel is divided into two Parts, which correspond generally – though not in any rigidly dogmatic way – to the two arms of this balance. Part One shows the world, of family and also of larger community, into which Paul is born and begins his own history of individual development; Part Two looks more intensely at the emotional problems of his adolescence, when he is on the threshold of what may be either mature manhood or the collapse of his quest for fulfilment.

The structure of Part One is underlined by the titles given to each chapter. Chapter 1, 'The Early Married Life of the Morels', shows the dual elements in that marriage which foreshadow the elements later to be found in the character of Paul: the intellectual Puritanism of the mother and the sensuousness of the father. It shows also the fascination each of these has for the other, thus implying a standard of harmony which, though it is only attained for a brief honeymoon period, becomes a measure for the subsequent development of Paul. Chapter 2, 'The Birth of Paul, And Another Battle', introduces the baby Paul into this context; and two scenes in particular – the lifting of the child to the sun, followed by withdrawal, and the quarrel which ends with blood dripping on to the baby's white shawl – symbolically link his future to the growing frustration of the parents' marriage. Chapters 4 and 5, 'The Young Life of Paul' and 'Paul Launches into Life', give Paul greater emotional prominence both within and outside the family; while the development of William's business career and love-affair ominously preludes the tensions of his younger brother's life. (This is not mere repetition; like the doubling-up in *King Lear* of Lear's relationship with his daughters and Gloucester's relationship with his sons, it unversalises the family situation.) The concentration on William in Chapter 6, 'Death in the Family', brings this prelude to a tragic climax, which stands as a warning of the dangerous imbalance that can be inflicted on a cherished son by a split between his parents; and the near-echo of William's death in the serious illness of Paul deepens this sense of menace. This concludes Part One; but not with decisive finality. By introducing Willey Farm and Miriam in the last chapter Lawrence also suggests the opening up of new and different possibilities for Paul, while his mother's nursing him back to health after the loss of William counterpoints death with life.

Part Two, as already mentioned, is marked by a shift to a more analytical style as the love-affairs of Paul, first with Miriam and then with Clara, are explored more introspectively than any of the relationships in Part One. But the rhythms of the preceding Part are constantly felt as conditioning elements in the second Part, and characters and scenes inevitably recall earlier ones. The 'Lad-and-Girl Love' of Chapter 7 is an initiation into love between male and female which has structurally the same position in Part Two as the courtship of Mr and Mrs Morel in Part One. Significantly, however, it lacks even the short-lived poise of the Morels' early relationship, and its possibilities of growth are weighed upon from the beginning by the jealousy of Mrs Morel. Miriam's own inhibitions, deriving from a different aspect of the Puritanism which operates in Mrs Morel, complicate and increase the frustration of her and Paul's relationship; and the resulting 'Strife in Love' (Chapter 8) echoes the 'battle' in the Morel household. It is not, of course, expressed in similar physical violence, but there is an underlying psychological violence suggestive of involvement in a conflict, the nature of which they do not understand – just as the Morel parents were unaware of the forces which operated within them. Nevertheless, in Part Two (and this makes the increasingly analytical style especially appropriate) there is also a gradual heightening of consciousness with regard to the psychological condition that the characters find themselves in. Hence we find Paul probing the causes of his dissatisfaction with Miriam, and Miriam criticising the 'high' and 'low' elements in Paul's nature. The 'Defeat of Miriam' (Chapter 9) emerges from this process, and so does Miriam's introduction of Paul to her friend, Clara, which in turn leads to the development of a complementary relationship in Chapter 10 that has subtle affinities with the earlier complementing of Mrs Morel's spirituality by the sensuousness of Mr Morel. A rhythmical alternation now becomes the structural principle: Chapter 11, 'The Test on Miriam', is a doomed attempt at a sexual relationship between Paul and Miriam which has been precipitated by the growing sexuality in Paul's feeling for Clara; and with its inevitable failure the imaginative pendulum of the novel swings to the other extreme in the intensely physical, and for the first time deeply satisfying, 'Passion' (Chapter 12) experienced by Paul and Clara in their love-making. As this begins to lapse, however, the limitations of the physical are emphasised by Clara's sense of being excluded as an individual – functioning only as impersonal 'woman' for Paul; and in Chapter 13 a kind of retribution overtakes Paul in the form of Baxter Dawes's attack, which, in an emotional rather than a logically connected manner, is echoed in the collapse of Mrs Morel with cancer. This leads on to what is the greatest psychological crisis of all for Paul – the death of his mother; but, again, even in this chapter (14) the strands are complex rather than simply focused on the sufferings of Mrs Morel and her son. Much of the chapter is concerned with the tentative development of a new relationship between Paul and Baxter Dawes; the major theme of death thus has, as it were, an accompanying minor theme of a different, and, again, complementary, development in the area of the living. And even if Paul's manœuvres to bring Baxter and Clara together again are the manifestation of his (unconscious) desire to rid himself of her now, this can be also be seen as having an imaginative connection with the death of Mrs Morel, since this is Paul's 'Release', effected by a mercy killing, which, again, may be the expression of an unconscious wish to be rid of the still greater burden of mother-domination. Finally, in Chapter 15, 'Derelict', death and life are once more in contrapuntal relationship to each other, since Paul, though devastated by the loss of his mother, is still unwilling to capitulate to Miriam; and at the very end he is determined not to follow his mother into the darkness, but to walk 'towards the faintly humming, glowing town, quickly'.

Thus the structural development of *Sons and Lovers* shows a cumulative and forward movement, but one that has its eddies and backward-flowing currents as well. There are reversions to earlier scenes and motifs, and anticipations of what is to come; and particularly in Part Two Lawrence establishes a process of rhythmical alternation, modified by subtle interconnections, which focuses the reader's attention on both the positive and negative aspects of Paul's emotional development. But that is not all. Vignettes of working-class life, glimpses of the lives of minor characters such as Annie and Arthur, and elements in the growth of Paul's career as an artist are also interwoven with the central theme in a way that heightens the sense of there being a more ordinary, less complicated and 'normal' pattern of life, which provides the context for his particular struggle towards fulfilment, and against which his success or failure is to be measured. The skilful way Lawrence keeps this supporting material constantly available to his readers is another feature of the plotting of the novel. There are occasions when it can be regarded as mere padding, but these are rare. For the most part it is both interesting in its own right and a necessary means of filling in the sense of a healthy, living medium without which Paul's difficulties, and moments of vital satisfaction as well, could not be viewed in proper perspective. They are the atmosphere which the novel's theme must breathe, and the soil in which it must grow.

4.3 CHARACTERISATION

Sons and Lovers is a novel which both belongs to the realistic tradition dominant in the nineteenth century and transcends it. The characters are accordingly at once true-to-life and yet endowed with an imaginative dimension which gives them a larger poetic significance. Thus in Chapter 1 the young Mr and Mrs Morel are described in terms that might be used in a biography. *Mrs Morel* is seen as inheriting certain features of her father's family, the Coppards: she has their 'clear, defiant blue eyes and their broad brow'. She is like her mother in her small build, but her pride and Non-conformist independence come from her father's side. She has a lively intelligence and enjoys intellectual debate. She has a large brow, brown curly hair, blue eyes ('very straight, honest, and searching'), and there is a puritan touch about the way she dresses herself, always subdued, and making sparing use of ornament.

Morel's family receives less attention; it is merely mentioned that his grandfather was 'a French refugee who had married an English barmaid – if it had been a marriage'. Instead, focus is on his physical appearance – red cheeks and mouth, large wavy black beard and erect stature – and his great love of dancing. We are also told that he has 'a rich ringing laugh' and a sense of the comically grotesque, which is devoid of satire.

So far these are effective, but essentially conventional, character-sketches. However, as Lawrence is drawn on to compare and contrast the two, his language becomes more figurative and evocative (when Morel dances, for example, his face is said to be 'the flower of his body'), and the comparison at last issues in the richly suggestive image of the flame:

> Therefore the dusky, golden softness of this man's sensuous flame of life, that flowed off his flesh like the flame from a candle, not baffled and gripped into incandescence by thought and spirit as her life was, seemed to her something wonderful, beyond her.

The two persons concerned now become not just characters, but complementary aspects of the life-principle. The image of the flame unites them, while its different manifestations suggest radically opposed qualities of being. It may be that at the back of Lawrence's mind is the difference between a candleflame and the sharper and brighter light of a gas jet; if so, this also carries with it the further suggestion of contrast between traditional and more modern forms of illumination. Mrs Morel's is the new technologically-produced flame, Morel's the old-fashioned one that flickers and flows in the wind. He follows natural rhythms, but has little assertive power of his own; she has the brightness and energy of the will, but at the cost of an effort which, as hinted by the uncomfortable verbs 'baffled' and 'gripped', is painfully, and perhaps damagingly, intense. We cannot define exactly what the image means, but we are made to feel that Mr and Mrs Morel are more than just two different kinds of person. They reflect two different ways of responding to, and directing, the very pulse of life itself.

This combination of psychological realism and wider meaning is also to be found in the treatment of *Miriam*. She is a girl of dark complexion, with short black curls, 'very fine and free', but also rather awkward, maladroit movements which betray a lack of adjustment to the world in which she lives. Although a farmer's daughter, she has been conditioned by her mother to such reticence about sex that in her conversations with Paul 'It could never be mentioned that the mare was in foal;' and she cultivates a compensatory dream-world of literary romanticism ('Everywhere was a Walter Scott heroine being loved by men with helmets or with plumes in their caps') into which she can escape from the crude, physical realities of ordinary life. Beyond this, however, she also represents a whole tradition of Victorian Christian idealism, which emphasises the spirit rather than the body, and exalts moral duty to a level of religious devotion. For her the noblest achievement is a high-minded communion between man and woman, with sexuality admitted only in the form of self-sacrifice.

Clara, with her high-piled hair and whiter, though coarser, skin and prominent breasts, is immediately recognised as a more sensual woman than Miriam. She is a natural sexual partner, and her initial aggressiveness and militant feminism are quickly perceived as little more than a protective screen thrown up after the disappointment of her marriage to Baxter Dawes. She is not a particularly complex character. Her inner world is less convincingly portrayed than Miriam's, and in her love-affair with Paul she perhaps slides too readily into the 'poetic' role that Lawrence has designed for her. She is most vividly realised in the scenes at her home in Sneinton and in the love-making scene by the River Trent. It is in the latter episode especially that the more ordinary level of characterisation is superseded and she acquires a sensuous aura which makes her for a while representative of the principle of the 'Flesh'; though, as we have seen, it is also here that the love between her and Paul is expressed with the most vivid, naturalistic detail and persuasive tenderness. The more ambitiously evocative passages in Chapter 13 confirm this wider meaning, but they also show Clara drawing away from it. The combination of the two begins to separate out again. During her last appearances in the novel she becomes less of a sensuously suggestive figure and more of an ordinary, insecure woman. Her return to Baxter perhaps ties up the loose ends of plot too tidily, but as an expression of her final dissatisfaction with Paul it is at least connected to what Lawrence has shown - almost reluctantly, it would seem, and against the grain of his own developing interests - to be her need for a real and lasting relationship. This may lack the imaginative dimension which she has known with Paul, but it promises her greater permanence and stability.

Baxter Dawes is the most prosaic of the major characters. He is introduced late in the novel, and at first is only a rather shadowy figure, referred to in conversations between Paul and Miriam and Clara. In one of these Paul (somewhat ridiculously, though Lawrence probably does not intend it to be felt that way) analyses the failure of Baxter's marriage with Clara, suggesting that he never really 'awakened' his wife, with the result that she developed into a self-consciously 'misunderstood woman' who 'treated him badly'. Baxter's jealousy of Paul's affair with Clara - despite the fact that he is the one who has already deserted the home and taken a mistress - reflects the conventionally masculine view of marriage, and his subsequent violence is related more to a sense of injured dignity than thwarted love for Clara. He only comes to life as a more interesting character when he is ill in hospital and subsequently convalescent. Then, although he has lost his earlier brutal energy, he acquires a resignation which allows a change to take place. In the lodgings at Skegness it seems to Clara that 'Dawes now carried himself quietly, seemed to yield himself, while Paul seemed to screw himself up'. Even allowing for the distortion of Clara's point of view, this seems to indicate a capacity for adjusting to circumstances that Paul lacks. His final return to Clara confirms previous hints that there is a bond between them which has only been dormant, not severed, during the Paul affair; but it is a bond involving submission rather than assertion. The formerly swaggering Baxter is a 'broken', and in some respects pathetic, figure, but he is not without hope for the future. He is like a man whose bluff has been called, but who has found strength through recognising his own weakness.

Although there is obvious contrast between Baxter's and Paul's development, it is nevertheless *Paul* who is mainly instrumental in helping Baxter to his curious victory-in-defeat. Is this a tribute to Paul's insight, or is it a convenient device for ridding him of Clara? The reader is left rather unsure what to make of it. And this points to a central problem in the characterisation of Paul. He is the novel's most important character – we remember that in the earlier stages its title was *Paul Morel*; and he is also perilously close to Lawrence himself. It is most often through his eyes that we see what is happening, and his mental processes and judgements, though far from being the only ones available to us, are the ones we share most fully. The slightly odd result, however, is that we view him as a character less clearly than anyone else. He is not presented uncritically, and we are not unaware of his strengths and weaknesses; but we are not able to assess them with the same surety.

It is possible, in fact, to construct two different portraits of Paul: one heroic, and one less heroic – even un-heroic. The heroic Paul is lively and creative; he has the sensitivity of the artist. In Chapter 5, when he is fourteen and about to look for work, we are reminded that, though small, he was a 'rather finely-made boy' and that his face was 'extraordinarily mobile'. Then comes the comment:

> Usually he looked as if he saw things, was full of life, and warm; then his smile, like his mother's, came suddenly and was very lovable; and then, when there was any clog in his soul's quick running, his face went stupid and ugly. He was the sort of boy that becomes a clown and a lout as soon as he is not understood or feels himself held cheap; and, again, is adorable at the first touch of warmth.

Here is sketched in the vital potentiality of the later man, with positively charged words like 'life', 'warm' (plus 'warmth') and 'quick'. Adverse characteristics are also acknowledged ('stupid, 'ugly', 'lout'), but they are subordinated to the primary vitality, and they are attributed to the imposition of some inhibitive, 'clogging' force rather than defects in Paul's character. In his subsequent career the implications of this are worked out in his relations with his girl-friends; he arouses their admiration by his zestful appreciation of the world around him, but when he is harsh or cruel it is because he is impeded by their inability to match his flexibility and emotional freedom. The un-heroic Paul, on the other hand, is an egoist. Fed by his mother's over-intense love and encouraged to side with her against his father, he becomes a prig; in his relations with women he is both demanding and high-handed, and with Miriam, in particular, he is incapable of the sympathetic understanding which might find a constructive way out of the impasse of their relationship. He claims the leadership role for the male (jokingly, it is true, in his response to Clara's feminism), but is in reality dependent on women – most of all his mother; and his three crucial assertions of independence (his breaking with Miriam, and then with

Clara, and, finally, his mercy-killing of his mother) are all rejections rather than positive affirmations.

Of course, neither of these portraits represents the whole truth about Paul. On the other hand, neither is a complete falsification. Perhaps the first is nearer Lawrence's intention, but the second is certainly incorporated in the text as well. There are, indeed, even moments when the less flattering view seems to surface in Paul's own consciousness – though for the most part, as Miriam rightly observes, he seems to be fighting off what he regards as the restrictive influence of others. One such moment is when he admits to his mother that he feels as if he 'wronged' his women, and goes on to say: 'They seem to want *me*, and I can't ever give it them.' The mother's comment is that he hasn't yet met the right woman, to which he replies: 'And I never shall meet the right woman while you live'.

The most straightforward way of reading this is to see it as an endorsement of the novel's mother-domination thesis: Paul cannot give his self because it is usurped by his mother. Even here, however, Paul betrays his deep-rooted habit of transferring the blame for his own deficiency on to someone else – preferably a woman. The question inevitably arises: is the influence of the mother a convenient excuse for some other, still unacknowledged, defect in Paul? Or is the failure to 'give' not a disability, but refusal to capitulate? At the heart of this puzzle lies a problem of values rather than character. It may be that Paul is not merely unable to transcend his egosim, but fundamentally unwilling to do so. He is perhaps to be understood as groping his way towards a different moral standard from the traditional one of unselfishness, and seeking, instead, for a new criterion of behaviour based on the preservation of the integrity of the self. Lawrence certainly did move towards such a new standard in the work he wrote after *Sons and Lovers*. For example, in his *Study of Thomas Hardy* (1914) he declared: 'The final aim of every living thing, creature, or being is the full achievement of itself.' There is nothing quite so clear and emphatic in *Sons and Lovers*, but occasionally views are attributed to Paul which point in that direction, as when he rebels against Miriam's overemphasis on religion:

> 'It's not religious to be religious,' he said. 'I reckon a crow is religious,' he said. 'I reckon a crow is religious when it sails across the sky. But it only does it because it feels itself carried to where it's going, not because it thinks it is being eternal.'

Implicit in this – though it is not fully worked out – is a new religion of vitalism, opposed to the old one of Christian transcendentalism. As we have already seen, Paul's belief in the impersonality of sexual experience, as opposed to Miriam's (and later, Clara's) demand for personal recognition, also carries with it a challenge to conventional assumptions. Both look forward to developments which come after *Sons and Lovers*. Here, however, they are, at the most, only tentative suggestions presented as latent ideas in the expanding consciousness of Paul Morel.

The effect is of something stirring within him, which he struggles to articulate, but which he cannot, as yet, properly understand or judge. And – to carry speculation a little further – it may well be that the process of change which Lawrence was himself undergoing at this time, led to the projection of his own uncertainty on to the character of Paul. The result is a certain degree of ambiguity, which, if it is a fault, is a fault that carries with it a quality of virtue as well, since it heightens the sense of mental turmoil which is appropriate to such a sensitive, adolescent character.

Apart from these major figures there is also a wide range of minor characters in *Sons and Lovers* who deserve critical attention. These include Paul's sister, *Annie*, his younger brother, *Arthur*, the tom-boyish *Beatrice*, the stolid, sensible miner, *Barker*, the well-intentioned but out-of-touch minister, *Mr Heaton*, and all the people at Jordan's – *Mr Pappleworth*, the 'Spiral' overseer, *Fanny* and *Polly*, and the self-important employer, *Mr Jordan* himself. The primary function of these characters is to fill out the life of the mining community, or to provide a foil for the major characters. They also, however, exist as characters in their own right. Beatrice, for example, embarrasses Miriam with her quick, mocking wit, and in so doing illustrates the no-nonsense, down-to-earth bias of working-class people towards those who are shy and sentimental. She is also, however, involved in a love-affair of her own with Arthur in a way that reveals feelings uninhibited either by convention or gawkiness: 'She acted of her own free will. What she would do she did, and made nobody responsible.' Mr Heaton and Mr Jordan are more in the mould of Dickensian caricatures, especially as their middle-class propriety is seen in relation to the more brutal manners of Morel and Baxter Dawes respectively; but Mr Heaton at least acquires more depth as we learn about the loss of his young wife and his kindness in teaching Paul French. The one thoroughly unsatisfactory minor character is William's fiancée, *'Gipsy'*. Her full name is Louisa Lily Denys Western – a name which, it seems, is created only to poke fun at her (witness Morel's reaction to it: ' "An' come again to-morrer!" exclaimed the miner. "An' is'er an actress?" '). Her empty-headed silliness, obsession with dress and carelessness about money are simply the antithesis of Mrs Morel's domestic virtues; she too obviously illustrates the thesis that 'William gives his sex to a fribble, and his mother holds his soul.'

4.3 LANGUAGE

The prose style of *Sons and Lovers* is based on the loose, aggregative syntax which is typical of ordinary, relaxed conversation. Sentences tend to be either short and simple or, when longer, to be built of readily understood units. For example, the following passage describing Mr Morel consists of a series of brief, almost independent, units connected by the conjunctions 'and' and 'but': 'He had signed the pledge, *and* wore the blue ribbon of a teetotaller: he was nothing if not showry. They lived, she thought, in his own house. It was small, *but* convenient enough, *and* quite nicely furnished, with solid, worthy stuff that suited her honest soul.' (Chapter 1)

Subordination is used sparingly and hardly ever in such a way as to interrupt the natural flow of a sentence or cause the reader to have to go back and puzzle out the meaning. For example, in the following sentence about Baxter Dawes' mistress, 'She was a handsome, insolent hussy, who mocked at the youth, and yet flushed if he walked along to the station with her as she went home' (Chapter 8), the subordinate clauses introduced by 'who, 'if' and 'as' come as an easily grasped sequel to the main clause ('She . . . hussy'), expanding it with further information. There are, of course, sentences which are more complex than this. For example, Paul's frustration in his relationship with Miriam is expressed as follows: 'But still again his anger burst like a bubble surcharged; and still, when he saw her eager, silent, as it were, blind face, he felt he wanted to throw the pencil in it; and still, when he saw her hand trembling and her mouth parted with suffering, his heart was scalded with pain for her.' (Chapter 7) Obscurity is avoided, however. The main statement about Paul's anger is made in the opening words, and consequently little difficulty is caused by the fact that the two subordinate 'when' clauses keep the reader waiting for their main clauses ('he felt . . .' and 'his heart was scalded . . .'), since they are only further elaborations of the annoyance and guilt already implicit in the sentence's beginning.

It is also characteristic of Lawrence to prefer the active to the passive voice: in the sentence just quoted there is an example of a passive construction in 'his heart was scalded', but such verbs as 'burst', 'saw', 'felt' and 'wanted' are all active. Likewise, Lawrence tends to prefer transitive verbs, transferring energy from subject to object, rather than intransitive, as can again be seen in the same sentence in such examples as 'he saw her . . . face', 'to throw the pencil' and 'he saw her hand . . . and her mouth'.

In choice of words Lawrence prefers the familiar and colloquial to the learned and abstract. Words of native English derivation tend to predominate rather than academically latinate words, though the vocabulary is wide-ranging and varied according to the needs of context. There is, for example, a higher incidence of latinate words in analytical passages than in the narrative, which is rooted in the specific details of everyday life. When at the end of Chapter 1, Mrs Morel makes her usual preparations before going to bed the language in which her actions are described is precise and concrete: 'In her weariness forgetting everything, she moved about at the little tasks that remained to be done, set his [Morel's] breakfast, rinsed his pit-bottle, put his pit-clothes on the hearth to warm, set his pit-boots beside them, put him out a clean scarf and snap-bag and two

apples, raked the fire, and went to bed.' The repetition of 'pit' in com-
pounds with 'bottle', 'clothes' and 'boots' both emphasises the steady,
mechanical routine which is being performed and brings its matter-of-fact
quality into focus. The local word for lunch, 'snap', also drops naturally
and easily into this context, increasing the sense of familiarity and immediacy. On the other hand, the following sentence from Chapter 7
analysing the behaviour of the Leivers family is generalised and abstract:
'And so they were unaccustomed, painfully uncouth in the simplest social
intercourse, suffering, and yet insolent in their superiority.' Words of Latin
derivation are more prominent, e.g. 'intercourse' (from *inter* between and
currere to run), 'insolent' (from *in* not and *solere* to be wont) and 'superiority' (from *superior* higher). These are words which invite the reader to
consider a certain quality of feeling and, while sympathising, also to form
some sort of judgement. Both kinds of language are essential for the purposes of *Sons and Lovers*. It is the recurrent presence of the first, however,
which keeps the reader close to the community in which the novel is set,
and it is this which provides the linguistic norm of the novel.

In the dialogue of the characters there is a still more noticeable contrast between two different levels of language. The Nottinghamshire and
Derbyshire dialect is the usual language of the working-class characters
– as it was in the Eastwood of Lawrence's childhood. It is the natural
speech of Mr Morel and his mates. Mrs Morel, however, coming from
the south and a more educated background, speaks 'with a southern
pronunciation and a purity of English which thrilled [Morel] to hear'.
This 'received standard' is also the language of Mr Heaton and, it would
seem, of Miriam and Clara as well – it is the language of the middle-class
and those who see education as a social passport to the middle-class. Mrs
Morel's children, including Paul, seem to follow her, but they also drop
into the dialect when they wish. This, too, reflects Lawrence's own situation, as he mockingly recalls it in the poem 'Red Herring':

> We children were the in-betweens
> little non-descripts were we,
> indoors we called each other *you*,
> outside, it was *tha* and *thee*.

Dialect does more, however, in *Sons and Lovers* than simply provide
authentic local colour and an index of class. It is a reservoir of vivid
speech, by comparison with which the universally acceptable 'received
standard' is a rather dull, imaginatively unexciting language. Mr Morel,
for example, has a store of dialect phrases which are metaphorically much
more alive than those of ordinary speech. Thus, in his courtship of Gertrude
Coppard he tells her cheerfully, 'Tha'rt not long in taking the curl out of
me,' and when his talk of mining makes her 'feel blind', he exclaims: 'Like
a moudiwarp! [mouldwarp, or mole] . . . Yi, an' there's some chaps as
does go round like moudiwarps.'

The dialect is also a warm and affectionate medium. Gertrude is startled when Morel offers to let her see what a mine is like: 'Shouldn't ter like it?' Morel is quoted as saying; and he adds, "Appen not, it 'ud dirty thee.' This reply is not jeering, but, on the contrary, considerate (it is spoken 'tenderly'). It is a way of expressing the respect, and growing love, which the miner feels for this 'thing of mystery and fascination, a lady'. The narrator's laconic comment: 'She had never been "thee'd" and "thou'd" before,' is also a more effective way of suggesting the powerful emotional effect of the dialect than a lengthy description of Gertrude's feelings could be.

Dialect is the attractive medium likewise for Morel's tales of life down the mine; and it is the language of the children when they are excited and enthusiastic, as with William at the wakes in Chapter 1. As they grow up they seem to discard it. William as a young man even adopts the public-school habit of calling his mother 'Mater', and the adult Paul shows slightly affected traits, such as his use of the French phrase *femme incomprise* (misunderstood woman) to describe Clara (Chapter 12) and his curious statement. 'I'm not daggeroso', when he refuses to carry a weapon to protect himself from Baxter Dawes. The dialect remains, however, the language which is associated for him with tenderness and intimacy, so that he naturally slips into it again with Clara by the River Trent. There is at least a hint of it, too, in the conspiratorially intense scene between him and Annie in Chapter 14 when they administer the overdose of Morphia to their dying mother. The dialect is the natural language of strong feelings.

4.4 IMAGERY AND SYMBOLISM

Jessie Chambers praised the domestic scenes in *Sons and Lovers*, particularly Mrs Morel's ironing. This household task is a commonplace occurrence, which is made to seem fresh and arresting by Lawrence's description of it: 'She spat on the iron, and a little ball of spit bounded, raced off the dark, glossy surface' (Chapter 4). The observation of what happens when the spit hits the surface of the hot iron is precise (the woman does this to test whether the iron, which is heated by the fire, is at the right temperature), but what makes it so memorable is the force of the verbs 'bounded' and 'raced off' which transfer an impression of animal energy to the 'little ball'.

The novel is full of this kind of vivid imagery. Other examples are: the description of the mines at the beginning of Chapter 1 as 'black studs' and the connecting railway line as 'a loop of fine chain'; the view of the valley from the Morels' new house, to which they move in Chapter 4, 'spread out like a convex cockle-shell, or a clamp-shell'; the celandines in Chapter 7 seen as 'scalloped splashes of gold'; and the vision of the sunrise in Chapter 13 'drilling fierily over the waves in little splashes, as if someone had gone along and the light had spilled from her pail as she walked'.

Occasionally, as in this last example, the figurative expression can seem a little too self-conscious, but it is the cumulative effect rather than the success or failure of particular examples which matters most. The constant recurrence of such metaphorical language heightens the reader's sense of being in a world which is shot through with energy; he cannot be coolly aloof, but is stimulated to awareness and emotional involvement.

Even the more abstract, analytical passages, which do seem to require a more detached response, are given a degree of personal immediacy by the image-making faculty which is so natural to Lawrence. For example, when William goes to London the psychological effect of his move is evoked in the following words: 'He was unsettled by all the change, he did not stand firm on his own feet, but seemed to spin rather giddily on the quick current of the new life' (Chapter 5). His uncertainty and instability become a whirlpool which confuses him and carries him away. Similarly, Paul's relationship with Miriam, though it is analysed in terms of the conflict between physical and spiritual needs, is converted into matter for keen, immediate feeling rather than detached contemplation through the image of fire and steam in the following sentence: 'With Miriam he was always on the high plane of abstraction, when his natural fire of love was transmitted into the fine steam of thought' (Chapter 7). And at their final interview in Chapter 15 Miriam's despairing sense that there is a restless elusiveness about Paul which means that he will never submit to her, is given memorable expression in the simile, 'He would escape like a weasel out of her hands'.

Such examples of imagistic immediacy are reinforced across the whole range of the novel by details and motifs, which, while not necessarily seeming particularly important in themselves, build up significance, like a theme in music, through repetition and variation. For example, there is the typically Lawrentian fondness for the words 'dark' and 'darkness'. In Chapter 4 the children of Scargill Street choose to go out to play only when it is 'thick dark'. In Chapter 11 when Paul's feelings are aroused by Miriam he wants her to go with him where it was 'very dark among the firs'; she is afraid, but he asserts that he likes the darkness: 'I wish it were thicker – good, thick darkness'. And in Chapter 13 his love-making with Clara becomes associated with darkness; as he looks into her eyes, 'They were dark and shining and strange, life wild at the source staring into his life . . .' Through this kind of repeated use (some less friendly critics would say 'repetitious abuse') darkness becomes identified with a primitve vitality which is felt to be somehow essential to the deepest human satisfaction.

The colour red – often in conjunction with darkness and blackness – also recurs throughout the novel, acquiring a similarly cumulative force. Thus, in the opening chapter Morel's hair and beard are described as black and his cheeks as red, and the redness of his mouth is made specially noticeable by his frequent laughter. In an early quarrel with his wife 'his red face, with its bloodshot eyes,' is thrust forward at her; and in the scene where he throws the drawer at her the same characteristics are singled out, redness being echoed again in the blood which drips from the cut on Mrs Morel's forehead down on to the child. Again, in the scene of the tea-party for Mr Heaton, Morel's 'great black moustache' is especially prominent, and as he leans across to the minister his mouth appears 'very red in his black face'.

Of the three Morel sons the one most like his father is Arthur, and he is specifically described as having the same 'full red mouth' (Chapter 9). But Paul also has links with the ruddy vitality of his father, as suggested, for example, by the 'big red moon' which he sees after fighting with Billy Pillins (Chapter 4). This, we are told, makes him think of the Bible, 'that the moon should be turned to blood' – a reference to Revelations 6:12, where, interestingly, hairy blackness is also part of the association ('. . . and, lo, there was a great earthquake; and the sun became black as sackcloth of hair, and the moon became as blood'). The same motif likewise recurs in Paul's love-making in Chapter 12, via the red clay of Clifton Grove and the carnations which he has given to Clara. Here red and black are mingled together, with a perhaps unconscious echo of the dripping blood of the quarrel in Chapter 2: 'When she arose, he, looking on the ground all the time, saw suddenly sprinkled on the black, wet beech-roots many scarlet carnation petals, like splashed drops of blood; and red, small splashes fell from her bosom, streaming down her dress to her feet.'

These motifs constantly overlap and even blend together. Thus the carnations just mentioned are part also of a recurrent use of flowers, and the theme of sensual redness is inseparable from repeated references to fire and flame. Morel is said to have a face which is 'the flower of his body' (Chapter 1), and – naturally enough for a miner accustomed to working in very hot conditions at the coal-face – he must always have a roaring fire in the grate to keep him warm. As far as Paul is concerned, this fiery ruddiness seems to be extinguished at the end of the novel; but in fact it is still there, even though reduced to the merest 'spark'. It remains a sign that he is still clinging to life (as does, perhaps, the 'bowl of freesias and *scarlet* anemones' [my emphasis] in his room at Holme Road).

Flowers are also at the centre of several powerfully evocative scenes in the novel, such as the night scene in which Mrs Morel is shut out in the garden after quarrelling with her husband (Chapter 1) and the scene of Paul and the madonna lilies (Chapter 11). In such scenes Lawrence describes a situation which is entirely plausible on the realistic level, but which yet seems to tap obscure feelings beyond that level. Thus the garden in each case is precisely and vividly evoked. In Chapter 11, for example, we are sharply aware of the lilies and pinks in the garden, of the sycamore tree at the end, and of the sound of a corncrake nearby; and in Chapter 1 the details are still more specific: rhubarb grows near the door at the back, there are currant bushes in the side garden, and lilies, phlox and roses grow at the front, while a 'train, three miles away, roared across the valley'. But the states of aroused emotion felt by Paul and Mrs Morel respectively suffuse each scene till it becomes transformed – though still recognisably an ordinary, familiar setting – into something strangely exotic.

The garden in Chapter 1 is bathed in moonlight, and the commonplace rhubarb becomes 'the glistening great rhubarb leaves'. Mrs Morel stands there 'as if in an immense gulf of white light, the moon streaming high in face of her, the moonlight standing up from the hills in front, and filling the valley where the Bottoms crouched, almost blindingly'. In this passage the language becomes virtually that of poetry. Repetition – not only of the words 'moon' and 'light', but also of similar sounds (e.g. wh*ite*/l*ight*/h*igh*/moonl*ight*/bl*in*dingly, h*ills*/f*ill*ing) – produces an incantatory, hypnotic effect to match Mrs Morel's unusual state of consciousness. Furthermore, the air is said to be charged with the perfume of the lilies 'as with a presence', and in 'the mysterious out-of-doors' Mrs Morel is said to feel 'forlorn' – phrases which, perhaps unintentionally, recall Wordsworth's 'A presence that disturbs me with the joy/Of elevated thoughts' ('Tintern Abbey', 94-5) and Keats's 'faery lands forlorn' ('Ode to a Nightingale', 70).

In the episode from Chapter 11 Paul's experience in the garden becomes one of intense awareness of life: 'the air all round seemed to stir with scent [of the lilies], as if it were alive'. The phrasing is such that the scents of the flowers seem to acquire a strange capacity for motion: 'He went across the bed of pinks, whose keen perfume *came* sharply across the *rocking*, heavy scent of the lilies, and stood alongside the white barrier of flowers' [my emphasis]. Personification intensifies this effect still more: the lilies 'flagged all loose, as if they were panting', and 'leaned as if they were calling'; the moon slid down 'growing more flushed' (as if its face were reddening with emotion); the irises seemed to have 'fleshy throats' and 'dark, grasping hands'. Again, this is the evocative language of poetry, in which the usual distinction between the categories of human and non-human is broken down in order to express an experience which goes beyond ordinary rational understanding.

Both Mrs Morel's and Paul's experiences are represented as forms of intoxication; the scent of the lilies is said to make Paul 'drunk', and there is a similar suggestion in the language applied to Mrs Morel: 'Then she drank a deep draught of the scent. It almost made her dizzy.' But this, of course, is not to be taken literally. Their 'intoxication' is a metaphor for the emotionally aroused and excited state which gives them such heightened awareness of their surroundings. They are 'drunk' only in the sense that they are carried away by the special mood of the moment; and what they perceive in this state is not the drunkard's blurred distortion of reality, but something which strengthens their contact with it. Thus at the height of her experience Mrs Morel enjoys a feeling of unity with the natural world, as if 'she rested with the hills and lilies and houses, all swum together in a kind of swoon'; and Paul's experience gives him a sense of the sharp, even 'brutal', reality of the flowers: 'At any rate, he had found something'.

For want of a better word such experiences may be called 'symbolic.' That is to say, they are the means of expressing something which cannot be translated into the terms of rational prose discourse – something which has deep psychological reverberations beyond the grasp of ordinary understanding. As Lawrence wrote in his Introduction to Frederick Carter's *The Dragon of the Apocalypse*: 'You can't give a great symbol a "meaning", any more than you can give a cat a "meaning". Symbols are organic units of consciousness with a life of their own, and you can never explain them away, because their value is dynamic, emotional, belonging to the sense-consciousness of the body and soul, and not simply mental.' All one can say about these experiences of Mrs Morel and Paul is that the language in which they are embodied suggests that they are profound and authentic, and that they are in some way connected with a capacity to make living contact with the natural world. They perhaps reveal that positive element in Mrs Morel which is handed on to Paul, and which is a vital counterbalance to her destructive influence.

There are, however, certain other scenes in *Sons and Lovers* which, though likewise possessing an element of this mysteriously symbolic quality, are somewhat more amenable to interpretation as expressions of the psychological forces operating within the characters of the novel. Examples are the scene in Chapter 2 where Mrs Morel has an impulse to hold the baby Paul up to the sun; the episodes of Paul and Miriam with the swing (Chapter 7) and the cherry tree (Chapter 11); and the incident of the stallion (Chapter 9). All of these, except the first, have strong sexual connotations. They follow the precedent set by Thomas Hardy in, for example, the scene in *Far From the Madding Crowd* where Sergeant Troy demonstrates his sword exercises to Bathsheba Everdene; the force of sexual attraction is conveyed obliquely, but powerfully, without specific reference to sexuality as such. Thus the to-and-fro movement of the swing in Chapter 7 has erotic overtones, and Miriam's fear of going too high suggests her inhibition. Paul's more spontaneous reaction, on the other hand, communicates his greater capacity for sensuous enjoyment of life. For him it is a means of escape from the puritanical restrictions of Victorian moral convention. It is an experience of freedom – as further hinted by the symbol-within-symbol represented by the swallow which stoops down from the roof of the barn, where the swing is situated, and flies out of the door.

4.5 ALLUSIONS

Lawrence also uses a number of literary, artistic and biblical allusions to enhance his themes. Thus, Miriam's romantic inclinations are expressed in the opening paragraphs of Chapter 7 with a concentrated series of references to novels by Walter Scott. Some pages later we learn that she has a reproduction of Veronese's painting of the martyr, St. Catherine, on her bedroom wall – a hint of the religiose, self-sacrificing element in her temperament which becomes more marked as her affair with Paul develops. When she studies French poetry with Paul one of the texts is Baudelaire's 'Le Balcon', which Paul reads in a voice which is 'soft and caressing, but growing almost brutal'. Baudelaire's poem is not explicitly sexual, but it has phrases of a rich, at times almost glutinous, sensuality which provoke the frustrated desire that Paul feels in such close proximity to his sweetheart. Miriam, however, cannot understand this 'tumult and fury'; and, typically, she prefers less disturbing poems, such as Thomas Hood's 'Fair Ines,' and Wordsworth's 'The Solitary Reaper' and his sonnet, 'It is a beauteous evening, calm and free'. (Note that the Penguin text of 1981 prints what seems to have been Lawrence's misquotation of the ending of this line: 'calm and pure', while earlier Penguins correct it. The misquotation is itself significant, as 'pure' increases the impression of sexlessness which goes with the reference in the second line to 'a nun'.)

Biblical allusions, as one might expect, given Lawrence's Congregational background, are fairly frequent. They include the references to Exodus 13:21.2, John 2: 1–10 John 19:34 and Genesis 37:7 already discussed (see above pp. 35, 28 and 40), and further allusions such as Beatrice's joking remark in Chapter 8 about Paul's girl-friends and the judgement of Solomon (I Kings 3: 16–27) and Fanny's satirical reference in Chapter 10 to Clara as the Queen of Sheba (I Kings 10: 1–13). Some of these are, of course, simply the currency of a community where chapel-going and bible-readings are a part of everyday life, and not necessarily of great significance in themselves. But even such trivial allusions help to keep the reader of *Sons and Lovers* aware of its Nonconformist background.

Similarly, the choice of biblical names for such characters as Miriam and Paul is a reminder of the religious values permeating the novel. Miriam is the name of the sister of Moses and Aaron (see Numbers 12: 1–15), and Paul is the name of the chief apostle to the gentiles (hence William's nickname of 'Postle', for his younger brother, Paul). Above all, 'Paul' is a name of great significance for his mother. It is associated with her father, George Coppard, who 'drew near in sympathy only to one man, the Apostle Paul' (Chapter 1); and it is a name which comes to her as a sudden, inexplicable inspiration ('she knew not why') as the one she should give her second son in the immediate sequel to the episode of the baby and the sunset in Chapter 2. It thus inevitably carries some of the symbolic implications of that scene. It suggests the great hopes Mrs Morel has for some kind of vicarious spiritual achievement through her child, but also the potential burden which this imposes on him. Paul's biblical name is thus a significantly distinguishing mark which he carries with him throughout the novel.

4.6 SICKNESS AND HEALTH

The accidents and illnesses of various characters provide much of the basic material of the plot of *Sons and Lovers*. Cumulatively, however, they seem to acquire a significance which perhaps justifies a brief discussion of these too under the heading of 'Techniques'.

As a miner, Morel inevitably suffers a number of accidents, one of which is recorded in Chapter 5. The pain which he suffers on this occasion is not disguised, but his tendency to moan gets more emphasis than his suffering. This is still more evidently the case with the presentation of his illness in Chapter 3, where it is stated that 'He was one of the worst patients imaginable'. He enjoys being spoilt, and he tries to prolong his wife's indulgent treatment of him even when he is well on the road to recovery. Sickness, in fact, reveals his lack of inner strength and independence; it is a sign of that weakness which makes him unable to stand up to his wife (notwithstanding his bullying), and which shows itself most contemptibly in his inability to face her when she is dying.

There is also a tell-tale quality about the illnesses of William and Paul. William's is not just the result of chance, but an expression of the psychic division brought about by his mother's dominance. The boyhood illnesses of Paul may not have such specific meaning as this, but they reveal a closeness of relationship between him and his mother which is at least ambiguous – one that is at once necessary to his survival, and yet dangerously over-intense. The illness he suffers after his fight with Baxter Dawes is, on the other hand, more comparable with that of William since it is connected with a similar inadequacy inherent in his affairs with Miriam and Clara; and his near-despairing state of mind after his mother's death, though not an illness as such, is, effectively, a psychological affliction which threatens him with the loss of his essential manhood.

The most dramatic of all the illnesses in the novel is that of Mrs Morel. We are first made aware of its possible existence at the height of the quarrel between father and son in Chapter 8; it becomes more apparent in Chapter 9 when she visits Lincoln with Paul; and it is virtually acknowledged between them when Paul makes the significant statement in Chapter 13 that he will never meet a woman whom he can marry while she lives. Her illness thus takes on the quality of a physical reaction to the psychological impasse between her and her son – an overt manifestation of the damaging force that their relationship has become.

How far this explains Paul's conduct during the last, painful stages of her illness, it is hard to tell. It is unlikely that his mercy-killing of his mother is other, deliberately, than the expression of his desire to save her from further suffering. When, however, we look back to the strange little episode at the beginning of Chapter 4 in which he makes a game of sacrifice out of the destruction of the doll so much cherished by his sister Annie, it would appear that there is at least a hint of similarity between the two. Both episodes share a curiously ambiguous – even slightly hysterical – quality; and the underlying purpose in both seems to be to remove a psychological burden – Paul's guilt for having broken the doll in the one instance, and his sense of the crippling effect of his mother's love in the other. The two levels of seriousness are, of course, quite different; one cannot simply apply the childish Paul's comment, 'An' I'm glad there's nothing left of her', from the burning of 'Missis Arabella' to the death of his mother. But there is at least the possibility of a double meaning in the mother's 'release', which would lend support to the idea that Paul sacrifices her, too. If so, we should not think of him as being callous or hypocritical; he is clearly prostrate with grief at the loss of his mother. Rather it would be a further comment on the peculiarly tragic nature of a relationship which is so compounded of sickness and health.

5 SPECIMEN PASSAGE AND COMMENTARY

This chapter is devoted to a detailed critical commentary of a passage from Chapter 5 of *Sons and Lovers*.

5.1 SPECIMEN PASSAGE

'Then,' said his mother, 'you must look in the paper for the advertisements.'

He looked at her. It seemed to him a bitter humiliation and an anguish to go through. But he said nothing. When he got up in the morning, his whole being was knotted up over this one thought:

'I've got to go and look for advertisements for a job.'

It stood in front of the morning, that thought, killing all joy and even life, for him. His heart felt like a tight knot.

And then, at ten o'clock, he set off. He was supposed to be a queer, quiet child. Going up the sunny street of the little town, he felt as if all the folk he met said to themselves: 'He's going to the Co-op. reading-room to look in the papers for a place. He can't get a job. I suppose he's living on his mother.' Then he crept up the stone stairs behind the drapery shop at the Co-op., and peeped in the reading-room. Usually one or two men were there, either old, useless fellows, or colliers 'on the club'. So he entered, full of shrinking and suffering when they looked up, seated himself at the table, and pretended to scan the news. He knew they would think, 'What does a lad of thirteen want in a reading-room with a newspaper?' and he suffered.

Then he looked wistfully out of the window. Already he was a prisoner of industrialism. Large sunflowers stared over the old red wall of the garden opposite, looking in their jolly way down on the women who were hurrying with something for dinner. The valley was full of corn, brightening in the sun. Two collieries, among the fields, waved their small white plumes of steam. Far off on the hills were the woods of Annesley, dark and fascinating. Already his heart went down. He was being taken into bondage. His freedom in the beloved home valley was going now.

The brewers' waggons came rolling up from Keston with enormous barrels, four a side, like beans in a burst bean-pod. The waggoner, throned aloft, rolling massively in his seat, was not so much below Paul's eye. The man's hair, on his small, bullet head, was bleached almost white by the sun, and on his thick red arms, rocking idly on his sack apron, the white hairs glistened. His red face shone and was almost asleep with sunshine. The horses, handsome and brown, went on by themselves, looking by far the masters of the show.

Paul wished he were stupid. 'I wish,' he thought to himself, 'I was fat like him, and like a dog in the sun. I wish I was a pig and a brewer's waggoner.'

Then, the room being at last empty, he would hastily copy an advertisement on a scrap of paper, then another, and slip out in immense relief. His mother would scan over his copies.

'Yes,' she said, 'you may try.' (Macmillan edn, pp. 92–3)

5.2 COMMENTARY

Paul, now on the brink of fourteen, has just left school and is about to look for employment. He does not have any very definite ideas of what he wants to do, and so his mother takes charge of the situation. She tells him that he must go to the reading-room of the local Co-operative Society and study the advertisements in the newspapers.

As he had been when he went to fetch his father's pay at the colliery office (Chapter 4), Paul is shy and self-conscious. The prospect of exposing himself to public gaze makes him extremely tense – a condition which Lawrence expresses through the sharp immediacy of the phrase 'knotted up' (repeated again in the taut, monosyllabic sentence: 'His heart felt like a tight knot'). He himself is obsessed with the thought, 'I've got to to and look for advertisements for a job', and he imagines that everyone who sees him as he goes through Bestwood to the reading-room is harping on the same theme. The other thing that preoccupies him – it has reverberations throughout the whole novel – is his relationship with his mother, and he likewise imagines that everyone will be saying that he is living on her. There is no evidence to warrant this supposition, which is merely a projection of his own self-consciousness; but it is interesting to note that he thinks of people as mocking him for dependence on his mother, not his father, though the father is the bread-winner. The very absence of reference to the father is an implicit comment on the relationship between Paul and his parents.

Going into the reading-room is for Paul something like going into a prison. It signifies the beginning of a process which he fears will cut him off from the natural world and subject him to the dictates of industrialism; the 'freedom' he has hitherto enjoyed in 'the beloved home valley' is, he feels, about to be eroded. Given what we know of Lawrence's later views on the inimical influence of a mechanico-industrial society, and given the admitted closeness of the fictional Paul's experiences to those of the young Lawrence himself, it is tempting to regard a statement like 'Already he was a prisoner of industrialism' as an authorially endorsed expression of hostility to the industrial world. And it would seem to be supported by the emphasis in the sixth and seventh paragraphs on the bright, shining liveliness of everything outside, as opposed to inside, the reading-room. For example, in the description of the scene the word 'sun' becomes a powerfully repeated motif (*'sun*flowers, 'corn, brightening in the *sun*', hair bleached almost white by the *sun*', 'almost asleep with *sun*shine'); and it is coupled with repetition of the word 'red' ('old *red* wall', 'thick *red* arms', '*red* face'), which increases the effect of warm colourfulness by bringing into this particular passage the associations of sensuous satisfaction which it has accumulated elsewhere in the novel. The personification of the flowers implicit in 'stared' and 'looking in their jolly ways' further adds to the impression of gaiety and life, as does the imaginative, almost explosive, energy contained in the simile of the beer-barrels as 'beans in a burst bean-pod'.

Nevertheless, we are always aware that this is Paul's view of things. It is he who looks 'wistfully' out of the window; and the very arrangement of the picture-like landscape – with garden and street in the foreground, cornfields and collieries in the middle distance, and woods in the background – presupposes a person looking from a given point of vantage. At the end of the sixth paragraph we are reminded of Paul's feelings of 'bondage', and in the middle of the next his position as onlooker is again brought to our attention by the reference to the driver who comes rolling by on his waggon as being 'not so much below Paul's eye'. Finally, the eighth paragraph returns to Paul's thoughts, which have the slightly comical naiveté ('I wish . . . I was fat like him, and like a dog in the sun. I wish I was a pig and a brewer's waggoner') appropriate to a boy of thirteen or fourteen rather than a fullgrown man.

Lawrence is not, as a matter of settled principle, the kind of author, like Henry James or James Joyce, who deliberately avoids personal expression, preferring instead to present his story only as it is seen and understood by one or more of his characters. But the point-of-view method is important in this particular extract. The vision of the world seen from within the Co-op reading-room is carefully adjusted to the state of mind of the young Paul Morel, conditioned as he is by his self-consciousness and his quite natural anxiety about embarking for the first time on the business of earning a living. His thoughts of himself as 'a prisoner of industrialism' should not therefore be taken as a straightforward expression of Lawrence's own thoughts. There is, after all, some inconsistency between what Paul is made to think and what he is described as seeing. For example, the 'two collieries' represent the most pervasive, insistent and relevant form of industrialism in Paul's 'home valley', but they are in no way felt to be an intrusion on, or incongruous with, the rest of the scene. On the contrary, they are situated quite simply 'among the fields', and the metaphorical liveliness which presents the steam rising from their engine-houses as 'small white plumes' is of the same order as that applied to the personification of the sunflowers. Paul does not think of them as prisons in which miners are condemned to spend the hours of sunshine doing dirty and dangerous work. To him they are a normal, even attractive, part of everyday life; and this is true of the way he sees them at other times, notably in Chapter 12, where he defends them against Clara's view that they spoil a pretty place. Nor does he think of a waggoner's job as soul-destroying, or of dray-horses as animals degraded in the service of man – quite the reverse, they look 'by far the masters of the show'. There is nothing doctrinal or didactic in this view of man and beast at work; it is appreciative rather than critical. If Paul gazes longingly, or, rather, 'wistfully', at the scene from his reading-room 'prison', it is because he exaggerates the disagreeableness of what he is about to do – and perhaps over-romanticises the delightfulness of what he imagines himself to be on the point of losing. Looking beyond this passage to the pages that later describe his actual employment at Jordan's, we find that it is not nearly so bad as Paul feared. In fact, he quite enjoys himself there, and he positively relishes the company of his adoring female fellow-workers. Industrialism in that form at least is not so terrible.

The passage ends, however, with Paul's copying out a few advertisements, and then receiving his mother's laconic permission to 'try'. We are now back in the crisp, practical, down-to-earth world of Mrs Morel's managing concern for her son's future. She is the one who wants him to get on, and wants him to be something 'better' than a miner. Logically it is she whom Paul ought to blame for the threat he feels to the enjoyment of his 'freedom in the beloved home valley'. But, of course, he never voices, or even conceives, such a criticism. What he has to do may be 'bitter humiliation' and 'anguish', but he does not question whether it should be done; his mother's word is law. In the novel as a whole the influence of the mother is shown as being far more complex than it appears to be in this passage. It is not, therefore, fair to draw conclusions about her driving force and the vision of 'freedom' which Paul constructs as he looks out of the reading-room window. But one last point should be made; and it is a point which carries with it a curious kind of irony. The father, we have noted, is absent from this passage, yet several of its sensuously evocative elements, including the thematic recurrence of redness, seem to have a poetic affinity with him. One of the two collieries which blend so easily with the landscape may even be where Morel is working at that moment. In other words, his presence is felt, even if he himself is not there; and it is felt in association with the vision which Paul finds such an attractive contrast to the reading-room and his job-hunting. It may well be, in fact, that Paul is responding to the unrecognised appeal of the father. If so, the passage has a kind of imaginative sub-text, which calls in the associations of the neglected father-figure to redress, at least imaginatively, the imbalance in Paul's relationship with his mother.

6 CRITICAL APPRAISALS

6.1 EARLY REVIEWS

When it was first published *Sons and Lovers* had a mixed reception, though Lawrence himself was not displeased with the reviews. Several critics found it too outspoken in sexual matters. Among these the essayist, Robert Lynd, though recognising Lawrence's 'curious eagerness for the beauty of words', thought that he had 'an exaggerated sense of the physical side of love' (*Daily News*, 7 June 1913); and another critic shrank from what he felt to be Lawrence's excessive frankness, and deplored his lack of spiritual uplift: 'Mr Lawrence strips everything naked; there is no delicacy nor reticence about his work . . . His people are animals – highly developed, it is true – and very fine mentally, but throughout all the book there is no glimpse of spirit – Paul and the circle of people among whom he moves live by sense and sense alone' (*Academy*, 28 June 1913).

The powerful realism of the novel and its fine descriptive passages were appreciated, but few reviewers could grasp its structure. In the opinion of Harold Massingham, an otherwise sympathetic critic, it had 'no pretensions to plot-architecture' and was 'simply an objective record of a collier's family in the Midlands, over a period of twenty to thirty years.' He did, however, note a difference in manner between Parts One and Two, the latter being 'more impressionist, and more coloured than the first part', and he also suggested that the 'ego' of the author was more involved in the second part (*Daily Chronicle*, 17 June 1913). Lascelles Abercrombie likewise criticised the book's construction: 'It has no particular shape and no recognizable plot; themes are casually taken up, and then as casually dropped.' All its faults, however, were of little importance beside its imaginative brilliance, and Abercrombie – without knowing it, echoing Jessie Chambers' praise when she saw the early chapters in manuscript – concluded his review with a glowing tribute to Lawrence's 'power of lighting a train of ordinary events to blaze up into singular significance' (*Manchester Guardian*, 2 July 1913).

The theme of mother-domination was not immediately apparent to early reviewers. Indeed, several tended to see Mrs Morel as the heroine. One critic wrote that the novel 'tells the story of the life of a refined woman wedded to a clod' who does not appreciate her, and went on to reveal how completely he had missed its purpose by adding that '*Fortunately* [my emphasis] one of her children fills that gap in her life which her husband is quite incapable of supplying' (*Sunday Times*, 1 June 1913). And the American critic, Louise Maunsell Field, approvingly saw the tenderly portrayed love between mother and son as 'the mainspring of both their lives'. This critic also accepted Mrs Morel's judgement on the relationship between Paul and Miriam at its face value. Nonetheless, she was intelligent enough to recognise that Miriam was an effective character-study of an intensely 'over-spiritualized' woman, and her comment on Lawrence's psychological insight in portraying the affair between the girl and Paul was unusually perceptive: 'The long, psychic battle between the two, a battle blindly fought, never really understood, is excellent in its revelation of those motives which lie at the very root of character – motives of which the persons they actuate are so often completely ignorant' (*New York Times Book Review*, 21 September 1913).

The Freudian critic, Alfred Kuttner, was the first to appreciate the full implication of the mother's intense love for her sons as a destructive influence; but it must be said that he saw her influence in its negative aspects only. In a review originally published in the *New Republic* (10 April 1915), and later expanded into an article in the *Psychoanalytic Review*, he related the story of *Sons and Lovers* to the recently propounded theories of the great Austrian psychoanalyst, Sigmund Freud. The Freudian view hinges on the idea that infantile sexuality is focused on the parent of the opposite sex. A boy's unconscious desire is to possess his mother and exclude his father (hence the term 'Oedipus complex' – so named from Oedipus, a figure in Greek myth, who unknowingly killed his own father and married his own mother). Society demands, however, that this desire be suppressed, and in the normal process of maturation: (a) the boy learns to imitate the father, because he sees that the mother loves the father; and (b) he transfers his sexual desire from the unattainable mother to an attainable woman who resembles her as much as possible. When this process is impeded, as it is for Paul by his mother's excessive emotional demands and the example of her contempt rather than love for the father, the consequences for the son's ability to form a normal love-relationship in early manhood are catastrophic. Kuttner applied this argument to *Sons and Lovers* in the following manner:

> In Paul this salutary process never takes place because he cannot free himself from the incubus of his parents long enough to come to some sense of himself. He remains enslaved by his parent complex instead of being moulded and guided by it. One returns back to that astonishing scene at Lincoln Cathedral. Here Paul goes to the roots of

his mother's hold upon him. For his passionate reproaches hurled at his mother because she has lost her youth, prove that the mother-image, in all its pristine magic, has never diminished its sway over him; he has never been able to forget or to subordinate that first helpless infatuation . . . Miriam feels it when she calls him a child of four which she can no longer nurse. Nor can Clara help him by becoming a wanton substitute for his mother. Only the one impossible ideal holds him, and that means the constant turning in upon himself which is death. Paul goes to pieces because he can never make the mature sexual decision away from his mother, he can never accomplish the physical and emotional transfer.

(Psychoanalytic Review, III, No. 3, July 1916)

Lawrence read this review and said that he hated it: 'You know I think "complexes" are vicious half-statements of the Freudians: sort of can't see wood for trees . . . My poor book: it was, as art, a fairly complete truth: so they carve a half lie out of it, and say "Voila." Swine!' (Letter to Barbara Low, 16 September 1916.) Clearly, Kuttner annoyed him because his interpretation of *Sons and Lovers* seemd to Lawrence reductive, though Kuttner praised it as a great and universally representative work. As we can see from Lawrence's later excursions into psychological analysis, in *Psychoanalysis and the Unconscious* (1921) and *Fantasia of the Unconscious* (1922), what he disliked about the Freudian theories was that they treated the unconscious as a kind of dustbin for unpleasant facts which the conscious mind preferred not to know about, whereas Lawrence thought of the unconscious as a store-house of energy and creative vitality. Not only does Kuttner's view ignore the tentative 'quickness' still detectable at the end of the novel, but it also takes no account of those symbolic passages which hint at a richer unconscious life shared by both Paul and his mother. For the 'complete truth' these, and other, more positive, features must be heeded, as well as the negative aspects of mother-fixation.

6.2 LATER CRITICISM

So much has been written on *Sons and Lovers* during the last forty years that it would need a study at least the length of the whole of this book to give an adequate account of it. All that can be done here is to indicate some of the themes that have attracted attention, and the way in which assessment of the novel has been changed.

Among critics who have reacted against the generally received Freudian view of the novel one of the most interesting is Mark Spilka. In *The Love Ethic of D. H. Lawrence* (1955) there are two chapters which particularly concern *Sons and Lovers*: Chapter 3, 'How to Pick Flowers', and Chapter 4, 'Counterfeit Loves'. Chapter 3 contrasts the soulfully adoring way

Miriam responds to flowers with the more detached, but also more vital, way of Paul – and of his mother, too (an alliance which emphasises the more creative side of their relationship). In Chapter 4, however, Spilka presents all the three kinds of love – that of Clara and the mother, as well as Miriam – as being restrictive, or 'counterfeit', influences from which Paul needs to free himself. According to Spilka, this is the essentially Lawrentian psychology on which *Sons and Lovers* is founded, the Freudian being added only in the final, rather garbled, revision of the novel. The influence of the mother is conceded to be destructive, but only in the later stages; earlier it is described 'in completely wholesome terms'. Above all, Spilka argues, it is not the 'split' associated with the mother's dominance which accounts for the break-down of the affairs with Miriam and Clara, but the unsatisfactory nature of the kind of love which each of these women respectively can offer. Nor is Paul to be seen as one who is 'derelict' at the end, but as one who 'has achieved a kind of half-realized, or jigsaw success, consisting of mixed elements of life-warmth, creative vision, incipient manhood, and most of all, a belief (almost) in life itself'.

Spilka's feeling that the late, 'Freudian', stage of the novel is somehow at odds with an earlier, more independently Lawrentian version is followed up by several other critics. Julian Moynahan, for example, in *The Deed of Life* (1963), finds three centres, or 'matrices', in the novel: (1) 'autobiographical narrative' which is 'articulated in terms of historical sequence;' (2) psychoanalysis (i.e. the Freudian Oedipal theory); and (3) the 'vital' or 'passional' matrix. Paul, according to Moynahan, is a new kind of fictional hero – 'a passionate pilgrim whose every action and impulse is a decision for or against life'. Paul is doomed in terms of the second matrix, but in terms of the third matrix he is still left at the end of the novel with the possibility of a way out, because 'he accepts freely his responsibility for action in conformity with an instinctive morality of life'.

Two other scholarly critics, John Worthen and Keith Sagar, attempt to plot the sequence of the novel's composition more precisely. In *D. H. Lawrence and the Idea of the Novel* (1979) Worthen finds a variety of strands in *Sons and Lovers* which, owing to Lawrence's changing interests and circumstances at the time of writing it, are imperfectly woven together; and he concludes, in particular, that the theme of the dominant mother is 'simply the final divisive and cohesive force in the book: cohesive in drawing together the various stages of Paul's emotional life under a common influence, and divisive because it operates in the book with the force of a prejudice, breaking up the social complexity of the novel in favour of moralised respectability and social ambition.'

Sagar likewise detects at least three different strata in the novel, including a final Freudian layer. For him, however, the ultimate result is more successful. Precisely because the last revision was not totally comprehensive the book as we now have it is – 'almost by accident' – one in which 'the mother is presented as neither absolutely right nor absolutely wrong,' but 'holds in creative tension the opposing attitudes'. Similarly with regard to Miriam he rejects interpretations which either would fasten on her the blame for the failure of her affair with Paul, or completely exculpate her. 'Can we imagine that the novel could have ended with Paul and Miriam happily married?' Sagar asks, and his own answer is: 'Surely such a marriage could only have been, for Paul, a capitulation.' (Introduction to the Penguin edition of *Sons and Lovers*, 1981).

In his 1966 study, *The Art of D. H. Lawrence*, Sagar also emphasises the need for *Sons and Lovers* to be recognised as not just 'a case-history', but a work of art, and he points out that Lawrence's 'distinctive use of imagery carries a great deal of the novel's significance'. A similar concentration on form – with a still more emphatic rejection of earlier opinions that it lacks structure – is also the basis of Gamini Salgado's chapter-by-chapter analysis of the novel in the Studies in English Literature series (1966). Salgado's essay is especially valuable for its strong sense of the way both personal and social material is integrated in the novel, and for its recognition of Lawrence's 'modernity' as something already firmly established in *Sons and Lovers*. Like much 'contemporary' literature this novel has 'a crippled hero', says Salgado, 'who is victim rather than agent'. And this change in the nature of the hero brings about a change in the form of the novel, for 'such a hero's view of the world is appropriately presented not through the orderly chronological sequence of most nineteenth-century fiction, but through a freer and more introspective form, where the emphasis is constantly on the emotional predicament of the protagonist'.

Finally, there is the question of the assessment of *Sons and Lovers* in relation to the rest of Lawrence's work. There is no detailed study of this novel by the most distinguished of Lawrence's critics, F. R. Leavis, who is preoccupied with what he sees as the much greater achievement of the later work. But as James Gibson points out, it 'has always been the most popular, has been much admired, and has been preferred by some critics to Lawrence's later work' (Introduction to Macmillan edition, 1983). The verdict of Gamini Salgado seems to be as sound as any; and it provides a suitable note on which to end: 'I have no wish to deny that both *The Rainbow* and *Women in Love* are greater novels than *Sons and Lovers*, nor that the earlier novel often illuminates the later ones. But my own concern has been to show in what way *Sons and Lovers* is an enjoyable and important novel in its own right.'

REVISION QUESTIONS

1. Consider the way in which Lawrence contrasts Mr and Mrs Morel in Chapter 1. What significance does this contrast have for the rest of the novel?

2. Why does Lawrence precede the story of Paul's relationship with his mother by that of William's? Is the outcome the same for both?

3. Discuss two or three scenes which contribute to *Sons and Lovers* as a portrait of a mining community.

4. Salgado calls Paul 'a crippled hero'. In what ways is Paul different from more conventional heroes of fiction?

5. What is the evidence for and against regarding Mrs Morel's influence on her sons as wholly destructive?

6. Who is more to blame for the failure of their relationship, Paul or Miriam?

7. What is the nature of the relationship between Paul and Clara, and by what means does Lawrence seek to communicate its special quality?

8. Compare and contrast the relationship between Paul and Miriam with that between Arthur and Beatrice.

9. Discuss the different ways in which flowers are used in *Sons and Lovers*.

10. Write a detailed commentary on the scene in which Mrs Morel visits Bestwood market and afterwards shows Paul her purchases (Chapter 4: 'Mrs Morel loved her marketing . . . "Yes!" she exclaimed, brimful of satisfaction.') What does it reveal, (a) about the kind of life ordinary

people lead in Bestwood; and (b) about the relationship between Mrs Morel and Paul?

11. One early reviewer of *Sons and Lovers* wrote that 'Odi et amo' [I hate and I love] should have been on the title-page of the novel. Examine one or two episodes in which you can detect both love and hate in the feelings of one character for another.

12. Lawrence wrote several plays as well as novels. What evidence can you find in *Sons and Lovers* to suggest that the author has a good dramatic sense?

13. What does Lawrence's use of dialect contribute to the overall effect of *Sons and Lovers*?

14. What are the main features of Lawrence's style?

15. Write a detailed commentary on the swing scene in Chapter 7 (' "Have you seen the swing?" . . . It were almost as if here were a flame that had lit a warmth in her whilst he swung in the middle air.') What does this suggest about the characters of Paul and Miriam respectively? What elements in the passage suggest that it is not merely descriptive but has symbolic overtones?

16. Discuss the significance of the fight between Baxter Dawes and Paul. How is it that they become friends afterwards?

17. Why is the novel divided into two Parts? What episodes provide the main material of each?

18. Is *Sons and Lovers* a tragedy?

19. Paul is represented as being a painter in his spare time. Are there any ways in which *Sons and Lovers* might appropriately be called 'a portrait of the artist as a young man'?

20. Jessie Chambers wrote of Lawrence: 'It was his power to transmute the common experiences into significance that I always felt to be Lawrence's greatest gift.' Would you agree that this is his greatest achievement in *Sons and Lovers*, or would you rate other qualities in the book more highly?

FURTHER READING

Text

Two texts can be recommended: the Penguin English Library text, edited by Keith Sagar (1981) and the Macmillan Students' Novels text, edited by James Gibson (1983). Both contain excellent Introductions, valuable Notes and useful Glossaries.

Biography, memoirs, letters

Boulton, James T. (ed.), *The Letters of D. H. Lawrence*, vol. I, 1901-13 (Cambridge University Press, 1979).

Boulton, James T. and Zytaruk, George J. (eds), *The Letters of D. H. Lawrence*, vol II, 1913-16 (Cambridge University Press, 1981).

Chambers, Jessie (E. T.), *D. H. Lawrence, A Personal Record*, 2nd edition, ed. J. D. Chambers (Frank Cass, 1965 – originally pub. Cape, 1935).

Lawrence, D. H., 'Nottingham and the Mining Countryside' and 'Autobiographical Fragment', in *Phoenix*, ed. Edward D. McDonald (Heinemann 1936; reprinted, 1961).

Lawrence, D. H., 'Return to Bestwood', 'Autobiographical Sketch' (Miscellaneous Pieces), 'Autobiographical Sketch' (Assorted Articles), and 'Hymns in a Man's Life', in *Phoenix II*, ed. Warren Roberts and Harry T. Moore (Heinemann, 1968).

Lawrence, Frieda, *Not I, But the Wind* (Viking Press, 1934).

Moore, Harry T., *The Priest of Love* (revised edn, Heinemann, 1974; Penguin Books, 1976).

Nehls, Edward, *D. H. Lawrence, A Composite Biography*, 3 vols (University of Wisconsin Press, 1957, 1958, 1959).

Criticism

Coombs, H. (ed.), *D. H. Lawrence: Penguin Critical Anthologies* (Penguin Books, 1973).

Draper, R. P., *D. H. Lawrence* (Twayne, 1964).

Draper, R. P., (ed.), *D. H. Lawrence: The Critical Heritage* (Routledge & Kegan Paul, 1970).

Moynahan, Julian, *The Deed of Life* (Princeton University Press, 1963).

Sagar, Keith, *The Art of D. H. Lawrence* (Cambridge University Press, 1966).

Salgado, Gamini, *Sons and Lovers: Studies in English Literature* (Edward Arnold, 1966).

Spilka, Mark, *The Love Ethic of D. H. Lawrence* (Indiana University Press, 1955).

Spilka, Mark, (ed.), *D. H. Lawrence: Twentieth Century Views* (Prentice-Hall, Inc., 1963).

Tedlock, E. W. (ed.), *D. H. Lawrence and 'Sons and Lovers': Sources and Criticism* (New York University Press, 1965).

Worthen John, *D. H. Lawrence and the Idea of the Novel* (Macmillan, 1979).

Mastering English Literature
Richard Gill

Mastering English Literature will help readers both to enjoy English Literature and to be successful in 'O' levels, 'A' levels and other public exams. It is an introduction to the study of poetry, novels and drama which helps the reader in four ways – by providing ways of approaching literature, by giving examples and practice exercises, by offering hints on how to write about literature, and by the author's own evident enthusiasm for the subject. With extracts from more than 200 texts, this is an enjoyable account of how to get the maximum satisfaction out of reading, whether it be for formal examinations or simply for pleasure.

Work Out English Literature ('A' level)
S.H. Burton

This book familiarises 'A' level English Literature candidates with every kind of test which they are likely to encounter. Suggested answers are worked out step by step and accompanied by full author's commentary. The book helps students to clarify their aims and establish techniques and standards so that they can make appropriate responses to similar questions when the examination pressures are on. It opens up fresh ways of looking at the full range of set texts, authors and critical judgements and motivates students to know more of these matters.

MACMILLAN STUDENTS' NOVELS

General Editor: JAMES GIBSON

The Macmillan Students' Novels are low-priced, new editions of major classics, aimed at the first examination candidate. Each volume contains:

* enough explanation and background material to make the novels accessible — and rewarding — to pupils with little or no previous knowledge of the author or the literary period;

* detailed notes elucidate matters of vocabulary, interpretation and historical background;

* eight pages of plates comprising facsimiles of manuscripts and early editions, portraits of the author and photographs of the geographical setting of the novels.

JANE AUSTEN: MANSFIELD PARK
Editor: Richard Wirdnam

JANE AUSTEN: NORTHANGER ABBEY
Editor: Raymond Wilson

JANE AUSTEN: PRIDE AND PREJUDICE
Editor: Raymond Wilson

JANE AUSTEN: SENSE AND SENSIBILITY
Editor: Raymond Wilson

JANE AUSTEN: PERSUASION
Editor: Richard Wirdnam

CHARLOTTE BRONTË: JANE EYRE
Editor: F. B. Pinion

EMILY BRONTË: WUTHERING HEIGHTS
Editor: Graham Handley

JOSEPH CONRAD: LORD JIM
Editor: Peter Hollindale

CHARLES DICKENS: GREAT EXPECTATIONS
Editor: James Gibson

CHARLES DICKENS: HARD TIMES
Editor: James Gibson

CHARLES DICKENS: OLIVER TWIST
Editor: Guy Williams

CHARLES DICKENS: A TALE OF TWO CITIES
Editor: James Gibson

GEORGE ELIOT: SILAS MARNER
Editor: Norman Howlings

GEORGE ELIOT: THE MILL ON THE FLOSS
Editor: Graham Handley

D. H. LAWRENCE: SONS AND LOVERS
Editor: James Gibson

D. H. LAWRENCE: THE RAINBOW
Editor: James Gibson

MARK TWAIN: HUCKLEBERRY FINN
Editor: Christopher Parry

AGILITY
DOG
TRAINING

MARY ANN NESTER

AGILITY

DOG TRAINING

INTERPET PUBLISHING

Published by
Interpet Publishing,
Vincent Lane,
Dorking,
Surrey RH4 3YX,
England

© 2007 Interpet Publishing Ltd.
All rights reserved

ISBN 978-1-84286-164-6

Editor: Philip de Ste. Croix
Designer: Philip Clucas MCDS
Photographer: Mark Burch
Cartoons: Kim Blundell
Diagram artwork: Martin Reed
Index: Richard O'Neill
Production management:
Consortium, Suffolk
Print production: Sino
Publishing House Ltd, Hong
Kong

The Author

Mary Ann Nester arrived in England from New York in the early 1970s and never went home. In 1977 she set up Aslan Dog Training, a dog training school named after her first agility dog, a lurcher. She holds puppy parties and offers classes in obedience and agility in her home town of Northampton and conducts training days and workshops throughout Britain and abroad.

Her credentials are impressive. Mary Ann is a member of the Association of Pet Dog Trainers as well as an Agility Club Approved Instructor. As a licensed SAQ® trainer and accredited trainer in the DAQ® method, she is qualified to design functional training programmes for agility handlers and their dogs.

Mary Ann's most successful agility dogs have been her miniature poodles, Brillo Pad and Daz. They have both been finalists at Olympia and Crufts and have competed at international level. Brillo represented Great Britain at the World Agility Championships in Portugal 2001 and Daz in Germany 2002 and France 2003. When not competing, Mary Ann accepts judging appointments throughout the year.

Committed to promoting agility to anyone who has a dog, Mary Ann has been a guest expert on BBC Radio Northampton answering listeners' canine queries and, for many years, has posed as the Agility Auntie for the internet magazine, Agilitynet. She has written for Britain's most popular agility magazines, *The Agility Voice* and *Agility Eye*, and served as a committee member for the British Agility Club as well as the Poodle Training Club. In addition, Mary Ann is an official measurer for the Kennel Club.

When not chasing her own dogs around the agility course or teaching other people how to catch theirs, Mary Ann works as a part-time receptionist at an out-of-hours veterinary emergency service.

Contents

If you've already tried agility with your dog, you'll know that it's fast and furious fun. But also you'll know that it's not as easy as it may first appear. Problems can and do occur and many a promising round ends in frustration when a silly mistake undoes all the good work. But don't despair … that's where this book comes in. I've suffered those disappointments just like you and I hope that the answers to the questions outlined in the following pages may help you to reach the promised land – a clear round!

Introducing the sport

I will never forget my first agility dog. She was a lurcher named Aslan, a dog that had the elegance of a glamour model and the speed of a bullet. I can't help but compare all the dogs that have come after to Alsan. Do they have her willingness to try something new? Do they have her sense of humour? Why are they missing the contact on the A-frame? Aslan never did! In agility, handlers get a lot of things right through good training and practice. Aslan was born good and I was lucky to have her. I didn't know how lucky I was until I got my second agility dog and had to start problem-solving in earnest.

I loved Aslan with all my heart, but I won't mention her again. This book is not about dogs like her that have impeccable manners and perform perfect agility. It is about the mistakes, problems and goof-ups. Despite the best intentions to get things right, things can end up terribly wrong. Dogs miss weave entries, bark at judges in rain hats and run under jumps. No matter how well you prepare yourself and your dog for competition, you will encounter the unexpected. Your dog emerges from the tunnel backwards or the zip on your trousers breaks just as you reach the fourth obstacle on the course. What are you going to do?

# of AGILITY

Each time I open the gates to my agility field to welcome a new intake of beginner handlers I anticipate a number of familiar problems. I can guarantee that there will be one dog that barks at everything and one handler who hasn't brought any treats for his pet. But I'm bound to get a few surprises too. "What do I do with my false teeth when I'm running?" This is one unforgettable question that momentarily stopped me in my tracks.

And these are the questions that this book tries to answer. They have come from first-time pet owners or from handlers on their third or fourth agility dog. When I started writing, I thought I would be pushed to find 50

questions. When I reached the 70 mark, I thought I had exhausted the subject. Then I got my second wind and I couldn't stop. My task became one of limiting the number of questions that I would address in one book.

Sitting in front of my PC, a dog curled on each foot, has been bliss. Writing about agility is almost as satisfying as doing it. If any of the answers to these questions have helped a reader solve a training problem or understand their dog a little better, I can pat myself on the back for a job well done. My dogs have enjoyed the break, but they would rather jump fences than be foot warmers. Can you blame them?

LEARN TO SPEAK AGILITY

consists of two ramps hinged at the apex 5ft 7in (1.7m) from the ground. Each ramp is 9ft (2.74m) long and 3ft (914mm) wide. At the bottom 42in (1.067m) of each ramp is a contact area which is painted in a different colour from the rest of the A-frame.

B

Back chaining Training the last behaviour in a chain of actions first.

Back cross See **rear cross**.

Back jumping Jumping a hurdle in the wrong direction.

Note: The dimensions of the obstacles listed in this glossary and the appropriate metric conversions conform to the specifications set out in the Kennel Club regulations governing agility competitions in the United Kingdom.

A

ABC An ABC (Anything But Collies) is any breed or type of dog except a collie or collie cross. Classes that limit entry to non-collies are called ABC classes.

Agility course An agility course will include contact obstacles in addition to jumps, weaves, tyre and tunnel.

A-frame This obstacle is also known as the **A-ramp**. It

A-frame

Back weaving Performing the weave poles in the wrong direction.

Banking When a dog pushes off the top of an obstacle with his hind feet.

Baton The baton can be a stick of wood or pipe that is exchanged in pair or relay classes. Fun classes are renowned for imaginative batons such as balloons or spoons.

Blind cross The handler changes sides and crosses in front of his dog with his back to him. The handler is running blind unless he turns his head to look over his shoulder to look at his dog.

Blocking When the handler stands in front of an obstacle, he is physically blocking it from his dog and prevents the dog attempting it.

Box Four jumps set out in the shape of a square box, one on each side.

Briefing The judge will hold his briefing immediately before starting his class. He will give the course time, scoring and answer any questions.

Brush jump A hurdle that is made with a

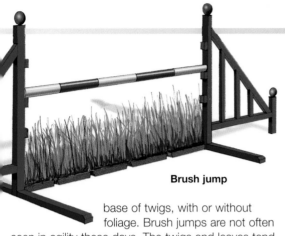

Brush jump

base of twigs, with or without foliage. Brush jumps are not often seen in agility these days. The twigs and leaves tend to dry out or disintegrate and so need regular renewing to keep the hurdle looking attractive.

C

Call off A handler will call his dog off an incorrect obstacle. He will use a call-off if the obstacle is part of a trap in the judge's course or if his dog is taking his own line through the equipment.

Caller The person who is responsible for booking in competitors and sending them to the start line in the approved running order.

Carousel An arrangement of jumps in a circle. The dog rotates around the handler in the middle as if he is a horse on a merry-go-round.

Channel weaves Channel weaves are a training aid consisting of two lines of poles that form a channel for the dog to run through. The two lines can be moved closer together or further apart. Guide wires running down the sides from one pole to the next keep the dog within the channel.

Clear round The dog and handler complete the course without faults and within the course time.

Clicker A clicker is a small hand-held device that makes a clicking noise when you press a button or tab. It is used as a training aid.

Collapsible tunnel The collapsible tunnel is also known as the **cloth, soft** or **chute tunnel**. The entrance is

made from rigid material so that it stands upright and the chute is usually made from plastic, nylon or soft material.

Come This is the recall command used by handlers when they want their dog to come towards them.

Contact The contacts are the demarcated areas at the base of the seesaw, dog walk and A-frame. The dog must touch them when they mount or dismount these obstacles or incur faults. They are always painted in a contrasting colour, most often yellow.

Course The course will contain at least ten obstacles, but not more than 20, and is designed by the judge.

Course builders The people who help set up the equipment in the ring in the morning and take it all down again at the end of the day.

Course time The judge assigns his course a maximum time in which it must be completed. The competitor will receive one fault for each second that this time is exceeded.

D

Directional command A command given to the dog to turn or send him in a specific direction.

Dog walk The dog walk is composed of three planks that are at least 12ft (3.66m) but no more than 14ft (4.267m) long and not less than 10in (254mm) but no more than 12in (305mm)

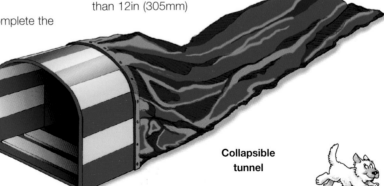

Collapsible tunnel

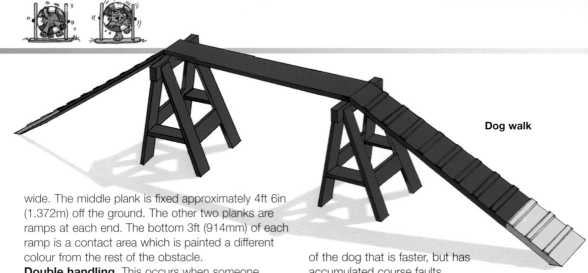

Dog walk

wide. The middle plank is fixed approximately 4ft 6in (1.372m) off the ground. The other two planks are ramps at each end. The bottom 3ft (914mm) of each ramp is a contact area which is painted a different colour from the rest of the obstacle.

Double handling This occurs when someone outside the ring attempts to help the handler and dog inside the ring. Double handling will be penalized by the judge.

E

E The abbreviation for **Elimination**. Some would argue that it also stands for entertaining, enthusiastic or energetic. Elimination is a result of the dog taking the wrong course or moving on to the next obstacle before completing the preceding one. A dog that is given three refusals will be eliminated as will the dog that is out of control or fouls in the ring.

Electronic timing The dog's time is recorded by electronic equipment when the dog breaks a beam at the start and finish of the course.

Elimination and out This is enforced at the judge's discretion. Handlers will be forewarned at the judge's briefing that if they are eliminated on the course they will be required to leave the ring immediately. This restriction is most likely to be imposed when time is running short.

F

Faults Penalties are awarded for both course and time faults. Course faults are awarded in units of five. It occurs when a dogs fails to perform an obstacle correctly, for example knocks a pole, misses a contact, or refuses a jump. Time faults are awarded at a rate of one fault per second if the competitor's dog exceeds the course time. The dog that has run clear and under the course time will be placed ahead of the dog that is faster, but has accumulated course faults.

Fence See **hurdle**.

Flick flack See **snake**.

Front cross The handler changes sides and crosses in front of his dog while facing his dog.

G

Go on A directional command telling the dog to go straight ahead and away from the handler. Also known as a **send away**.

H

Handler focus When the dog focuses on the handler rather than the obstacles.

Heel position The dog's heel position is on the handler's left side.

Hoop See **tyre**.

Hurdle Also known as **jumps** or **fences**. The height will vary. Large dogs jump between 1ft 9.6in (550mm) and 2ft 1.6in (650mm), medium dogs jump between 1ft 1.75in (350mm) and 1ft 5.7in (450mm) and small dogs jump between 9.8in (250mm) and 1ft 1.75in (350mm). The width of a jump should be a minimum of 4ft (1.219m). If the dog knocks the pole or bar, it should fall out easily.

Hurdle or fence

I J

Judge This is the person who has designed the course and will judge each dog and handler at a competition. He will indicate faults to his scribe or scrimer.

Jump See **hurdle**.

Jumping course The course will include jumps, tunnels, tyres and weaves but no contact equipment.

K

KC registration In the United Kingdom, dogs must be registered with the Kennel Club in order to compete at Kennel Club-licensed shows. There is a working register for non-pedigree dogs.

KC licensed agility In the United Kingdom, only agility clubs registered with the Kennel Club may hold and run a Kennel Club agility show.

L

Large dogs At shows licensed by the Kennel Club, dogs that measure over 1ft 5in (430mm) at the withers are classified as large. Height classifications will vary depending on which organization licenses the show.

Lead-out When the handler leaves his dog at the start line in a wait and walks out on to the course, positions himself and then calls his dog.

Lead runner The person who collects the competitor's lead from the start line and takes it to the finish for collection by the competitor after the run.

Long jump The long jump is made up of three to five units, each of a minimum width of 4ft (1.219m). The total length of the long jump will vary. Large dogs will jump 3 to 5 units with an overall maximum length between 3ft 11.2in (1.2m) and 4ft 11in (1.5m). The height of the front unit should be 5in (127mm) and the height of the one at the rear should be 15in (381mm). Medium dogs will jump 3 to 4 units with an overall maximum length of between 2ft 3.8in (700mm) and

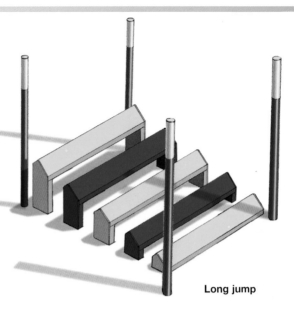

Long jump

2ft 11.4in (900mm). The height of the front unit to be 5in (127mm) and the rear to be 12in (305mm). Small dogs will jump 2 to 3 units with an overall length between 1ft 3in (400mm) and 1ft 7.7in (500mm). The height of the front to be 5in (127mm) and the rear to be 9in (229mm). In addition, poles of a minimum height of 4ft (1.219m) should mark each corner independently of the units.

M

Manual timing When the time keeper records a dog's time on the course with a stop watch.

Medium dogs At shows licensed by the Kennel Club, dogs that measure over 1ft 1.75in (350mm) and measuring 1ft 5in (430mm) or under at the withers compete as medium dogs. Height classifications will vary depending which organization licenses the show.

N

NFC This stands for Not For Competition. Dogs can be entered at a show even if they are not going to compete.

Nonstandard class These are **special classes**; for example, veterans classes (dogs over a certain age), knock-outs (two dogs

compete against each other on the course) or gamblers (in addition to accruing points on the course, competitors must perform a gamble, usually a specific sequence of obstacles in a short space of time). Any variation from standard marking will be explained at the judge's briefing.

O

Obstacle discrimination When a dog can tell the difference between one obstacle and another on the basis of the handler's verbal command or body signal.

Obstacle focus When the dog focuses on the obstacles rather than the handler.

Off-course When a dog deviates from the course set by the judge by taking the wrong obstacle, he is off-course.

Off side The dog's off-side position is on the handler's right side.

P Q

Pad runner This is the person who is responsible for making sure each competitor has the correct sheet from the score pad. The pad runner will give it to the scrimer and scribe to fill out and then give it to the score keeper.

Paddling This term refers to dogs that step on the units of the long jump. Instead of leaping the obstacle, they try to walk over it using each unit as a stepping stone.

Pivot When the handler turns on the spot. He can either pivot towards his dog or away from him.

Pole This is the horizontal bar on a hurdle that the dog has to jump.

Pole picker This is the person who sits at the edge of the ring during a competition. If a pole is knocked to the ground, it is his responsibility to replace it when it is safe to do so. He must not get in the way of the competitor, dog or judge. The pole picker keeps his eye on the course and may also straighten the collapsible tunnel if it gets twisted or re-peg the weave poles if they become loose.

Pull-off This is the opposite of pushing the dog

forward onto the obstacles. The handler pulls his dog away from the obstacle instead of towards it by verbal command or body signal. A pull-off may be intentional or accidental.

Pull-through This is a manoeuvre that takes place between two fences. The handler sends the dog over the first fence, calls him back through the gap between the wings of two hurdles and then turns the dog back and over the second fence.

R

Rear cross The handler changes sides and crosses behind his dog. This manoeuvre is sometimes called a **back cross**.

Refusal If a dog fails to attempt an obstacle, for example if he runs by a jump or goes underneath it, he will be marked with a refusal.

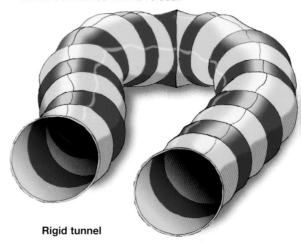

Rigid tunnel

Rigid tunnel Sometimes called the pipe tunnel. The opening should have a minimum diameter of 2ft (609mm) and the tunnel should be at least 10ft (3.048m) long.

Ring This is the test area where competitors are judged. It should be a minimum of 35yd x 35yd (32m x 32m) at outdoor venues.

Ring party Everyone who helps the ring run smoothly. This includes scrimers, pole pickers, callers, lead runners, show manager, pad runners and scorers.

Ring number Each competitor will have a ring number that identifies him and his dog.

Run This is the handler's competitive round on the course.

Run by This is a type of refusal. The dog runs past the obstacle rather than attempting to perform it.

Running order Dogs will receive a numerical running order randomly drawn for each class entered at a competition.

S

Schedule This is the printed notice of an agility show and will contain information such as host club, venue, entry fees, and so on.

Score keeper A show official responsible for posting, ranking and recording the performances of the agility competitors.

Scribe The person who records the dog's faults as signalled by the judge as well as the dog's time on the course.

Scrimer This word is a recent addition to agility vocabulary. The scrimer is the person who records faults as signalled by the judge as well as the times measured by electronic timing equipment. It is a combination of "scribe" and "time keeper".

Seesaw The seesaw's plank is a minimum of 12ft (3.66m) and a maximum of 14ft (4.276m) long with a width between 10in (254mm) minimum and 12in (305mm). It is mounted on a central bracket a maximum of 2ft 3in (685mm) from the ground.

Seesaw

At each end of the plank is a contact zone measuring 3ft (914mm) from each end and painted in a contrasting colour from the rest of the seesaw.

Send away See **go on**.

Show manager The person who is responsible for organizing and running the show.

Small dogs At shows licensed by the Kennel Club, dogs that measure 1ft 1.75in (350mm) or under at the withers are classified as small. Height classifications will vary depending which organization licenses the show.

Snake Three or more jumps in a line that the handler must send his dog over in a back and forth action. Also known as a **flick flack**.

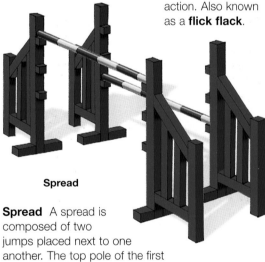

Spread

Spread A spread is composed of two jumps placed next to one another. The top pole of the first jump must be at least 5.9in (150mm) to 9.8in (250mm) lower than the pole on the second jump. The maximum spread will vary according to the size of dog. Large dogs – 1ft 9.6in (550mm), medium dogs – 1ft 3.7in (400mm), small dogs – 11.8in (300mm).

Standard classification Each organization will have a classification system. Entries to classes will either be based on previous wins or points gained.

Standard marking These are the rules and regulations as defined by the Kennel Club.

Star This is an arrangement of fences that mimics a star, a fence at each point. A three-fenced star is also known as a **pinwheel**.

T

Table The table needs to be solid with a non-slip surface. The table top is a minimum of 3ft (914mm) square. Its height will vary – large dogs will have a table 1ft 11.6in (600mm) high, medium dogs 1ft 3.75in (400mm) and small dogs 11.8in (300mm).

Table

Target Popular choices include plastic lids, mouse pads or squares of carpet. A target may be big enough for the dog to lie down on or so small that he can only touch it with his nose.

Threadle A threadle is a series of **pull-throughs** on a course.

Time keeper The person who holds the stopwatch and times each competitor's run.

Trap Traps can occur anywhere on the course. To avoid them, handlers must have good directional control over their dog and confidence in their dog's obstacle discrimination.

Tyre Its aperture is a minimum of 1ft 6in (457mm) and its height from the centre of its aperture to the ground will vary – large dogs jump through the tyre at 2ft 7.5in (800mm), medium dogs at 1ft 9.6in (550mm) and small dogs at 1ft 7.3in (490mm). The tyre is sometimes called the **hoop**.

Tyre

U V

V-weaves Weaving poles that are set in a base that allows them to pivot to different angles. They are used for training rather than competition.

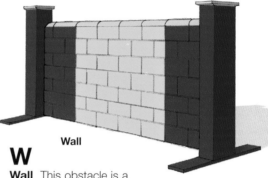

Wall

W

Wall This obstacle is a hurdle but it is built to look like a wall and is often painted to look as if it is constructed of bricks. The height is determined in the same way as a hurdle to accommodate small, medium or large dogs. The wall has displaceable units on top. If one of these units is knocked off, the dog is faulted just as if he had knocked a pole off a hurdle. If one of the units is touched but doesn't fall to the ground, the dog is not marked.

Weaving poles The dog has to wiggle in and out of the poles. There should be at least five poles but no more than 12. The poles should be set at least 1ft 6in (457mm) but no more than 2ft (609mm) apart. The poles themselves should be sturdy, between 0.75in (19mm) and 1.5in (38mm) in diameter, and with a minimum height of 2ft 6in (762mm).

Walking the course There will be time set aside before the class starts for competitors to walk the course. They must use the time to learn the sequence of the obstacles and plan their handling strategy.

Wings These are the bits on the

Wishing well Sometimes called the lych gate, this obstacle has a little roof not less than 5ft (1.524m) from the ground and a displaceable top pole that the dog must jump over like a hurdle. The pole will be set at the height appropriate to the category of dog. The wishing well should be sturdy and of solid construction and have a minimum width of 2ft 8in (813mm). There's not really any water at the bottom!

Zoomies When a dog has lost the plot and the handler has lost control of him, he will zoom around the ring at a hundred miles an hour. The dog has the zoomies.

Wishing well

Above: *A dog must always enter the weaving poles with the first pole on his left side. If he fails to do so, he will be marked by the judge with a refusal. And three refusals will result in an elimination.*

hurdle that hold up the pole. They are usually fashioned to look like a section of picket fence but they may be shaped like anything else, even a tin of dog food.

Below: *A dog with the zoomies doesn't always look where he is going and may run under or around the obstacles!*

Weaving poles

Chapter One

INTRODUCTORY QUESTIONS

You've seen a bit of dog agility on television and you've heard a little about it from a friend. But what exactly is agility training? Is it a form of canine callisthenics or is it more relaxing like yoga? And just how long have dogs been leaping over fences at agility competitions? Have you just not noticed or are these events a recent addition to the canine sporting calendar? There are so many activities for dogs these days, why should you choose to go to an agility class rather than something else? Your friend must be having a good time as nothing will make her miss a date with her dog and the agility equipment. Time to get some answers to your questions. Agility is not just about physical fitness or training techniques. It's not just about winning rosettes. It's about having fun with your dog. Find out for yourself!

The Agility Game

Q *What is dog agility? Please explain it to me in simple terms so that I can relay it to my grandmother who thinks that a good dog is one that earns his keep by culling the rat populations or working sheep. She lives on a farm and just can't understand why I love my "useless" Cavalier King Charles Spaniel, Tulip, so much and want to learn agility!*

A I don't think that you will be able to convince your grandmother that dog agility will add to the family coffers, but you might be able get her to admit that Tulip is much more than a lap dog!

The obstacles Agility is a canine assault course over obstacles. There are obstacles to jump like the hurdles, tyre, long jump, walls or spreads. There are the rigid and collapsible tunnel to run in one end and out the other. These are my dogs' favourite pieces of equipment. There are also the weaving poles to wiggle in between. The contact equipment includes the A-frame, dog walk and seesaw. Learning how to perform all the obstacles correctly is just the first step. The next is stringing them all together.

Sequencing When you can execute each obstacle competently, you will start learning how to put them together in a sequence, one after the other. For example, you might start with a line of hurdles and then progress to a box or a star of hurdles. Your instructor will want to familiarize you with the different patterns of obstacles that you will find on a course. When you and Tulip are stringing together more than ten obstacles at a time and consistently performing them faultlessly, you are ready to try an agility course.

The course The course is set by the judge and will consist of ten to 20 obstacles in a 32m (35yd) square test area. The jumps will be set at a height appropriate to your dog's height classification. Tulip will either be Small or Medium and will have to be measured before her first Kennel-Club-licensed show

to determine in which category she will compete. The distance between the jump obstacles will be not less than 3.6m (4yd) except on 90 degree turns when it may be reduced to a minimum of 2.74m (3yd). If it is an agility course, it will contain contact obstacles. If it is a jumping course, it won't. The challenge will be to perform the obstacles in the correct manner and in the correct order within the course time. Obstacle three must follow obstacle two.

The classes You must enter the lowest class for which you are eligible so start with elementary classes that have simple courses. You can qualify into more difficult and challenging classes as you gain more advanced handling skills and experience. Most shows will have a choice of types of class that people can enter.

Above: *There are more hurdles on an agility course than any other piece of equipment and dogs love jumping them.*

- Jumping classes will include jumps, tunnels, and weaves but no contact equipment.
- In addition to jumps, weaves and tunnels, agility classes will include the contact obstacles, the A-frame, dog walk and seesaw. These obstacles have contact areas at each end painted in a contrasting colour, usually yellow. Tulip must touch the contact area when she mounts or dismounts or else she will be faulted. A toenail will do! However, it is good practice to ensure that, in training at least, the dog performs a solid contact – either stopping on it or passing through it with four feet. Dogs that are allowed to jump over the yellow areas are risking injury.
- Special classes include pairs competitions, veterans classes (dogs over a certain age), knock-outs (two dogs compete against each other on the course) or gamblers (in addition to accruing points on the course, competitors must perform a gamble, usually a specific sequence of obstacles in a short space of time).

From start to finish If you have entered a Kennel-Club-licensed show, Kennel Club marking will apply. The judge will mark you as you run from start to finish. Your aim will be to get around all the obstacles without getting eliminated or incurring course or time faults.

Elimination Tulip will be eliminated if she pees or poos in the ring, so make sure she has an opportunity to relieve herself before you join the queue. She will be eliminated if she is out of control; for example, if she runs merrily around the judge snapping at his ankles or if she leaves the ring and won't come back. And Tulip will be eliminated if she makes up her own course. She must take the obstacles in the order decreed by the judge even if the tunnel is her favourite and she wants to do it first. Finally, if Tulip collects three refusals on the course, she will be eliminated.

Course faults Kennel Club marking awards course faults in units of five. Each obstacle on the course must be attempted. If Tulip runs by a jump, misses the mouth of the tunnel or fails to find the correct entry to the weaving poles, it counts as a refusal. And the obstacles must be performed correctly. So, if Tulip knocks a pole off a hurdle, leaps off the seesaw before it touches the ground or jumps over the contacts on the A-frame, she will be faulted. You will also incur faults if you touch Tulip while she is on the course or touch the equipment.

Time faults Hurrah! Tulip has made it around the course without a single mistake. You are clear, but are you in the course time? The judge will have set a maximum time on the course and time faults are awarded in units of one fault per second if the competitor's dog exceeds the course time. The dog that has run

clear and under the course time will be placed ahead of the dog that is faster, but has course faults.

Take your grandmother to an agility show and let her see for herself dogs in action on a course. She will be impressed by the number of well-trained dogs with wagging tails And she can't fail to notice how delighted the handlers are with their agility accomplishments, no matter how large or how small. I'm sure your grandmother will be very proud of you and Tulip although she might not admit it at first!

Born Jumping

Q *Whenever I visit Crufts, I watch the agility contests. The dogs love it and so do the crowds. Whoever thought of putting a dog and his handler with some jumps in one ring was on to something! How old is agility?*

A Some of us are pre-programmed to find an animal that they can partner over an obstacle course. As a child, I guided my pet terrapin over pencils laid on the floor. My next victim was an athletic hamster. No wheel for him, but rows of toilet rolls and matchboxes. Thank heavens I was eventually allowed to have a dog and go to training classes.

I'm sure that dog owners have been teaching their pets to leap over fallen logs in the woods for centuries, but agility as we know it was first seen at the Crufts Dog Show in England on 10 February, 1978. There was a gap in the schedule between the Obedience Championship and the Group Judging in Breed and the organizers needed something

entertaining that would keep people in their seats. Show-jumping certainly wowed the horsey set, so why not a canine version? The Crufts crowd loved it!

And they couldn't wait to get home and try agility with their own pets. Dog training clubs started to set up obstacle courses following the Crufts example and the British Kennel Club responded by developing a scoring system and a set of rules and regulations to govern competitions. It didn't stop there. Good news spreads. Agility is fun! Countries as far away as Brazil, Korea, and Canada have their own governing bodies for the sport and competition is now international with teams vying for the title "World Agility Champions".

Agility has come a long way since it first appeared at Crufts and it continues to grow in popularity. Terrapin agility? It never would have caught on.

Below: *Weaving can be a challenge to teach but, once proficient, dogs find it fun right to the very last pole!*

What's The Buzz?

Q *My Staffie cross, Buzz, is very clever and I think he would like agility. I'm tempted to have a go but I live on a tight budget and have to count my pennies. How expensive is it to get started?*

A Agility is accessible to people from all walks of life no matter what their incomes or lifestyle may be. My star pupil came to his first class with his sheep dog tied to a piece of binding twine.

He is a farmer who never normally has his dog on a lead and I've never been able to convince him to buy one. The dog follows the tractor when he's ploughing and roads are few and far between in his neck of the woods, so who needs a lead?

The dog You already have the most expensive part of the agility package – the dog. Even if you rescued your dog from a lay-by and named him "Freebie", he won't be cheap. There is no such thing as a low-maintenance dog and even the most routine health care can be costly.

The clothes The track suit and trainers you already have in your wardrobe are perfect, provided you don't mind them getting dirty. The important thing is to have clothing that is comfortable and washable. You don't want to feel cold and wet or hot and sticky. Shoes with soles that have plenty of grip are ideal. Falling over hurts and you don't want any more mud on your knees than necessary.

The classes It's worth shopping around to find an agility club that will suit your pocket as a night out with Buzz will be good value for money. There are a number of charging systems – pay as you go, pay for a course of six lessons or pay a single lump sum for the year. Some clubs ask you to pay a membership fee as well as class subscriptions. Remember, the most expensive classes will not necessarily be the best.

Put some money aside for mixing with your new friends after class in the pub. The talk will be all about dogs – Shelia's new puppy, what Molly the collie ate out on her afternoon walk or the handsome new vet at the local surgery. You don't need to dress in Armani or buy Buzz a diamante collar to do agility. But do please buy him a lead. Binding twine is so out this year! Go ahead. Look for some beginner classes and try your luck. You will not regret it.

Above: *Agility handlers come in all shapes and sizes. The attraction of agility is hard to resist whatever is in your wardrobe. People from different social backgrounds are united by their love of dogs and enjoyment of agility training.*

Collies Rule OK?

Q *I have a beautiful nine month old Border Collie puppy. I know that Tara is a working dog that needs mental stimulation and I want to make sure she gets it. I visited Crufts last year and saw that collies were participating and excelling in every sport available to dogs. Why should I choose to train Tara in agility rather than obedience, flyball, or heelwork to music?*

Left: *Having one blue eye and one brown eye won't affect this little merle pup's ability to learn quickly.*
Right: *Collie owners quickly find out that their pet's feet rarely touch the ground. They are ideal agility dogs.*

A Because agility will be more fun! But I'm bound to say that because agility is my passion. Ask the same question to a flyball competitor and they will say flyball, an obedience competitor will say obedience and a heelwork to music competitor will say heelwork to music. Each will try to persuade you that their chosen discipline is superior to all others. There are two reasons why I love agility more than anything else.

It's just me and the dog When I compete in agility, I have to work out how to get the best out of my dog over the course set by the judge on the day and I love that challenge. It's like doing a crossword

puzzle. I might get it right or I could fluff it, but I'm in command and the onus is on me. I don't have to worry about the performance of flyball team-mates. I don't have to listen to an obedience steward saying "forward, left turn and into slow pace". I don't have to follow the rhythm of a tune as I would in heelwork to music. The only person I listen to is me and hope my dog is doing likewise.

Speed is intoxicating I get a real buzz from running in partnership with my dog over a course. There is nothing more exhilarating than pushing yourself to the limits and biting the wind with your canine friend. Time is important in agility and "slow down" and "steady" are not in the vocabulary. The fastest dog clear takes home the trophy. Although speed is important in the other canine disciplines, handlers aren't expected to run with their dogs in competition. You won't see anyone sprinting with their dog to a flyball box or racing ahead of their pet to a send away marker. None of them will collapse over the finish line gasping for oxygen like I do.

But what is to stop you from trying more than one sport with Tara? There are many handlers who have trained their dogs in two or three disciplines and are successful competitors in each. The more you do with your dog, the more your relationship with her will be tested and enriched. Obedience, flyball and heelwork to music all have something of special value to offer, but I'm sure that agility will be your favourite. Not that I'm biased...

Left: *Border Collies are commonly black and white although other colour combinations are seen. Regardless of markings, all collies love to work and need mental stimulation.*

Hooked On Agility

Q *I am going to my first agility lesson next week with my Standard Poodle, Bella. My friend who already does agility with her dog has been teasing me that it will change my whole life and I'll wonder what I did with myself before I took it up. She can't be serious?*

A I'm afraid she is. It has certainly changed mine. The number of dogs in my household has grown to five and there is an A-frame in the garden. I'm rarely at home. I never have time to do the dishes, wash the laundry or mow the grass. I'd rather miss a party than an agility show. And that's because agility is more fun and it is very addictive.

You teach your dog to jump a line of hurdles. Wow! Look at that dog go! So you sign up for the next set of lessons. Your dog can do a course and he has lovely contacts. You enter a show and he goes clear in the time! You enter another show, then another. Soon you have a pinboard full of rosettes. You look for another club so you can get an additional night's training. It's worth the extra work because you win your first trophy! If you don't get to Crufts with this dog, then you surely will with your new puppy! He will be easy to socialize because all your new friends are eager to meet him.

And your new friends will be many. You will meet people from all over the country and from all walks of life. And most of them will believe that their dog is the best dog on the circuit – no matter how many times their pooch has been eliminated! You will meet large families with children, newly married couples and confirmed bachelors – all competing in agility with dogs that double as family pets. Agility people are very sociable and love to talk about their dogs or the meaning of life over a cup of coffee or a beer. I would rather train my dogs than watch TV and my best friends are my agility friends. I'm hooked. Agility has changed my life and for the better!

Below: *Don't be fooled by this poodle's exquisite grooming. He is perfectly willing to muss his hair to get the contact on the A-frame.*

Olympic Gold

Q *Agility looks simple and lots of fun. The dogs are really keen to be off and run around the course. Can you call something that looks so easy a "sport"?*

A Yes, you can and I'm all for seeing dog agility at the 2012 Olympics! Of course it's a sport and here are three reasons why…

It is a physical activity Running around a field with your dog means wearing trainers and getting out of breath.

It is a mental activity Handlers are challenged by the test set by the judge and must develop a strategy to steer their dog over the course in the shortest time.

It is governed by a set of rules Many people take up agility as a hobby, but handlers who enter shows are marked by a judge whose decision is final. If the judge's hand goes up, five faults go down on the score sheet.

Done well, agility looks easy. Horseback riding looks easy once you know how, so how much greater is the accomplishment of directing your dog over jumps and walls without a saddle or reins? Intensive training ensures a dog is focused and responsive, not sitting in the middle of the ring scratching itself for fleas. If everything goes to plan, the handler should be a competition winner.

But often it doesn't work out that way, no matter how many hours are put in perfecting contacts or tightening turns. A run will last approximately 30 seconds and you can make a lot of mistakes in 30 seconds. If you shout a command a split-second too late, you risk losing your dog in the wrong end of the tunnel. Or worse, the dog is just having an off day and decides to head for the ice cream van instead of the jumps. Herein lies much of agility's spectator appeal – you never know what is going to happen. Even the elite handlers can trip over their own feet.

Tennis? Football? Athletics? Those don't keep me on the edge of my seat. Give me the sport of dog agility any day. It's as fun to do as it is to watch.

Above: *Four feet are usually faster than two. But while speed is important, to cross the finish line first you also need a course strategy.*

Chapter Two

STARTING OUT

Are you and your dog up to a bit of agility? Do you need to be a super fit to stay the course? Are black and white collies essential for success? The best thing about agility is that it is open to anyone and any dog – regardless of age or breeding. If you own a pair of trainers and a dog with a leg on each corner, you can learn how to teach your pet to zoom through tunnels or wiggle between weaving poles. However, there are important questions to be asked before you sign up for a class. Is your puppy too young to start jumping fences? Can you bring your dog's treats with you to training? To get the most from agility, you need to be prepared. Dogs who have learned the basics of obedience and who are good canine citizens have a head start, but anyone can catch up and have fun learning to play the agility game.

Age For Agility

Q *What is the best age to start training my dog for agility. My Springer Spaniel, Tinker, is ten weeks old and I can't wait to start jumping.*

A Puppies are such a joy! It's so much fun rediscovering the world through their eyes. Tinker has a lot to learn before he gets down to the nitty-gritty of serious agility training. It will vary, but most agility clubs insist that new dogs should have finished growing before they start training. This usually occurs when a dog is about a year old, a little earlier for miniature dogs that tend to mature more quickly than the larger breeds.

While still a puppy, Tinker will naturally be pursuing his own fitness programme just by the way he behaves. He will be busy climbing stairs, balancing on the furniture and turning somersaults chasing leaves in the garden. He doesn't need to visit the gym. In addition, Tinker will be exploring his surroundings. One minute he'll be startled by a daisy, the next he'll be sniffing it and then he'll decide to eat it! Little puppies don't have the stamina for an hour's class or the strength and co-ordination for jumping hurdles or climbing the A-frame. Save these exercises for later when Tinker is a big boy.

Time flies when you have a puppy but for now Tinker is just a baby and agility is beyond his capabilities. You wouldn't enter a toddler for a triathlon, would you? Don't compromise

Tinker's future. What if he fell off the dog walk, landed badly after a jump, or tumbled down the A-frame? Puppies don't bounce. Be patient.

There are, however, lots of things that you can teach Tinker while you wait for him to grow up.

Become your puppy's best friend and play mate.

Don't assume that just because you are putting food in his bowl that Tinker will love you. Have fun together – a game of fetch or tug. Develop a bond. If you have a good relationship with your dog, Tinker will enjoy working with you and want to please you.

Socialize your puppy Do you want a hooligan as your best friend? Make sure your spaniel is getting out and about and meeting new people and dogs. Ride on a bus with him or visit the Post Office. Manners are important in agility. You don't want Tinker to jump up at people the moment you open the door to your house, so he will need training and socialization. Helping Tinker to mix socially now will pay dividends later on.

Have some basic obedience lessons Put your name down for a puppy party at your veterinary surgery or join a puppy class at your local obedience club. Learn the basics. A dog that will sit, go down and come on command is easy to control. These exercises are all fundamental to agility and have practical implications for everyday life.

Tinker will soon be old enough to join an agility class. At ten weeks old, make toilet training your immediate priority!

Left: *Teaching your puppy to sit for a treat or toy is rewarding and fun.*

Picking A Puppy

Q *I am finally in the position to have a puppy! In the past I have always adopted older dogs because I was working full-time, but now I have taken early retirement and I can indulge myself! What should I be looking for in a puppy?*

A Every puppy is a surprise package. As soon as you first get him through the front door, anything can happen and it often does. Health and temperament are important in agility and there are a number of things to consider when choosing a potentially suitable dog.

You can get a puppy from almost anywhere
They are advertised on the internet, on the newsagent's board and in the local paper. They are sold from breeding kennels, pet shops and people's homes. I like home-bred puppies because they are accustomed to the sound of the TV, the vacuum cleaner and pots and pans rattling on the cooker. They are more likely to meet lots of different types of people – the milkman, other family members and all the neighbourhood kids. The puppy's education and socialization have started before you bring him home.

Make sure your puppy "has a leg on each corner". Does he look healthy? Ask the breeder when he was last wormed and if he has been treated for fleas. Pick the pup that looks to have the best chances of a disease-free life in the future. If you are choosing a pedigree dog, talk to your breeder about inheritable diseases and whether the sire and dam have been screened for these conditions. You don't want to spend any more time at the vet than you have to!

Ask to see the parents and as many of your intended puppy's relatives as possible You will get a good idea of what your puppy will look like when he grows up, as well as an indication of likely temperament. Will he have short legs like his aunt or be grumpy like his uncle?

Think of how your puppy will fit into your family when making your choice If you still have other dogs, will they be more welcoming to a bitch or a dog? Do you want a submissive character or someone who will rule the roost? If you already have small dogs, do you think it would be fair to get a large breed?

And, finally, what sort of trainer are you? Try to pick yourself a good match. Are you a little inhibited and find it difficult to motivate and excite your dogs? Don't pick the laid-back puppy in that case. When you stand up, do you exude authority? If not, you may be storing up a lifetime of trouble if you take home the puppy that wants to be the leader of the pack.

When you choose a puppy, all you can do is try to stack the cards in your favour. No-one will promise you a winner and good breeding will not guarantee you reliable contacts on the agility course. Despite the odds, a sickly pup may turn out to be an agility champion. In the end it's not so much which one you pick, but what you do with him that really matters!

Breed Of Choice

Q *I would love to get a dog and do agility but whenever I have seen it on TV everyone has collies. Do other breeds of dog compete in agility? Would I have to get a collie if I wanted to do well?*

A Collies are the breed of choice for dog agility. They are agile athletes, independent workers and quick learners. All the ingredients are there to make an agility winner. Collies are great dogs, but there is no guarantee that they will be star performers and could you live with one? Just consider the following factors.

Mental stimulation
Collies like to flex their mental muscles. Out all day? Your bored collie might decide to entertain himself by ripping your settee into little pieces and trying to put it back together again before you come home from work. A dog lacking mental stimulation can become a destructive presence in the home.

Keen learners Collies pick things up very quickly and they are easy to train. This means that they will learn the wrong things as fast as they will the right ones. You might anticipate a speedy ascent onto the winner's podium if you get a collie, but the reality can be elimination after elimination on the course.

Need a job Collies hate being unemployed. If you don't have sheep, a collie will happily box and pen your children, perhaps even giving them a little nip for encouragement if they don't move fast enough!

Collies meet the job specification for agility dog, but they are not the only dogs competing in the sport of agility. Belgian Shepherd Dogs, Golden Retrievers and Cavalier King Charles Spaniels do well too. Large dogs, medium dogs and small dogs all enjoy flying over the jumps and racing through tunnels. Consider other types of dogs and their breed traits. Get a dog that you like and that fits in with your lifestyle. If you live in a flat, think about a miniature breed like a Papillon. If you hate dog hair, consider a non-shedding type like the Poodle. If you like spots, put your name down for a Dalmatian

Above: *This spaniel proves that small size and flyaway ears are no impediment to being a great agility dog.*

Physical exercise Collies are not the type of dog that likes to slob around at home. They need daily exercise and love long walks or chasing balls. If you live in the town, you may find it difficult to provide enough of these activities.

Above: *Jumping fences is just as much fun as chasing foxes. Beagles are one of the many small breeds that can excel at agility.*
Left: *Will this collie hit or miss the contact at the bottom of the dog walk? It's all in the training!*

puppy. Don't choose a breed just because of its popularity as an agility dog. Pick one you like through and through.

Other breeds might take a little longer to train to become proficient in agility, but they will get there in the end and many of them eventually turn out to beat the collies! Visit an agility show. You'll be surprised by the variety of dogs in the ring. Stay open minded. You may end up losing your heart to a bouncy Springer Spaniel!

Agility To The Rescue

Q *I have just re-homed a collie. I couldn't resist her big eyes and I've named her Shona. She is about eight to ten months old and loves everybody and everything. I've had her about four weeks and it's just like she has always lived here. She is such an active dog that I would like to take her agility training. Are rescue dogs accepted?*

A I'm so glad to hear that Shona has been given a second chance. There are so many waifs and strays out there. Working breeds, like collies or lurchers, often end up in rescue centres because they don't always settle down to family life. They want to round up and pen the children or chase the cat. Happily there are many successful rescue dogs in agility and they are a popular choice for many agility handlers because:

Above: *Give me a home and I'll be your agility dog – provided you give me lots of love, toys and treats too!*

Agility handlers have big hearts Who could fail to feel good about themselves after adopting a dog? Rescue organizations work hard to keep their animals happy and to make them comfortable, but a kennel cannot compete with a loving home.

Agility handlers love training their dogs Most of the dogs offered for re-homing are past puppyhood. Those that are ten months plus and well balanced individuals are ready to start agility training as soon as they are settled into their new surroundings. For those handlers who can't wait, they are the perfect choice for a new dog.

Size and shape matters You know more or less what you are getting with a rescue dog. Don't fall into the trap experienced by the agility handler who bought a puppy believing it would compete in the Small height category. It grew and grew and kept on growing. It ended up competing as a Large dog. Re-homing an adult dog that has already reached maturity takes the guesswork out of the equation.

Agility handlers love a challenge A rescue dog may have a number of behavioural problems and gaps in his education. You will never know why he is up for re-homing. Is it because his owners divorced or is it because he tried to bite the mother-in-law? Perhaps he simply barked too much? A rescue dog might understand the commands "Sit" and "Down" but may have missed the lesson on coming back when called. Bad habits like food bowl guarding won't be revealed until his first meal. These problems will have to be addressed before the rescue dog can begin agility training.

You are very lucky to have found Shona. She sounds the perfect companion and a real gem. And she has agility potential – the right age to start a little training and the right breed to excel at canine sports. Shona will keep you on your toes and you will have loads of fun with her. Have a look at the different agility clubs in your area and sign up for some classes. But beware … agility is very addictive!

One Of A Kind

Q *My dog is a real cultural hodge-podge. She has a little German Shepherd, a dash of Japanese Spitz and more than her fair share of Italian Spinone. Who knows what else went into the making of Minkie. You will never see another dog that looks like her and she is a fine example of a mongrel. Can Minkie try agility or is it only for pedigree dogs?*

A Agility is for all sizes and for all breeds of dogs and their crosses. If Minkie is in good health and at least a year old, there is no reason why she shouldn't try agility.

Not everyone wants a pedigree dog. You can be on a waiting list for a puppy for years and some blue-blooded dogs are exorbitantly expensive. Puppies from an accidental mating of your neighbour's pet can be had more quickly and are usually a cheaper option. You won't be able to anticipate what the pups will look like when they grow up, but you do know that they will be individuals that stand out in a crowd.

You will be surprised to learn that many agility folk actually choose a crossbreed over a pedigree dog. They see a combination dog working in the ring, admire the dog's style and set out to find a pup with a similar make-up. In Britain, Border Collie crossed with German Shepherd, Poodle and Bearded Collie have all been popular mixes and sometimes are deliberately bred for obedience and agility handlers. In addition, some crosses have been planned with size in mind. Small dog handlers have tried to miniaturize Border Collies by mating them with Jack Russells. Sadly, just because a dog sports black and white markings doesn't mean he will have the trainability and work ethic of a collie! There is no guarantee that the best traits of both breeds will dominate in the pups of a cross-mating.

In the UK you will see crossbreeds at every

Above: *Sometimes it's easy to confuse a pedigree dog with a crossbreed. The owner of this championship-winning Pyrenean Sheepdog would be most upset if you mistook her pet for a mixed-up mongrel!*

agility show including Crufts. And sometimes you will see them beating the pedigree dogs! To compete at Crufts or any other Kennel-Club-licensed show, your crossbreed must be enrolled on the Working Trials and Obedience Register at the Kennel Club of Great Britain. There are also a number of independent organizations that welcome crossbreeds – for example, UK Agility or East Midlands Dog Agility Club – that will have their own registration policies and rules and regulations governing competitions. Not all countries are so welcoming and regulations may vary in other countries. For example, a type of dog may be recognized as a pedigree in one country, but not in another. In addition to a national Kennel Club, a country will probably host a number of alternative agility organizations and each will have their own registration policies regarding crossbreeds and competition events. Who knows what went into making Minkie, but she's sure to have a jumping gene somewhere!

Agility Ability

Q *I've had my dog now for about a month. Zipper is from a rescue organization and I believe he is about a year old. He's a medium-sized mongrel that will do anything for food. I have always been interested in agility and thought that if he showed some aptitude for it, we would have a go. Well, his latest trick is to get up on the kitchen worktop to look out of the window! In view of his acrobatic leanings, do you think agility is a good idea or will it create more problems at home?*

A Zipper is the ideal candidate for agility training. He's handsome, quick to learn and athletic. He just has to learn that the items of furniture in your living room are not obstacles on an agility course.

Above: *No piece of furniture is too tall or too wide for this appealing rescue dog to jump or climb. He's an ideal candidate for agility.*

Discrimination
Agility can provide a constructive channel for Zipper's energy and turn him into a discerning dog. He has probably already learned to discriminate between the things in the house that he must not touch, like your slippers, and what he can play with to his heart's delight, like his squeaky toy. Similarly, he will quickly catch on to what behaviour is appropriate for an armchair at home and what is appropriate for an A-frame in agility.

Control Acrobatic ability is not the only prerequisite of agility. In addition to the obedience basics, dogs are trained to jump, climb or weave only when commanded to do so. If a dog takes his own line on an agility course because he prefers the blue jump to the red one, he will be eliminated. Zipper should only vault over the garden fence to visit his friends if you give him permission by saying, "Zipper jump!"

Agility rarely creates more problems than it cures. Find your nearest agility club and sign up for a course of lessons. You'll make new friends and Zipper will delight you with feats of athleticism that have nothing to do with the kitchen work surfaces. At the very least, Zipper should be too tired after training to get into mischief, but if he does still have enough energy to wonder what's passing the kitchen window, buy a blind!

A Rough Start

Q *I would like to start agility training with my rescue dog, Benny. Benny did not have the best start in life. He is very hand-shy and I think he must have been beaten as a puppy. He is very loving to me, but suspicious of people, especially men. He's a very handsome dog that attracts notice and he once nipped someone who only wanted to stroke him. Will agility help him overcome his fears?*

A Benny is very lucky to have found a home with an owner who understands his anxieties. Agility will certainly give Benny something different to think about, but it is not a cure. Care must be taken to make sure that your dog has professional help to overcome his problems and that they are not compounded by the stress or anxiety that Benny could experience on his encounters with agility. You need to be aware of the following factors.

The early stages of agility are hands-on There will be a number of occasions when your instructor will want to touch Benny. He might hold Benny for you while you call him over a fence or he might help you lift Benny into a position on a contact. If Benny looked unsteady on the dog walk, your instructor could reach out to steady him so that he didn't fall off. Do you think Benny would be frightened and protest at this kind of handling?

Right: *Two pairs of hands are better than one to keep this dog on the seesaw. They guide him up the trail of cheese and are ready to catch him if he decides to jump off too soon.*

It's hard to learn when you are thinking of something else Agility classes can be stressful. If Benny is worried because he can't keep track of all the new people he is meeting and is getting a headache from all the barking dogs around him, he won't be able to pay much attention to what you are trying to teach him. And you may well become worried about how Benny will react to the class environment which will compound his anxieties and make him even more nervous.

Agility is a very sociable sport Although Benny might relax and make friends with your trainer and the other students in his class, he will inevitably continue to meet new people as classes progress. What if one of your classmates brings her young children to a lesson during the summer holidays, and they want to pet Benny?

It is never too late to socialize a dog to new people, different dogs and strange places, but an agility class is not the best place to start. Benny might have very good reasons to be distrustful of people, but he can learn that not everyone is bad. Begin by talking to a canine behaviourist who will be able to assess your dog and find practical solutions. Not all agility instructors are qualified to give advice on problem dogs, but they are usually happy to support and help implement recommendations from those that are. There are many dogs enjoying agility today that have had a rough start and overcome their fear of people. Benny has already taken the first step. He has found an owner who loves him and wants to help him enjoy life.

Many Happy Returns

Q *Sammy my lurcher loves running. When I take him out he disappears over the horizon and I may not see him for ages. Often he brings back a rabbit. Then we go home and he sleeps. Would agility be a better way to exercise him and tire him out?*

are needed, both to give you some control and to help you become a team. And also for safety. When Sammy is off over the fields hunting, you don't know what he is doing. An out-of-sight dog is a dog courting trouble. Is he raiding a dustbin for scraps? Is he terrorizing someone's cat? Is he stopping to

A From the rabbit's point of view, agility is the choice option.

Lurchers are a type of crossbreed found in Britain. It is said that they were developed in the Middle Ages by gypsies to be used for hunting and poaching. They are usually sighthounds crossed with a collie or terrier type – an attempt to combine speed and brains – and they can be exceptionally beautiful and athletic dogs. My first agility partner was a lurcher and I have always had a soft spot for this type of dog.

Agility would be something that you and Sammy could do together – then you could both go home and have a snooze – but first I think a few lessons in basic obedience

Above: *Lurchers are speed demons. They make great agility dogs, provided they are pointed in the right direction – at the jumps and tunnels, not the rabbits.*

look both ways before he crosses the road? He may already have had a few lucky escapes. If Sammy does not come when you call him, he might decide to go hunting rather than jumping the first time you take his lead off in agility class.

Yes, agility will be great exercise for Sammy once he has a recall under his belt and he will still enjoy his walks with you. Every dog should have his training supplemented with time off to relax and do the things that dog do. Dogs love to smell where other dogs have been, roll on their backs with their legs in the air or play with their doggie pals. These are all acceptable behaviours in free time ... as long as the dog comes back securely when he is called.

Agility Best Buys

Q *My husband has offered to take me out for the day shopping. He thinks he will be buying me a little black number for Saturday nights, but I will be looking for something sporty and practical for my first agility lesson with Penny our Cocker Spaniel next week. What would you suggest?*

A Oooh shopping! After agility, shopping is my favourite hobby and what a lucky lady you are to have a husband generous enough to foot the bill. Convince him that you can look just as good in waterproofs as you can in silk!

Above: *Footwear is important in agility. You don't want to fall over and end up sitting on your bottom. Leave your wellington boots and high heels at home and buy a good pair of running shoes.*

Shoes Your first port of call should be the shoe shop. You want something that you can run in comfortably and that will cushion your feet. Shoes that grip all types of surfaces in all types of weather are ideal. Many agility enthusiasts wear field hockey shoes with rubber studs. Avoid shoes with metal studs – you may accidentally step on your dog. Don't buy anything that may give you blisters.

Clothes Make sure that whatever you buy allows you to move around freely and protects you from the weather. You will need something to keep you warm and dry if you are training outdoors in winter. Don't forget hats and gloves. If it's summer and the sun is shining, look for shorts and T-shirts. I try to buy clothes with lots of pockets to accommodate my dog's treats and toys. I look out for things that wash well and dry quickly. I'm a big fan of sporting/camping shops and practical leisurewear outlets as their clothing is practical rather than fashionable. I also have a number of sweatshirts and fleeces embroidered with my club logo, agility slogans and favourite breeds.

Underwear Don't forget to visit the lingerie department. If you are a well-endowed lady, you should consider investing in a sports bra. It should be the dog that is doing all the bouncing around on the course, not you.

Accessories What else? If you have long hair, you will probably want something to tie it back so you can see where you are running. And something just for fun – how about a pair of paw print earrings?

Best buys The two things I can't do without are my silk long underwear and my waterproof socks. OK, they don't make me look sexy or improve my handling skills but I feel like a hundred bucks when I wear them.

Room To Manoeuvre

Q *You need lots of room to do agility, don't you? I'd like to have a go with my Cocker Spaniel Barclay, but how could I practise? I have a small garden – there is no room for a lot of jumps and an A-frame.*

A Few of us have the room to lay out a full agility course. Our gardens are for flower beds and sun loungers. But that is no excuse for not practising. Basic obedience exercises and target training requires only a little space and can be perfected indoors. And you'll be surprised at what you can accomplish without "proper" agility equipment by using lots of imagination.

Contact position Is there a step out of your back door into your garden? Make it a "contact" step. Teach Barclay a two foot on/two foot off position (back feet on the step and two front feet on the ground). If he holds it for a few seconds, praise and release him into the garden to play.

A-frame Your stairs are an A-frame. Whenever Barclay comes down the stairs ask him to wait on the "contact" step at the bottom. Praise and release him into the room. Not all staircases are ideal for this exercise; for example, spiral or open tread

Below: *Walking along the top of a wall is just like walking along the top of the dog walk. The views over the lake may be lovely but watch your step or you could fall in!*

staircases are not recommended. You will have to use some common sense assessing their safety and suitability.

Dog walk Walk a wall with Barclay. I lift my young dogs up onto a brick wall that divides one side of my local park from the other. They walk along while I hold their collar, just like on a dog walk. Choose a wall that is wide enough for Barclay and, again, think about safety. Avoid walls that are too tall or have crumbling brickwork. Check what's on the other side – a steep drop onto a busy lane of traffic or a rose bed would be hazardous.

Hurdles You will find loads of these in your local woods. Logs and branches that have fallen down are perfect hurdles. The best time to find them is after a storm. There are lots of jumping exercises you can practise over a few well placed logs, but remember that Barclay is supposed to jump them, not crawl over or dive under them.

Miniaturized equipment Not all agility equipment is huge or heavy. I have a mini A-frame that I use to practise contacts and I can lift it with one hand. I also have a mini-tunnel which is only a few feet long. Neither is as big as the real thing, but perfectly fine for giving my dog a taster of the sport. Both can be folded away in minutes and stored out of sight in the garage.

Above: *Is it a poodle masquerading as a curly coated squirrel? No. It's an agility dog practising his climbing technique during a walk in the woods.*

There are also lots of potential agility obstacles in children's play areas and fitness circuits in neighbourhood parks. Remember, however, that these are for humans and resist the temptation of taking Barclay down the slide. Think about campaigning for a dog "play" area in your community instead. I'm sure it would be popular.

Absolute Beginner

Q *I rang my local agility club to find out the times and dates of classes for absolute beginners. I'm eager to do some training with my Patterdale Terrier, Zena. I thought I'd be the one asking the questions, but they wanted to know what kind of dog I had, how old she was and whether she had attended obedience classes. I thought I could do agility classes instead of obedience classes.*

A I'm sorry if you felt you were being interrogated by your agility club. It's not only important for you to ask a lot of questions when you are looking for classes but for the club to find out as much as possible about you so that they can decide where you will fit in best. Otherwise you could end up the smallest dog in a class of Irish Wolfhounds!

Dogs that have attended obedience classes are usually under control and receptive to learning new things. They will have already covered some of the basics such as:

Heelwork It is important in agility that dogs are able to walk on or off lead by their handler's side. If Zena pulls you through doorways, she is likely to pull you through the tunnel.

Recall Everyone likes their dog to come back to them when they call. And right away, not after the dog has disappeared down a rabbit hole. If Zena ignores your call, you could end up spending the first ten minutes of every agility class trying to catch her.

Positions The "Sit" and the "Down" are the agility handler's favourite positions and are used in a variety of ways. A dog can be told to go "Down" on a contact or to go "Down" when waiting in the queue for her turn. She can be told to "Sit" at the beginning of a new exercise or to "Sit" on the start line at a competition. Can Zena "Sit" and "Down" on command?

Wait or Stay The keener an agility dog becomes the harder it is to "Wait" your turn! Agility handlers get a head start on the course by telling their dogs to "Wait" behind the first fence. Or they place their dog in a "Stay" while they return to a jump and pick up a pole that has been knocked down. Will Zena stay put?

Zena may have received no formal obedience training yet still be able to perform these exercises proficiently. Each exercise has practical implications for everyday life and a well mannered dog is easier to live with than a hooligan. And just because a dog receives an "A" grade at obedience class doesn't mean she will remember all her lessons when she gets onto the agility field – much to her owner's stupefaction!

Obedience basics are a prerequisite for agility. While some agility clubs will incorporate a number of control exercises into their beginners' courses, others leave teaching the basics to the obedience clubs.

Below: *Waiting for your turn can be the hardest lesson in agility.*

The Sky's The Limit

Q *I have a collie cross called Sky and I want to do obedience and agility with her. I've already taught her to "Sit", "Down", "Walk to heel" and "Come" on command. What are the training techniques used in agility and how are they different from those used in obedience?*

A Agility dogs are not only trained to jump fences, but to be good canine citizens with a degree of proficiency in most obedience exercises. The training methods used by a handler to teach his dog the basic obedience exercises will usually be the same ones used to teach more specialized agility activities. If you take up agility with Sky, you will have an advantage because you are already familiar and practised with some of these training methods.

Take the A-frame contact as an example. The A-frame has a contact area at the end of its ramp measuring 106.7cm (3ft 6in) up from the bottom and the dog must touch this or be faulted by the judge. How the handler chooses to teach his dog to hit the contact area demonstrates a choice of training techniques. You may have already used one of these techniques to teach Sky to lie "Down" in obedience.

Above: *Dogs will follow a treat anywhere and luring a dog into the contact area can be a successful training method.*

Hands-on shaping When training the A-frame contact, the agility handler physically places the dog in the position he wants the dog to adopt on the contact. While she is in this position, she is rewarded with praise and a treat. Did you teach Sky to lie down by starting in the Sit, then lifting and lowering her front legs to the ground and finally rewarding her with praise and a treat when her tummy was flat on the floor? That is an example of hands-on shaping

Barrier shaping The agility handler places a hoop at the bottom of the A-frame that the dog must run under as she exits the contact. He hopes that enough repetitions of this action will embed it in the dog's muscle memory. Perhaps you got Sky to crawl under a table so that similarly she had to lie down?

Luring Armed with his dog's favourite treat or toy,

the agility handler lures the dog to the very bottom of the contact. Dogs will follow a treat anywhere! Did you hold a treat just above Sky's nose and then slowly lower it to the floor so that she was lured down into the flat position?

Click and treat The agility handler clicker-trains his dog to nose-touch a target. He places the target at the bottom of the A-frame and asks his dog to touch it. You may have used a clicker to teach Sky to lie down. Click means the same thing in any discipline – a treat is coming.

Training techniques often cross divides. Some are better suited for specific actions than others. Choose one that works for you and your dog to get the results you want.

Pre-Agility Classes

Q *I have a lively and exceptionally clever six-month-old Border Terrier, Nellie, that I believe would be great at agility. I have never done agility before but understand that although she is too young to do it properly, some clubs run pre-agility classes for youngsters. Have you heard of these classes? What should I expect?*

A There are a number of clubs that run pre-agility classes, sometimes called "foundation classes" or "fundamentals for agility". They are ideal for youngsters that are too young to jump high hurdles but are old enough to master some basics. The classes concentrate on the agility essentials like motivation, control and attitude. Graduate dogs are receptive to further agility training and progress quickly. A good pre-agility class will cover some of the following:

Motivation You will learn how to use a toy or food as motivational aids. Nellie may like to chase a tennis ball but will she bring it back to you? She may love to rag a tug toy, but will she let go of it on command? A high play drive can make teaching your dog new things in agility a lot of fun.

Distractions If your dog is going to do agility, she must learn to ignore distractions such as other people, dogs or food – no matter how tempting. Will Nellie walk by your side or wander off to hunt squirrels? When you call her, will she come straight back to you or will she make a detour to the food bin?

Socialization Some dogs are nervous in mixed company. They can be overwhelmed by new environments. Pre-agility classes can help Nellie relax and take things in her stride. Dogs find it easier to learn when they are not stressed or anxious.

Tricks In addition to some of the obedience basics, Nellie may be taught a few tricks like walking backwards, waving a paw or taking a bow. Tricks will amaze your friends, but more importantly, they will engage Nellie's brain, improve her flexibility and give her confidence in you. Just what you need for agility.

Flat work There are many agility exercises that can be done without the equipment like directional commands, target training or teaching Nellie to run on both your left and right side. And, Nellie can learn to run between the hurdle wings – on the left and right, as a recall and as a send away. This is a good preparation for jumping later on.

Partnership The aim will be to make sure that you and Nellie are having a good time. Doing things together will strengthen the rapport you have with your dog.

I would like to see more agility clubs offer classes like these, but until there is a sufficient demand, pre-agility classes won't appear on your club's timetable and they will rely on local obedience schools to teach traditional exercises like "Sit", "Down" or "Stay". I do hope you will be able to find a pre-agility class near you.

Left: *Puppies too young to start jumping can still learn a trick.*

Getting A Head Start

Q *I have a ten-month-old collie cross spaniel named Charlie. I have competed in obedience with my other dogs, but would like to have a go at agility. We live on a remote hill farm and my nearest training club is 60 miles away. Their "Introduction to Agility" class doesn't start for another 12 weeks and I may have to miss some of these if we get snowed in. Is there anything I can teach Charlie now so that we can make a good impression on our trainer? We don't have any agility equipment.*

A You can introduce Charlie to a great deal in agility without him touching a piece of proper equipment. Keep your training at ground level so that Charlie will avoid accidents and continue growing into a confident, bold adult.

The plank Put a two-metre (6-8ft) plank of wood on two bricks on the ground and teach Charlie to walk along it. Gymnasts practise new moves and routines on a balance beam laid on the floor before they move to a competition-height beam. Charlie will become a confident performer on his plank and be better prepared for balancing on a real dog walk. Make sure there are no nails or splinters sticking out of the plank before you begin any exercises.

The wobble board Put a small log under a flat square of wood so that one side rests on the ground and the other is raised about 15cm (6in). Voilà, a miniature seesaw! Charlie will have to get accustomed to the ground moving under his feet and keeping his balance while you lead him from one side to the other.

The ladder
Lay six poles (broom handles or PVC tubing cut into lengths) on the ground about 1 to 1.2m (3 to 4ft) apart

like a ladder and walk Charlie up through the middle. Charlie's co-ordination will improve and he will learn to pick his feet up to avoid the ladder's rungs – just as he will have to pick up his feet to avoid knocking a pole when he is old enough to start jumping.

Running through the wings Put a pole on the ground between two chairs that act as hurdle wings. You can teach Charlie to run over the pole with you positioned on either his left or on his right. You can recall him over the pole or you can send him away to fetch a toy. Charlie will be learning to run between the wings of a hurdle rather than running around them.

Left or right You can start teaching Charlie directional commands. If he has been clicker-trained, you can click and treat when he looks right or left and give these actions directional commands. Or teach Charlie to spin to the right or twist to the left, luring him with a toy.

Start as you mean to continue. Build his confidence. You want each exercise not only to be fun and successful, but to lay solid foundations for subsequent agility training in a few months time.

Top Dog

Q *I'm not ashamed to admit that I'm very competitive. Whether at work or at play, I take the time to make sure I come out on top. What are the characteristics of a great agility dog? What should I be looking for if I want to end up on the podium in a few years time?*

A A truly great agility dog will be the one that the judge has been waiting for all day. As the dog steps onto the start line a hush will descend over the crowds. Everyone will hold their breath while the dog takes centre stage. His handler will be rallying every ounce of grit and determination in order to do the dog justice. This dog is likely to cross the finish line with either the fastest clear run of the day or the biggest elimination points tally. The characteristics of a great agility dog are:

Peak physical condition The dog will be in his prime; fit and healthy. He is a superb canine specimen with a sparkle in his eye.

Above: *If your dog doesn't skip the last pole, a tight turn exiting the weaves can cut seconds off your course time.*

Bold and fearless If this dog falls off the dog walk, he dusts himself off and gets back on again. He is prepared to take risks as he flies around the course

– getting contacts by a toenail or tightening a turn so much he almost knocks a pole. He is not afraid to take the initiative if his handler is too slow.

Drive Acceleration is not a problem, slowing down often is. A great agility dog will have drive and work in top gear even if his handler has a hangover.

The "I want" factor A top class agility dog is always hungry for the jumps and contact equipment. The minute he sees the training venue or show ground, he begins to pull on the lead.

As a judge, this is the kind of dog that I like to see step into my ring. Whether the handler loses control or goes on to win the class is irrelevant. I can appreciate not just the fine agility dog in front of me but the work that has gone into making him so formidable. I know appearances are deceptive. Who expected that the "jump everything in sight" Sheltie would be brought under control with no loss of enthusiasm? Who would have put money on the Papillon ever breaking out of a trot? And who would believe that a few months ago that terrier was badly spooked by an umbrella? Their handlers have succeeded in motivating their dogs and teaching them not just competency over the equipment, but a joy and love of agility.

Few top agility dogs are born ready made and even fewer land in the laps of experienced handlers. More often top agility dogs are the result of hard work, good training and a few embarrassing moments in the ring from which they happily learn.

Short In The Leg

Q *I've seen dog agility on TV. Everyone looks like they are having fun and I would like to have a go with Freya, my Bichon Frise. She's big on personality, but is she too small for agility?*

A No. She's probably the perfect size for a Bichon! Agility is for all shapes and sizes of dogs. In the UK, dogs are measured before they enter their first show and compete in three different height categories:

- **Small** – open to dogs measuring 350mm (13.75in) or under at the withers.
- **Medium** – open to dogs measuring over 350mm (13.75in) but under 430mm (17in) at the withers.
- **Large** – open to dogs measuring over 430mm (17in) at the withers.

And no one would expect your little Bichon to jump big fences. The respective jump heights are:

- **Small dogs** – jump obstacles will be 250-350mm (9.8-13.75in).
- **Medium dogs** – jump obstacles will be 350-450mm (13.75-17.7in).
- **Large dogs** – jump obstacles will be 550-650mm (21.6-25.6in).

Small dogs are as passionate about agility as the big dogs. A dog is a dog, regardless of size – they all jump, weave and miss contacts. They all have a trigger button that turns on their motors. Small dogs can do everything that the larger Border Collies can do. It's just sometimes a little harder because of their size, but their training will take their size into account.

Short legs Shorter legs mean that small dogs will have to take three to four times as many strides to cover the same ground as big dogs with longer legs. Consequently they can run out of steam quickly.

Small mouths A tennis ball can be too big to fit comfortably between their jaws so they aren't always

Above: *Good things come in small packages. Many miniature breeds enjoy competing in Small dog agility classes.*

keen to retrieve. Tug games need care. Pull a toy out of a small dog's mouth with too much gusto and you could extract a few teeth too! And many little dogs are fussy eaters turning their noses up at gourmet morsels. As a consequence, play and treat training can be hard work.

Small dog breed traits Dogs that were miniaturized to fit in your lap can be difficult to motivate and switch on. They worry about breaking their nails if you ask them to do a bit of work. On the other hand, small terrier-type dogs that have been bred to go down rabbit holes or kill vermin never stop. Offer this type of mini-dog a job and he will sign on the dotted line.

There are a number of small dogs on the agility circuit that should be given speeding tickets. They achieve course times faster than many of the large dogs. Do look out for an agility class near you. Agility is lots of fun and you won't be the only one with a small dog. Freya may be little, but inside there's a big dog waiting to be let loose on the jumps.

Big Is Beautiful

Q *I have a Great Dane called Pernod and I would love to do agility with her but have been told that my breed of dog is too big and heavy. Is this true? I just want to have some fun.*

A It doesn't matter how large or how small your dog is to have fun. However, Pernod is a big girl and you need to make sure that she has fun safely. You will both stop smiling if Pernod hurts herself and you end up with a big, big vet's bill to match your big, big dog. There are three areas that give me concern.

Tunnels Pernod would have to get down on her knees to fit in and crawl through the tunnel. Such a tight squeeze would not be very comfortable for her.

Weave poles These could be a problem, too. Most poles are a minimum height of 76cm (2ft 6in). The distance between the poles is a minimum of 46cm (18in) to a maximum of 61cm (2ft). If Pernod is taller than the poles she risks

being poked in her tummy. And bending one way with her front end while her back end is bending another way would not be easy.

Dog walk and seesaw I think these two pieces of agility equipment could be very challenging for Pernod. The plank for both has a width of between 25 to 30cm (10 to 12in) – probably considerably less than Pernod's shoulder width. For her, placing one foot in front of the other will be like tightrope walking. Moreover, I am not aware of any regulations regarding the weight-bearing capacity of the equipment. If the dog walk and seesaw are left outside in all weathers or are very old, they won't be particularly sturdy and could collapse under the weight of a big dog. But don't let this stop you. I suggest the following:

Talk to an agility instructor You would be taking Pernod to classes purely for her pleasure and entertainment. Why not ask if you could participate in class activities but abstain from those that would be uncomfortable or risky for Pernod?

Find a "big" dog agility club These clubs cater for the larger breeds like yours and train over purpose-built equipment to withstand the size and weight of Great Danes, Irish Wolfhounds, Bernese Mountain Dogs and others. They realize that big dogs are capable canines who love to run and jump as much as their smaller cousins.

Start your own "big" dog club Large breeds can do agility. Make your own reinforced, super-sized equipment and have some fun. Pernod could be your club's mascot! You will be setting a new trend in your area. Size is important and does pose some particular problems, but it shouldn't stop you from having fun with your dog.

81cm (32")

Below: *Samoyeds are built for pulling sleds in the Arctic, but are also valued as pets. If your dog is missing the snow, introduce him to agility. He'll soon dream of nothing else!*

15cm (6")

Size matters! And with a little forethought, agility can cater for all dogs, from the smallest to the very biggest.

How To Be A Champion

Q *Sometimes I look at my dog and feel sorry for him. I make so many mistakes and let him down. Turbo is a superb lad who always does his best for me. If he was someone else's dog, he would be an Agility Champion by now. What makes a good agility trainer?*

A There are three types of agility trainer who stand on the podium holding a clutch of rosettes and trophies.

The born good trainer A few people are born good trainers. The born good trainer has been blessed with perfect timing, great co-ordination and bags of patience. His intuition is always right and he appears to be able to communicate with his pets telepathically.

The trainer with a born good dog This trainer has a once-in-a-lifetime dog. God's gift. His dog learns despite the trainer's mistakes. The dog always gets his handler out of trouble on the course and people say that he must have been an agility dog in a previous life. God's gift would be on the podium no matter who owned and handled him.

The trainer who works hard Most of us have to work our socks off to be a good trainer. It's not easy and a good trainer can be years in the making. As time goes by, he will accrue a vast knowledge of canines and develop the skills to communicate clearly with his dogs. He will understand how to make learning fun and how to guide his dogs to make the right choices. And he will have spent hours practising agility to perfect his handling moves. If you want to follow in his footsteps, here are a few tips:

- **Be consistent** Consistency makes learning easy. Don't say "Over" one day and "Jump" the next.
- **Be patient** A good trainer knows how to be patient and will master the basic moves before trying advanced ones. Take it steady and don't try to run courses before you can do all the obstacles.

- **Stay up to date** A good trainer will arm himself with a sound knowledge of current training methods and learning theories. Curl up in your armchair with a good dog training book.

- **Perfect timing** A good trainer knows the importance of a few seconds. Make sure your commands and praise are spot on. Tell your dog he is a "Good boy" for sitting, not scratching his ear after his bottom hit the ground.
- **Learn from mistakes** Even the best dog trainers make them. Never blame the dog for your errors but adjust your training programme to make sure the same thing won't happen again.
- **Practice** A good dog trainer will make practice count. Spend time practising what you need to improve but stop before your dog reaches saturation point. There is just so much a dog can learn in one day.

Don't feel sorry for Turbo. He is lucky to have you. You don't love him any less for not being an Agility Champion and Turbo loves you despite your mistakes.

What's In A Name?

Q *I will be bringing home my first puppy in a few weeks time. He is going to be a star agility dog, but has so much to learn. What is the most important thing that I can teach him?*

A The most important thing that you will ever teach your dog is his name. He should be listening for his name even in his sleep. When he hears it, your dog should snap to attention in anticipation of some fun. His name will precede every command you give him. Listen to some of the top agility handlers when they are in action. Often the dog's name is the only thing they say when they run their dogs, so choose your dog's name carefully.

Keep it short Your dog may already have a fancy pedigree name like "Torrington's Mad Hatter Over Tabasco". What a mouthful! By the time you spit that out your dog could have taken the wrong turn on an agility course and been eliminated. Choose a pet name that is easy to say and rolls off the tongue.

Avoid people's names If you are standing in the middle of the park yelling for "Brian" and a good-looking young man approaches and asks how he can help you, how are you going to explain the mix-up?

Feel comfortable with your choice The kids might think that "Twit" or "Willy" is a cute name for your pup, but how happy will you be registering him at the vet or introducing him to your friends?

Think of everyone in the family when making your decision I have a friend who named her dog "Vodka". A few years later she got married and had babies. Her neighbours now believe the children have a drink problem because someone in the household is always shouting for Vodka.

Name and command Make sure that the name you choose does not sound like an agility command. If your jump command is "over", you don't really want to call your dog "Clover".

It's easy to teach your puppy his name. Put some cubed cheese or diced chicken in your pocket and when your puppy is looking away from you, say his name in a happy voice. If he looks at you, praise him and give him a treat. Practise in all the rooms in your house and out in the garden. When he is investigating under the sofa or sniffing daffodils in

Above: *Don't call your dog by his name unless you want him. If you shout your dog's name while he is weaving, he may leave the poles uncompleted to return to you.*

the back yard, call his name and offer a titbit as soon as he turns to you. Responding to his name gets the reward – not the names of your husband, children or other dogs. He will start listening for his name and giving you his attention when he hears it. And let's face it. Before you can teach your dog anything, you have to be able to get his attention!

Packing Your Bag For Class

Q *I am going to my first agility lesson next week with my dog, Tansy. I'm so excited! I don't know if I'll be able to get to sleep the night before because I'm already dreaming about it. What do I need to take with me to class?*

A I am so glad that you and Tansy are looking forward to your first class with such enthusiasm and, like a good boy scout, you want to be prepared. Here is a list of things that you should take with you.

Collar and lead Choose a flat leather or webbing collar (not a choke chain). Agility dogs in England are permitted to wear collars in competition provided there are no tags hanging from the D-ring and many handlers have their dog's collar custom embroidered with their pet's name and phone number. You will also need a lead to keep your dog under control and introduce him to the agility equipment. Avoid flexi or extra long leads. You don't want your dog to tie himself up or trip over.

Treats Take a selection of treats with you – diced cheese, sliced sausage, or biscuits. Used wisely, treats help a dog to make correct choices and encourage him to give his best performance. Make sure your treats are in a dog-proof container. Determined dogs will try to open or chew through treat pots to get to the yummies inside.

Toys Don't forget your dog's favourite toys. Does your dog like to tug on a piece of rope or fetch a ball? Use that instinct to your advantage. Dogs that love to play, love agility and toys will become an intrinsic part of their training.

Clicker and target If you have already trained your dog with a clicker, you will be ahead of the game. Clickers have many applications in agility and there are many different ways that a target can be used to teach new skills.

Diary Start as you mean to continue and buy a training diary. Record your progress, triumphs and disasters. A training diary is not essential, but it will make good reading later on when you are a superstar or get a second dog.

Poo bags Never go out without these. Your dog may want to go to the toilet before class starts so be prepared to pick up the faeces and deposit it in the bin provided.

Training bag Buy a bag for all your training gear. If you keep all your training paraphernalia in one place, you won't end up hunting through your pockets for a toy that you left in your car. Be selective and don't overload Tansy's training bag. You want to be able to carry it easily to and from agility.

Sense of humour Never leave this at home. It is the most important thing to bring to an agility class. Have a laugh and enjoy yourself.

Left: *Walk into any pet shop and you'll see that the shelves are filled with all shapes, sizes and colours of tempting toys.*

Picking A Toy

Q *I have been told by my agility instructor to bring a toy to agility class. I looked through my Troy's treasure chest and most of his toys are half chewed or filthy. I would be too embarrassed to be seen in public with any of them. I'm going to the pet shop today to buy him something new. What should I be looking for?*

Above: *These collies can't take their eyes off the tennis balls on a rope.*

A Manufacturers really know how to make adorable toys for dogs these days. I have a collection of little toy animals I bought at a pet shop. They live on my bedspread, match my wall paper and are forbidden territory. I wouldn't consider giving such sweet things to my dogs – they would cover them in slobber! When you shop for Troy, consider some of the following:

What does your dog like? Would Troy like a ball or a toy in the shape of a hoop or a bone? Does he have a passion for vinyl or rubber? Does he love soft plush toys? There are toys that squeak, jingle or make mooing noises. There are toys with pockets in which to stuff treats. Tug ropes come in different colours, widths and lengths. Despite this wealth of choice, Troy still may simply prefer a pair of old socks.

How big is your dog? What will fit comfortably into the mouth of a German Shepherd Dog will not fit into the mouth of a Papillon. The Pap will need something smaller and lighter. And never buy a toy that is so small that your dog might swallow it accidentally or choke on it.

What games can you play? Choose interactive toys. Some toys are easy to throw and great for games of fetch. Other toys are ideal for tug games. Small toys are great for hide and seek. The only limit on the number of games you can play is your imagination.

Is your toy easy to hold? If your dog's favourite toy is a big soccer ball, you'll have trouble holding it while you run an agility course. And it will be a difficult toy to fade from training because it's too big to tuck in your pocket. I like toys that fit in my hand or up my sleeve. My dogs never know for sure whether I have a toy on me so they work really hard, just in case I do. Sometimes it is so well hidden, I don't find it till I change for bed.

Wash and play Will the toy you choose go in the washing machine? Tennis balls bounce around a bit but come out looking brand new. It won't matter how many times Troy drops his toy in a puddle if it can be easily cleaned.

Can you make a toy valuable? You are halfway there if Troy has already fallen in love with his toy. Make him love it even more by making it an "agility only" toy. Restrict his access to his toys in the house. Don't leave them lying around for him to chew on in idle moments. My dogs would give their eye teeth for a toy animal off my bed. One day perhaps…

Tasty Treats

Q *I don't know what kind of treats to use at agility class with Tinsel, my Yorkshire Terrier. She is a fussy eater and I'm sure that some treats are better for her than others. What would you suggest?*

A Treats can be used in agility in a number of ways and are especially important for dogs that don't like to tug or fetch a toy. You can use a treat as a lure, a reward or an incentive. Something tasty will motivate a dog not only to learn something new but to perform existing behaviours faster. Treats are versatile. You can give your dog a lick of her favourite titbit or you can jackpot her with a handful if she has done something really spectacular. It's worth while finding something that Tinsel likes.

Yummy The perfect treat will be delicious – the greasier and smellier, the more attractive to your dog. Cubes of cheese and slices of frankfurter are popular choices with many dog trainers or you can buy readymade treats from the supermarket or pet shop. Experiment with different food types to see what makes Tinsel's eyes light up. How about diced carrot or chunks of cooked chicken? But do remember NOT to use human chocolate as a treat; this is harmful to dogs and even quite small quantities can be toxic.

Easy to eat Choose a treat that is quick and easy to eat. You don't want Tinsel to spend ages gnawing on a hard biscuit. She'll forget why you gave it to her. The rest of the class won't wait for her to finish eating and think of all the crumbs she'll be leaving behind that may distract the other dogs.

Small Little dogs have little mouths and stomachs. Don't use a whole chicken leg as a treat – a sliver will be enough! Remember that you will be treating Tinsel frequently in class and you want her to be able to run without feeling full or bloated.

Special A treat must be special. If you feed Tinsel dried biscuit everyday, she is unlikely to get excited when you try and tempt her over a jump with the same biscuit. How boring! Choose something different.

Bon appetit Is Tinsel's food bowl always full? She won't have much interest in food if it's on tap all day. Stick to regular meal times so that in between she will have a good appetite and appreciate a treat.

Sensitive stomachs Some dogs have sensitive digestive tracts and introducing a new food type can upset their stomachs. Other dogs are prescribed special diets due to medical conditions or allergies that should be fed exclusively – not even one day off for good behaviour! If Tinsel has a touchy tum, try setting aside a portion of her daily food ration to use as training titbits. Her tummy won't be upset by it and you'll be able to monitor her weight.

Stress Appetite is not just a good measure of a dog's physical condition but of a dog's mental state. If Tinsel refuses treats at training, it might be that she is worried or stressed. Try and help her to relax. Give her time to acclimatize to her surroundings.

Keep trying. It's only a matter of time before you find something that Tinsel likes.

Play Training

Q *As instructed by my agility trainer, I have bought my collie Zak a toy. I took Zak with me to the pet shop and he picked it out himself. It's a pink ball on a rope. Then he picked another toy, then another. This is going to cost me a fortune. Why do I need a toy for agility?*

A I must congratulate Zak on his first choice of toy. A pink toy is very visible and will be hard to lose in the green grass. It's multi-purpose, doubling either as a fetch toy or as a tug toy. And another bonus is that you will be able to throw your pink ball even further because it's on a rope. But do practise your aim. If you sling the ball too high up in the air near a tree, it may get tangled in the branches and you will have to plan another shopping expedition to replace it! You ask why toys are needed –

Playing with toys will arouse and stimulate your dog Toys make practice fun and exciting. They are the key to mental ignition. When dogs are playing, everything is turned on. You need that kind of excitement in competitive agility to obtain a tip-top course performance from your dog.

Toys are filters There are many things that can catch a dog's eye in agility – strange people, new dogs, strange scents. Having an exciting game with Zak's tug toy can filter out many of these distractions and focus his attention on you. He'll be too engrossed trying to win the toy from you to worry about the lady wearing a funny hat selling ice cream.

Toys can create distance between you and your dog Whenever you want Zak to accelerate away from you, throw a toy for him to chase. Zak will drive down a line of fences in order to catch a ball. It will be travelling much faster than you will ever be able to run. Just try and beat him to it!

Above: *Soft toys can be too delicate for tug games but they are ideal gobstoppers. A dog can't bark when he is holding one in his mouth or he'll drop it!*

Toys can bring your dog back to you If you want a sharp turn after the tunnel, call Zak to you and have a tug game with his toy. If you want to pull Zak through the gap between two fences, he will return to you more quickly if he gets a game of tug as a reward. If your dog wants to get his teeth into his favourite toy, he has to be within arm's reach. And don't let go of your end.

You will have as much fun playing with a toy as your dog That is the best reason for buying Zak a toy. Play is something you do together and a good way to learn about your dog. Toys are not for solitary individuals. Become Zak's favourite playmate. And remember, a toy can last forever. A titbit disappears in seconds.

Left: *Throw a toy for your dog to chase and hope that he will bring back to you to throw again! Games keep a dog motivated.*

He Won't Touch The Toys

Q *My beagle, Horace, has no interest in toys. I have filled a drawer in my kitchen with balls, rubber hedgehogs, plush mice, tug ropes and old slippers (he loved chewing them when he was teething). All of them, except for the slippers, are in pristine condition. He would rather have a worming tablet than a toy in his mouth. My agility instructor keeps telling me to get Horace interested in a toy. How?*

A Handlers who have dogs "born" with a tug toy in their mouths never really understand the difficulties of coaching a dog to play with a toy. If you want Horace to beg you to open your kitchen drawer, you'll have to work hard to make his toys interesting.

Keep the toy moving There is nothing more boring than a static ball. Drag it along the floor like it is a small dying bird. Throw it across the ground. Make the toy's actions mimic an injured prey animal. Praise him for looking at it and Horace might be inclined to show even more interest next time and stretch out a paw to touch it.

Right: *Where is that squeaking noise coming from? If I squeeze it between my jaws, will it squeak even louder?*

Squeak your toy If your toy makes a noise, it will attract Horace's attention. At the very least he will wander over to investigate. If you are lucky, he will think it is a small animal about to expire and dive in to put it out of its misery. You can join in as well by praising him.

Hide food in your toy Some toys have little pockets that you can stuff with titbits. If Horace likes food, he'll be keen to get inside. Give him a treat from the toy if he sniffs it. Cheer him on if he starts to disembowel it!

You play with the toy You might feel foolish throwing a rubber hedgehog up in the air, catching it and chuckling with glee, but don't stop. If you are convincing, Horace will want to join in the fun. It's like watching someone eat chocolates, you wish they would share them with you.

Left: *Stuffing a rubber food toy with treats will keep a dog occupied for hours. And when it's empty, he will bring it to you to fill up again!*

You become a toy Does Horace like to wrestle with you? Push him away from you. Does he bounce back? If you run up the garden, does he chase you? Have a toy in your hand ready to add into the game.

The right toy The most unlikely objects might elicit a response from Horace. Be prepared to praise him even if he's playing with the toilet brush.

There are many reasons why a dog will not play. Sometimes they are inadvertently taught to stay away from toys. A possessive older dog will teach a puppy "All toys are mine. Touch one at your peril."

Above: *Take a favourite toy to the beach, on a walk in the woods or out into the garden. You can have an energetic game with your dog anywhere and anytime and when you get home, spoil yourselves with a biscuit and a cuddle.*

A puppy may be scolded for ragging a dishcloth and he will never tug again. Or a puppy is teased with a toy but never given the chance to get hold of it so gives up trying.

Toys are an important tool in agility, but they are not the only ones. If Horace likes worming tablets, he's bound to like treats, so that may be the answer.

You're Never Too Old

Q *I'm no spring chicken. I'm a little fatter and a little slower than I was 20 years ago, but otherwise I'm a very fit senior citizen. My boxer, Barney, is in his prime and would love agility. Would my attempt to run around a field embarrass him and would I have to wear Lycra?*

A Don't let your age prevent you from joining an agility club. Start slowly if you are afraid of tripping over your shoe laces. After a few lessons, running will start to feel more natural and you'll be more confident in your own abilities. Everyone feels a little self-conscious at first running a dog, but this soon passes especially when you see how willing other people are to act silly to keep their dog's attention. It's people who get embarrassed, not their pets. Barney will love you no matter what. Speak to him in a funny voice or jump up and down on the spot if this is what he likes. He won't be able to take his eyes off you.

It's Barney that has to do all the running and jumping, not you. He's the one that your instructor and class will be watching. Especially if you teach him to work independently of you on the course. He'll be able to cover the distance to leave you far behind but you will be able to take all the short cuts so as to catch him up.

Running fast is not so important for the handler in agility, but knowing the course is. You must know that the weaves follow the A-frame or that there is a left turn after the tunnel. If you teach Barney to follow your directions, your speed won't matter. The clock stops when Barney, not you, crosses the line!

Above: *There is no age limit for agility. Strut your stuff with pride and show those youngsters how it's done. Your dog will love you all the more for taking him to agility classes. It's so much more fun than sitting on your lap watching TV.*

You don't have to wear Lycra if it makes you feel uncomfortable. Anything that allows you to move freely and keeps out the cold will do the job. As far as Barney is concerned, anything you wear with treats in the pocket is fashionable. I have seen many 20-year-olds that should have left their Lycra in the wardrobe, and I have been beaten by many pensioners who tell me that when I get to their age, I'll finally lose all my inhibitions and be a great handler! Let agility liberate you!

Agility's Juniors

Q *My 14-year-old year old daughter Judy has a pet Cocker Spaniel called Kylie and they are best friends. Judy would like to take Kylie to agility classes but I am worried that she may not be old enough to train a dog. Are there classes that cater for children?*

A If Judy is old enough to look after a puppy, she is old to join an agility club. It is committed children like Judy who become the agility handlers of the future. Young dog lovers need to be encouraged to get involved in an activity with their pet that will not only be fun but teach them something about the care and training of dogs. Agility has much to offer.

Above: *If you get a puppy, you will always have a best friend while you are growing up.*

Classes Judy will start with an introductory or beginner's course of agility lessons and once she has learned all the obstacles and is proficient at course work, she will be able to progress through the classes. Her classmates are likely to be other adults of all ages and backgrounds. Not all agility clubs run classes especially for youngsters, but more and more do, operating as weekend or afterschool activities. It depends on what is available in your area.

Sportsmanship Part of growing up is learning about winning and losing and entering an agility competition is a great way to start. Children have a choice of classes. They can compete in standard classes against adults (often beating them) as well as special classes whose entry is limited; for example, "handlers must be under 16 years of age". There are a number of tournaments, finals and league tables run just for young people. If Judy is ambitious, she could set her sights on qualifying to compete in the Young Kennel Club Final at Crufts.

New friends Agility is a great way to meet new people and share a passion for dogs. Many of the agility magazines have a section written for and by junior handlers. Here Judy will find all the information she needs – what shows are scheduled, what classes to enter, as well as special events for young people like weekend training camps. Judy will have plenty to do with her new buddies instead of homework.

Agility parents are keen that their kids should get involved and learn to run the family dog. But beware – agility kids often want their parents to take hold of the lead. Till Judy gets her driving licence, you will probably be chauffeuring Judy to training and shows.

Left: *Learning to care and train a dog can teach young people important life skills.*

His Highness and Her Majesty

Q *My husband and I have two Border Collies, one for him and one for me. Bliss is a dear sweet girl and my dog. Bonus is about two years younger. He's a bit of a delinquent but dotes on my husband. We are looking for a hobby to share and thought about taking the dogs to agility class. Is this a good idea?*

A It's a great idea! Agility will keep you both fit and give you lots to talk about over dinner. There are a number of successful husband-and-wife teams competing in agility. Here are some tips to make sure that you become the King and Queen of agility.

Below: When husband and wife agree, can there be any doubt in a dog's mind that "Stay" means "Stay"?

One handler, one dog It's hard for a dog to learn new things and it's even harder if more than one person is telling her what to do. Bliss is your baby so you stick with her and let your husband work with Bonus. Don't treat or fuss each other's dogs in class. It will confuse them if the commands are coming from one direction and the rewards appear from another.

Instructors instruct If the instructor is talking to your husband, don't interrupt. Let your husband offer his own excuses for not doing his homework. Never say, "Do it like this" or "This always works for me". It is the instructor's job to make corrections and suggestions. Your husband will be more receptive to criticism from the instructor than his wife which he is more likely to take personally.

Agility class is fun If you have been arguing all week about who left the top off the toothpaste, don't continue the fight at agility class. Your dogs will pick up on the discord and get stressed. Agility is not the place for domestics, so leave your troubles at home. It is also rather embarrassing for your classmates if you indulge in a shouting match.

Lend a hand Help each other. Take turns toileting the dogs, chopping up treats for training or filling

Right: *A dog's loyalty may lie with the agility equipment rather than the handler. This collie would work as happily for his mistress as he would for his master as long as he can beat them to the finishing line.*

in entry forms. Be supportive and sensitive. Dog training will always be plagued with highs and lows. Sometimes a run goes really well and at other times disaster strikes. If your husband is having difficulty teaching his dog a new obstacle, don't brag about how Bliss found it really easy. It won't help.

Wait your turn It is hard not to be a little jealous if your husband brings home trophy after trophy while your dog's only consistent quality is

getting eliminated. Friendly rivalry is one thing. Hiding his running shoes and the car keys is another. Your turn on the podium will come.

As you become more experienced agility competitors you might divide tasks even further. Perhaps one of you is better at training youngsters while the other has nerves of steel, a good competitor. Whatever happens, remember that you've taken up agility to enrich your marriage – not to end it with divorce!

Left: *Don't be tempted to shift the blame for a fault to your dog. Your wife told you the pole would drop if you continued to push for speed on the corner.*

Chapter Three

SOLVING PROBLEMS

Agility training is not always smooth sailing. Some problems are common and the result of youth and inexperience. With luck, they disappear with maturity. Other problems are unique and rare. You'll see them all if you attend an agility class and you'll start asking questions to learn about your pet. Why does your dog pee on the tunnel? Why does he try and limbo dance under the fences? At home, your dog is a quiet member of the household, but at agility club he won't stop barking. And you need an explanation for other odd quirks of canine personality. He is the only dog in the class that perches on the A-frame and won't come down and what's this obsession with hats? By trying to understand your dog's behaviour and find solutions to your problems, you will also find out about yourself…

Barking Mad

Q *I have just started agility with my very keen Labrador Spice who barks incessantly! In the beginning I didn't want to tell him off for barking because I was afraid it would dampen his enthusiasm. But now it is a real problem and any tips would be greatly appreciated.*

A Take out your ear plugs. What is Spice telling you? The barking can mean various things.

"I'm so excited to be here!" I think this type of bark is permissible in agility. It expresses joy in life and anticipation of good things to come. I don't object to this kind of barking in class. You hear it at every agility show, so get used to it. However, as an instructor, I would not compete with it during lessons. No woofs when I'm talking or my pearls of wisdom will go unheard. Teach Spice to speak and to be quiet on command, divert his attention with a toy or simply remove him temporarily from the training area which is triggering his excited barks.

"I'm so excited I could eat you!" This type of bark verges on the hysterical. Take it as a warning that Spice has wound himself up and could explode. He may even try to nip you. He won't mean to hurt you, but he just won't be able to help himself. Put Spice in a Down stay until he has gained control of himself.

"You are SO frustrating!" If you hear this bark, it is because you have slowed down on the course or lost your way. Make sure you know where you are going and what you are doing. Plan each run in advance and execute it confidently and positively. Your commands should be clear and your timing immaculate. Spice won't be baffled and he'll have to work to keep up with you.

"Come on, come on, COME ON!" Spice is pressurizing you to get a move on. He is even more frustrated and about to burst because you are hesitating again. There is a hint of desperation and his body posture might be a tad confrontational. If you don't hurry up and decide which fence to send him over, he'll decide for you. As your handling improves, these situations should reduce in number. In the meantime, turn your back on Spice. Go to the end of the queue till he has regained his composure. Leave the building if you have to. You don't do agility with dogs that try to handle you over the course. That is your job. When Spice is quiet, take up where you left off, on your terms. Teach him that silence is the starter whistle for agility.

For some dogs, barking is as natural as breathing. It can be as addictive as gambling, alcohol or drugs. Anti-bark collars or a spray of water will help break the barking habit. But if Spice is making noise because he is frustrated or confused on the agility course, you need to concentrate on sharpening your handling skills to help Spice become a quieter dog.

Below: *Given the choice would you rather bark or play ball? Encourage your dog to think with his mind, not his mouth.*

Snipping The Nipping

Q *I have a very fast and excitable collie, Smudge. Recently, he has started to nip me if I slow down or hesitate on the agility course. At the moment I grit my teeth and keep going. The biggest nip is saved for the end of the round when he's actually come close to removing items of my clothing. If this keeps up, I'm going to have to give up agility. Please help.*

A I see many dogs at shows nipping their handlers. Some people learn to live with it. They have mastered the art of crossing their arms to protect the more sensitive parts of their body as they surge over the finish line.

Herding sheep
Nipping is in a collie's job description. Giving a particularly dozy member of the flock a nip is all part of a day's work. When you slow down or hesitate in agility, Smudge is nipping you to get you to move faster or change direction. He is herding you round the course and, unlike sheep, we humans haven't any wool to protect our flesh. We puncture! Make sure that you are doing the shepherding. Don't give Smudge a reason to harass you.

Know where you are going Plan your run in advance. You won't have time to think on the course. Smudge is quick and impatient for instructions. If you get lost or hesitate, he will start pressing you with his teeth to make a decision. Smudge doesn't have the map. You do.

Tell Smudge what to do Smudge is not a mind reader. Fail to direct him with a command or body signal and he will start nipping to remind you that he needs orders. The better you are at steering, the less Smudge will nip.

Don't stop if you make a mistake If you halt, Smudge will have a reason to start complaining with his teeth. Finish and then, if necessary, re-start the sequence from the beginning.

Speed up your handling
Nipping often starts because the dog has become confident on the agility field more quickly than the handler. Don't try to slow Smudge down. Learn to drive your canine missile while he is in top gear. You won't have time to look in your rear-view mirror.

Don't anticipate a nip If you worry that Smudge is going to nip you, you will be less focused on the course and you'll slow down. You'll be thinking about your personal comfort rather than mapping the course. Smudge will know your mind is elsewhere and bring you back to the agility ring with a nip.

Still nipping? If Smudge forgets himself in the heat of the moment and nips, down him and stand still until he has regained his composure. You don't play agility with a dog that nips.

I am sure that with preparation and practice you will be able to improve your handling skills and Smudge will lose the urge to nip. Good luck nipping his bad habits in the bud!

Little Nipper

Q *I hope you can help me and my dog, Gunner. Gunner bites the end of the seesaw as he dismounts. He bites the last weave pole as he exits. He also bites the hurdle poles but not as often as when he started agility training. Gunner is a rescue dog and has always been difficult, but at least he has stopped biting my hands and feet. He loves agility.*

A If Gunner loves agility, he must stop sinking his teeth into the equipment. Take him out of the ring before he chips a tooth. Which of the following dog types is Gunner?

Below: *The dog knows where he wants to go but do you? Take the lead!*

Dog number one Dog number one starts well, but half way through the course picks a pole off the jump wings and proceeds to parade it round the ring in his mouth. No need for a rosette. He already has his trophy. The spectators love it. There is laughter and applause as the dog plays the clown and his handler begs him to drop it. I suspect that this dog has inadvertently learned that pole-picking is a good way to get attention. What might have started as a way to relieve stress has turned into a great act that has everyone laughing.

Do you see similarities between Gunner and this dog? If Gunner picks up a pole, leave the ring and go sit in the car park. Don't join in the game. In contrast, if Gunner negotiates the obstacles as the designers intended, be delighted. Fuss and praise him. Gunner will soon learn the new rules and will want to stay a player. Also address the problem of stress. Improve your handling skills and make sure you are always making the best of your communication channels.

Dog number two The dog drags his handler to the start, takes his own line on the course and attacks obstacles in his path, especially the ones that slow him down. He vents his frustration at his handler's inability to keep up directly onto the agility equipment. When the handler crosses the finish line and attempts to collect his dog to attach the lead, the dog snaps at him but misses. The handler is oblivious. I would guess that this dog is very sensitive to movement and has bitten his owner in the past. His bite has never really been inhibited, simply displaced onto the agility equipment.

Does this sound like Gunner? Gunner knows he can snap at the seesaw before you can stop him. Correction only fuels his desire to do it again. He loves agility but you frustrate him because you allow him to go his own way one minute and the next you are reprimanding him for something that happened earlier on the course. I think you have pushed ahead in agility too quickly and missed out many dog training fundamentals. Also, I wonder if your problems in the agility arena aren't tied up with more general problems at home. Consider consulting a canine behaviourist and shelving agility for a little while.

Left: *So many poles and so little time to collect them. Don't let your dog clown around. Poles are for jumping, not retrieving.*

Heel!

Q *Flynn, my big Border Collie, is doing well this season, but I have one problem. He attaches himself to my foot with his teeth at the end of each round. He never does it in training, but always at shows. I'm only five foot tall and weigh eight stone. You can imagine how difficult this makes it to leave the ring with any dignity! Should I tell him off in front of the judge? If I praise him for doing a nice round, he might think I'm praising him for grabbing my foot.*

A Puppies love to chew old trainers and chase dangling laces. No wonder they grow up with a foot fetish and take it with them to the agility ring. Flynn gets excited at training, but he can contain himself. The buzz of competition tips the balance. He is not nipping your trunk or arms, but grabbing your feet. It's not as daring, but it's still challenging. And, once Flynn has caught a foot, I bet the spectators chuckle at your predicament. So, not only has Flynn been allowed to chomp your trainers, he has been rewarded for it with laughter.

react if you praised him in the middle of the course at obstacle sixteen, thanked the judge for his time and left the ring (with your foot intact)?

Fake ring Set up a "competition" ring and have a friend wait at the finish with a water pistol to give Flynn a soaking if he dives at your shoes. If you think a water pistol would be ineffective, try a bucket of water. However, Flynn may be so determined that he won't mind getting wet.

Stand still Flynn will not have a moving target to chase. His attacks on your feet may continue for a while, but if they fail to get a response from you they should eventually cease.

Target a toy Encourage Flynn to have something in his mouth besides your foot. Offer him a toy at the end of his rounds in training and at shows.

Down After each round, whether in training or at a show, put Flynn in the Down. Wait a few seconds for him to collect his wits. Praise him and then release him onto a toy or give him a treat.

Try the unexpected I wonder how Flynn would

A nasty taste Spray your trainers with something unpalatable, like mustard or bitter apple spray. It may not stop the more aroused foot-fetish dogs, but it's worth a try.

Bare feet Run in bare feet. It will strengthen your resolve to find a solution to the problem.

Ignore it The more you try and push Flynn off your feet, the more firmly he will try to attach himself. Arguing with you is a rewarding game played at the end of an agility round that breaks all the rules of good behaviour. If you stop playing, it won't be fun anymore. But it will take time for the message to sink in.

What A Drag!

Q *I do agility and obedience with my young working sheep dog, Quasar. She's a good girl until we get to training. She's so excited to get to agility that she lunges and pulls on the lead. I'm afraid she is going to drag me into the ring. After about 15 minutes, she calms down a bit and starts working. What should I do?*

Ignore her Quasar gets excited in anticipation of having lots of fun in agility. If she is pulling on her lead at the start of your class, don't yank it or yell at her. You will only make matters worse. She'll be more determined to leap around and it will take longer for her to settle the next time you go to class. Loop her lead over a fence post and turn your back on her.

A I'm glad to hear that Quasar is enthusiastic, but her pulling must be checked or you could end up with one arm longer than the other!

Turning your back on your dog is the worst punishment you can inflict on your pet. You have withdrawn your attention and worse, he won't be able to see your face.

When she quits lungeing and is quiet, return to her and give her a treat. She'll soon get the message – loose leads are good. A dog that walks in a controlled way to the start line gets to run the course.

Work mode Like most collies, Quasar is keen to work. Help her don her thinking cap earlier by asking her to perform some tricks or basic obedience exercises before you start your agility class. Do some heelwork in the car park and continue working her through the door into your training venue. Teach Quasar to watch you on command. This is something that you can do quietly and calmly. It will encourage her to focus on you and give you a reason to reward her when she gives you eye contact.

Head harness There are a number of different types of head harnesses on the market; for example, the Halti or Gentle Leader. Not only do head harnesses prevent your dog from pulling you into traffic, but they seem to have a calming effect on the dog. Many dogs wear a head harness at agility shows on their way to the exercise area or while they are queuing to enter the ring. Their handlers can concentrate on the course rather than trying to stop their dogs lungeing on the lead. Buy one for Quasar.

I think your dog will settle down as she matures.

She sounds eager to please and still has four feet on the ground. Some dogs arrive at agility class excited and become increasingly demented. They throw themselves into orbit trailing their owners behind them. Quasar is dragging you to the launch pad. Teach her that a loose lead means that she will be first in the queue for the jumps and tunnels.

3 When the handler halts, the dog sits but is ready to move off again as soon as the handler steps forward.

2 The dog takes his cue from his handler and maintains his position by the leg, neither pulling ahead or to the side.

1 Dogs that learn to walk on a loose lead are a pleasure to own. Heelwork is a basic obedience exercise that teaches the dog to walk on the handler's left hand side.

Above: *All dressed up and ready to go for a walk to the park or training class. A head harness is the must-have accessory for every fashion-conscious dog that pulls on the lead. And they can be bought in a variety of colours for special occasions.*

Learning To Queue

Q *My problem is not with agility, but queuing. My rescue dog Felix turns into a demented monster and no one will stand next to me near the ring. I don't blame them. Can you help?*

A Queuing is an important part of agility. Dogs should be able to wait patiently and quietly for their turn whether they be at their local training club or at an agility show. It's not always easy. The sight of another dog working is very exciting and dogs that are sensitive to movement can be aroused to fever-pitch, expressing their frustration through barking.

A groom Ask a friend to hold Felix away from the ring while you queue. If he is a Mummy's boy, he will be looking for you rather than watching other dogs run. But remember that as soon as you have hold of the lead, Felix will turn his attention back to what's happening in the ring.

A head collar A head collar will give you more control in the queue. It will help you battle the more severe symptoms of Felix's fidgeting, while you work on attention exercises at home.

Attention exercises Teach Felix to pay attention and watch you, not the other dogs. Start in your living room where there are few distractions. Each time Felix looks at you, click and offer a treat. Use a high value food reward like diced cheese. A few seconds attention will do and training sessions should be short and intense. Once Felix gets the idea, he won't be able to take his eyes off you. Progress slowly. Will Felix look at you when he is sitting on your left, on your right and in front of you? Eventually you will be able to perform these attention exercises in a noisy queue at an agility show. They

don't take up much room and won't be disruptive. They will allow you to enter the ring with Felix by your side, relaxed and under control.

Sights and sounds Be aware that it is not only in the queue that Felix can hear and see agility. If he can watch round after round from the back of your car, he'll be truly frantic before you even attach his lead. He's lost it and so have you. Cover the windows of your car or park somewhere else out of view.

The experienced handler will practise queuing with their young dogs as part of their agility programme. Although their dogs may be too young to compete, they will walk their youngsters around the showground and practise a few obedience basics. They know that the earlier they train their dogs to pay attention and ignore exciting distractions in their environment, the easier it will be for them later. Felix already knows that hurdles mean agility and he demands to be let loose on them, so your task will be harder.

Help Felix relax in the queue and you will have a dog that listens for your commands and watches for your body signals. A clear round will be much closer.

Below: *Good manners in the queue ensures that everyone has a good time both at agility training and at shows.*

Maniac Collies

Q *My two-year-old collie, Blue, is manic. He gets more and more wound up as he travels round the course and ends up a slobbering wreck. It's worse at shows. He gets hyper and so do I. Blue knocks poles and he flies his contacts. The more excited he becomes, the less interested he is in me. How can I keep him calm? Is there something I can give him to help him relax?*

A Ah, those mad, manic collies! Blue is discharging his pent-up adrenalin in an exciting environment in the only way he knows how – by launching himself into orbit.

Herbal remedies Many handlers swear that herbal remedies such as skullcap or valerian help their dogs calm down. But before you give Blue any pills or potions, it's a good idea to have a chat with your vet first. He is familiar with your dog and best placed to advise you on different kinds of medication. And remember that although herbal remedies might help Blue relax, he still may be unable to contain himself in a highly charged, stimulating environment like agility.

Keep cool and calm Dogs are very quick to pick up and act on a handler's excitement. Don't let adrenalin turn you into a nervous wreck who paces the floor muttering to yourself. Sit down and shut up. Blue will follow suit.

Slow motion Don't aggravate Blue's excitement by trying to win the class. Forget your time. Don't hurry. Take giant steps instead of little busy ones. You will feel like you are running in slow motion, but you will be well within the course time. When you try to do things as fast as possible, your adrenalin levels rise. Keep them lowered by thinking "slow".

No reward For many agility-loving dogs, the next obstacle on the course rewards the previous. If Blue makes an error, mark it with a word or phrase like "Shame" or "Oh dear". Then leave the ring taking your dog with you. Blue will quickly come down to Earth. And use your marker phrase accurately. It's no good saying it because Blue has missed contact when he has already jumped the next set of hurdles. Moreover, make sure that the mistake is his and not yours. Did the dog go the wrong way because he was over-excited or because your command was late and you were out of position on the course?

Praise Take the time to praise your dog calmly if he gets it right. You do this in class; don't forget to do it in the ring. Blue needs some kind words to reinforce the correct behaviour when he is under a judge. Don't take something like good contacts for granted. You won't get eliminated if you smile and call Blue a "clever boy". If you have already been eliminated somewhere else on the course, why not take the opportunity to stroke him on the head too?

I think you are as much a victim of the excitement of a show as Blue is. You feed off each other. A little nervous buzz is good for you – too much and you and your dog end up out of control.

Ballistic Missiles

Q *My young collie, Pippin, loves agility. Too much! She knows which night we go to training and as soon as we set off in the car, she goes ballistic. We can hardly get through the door, she is so excited to have arrived. I spent a lot of time working on the lead over the A-frame, dog walk and seesaw, but off-lead she misses all her contacts. She is so fast – what can I do?*

A Count your blessings. You are lucky to have a dog with so much enthusiasm and energy. But don't let Pippin's excitement turn her into a raving lunatic.

Start as you mean to continue Before you leave home, make sure that Pippin is still on planet Earth and you are in control. Tell her to sit before you attach the lead or open the car door. Don't allow her to race or pull you into class – try a head collar. Don't let her run around the field or arena while the equipment is being set out for the lesson.

Class size Dogs that are susceptible to excitement can benefit from smaller classes or private lessons. The mere sight of other dogs having a good time can tip the balance and transform a well-behaved pet into a whirling dervish. When Pippin's feet are firmly on the ground and there are fewer distractions, you can learn more and gain confidence in your ability to train and handle your dog. This confidence eventually enables you to cope in any situation, with any number of exciting things going on in the background.

Short and simple Running long courses before Pippin has built up some mental stamina can blow her mind. It's similar to serving a feast to a famine victim – impossible to eat it all, but you try anyway.

Far better to praise and reward Pippin after she has successfully completed a short sequence than to start pulling your hair out when she has gone crazy over twenty obstacles and made five errors.

Bridge the gap There is a big jump between doing contacts on the lead and doing them without it. Bridge the gap. Can Pippin perform contacts without the lead in a short sequence? Think about what you will do if she jumps off. Doing course work too early encourages many handlers to ignore mistakes and carry on to the last obstacle. It's such a relief just to finish! But it can lead to bad habits and undo all the good work you have done in training.

Pippin is still young and has the most important ingredient for an agility dog – she loves it. Take your time and make sure that all her basic skills are sound so that you will have a firm foundation to build new ones. There is still lots for you both to learn. In the meantime, you and Pippin can still have lots of fun together without giving her your car keys.

Above: *Don't push too hard or fast with a young dog. Paying only lip service to the basics can create problems later on.*

Hot Pursuit

Q *How can I stop Trim, my Belgian Shepherd, acting aggressively when she sees other dogs running? She looks desperate to give chase and floor them, especially if it is a really fast, noisy dog. I have to hold on tight to the lead and it would be so embarrassing if she pulled out of my hands. She's normally such a sweetie, but I don't know what she would do if she got loose.*

A This is an embarrassing but common problem with dogs that are easily stimulated by agility. They see a fast dog whizzing his way around the course and they can't take their eyes off it. Who knows what would happen if the lead snapped. Would the dogs climb the A-frame together as a double act? Or would there be a big fight and bloodshed? Your problem is not just ruining your own enjoyment of agility, but it could potentially jeopardize the safety of dogs on the course.

Attention exercises If Trim is looking at you, she will be missing the visual stimulation of watching agility dogs that triggers her unruly behaviour in the queue. The "Watch" exercise is a good place to start and she should be rewarded generously with her favourite treats for looking up at your face. Whenever and wherever Trim hears the "Watch" command, she should fix her eyes on her owner. Is she watching you?

Above: *A Belgian Shepherd gaining speed with every jump. It's a race to the finish, not another ring!*

Turn away. Has she moved around so that she can watch you? Yeah! Give her a treat as a reward. Drop a ball on the floor. Did she look at her toy or did she continue to look up at you? Reward if it's you.

Concentration exercises You can't teach a dog anything unless you have its attention. If you have practised the attention exercises in different environments and gradually increased the number of distractions, Trim should be ready for action at agility training. Before starting a sequence of jumps, ask Trim to pay attention. If you get it, proceed. Concentration will be improved and you will find that Trim is keen to please you. She will learn new things more quickly and remember them for longer.

Movement and speed exercises Trim is aroused by the movement and speed of other dogs running agility courses. Make that work to your advantage by moving the focus from other dogs to you and the agility equipment. Make Trim chase you for her favourite toy. Are your legs faster than hers? Race her to the end of a line of jumps. Can you beat her to the other side of the dog walk? Give yourself a head start so she has to pull out all the stops to catch you. Don't let Trim waste energy chasing other dogs when she could be chasing you.

I am sure if won't take long to redirect Trim's focus. You are probably much faster and prettier than any of the dogs Trim has been watching at agility!

Herding Instinct

Q *I have just started to train Marvel, my Border Collie. He is a year old and works beautifully and I think he could be really good at agility. However, if there is another dog running on the course, he wants to herd it. I can't keep his attention focused on me. If he is not on the lead, he will rush over and try to round it up. What can I do?*

A Agility enthusiasts love Border Collies because of their herding instinct. It enables them to work independently and use their initiative on an agility course. But it can also land them in hot water if

Above: Collies need an occupation and their favourite games are chasing and herding – sheep, children or toys!

they decide to round up the children. Start thinking like a shepherd if you have a sheep dog. You want to be able to work your dog over fences with the same skill and control that a shepherd uses to direct his dog to box and pen a few lambs.

Shepherd's crook You don't need a shepherd's crook – just a good collar and lead. Keep Marvel on the lead when you are in class. You don't want him to interfere with other dogs and it's not his turn yet! When you are confident that he is waiting for your cue to start work, let him off his lead to perform an exercise.

Shepherd's hut Train at home where there are no distractions. Marvel is young and bound to be stimulated and excited by other dogs running around. Cultivate control, increase his attention span and teach him concentration through basic obedience exercises or trick training. As Marvel becomes more mature, educated and well-mannered, he will become less interested in distractions and more willing to focus on you and his agility. That's how he scores brownie points. Herding other dogs is a real non-starter.

The sheep In lieu of sheep, buy some tennis balls. Collies are often obsessed with toys and you can use a ball to keep his attention on you and not the other dogs in class. Play with the ball at home and use it as a reward for completing an exercise in class. The more agility you do, the more your dog will love not only the tennis ball but all the equipment, especially tunnels. Try treating him with his favourite obstacle instead of a ball at the end of a difficult jump sequence. Many collies are so equipment-orientated that they are oblivious to everything else going on around them.

Above: Two collies work as a team to keep the sheep in a bunch and eagerly await the shepherd's next command.

Above: *Agility is a good substitute for sheep. Some collies become so obstacle-driven that they think of little else.*
Right: *Toys are a great way to take your collie's mind off sheep and redirect his attention towards you.*

Honest shepherd Any honest shepherd will admit to having a few problems training his dog. So don't get disheartened. Marvel is bound to make mistakes and misbehave. Give him time to learn what is the right place to aim his energy and enthusiasm. Make sure you dish out big rewards when he is offering you his best behaviour and really trying to get it right on the agility course.

Be patient and keep training. Make your collie's herding instinct work for you rather than against you.

Shutting Down

Q *I have been training my terrier in agility for about 18 months. Millie is a good girl. However, sometimes she shuts down at shows. She sits in front of a fence and refuses to move. It can also happen at the start of training or if we are learning something new. Why is she doing this?*

A Millie is sitting on the start line and you give the signal to commence. Nothing happens. Has she gone deaf? Why is your keen and competent dog rooted to the spot? If Millie starts shutting down on a regular basis, your confidence in the ring will be shattered making matters ten times worse. Shut down happens for a number of reasons.

Stage fright Competitions are always a bit daunting for a young dog. You are expecting Millie to jump as well as keep an eye on what's going on around her – a hustling crowd, strange dogs and the burger van. She's not yet ready to multi-task in this way.

Perfectionist If this type of dog does anything at all, she wants to make sure she gets it right. Unfortunately, the learning process is fraught with pitfalls – especially in agility. Every course is different with so many variations based on 20 obstacles. Millie has to take risks and have the courage to make mistakes. The dog that is a perfectionist can shut down if there is the possibility of making an error.

Confidence The more confident Millie is in her own ability to execute the obstacles and in your skill at directing her over a course, the less likely she will be to shut down. Confidence comes with time, but it can also be fostered by training simple exercises which will give you an excuse to give her lots of praise. Repetition is another tool that you can use. If Millie performs an exercise hesitantly, do it again and then one more time for luck. She will know where she is going and get faster and surer-footed each time.

Motivation Once your dog has shut down, the lights are out. There is nothing on Earth that is going to switch them back on. It is too late to dangle a tug toy in her face or wave a treat under her nose. Treats and toys are positive training tools that should not become negatively associated with times of stress or confusion.

Bonding The more Millie trusts you, the better your working relationship will be. Spend quality time with her. Learn how she ticks and she will reciprocate by working out how to do her best for you. Instead of thinking "I can't do this. I'll get it all wrong", Millie will think "I'll have a go because you'll be there to help get it right".

Many handlers become frustrated and impatient when their dog shuts down. You are to be congratulated for not thinking that your dog is merely being naughty. Bravo for trying to understand why it happens before looking for remedies.

Above: *Refuse a jump? No, never! Switch your dog on to the joys of jumping with patience and understanding.*

Under Pressure

Ollie, my Belgian Shepherd, and I have been doing agility for two years now and lately he seems to hate being in the ring. When we started competing, Ollie was so excited that I had trouble keeping up with him. I've got him back under control, but now he enters the ring looking stressed and pressured. His head hangs down and his tail is tucked under. I've always been nervous which doesn't help and now I'm getting frustrated by Ollie's behaviour.

Dogs take their cue from their owners. I fall asleep and snore in front of the TV, so do my dogs. I stress and my dogs stress. We tend to forget how sensitive our pets are to our state of mind, our body language, the tone of our voice. The sweat on your palms tells your dog that you are nervous just like his tail tucked under his belly tells you that he's stressed. You aren't helping each other!

Have Ollie checked by a vet Whether the onset of Ollie's reluctance to jump was sudden or not, it is possible that there is a medical problem at the root of his behaviour. Have him checked before you start any retraining.

Learn to relax So easy to say, but so hard to do! But you need to take the lead. Learn to be cool, calm and relaxed and Ollie will follow suit. Recite a mantra, meditate on your navel or pet a rabbit's foot. Whatever will help you to be in control of you nerves.

Practise competing under show conditions
Enter a simulated show, sign up for a training day or

Above: *Agility competition is about being a performer. Make it look fun and your dog will take his cue from you.*

join a new club. All of these will get you and Ollie accustomed to performing in front of strangers on different equipment in strange venues. You'll have to learn to cope with a little bit of pressure and this is a good way to start.

Have fun Ignore Ollie's mistakes. Don't expect him to be precise. Encourage him to take risks and praise him for independent actions. If you want to have a game in the middle of a round – do it. Let him jump up on you or chase you round the seesaw. You'll both have a giggle and loosen up.

Start rewarding attitude in training If you want a dog with a wagging tail, give him a treat when he wags it. If you want a dog with enthusiasm, let your control slip. So what if Ollie misses a weave entry. Do you want a dog that zooms through the poles or one that reluctantly bends in and out? Reward enthusiasm and speed.

As Ollie's attitude becomes more positive, you will have less reason to feel nervous and you will both look forward to stepping up to the start line with renewed confidence.

21st Century Schizoid Dog

Q *I have a problem with my hound, Rowan. We start our run and all goes well. She is really good. A superstar. Then, she goes hyper. She messes about and runs around in circles at a hundred miles an hour. If I plead with her to come back and hold out a treat, she runs straight past me. Does Rowan have a split personality?*

A Rowan sounds a delightful challenge. A hound going loopy in the ring is funny at first, less so the next loop and eventually plain infuriating. I think Rowan is more misunderstood than naughty.

Above: *She's on track to finish the course but if the pressure is too much she could start playing loop the loop.*

When? At what point does your superstar lose her grip on the course?

- Does Rowan start messing about when you've made a mistake? If she has disappointed you, she'll provide you with a few mad moments to lighten the mood.
- Does Rowan play loop the loop towards the end of class? If she has been an angel for the first half of training, it may be that she just doesn't have the mental reserves to be good for a minute longer.
- Does Rowan go hyper when confronted by something new? It could be her way of letting you know that she is confused and puzzled. She doesn't understand what you want her to do.

Mistakes If Rowan runs past a jump in class, it's not the end of the world. Don't stop and shrug your shoulders in despair. The minute you do, Rowan will start orbiting the equipment. Instead of calling her back to redo the jump she has missed, keep going and finish the sequence. Go to the end of the queue, take a few deep breaths and ask your instructor how to get it right next time.

Concentration Build up Rowan's mental reserves. Concentration is hard work. If Rowan's had enough and is tired, she'll start messing about and acting the clown. Keep her focused with frequent rewards. Break up exercises with play so she can recharge her brain batteries for more learning. Shorten her agility sessions. Quit when she is still wanting more. If 18 obstacles blow her mind, train over ten or less. Add one more obstacle, then another until Rowan can complete a full course.

Confusion Rowan will stop acting like a lunatic when she is confident that she knows what you want her to do. Believe it or not, dogs try to please. Does it take you five attempts to get your weave entry on a course? Frustrated and confused, Rowan does a few laps of honour round the ring instead of making a sixth attempt. She's not being naughty. She doesn't understand what to do in the poles. Practise weave entries as a static exercise and she will reward you by getting it right on the course.

Relax Rowan doesn't have split personality. Running round the ring is her way of coping with stress. Relax and enjoy each other. Try and match her enthusiasm and I'm sure you will be bringing home a rosette soon.

Sniffy Dog

Q *My Jack Russell cross, Susie, is driving me mad! We've just started to compete and I never know what she will do in the ring. She measures only ten inches, so her nose is very close to the ground, which results in her finding interesting smells. She often ignores me and follows them. All she wants to do is sniff. What can be so interesting on the ground?*

A Sniffing is a big and important part of being a dog. Susie is not being naughty – just doing what comes naturally. She's not consciously trying to get you mad by tracking a mouse instead of climbing the A-frame. Try to figure out why she is sniffing.

If agility is boring... Susie will find something else that is interesting to do, like sniffing. Too many repetitions and too few rewards can make exercises tedious and dull. Make agility fun. Give Susie a reason to hold her nose in the air and reason to believe that there is nothing else she would rather be doing.

If you are boring... You will lose Susie's attention and she will start searching the ground for smells. Be an exciting companion and playmate rather than a stern disciplinarian. If you fall down in the mud and Susie jumps up and down on your tummy, try to see the funny side. Laugh with your dog.

If Susie is stressed... She will try and find some way to relax. Sniffing is a natural and comforting activity that, like most dogs, she does well. Confronted with an obstacle course at a strange venue with the whole world watching, young Susie may feel out of her depth. She sniffs to stress bust.

If you are stressed... Susie will pick up on your discomfort. She'll sniff in sympathy. You, like Susie, will find agility shows a bit daunting at first. But you will soon get used to it. Relax with your new agility friends. Sometimes talking about pre-competition nerves with someone else in the same boat makes them go away.

Dogs that think with their nose rather than their brain, can be a liability in agility. I've no doubt that the more agility you do, the more comfortable you will both feel and the less Susie will sniff. In the meantime,

- Train at a venue that is relatively smell-free. Do you train after the puppy class (more treats end up on the floor than in their mouths)?
- Teach Susie a "Watch" command so that she will look up at you and not at the ground.
- Add the "Leave" command to your tool box. Susie should withdraw her nose from whatever smell she is investigating when she hears it.
- And keep practising your recall. When Susie takes off on an olfactory trail, she will return to you before she reaches its end.

Be patient. Your dog will soon be demonstrating her true potential in the ring.

Below: *No sniffing! On the seesaw a dog must concentrate on balancing while putting one paw in front of the other.*

Party Animal

Q *I have an 18-month-old Labrador called Charlie. He started agility a couple of months ago and was brilliant, but lately he has turned into a social butterfly. He ducks and dives in front of me and then sprints out of the ring in great excitement looking for four-legged friends to play chase with him. As soon as he gets a little distance from me he runs off to party. What should I do?*

A Charlie is still a baby. He doesn't have years of agility behind him and the world out there still holds surprises and temptations.

Make agility fun Don't take it personally when Charlie accepts an invitation to boogie with a friend off course. Continue to teach Charlie that the best place to party is with you in the ring. Make training irresistible fun and call a halt to training sessions while Charlie still wants more – not when he's exhausted and has lost interest.

Distraction training The temptations at agility shows are many – squeaky toys, dropped titbits, new people and barking dogs. Start distraction training by inviting some friends to watch you in class. If Charlie leaves the ring to visit them,

call him back and give him a biscuit for returning to you quickly. When you are in the ring, reward him for being there with lots of play and treats. He will soon learn to keep his attention on you.

Stressed or confused If a dog is stressed or confused, distractions can be very hard to resist. If Charlie doesn't fully understand the rules of the agility game, he'll opt to play something easier that comes naturally, like rough and tumble with his canine buddies. Remember, he's confounded not naughty. Running out of the ring may be Charlie's way of telling you that your instructions have not been clear or that the task you have set him is too difficult.

Great expectations Charlie may feel pressured. Are you expecting too much of him? Just because he can do all the equipment doesn't mean he can run a course. Working the space between the fences is not as easy as it often looks. Perhaps Charlie is happy doing five obstacles in a row, but not ten? When you ask more of him than he is able to give, he takes off. Stick with shorter sequences. If Charlie looks uncertain, rebuild your basics and return to exercises that he finds fun and easy. Increase his confidence and yours will get a boost too.

Charlie sounds a very lovable Labrador. You will soon become not only his best friend but his favourite playmate. As soon as he understand all the rules of the agility game, he won't want to play anything else.

Below: *When you call your dog, make returning to you worthwhile. He will probably come back to you more quickly for a piece of liver cake than he would for a stale, dry biscuit. And he will come even faster if he hears a happy, rather than a scolding, voice.*

Doing A Runner

Q *I have been training my crossbreed, Abbey, in agility for about a year and I'm having trouble keeping her in the ring with me. She runs out to my husband and friends. She runs out to my handbag. She runs out to the score tent. She loves everyone and everything! Do you think she is just very smart and gets bored quickly in the ring? Any suggestions to help my runaway dog?*

A Oh dear! Abbey is a well-socialized individual with loads of geniality. So many people to meet and things to do. Abbey wants to share her successes with everyone. All you want her to do is concentrate on the task in hand so that she really has something to brag about. A span of 30 to 40 seconds in the agility ring is nothing to us, but for a dog it can be an eternity, especially if she is as happy chasing leaves as she is jumping hurdles. If you think that Abbey is bored in the ring, make it challenging and exciting to be there.

Centre of the universe That should be you. Become more attractive, interesting and exciting to be with than the distractions outside the ring. All the action should begin and end with you. Enhance your appeal with a toy or treats. Does your dog rely on you for the good things in life like food and exercise? Make sure you are the one putting foodstuff in her bowl and clipping on her lead.

Distractions Become a slob at training. Leave a jumper on the ground here and a bumbag over there. You will know where the distractions are in advance and you can work a little harder to get Abbey to run past them. Start with a few distractions of low interest and increase the number and level of their appeal as your dog gets better at ignoring them and concentrating on you.

Practical exercises Teach Abbey a "Leave" command. If she makes tracks towards someone's treat bag, tell her to leave. Teach Abbey to "Watch" so that you can direct her gaze to you and away from distractions. Improve Abbey's recall. She should be so keen to get to you that she runs past the dropped sweet.

Give it time As Abbey matures, you will get that 30 seconds of concentration in the ring. As her confidence in you as a handler and her own abilities grows, Abbey will become eager to work the obstacles instead of running to friends. She will remain a gregarious girl but she will want to share her bonhomie a little less often.

And, wouldn't you rather have a dog that loves everybody and everything than a dog that hates the world?

The Green Grass Of Agility

Q *I don't know what to do. My little crossbreed Cilla insists on grazing between the jumps. The minute we start doing agility she turns into a goat, snatching mouthfuls of grass and chomping her way around the course. It's driving me mad. How do I stop her being a lawn mower?*

A I don't know why dogs eat grass (and I don't know why we eat spinach), but it is a normal and harmless activity for dogs. Young tender shoots are a real delicacy in the Spring and dogs that gorge themselves on too much grass usually vomit it right back again. One explanation is that dogs eat grass to make themselves sick up unwanted or irritating substances from their stomachs. If Cilla is a real "grassaholic", do keep her away from grass treated with chemicals or exotic plants that may be toxic.

Left: *OK – put your nose in the grass and smell the scents of daisies and buttercups. But don't eat them!*

Cilla's taste for grass on the agility field is a surefire way of getting your attention. Do you spend more time trying to stop her from grabbing a mouthful of the green stuff than you do teaching her how to jump? Also, eating grass is a great stress-busting activity. It's comforting and reassuring – a bit like chewing gum. If Cilla is confused in her learning environment, she stops and eats a few blades of it.

Don't train outdoors There won't be any grass for Cilla to munch at an indoor riding school or sports arena. Try to be positive and do everything you can to boost Cilla's confidence on the agility course. Concentrate on getting the basics right before you progress to more difficult exercises. When you both forget that eating grass was once a problem, it will be time to move back outdoors.

Distract with tasty treats Would Cilla rather have a slice of frankfurter or a blade or grass? No contest. But you have to keep the tasty treats coming. Teach her to look up at you or a hand touch. She'll be too busy to have time to look at what's growing out of the ground at her feet.

Don't stop No time to eat and run. Don't stop when Cilla stops to have a snack of grass. She might think you are approving of her choice of snack. Keep going. Hurry to the finish line where there are better things to eat in your bait bag.

Keep moving Cilla should get praise and attention for running and chasing you. Play a catch-up game at home and in training. At first, Cilla shouldn't have to run too hard or too far to reach you and get her prize. When she gets the idea, go for it!

Try a toy Does Cilla have a favourite toy that she carries everywhere? She will find it impossible to hold it and eat grass at the same time so let her run over the course with it in her mouth.

Be patient. Cilla will become more sure of herself and what you want her to do. She will be less of a goat and more of an agility dog.

Keeping It In The Family

Q *I am 15 years old and my Dad drives me and my Golden Retriever Tyler to agility shows. Dad likes to watch me run and this causes problems. Tyler loves my Dad and he runs out to him in the middle of the round as if to say "Wasn't I great over there!". What should I do?*

A This is a tricky one! Your Dad provides your transport to shows which is great, so you want to keep in his good books. And I can understand him wanting to watch you. He believes that he is being a good parent by being there to support you. Unfortunately, his presence next to the ring is too much of a distraction for your Goldie. Every time Tyler runs out you risk elimination.

Hiding Your Dad can hide behind the nearest tree or score tent and watch you covertly. Out of sight can be out of mind. This ploy doesn't always work. Sometimes it just makes it more fun for the dog – agility plus a game of hide and seek for Dad. And sometimes the dog can become unsettled and worried if one of his family members suddenly disappears.

Ignoring Take your Dad to training. When Tyler runs out to him, tell him not to fuss your dog. Tell him to turn his back on Tyler and ignore him. Call Tyler back to you and give him lots of praise and

Right: *Sorry! No fuss or treats from me while you are doing your stuff at agility. But that doesn't mean that I don't love you …*

treats for returning. If Tyler wants attention, he gets it in the ring. This is where everything exciting happens. It will take Tyler a little while to catch on but he will start to lose interest in your Dad and will seek fun and approval from you.

Growling and shooing When Tyler runs out to your Dad, he could try growling at Tyler to show he is displeased and shoo him back into the ring. But Tyler may still see this as attention, even if it is negative. He'll continue to pay Dad a visit on his way round the course. Or your Dad could throw some noisy training discs (or a can full of pebbles) on the ground next to Tyler to startle him or squirt water in his face. But remember that Tyler loves your Dad too, and these actions may jeopardize their relationship.

Above: *Unless your dog passes his driving test, he'll never be able to take you to training class and shows. Keep in your Dad's good books!*

Keep practising Your Dad is not the only distraction, but probably heads a long list – the chip van, barking dogs, and people picnicking by the ring. Work through it. Make agility so fun-packed, fast-paced and engrossing that Tyler doesn't have time to wonder what is going on elsewhere.

Your father wants to see you succeed in your chosen canine sport. I'm sure he will help you overcome this problem by ignoring Tyler's visits. And I know he will continue to be very proud of all your accomplishments.

Tough Enough?

Q *I'm thinking of signing up my whippet Fleur for agility classes, but she is such a sensitive flower. She doesn't like to get her feet wet or walk across pebbles. She always has to sit on a cushion instead of the floor. If I slam a door, she disappears under the settee. Is she too much of a wimp for agility?*

A We can all be a bit sensitive about certain things, but it shouldn't stop us from trying something new that we might enjoy. Fleur's introduction to the equipment should take into account her sensitivities – you don't want a sensitivity to be traumatized so it turns into a phobia. Watch out for:

The seesaw Sensitive dogs loathe the seesaw. Not only does it move up and down but it hits the ground with a loud bang. Fleur might think the world is coming to an end. Don't try to teach Fleur how to perform this obstacle until she is comfortable with its noise. Introduce her to it gradually, starting with a dull thump and slowly working up to a crash. Build a pleasant association, by giving Fleur a titbit every time the seesaw hits the ground.

The collapsible tunnel It's dark inside and the chute material is heavy – so claustrophobic. Prepare Fleur for this sensation. Get an old blanket and play tents with your dog. Get down on your hands and knees and invite

Left: *Whippets appear to be delicate creatures. Don't be fooled! They make excellent ratters and can become accomplished agility dogs.*

her to chase you in and out. Hide toys and biscuits in the folds and make Fleur hunt for them. If she is having fun, she won't object to the weight of the blanket on her back.

Weaving poles Fleur might look at the weaving poles and think that the metal base has been expressly designed to stub toes and hurt dogs. Get Fleur accustomed to the feel of the poles on her body by using one to massage her ribs gently while you whisper sweet nothings or give her a treat to munch. Teach her on channel weaves. The two lines of poles can be kept wide open and gradually narrowed as Fleur gets used to them.

Jump poles Contrary to what many sensitive dogs think, jump poles do not leap out of the cups and

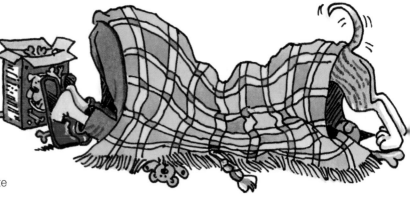

Above: *Whippets are simply miniaturized greyhounds. They can turn on the speed and possess the same elegance and grace over the ground.*

Right: *A fearless Italian Greyhound shows that jumping is just as much fun as running if you do it really fast.*

bite dogs on the knees. Knocking a pole probably hurts, but not that much. If Fleur hits a pole, check that she is all right but don't make a big fuss of her. You don't want to encourage her belief that poles are vicious. Get her back in the agility saddle. Have a game with her toy, do a piece of agility equipment she likes or try a different jump. Praise her for being brave. She will forget about her knee if you distract her with fun somewhere else.

Don't push Fleur beyond what she can comfortable tolerate. She'll soon learn that jump poles don't bite. When she relaxes and starts enjoying herself, you'll forget that she was a wimp!

Sore Tootsies

Q *I hope you can help my rescue collie, Ricky. When I got Ricky he was about five months old and his nails kept splitting on his front feet. This problem has now been resolved with the help of a diet supplement, but it has left him with very sensitive toes. The weaves are difficult to train because Ricky is very wary of the cross supports and metal base. I've never actually seen him stub his toes, but he always pops out as if he has and always at the cross supports. Any bright ideas?*

A Dogs can suffer from sore and tender feet for all sorts of other reasons. Ask your vet to have a look at Ricky's nails just to make sure that all is well and as it should be. If it is, think about the following:

It's time for a manicure Dogs walk on their toes, so if their nails get too long, even a few steps can be painful. Plenty of exercise and road walking will help keep them short and a vet or groomer will show you how to clip Ricky's nails or do it for you.

Go back to the beginning and re-teach the weaves You probably don't want to do this, but it would pay dividends. Use a different command and a different training method. Ricky should think he is learning a new exercise, not re-hashing an old one.

Hide the base of the weave poles Cover the base and cross supports with soil or sand. Slowly reintroduce the base by scraping away the soil over the next few weeks until it is again plainly visible. If Ricky starts popping out, replace some earth.

Consider training with channel weaves The poles and base are gradually moved closer together to make a

Above: *A dog that is worried about where he is putting his feet will inevitably slow down in the weaving poles.*

straight line which should allow Ricky time to get accustomed to touching or stepping on the base. If he baulks, just take a step back and widen them again.

Teach the base as a separate exercise It might be that keeping his eye on the poles as well as watching his feet on the base is too much for Ricky to worry about all at once. Take all the poles out, put Ricky on his lead and walk with him across the base. Praise or click and treat him for stepping over the metal base in a relaxed manner. As he becomes more confident, you can try criss-crossing it back and forth. When Ricky shows no fear or anxiety, you increase your pace to a trot and then a run.

It will take time and effort to turn around Ricky's thinking on the weaving poles. He may have stubbed his toe when you weren't looking and it's not easy to erase painful associations. They do fade in time and they can be supplanted with pleasant, positive ones given love and patience.

It's So Spooky!

Q I'm 13 years old and have a two-year-old Golden Retriever, Prince. He was really good at agility until a few weeks ago. Prince knocked a jump and then got spooked at training when it started to thunder and rain. Now Prince won't go into the equestrian centre where we train and he won't go over the equipment on the lead. Should I give up and do something else?

A Just when everything is going so well, something like this happens. Your dog's confidence has been knocked and so has yours. One single negative experience can jeopardize all your positive training. Try and rise above it. If you have laid good agility foundations, you and Prince will recover ground quickly and be back to winning rosettes and trophies soon.

Vet check Prince may be refusing to jump because something hurts. Have him checked by your vet. He may have bruised his toe or pulled a muscle when he knocked the hurdle. The only way he can tell you that something is wrong is by changing from a dog that excels at agility to one that is reluctant to even try to go over the jumps.

Take a break The association between jumping and the thunderstorm is fresh in his mind. Rather than training Prince every day, let him have a holiday. Give it time and the memory will fade. Do some obedience or heelwork to music so he has something different to think about. And you'll forget his fears too.

Don't force the issue The more you try to drag Prince over the jumps, the more he may resist. You could make matters worse. The equipment will become obstacles of confrontation rather than fun. Encourage, but don't coerce. Praise and reward Prince for what he offers you voluntarily.

Baby steps Don't expect Prince to take giant steps back to being a fully functional agility dog. He has had a frightening experience. Prince will make a speedier recovery if he takes baby steps, although he will have to take many more of them. If he looks at a hurdle, reward him lavishly with treats. Next time, he will take a small step towards it, next time two steps and so on until he is leaping over it.

Start at the very beginning Take Prince right back to the beginning. Lay poles on the ground, lower the A-frame, and shorten the tunnel. You won't be starting from scratch, but retraining the basics. It will be an opportunity for you to make each step a positive experience for Prince. Your confidence and trust in each other on the equipment will resurface.

I believe that you and Prince will be back on the agility field very soon. You obviously love Prince very much and I know that will give you the patience and understanding to help him overcome his fears.

At The Drop Of A Hat

Q *My German Shepherd Dog Dilly is a sweet girl, but she has this thing about hats. The one time we competed, she started barking at the judge who was wearing a baseball cap. She has never done it before. What can I do?*

A I agree with Dilly. People who wear hats look different. They look funny, frightening or surreal. And she's not sure how to react.

Aliens Dogs are freaked by people with hats because they look like aliens. However, as soon as the "alien" speaks, they recognize the voice as

human. This adds to their confusion. Take the hat off, and the dog realizes that it's not someone from another planet. It's the man from next door who passes biscuits over the fence. So embarrassing!

Dressing up I'm sure that your instructor or a class mate will help you with this problem by wearing a hat at agility lessons. Let Dilly sniff it before anyone wears it. And make sure that Dilly is comfortable with your helper before he puts a hat on his head. If she has been introduced to both, she should remain relaxed. Hats do not jump off people's heads and menace passers-by.

Out and about We can't dictate a dress code to judges but the more people Dilly sees wearing a hat, the more acceptable and mundane it will become. Take Dilly into town on a rainy or sunny day. Lots of people will be wearing something on their heads. These people will be going about their business, not staring at Dilly to see if she misses a contact. Dilly will soon understand that they are not interested in her and she will lose interest in them.

Introductions Once Dilly has started barking at someone with a hat, there is not much that you can do. She may be too frightened to be distracted by a treat or toy. And if you try to force the issue, she may become hysterical. Try laughing. Tell her she is a silly girl. The person wearing the hat has no fashion sense. They think they look glamorous? Ha! Laugh till your belly hurts and Dilly will take her cue from you. Yes, the hat is terrifying – terrifyingly funny.

One-off Perhaps you have developed a thing about hats and are misinterpreting Dilly's actions. It only happened once in competition and Dilly may have been objecting to the judge's choice of socks, not headgear. Worry about your course, not what the judge is wearing. The more experience Dilly gets in the ring, the more focused she will become on agility, and the less notice she will take of what is on the judge's head.

Above: *If you wear a hat that stays on your head while you are running, you can turn it into a toy at the last fence. Take it off for your dog to tug or throw it for him to chase.*

Toilet Trouble

Q *Please help me. My King Charles Spaniel Tina won't go to the toilet at agility shows. I've tried training her to relieve herself on command. I've tried jogging her up and down in the exercise area. Tina is a dynamo at training, but a snail at shows – I'm sure she would be able to run faster in the ring if she had been to the toilet first. As soon as she gets home, she runs into the garden to do her business.*

A Like Tina, I believe the toilets at shows are something to be avoided if possible – the facilities at home are much sweeter. However, nerves get the better of me and I spend as much time queuing at the Ladies as I do queuing to go into the ring.

If Tina is always fussy about where she squats, visit your vet for a check-up Her reluctance may be a sign of a medical problem and you need to rule this out.

If Tina is feeling vulnerable, she will not want to go to the toilet Many dogs don't want to go to relieve themselves in unfamiliar places. They like a bit of privacy and can't find it in the exercise area where there is a lot going on – dogs approaching and sniffing each other in greeting and lots of running around and barking. Help Tina by walking her somewhere that is quiet. Let her choose the pace. Give her time to get accustomed to the hustle and bustle of a show. When she feels comfortable in her surroundings and is relaxed, she will do her business.

If Tina feels pressurized, she will hold on Don't spend all day at an agility show trying to make Tina go to the toilet. That's not what you are there for. Give Tina an opportunity to do her business. If she

doesn't go after 15 minutes or so, take her to the ring and forget about toileting. She has had her chance. Concentrate on your run. Tina will be in the ring for about 40 seconds and should be able to wait until her next visit to the exercise area later.

If Tina is stressed, she won't run as fast as she does in training I don't think that Tina's reluctance to relieve herself is the cause of her change in

Above: *When a dog is mentally and physically comfortable in her surroundings, her true agility colours will show.*

performance on the agility course. Yes, it is hard to run on a full bladder, but I think it is more likely that Tina is unnerved by show conditions. There is so much to keep your eye on. Peeing and jumping are the last things on Tina's mind.

If you are relaxed, Tina will follow your lead You will both start to enjoy yourself. In time, Tina will relieve herself when you take her to the exercise area instead of holding on until you get home. She will gain confidence and you will see her start to work in the ring like she does at training.

Measuring Up

Q *I am currently competing with my small collie cross Morgan over different jump heights. It all depends on who is running the show that I've entered. At one show, he is classified as a medium dog and jumps over 51cm (20 inches) and at another he is considered a mini dog and jumps over 38cm (15 inches). Morgan doesn't seem to have any trouble adjusting from one to the other and back again, but he does knock a few poles now and again. Should I stick to just one jump height?*

A **Five inches can make a big difference to some dogs** If you have a dog that can make the transition from 15 to 20 inches and back again without a problem, you are very lucky. Five inches can make a lot of difference to some dogs. Morgan must check the height of the pole, adjust his take off to sail over the top and nail his landing. The taller the jumps, the more rounded and less flat he will be going over the poles. Morgan is either a natural jumper or you have trained him well.

And the extra five inches can make a lot of difference to some handlers! Morgan may be faster over lower jumps and it may be more difficult to keep up with him. You have to be quicker to get in position and you need to give your commands a little sooner. Over the higher jumps, you need to

reset your timing once again. There is a little more time to get where you want to be on the course. So often it is the handler who has the most trouble adjusting between jump heights and will favour one over the other. You do not seem to have a preference and can compete happily at either height.

Take a few practice jumps with you to the show Set them to the height at which you will be competing and do a few jumping exercises with Morgan. This will not only allow Morgan to set his

Above left and right: *Can a big sheltie compete against a small collie? The answer is yes. It all depends on the height classification for dogs at the show. Both dogs' handlers must adjust their handling to the size of the jumps in order to run the course in a good time without faults.*

sights on the height he will be working over, but it will give you the chance to brush up on your timing.

Sticking to one jump height would certainly make things easier for both you and Morgan, but if you enjoy going to different shows and have no problem competing over different jump heights, why stop? There are many other reasons for a pole dropping. If it happens only occasionally, I suspect that Morgan is knocking a pole because of one of these rather than being affected by different jump heights in his classes. When he becomes an old dog, Morgan may find the extra five inches more difficult. Then it will be time to reassess his jumping style and think about sticking to one type of class, but while he is fit and healthy I see no reason why you can't have fun doing both heights.

Limbo Dancer

Q *I started agility with my Staffordshire Terrier Tevo a few months ago. Did you know a Staffie could limbo dance? Tevo will run under the jumps no matter how low they are set. Sometimes this is really difficult and he has to duck to get underneath and crawl on his belly, but under he goes! My classmates think it's really funny. What should I do?*

A Your dog is so clever and so creative! Tevo is still new to agility and he is experimenting with the jumps. He thinks, "Hey! There's more than one way to get to the other side of a hurdle!" And Tevo gets a round of laughter for his antics if he goes under rather than over the pole. Which way would you choose?

When a dog is introduced to the hurdles, he has to learn that the object of the exercise is to jump between the wings and over the pole. It sounds as if Tevo is indeed targeting the pole and assessing its height, but failing to decide to jump it. It could be that the poles were raised too soon – before Tevo learned the right way to do it was up and over. Running underneath poles is a common fault in young or inexperienced dogs and many show real determination in picking this route.

Above: *Power and strength make Staffies awesome agility dogs. But their determination to do things their own way can cause problems for handlers.*

Put the poles on the ground Unless Tevo sticks his nose under the pole and lifts it over his back, he'll have to go over. It's the easier option, especially if there are a number of poles laid in a line.

Fill the gap underneath the pole Use a double poled, but low, jump. This might do the trick, but Tevo may try to jump between the two poles or try to crawl under the bottom one. Another method is to block the space under the pole with a board. Tevo will have no alternative but to take the high road. Praise him.

On your way up and over When Tevo has started to give up limbo dancing for jumping, he still might go under a pole every now and again. Put the pole on the ground and work your way back up again. Don't be tempted to lower it just a little. If Tevo stoops and scoots underneath, you will have to lower it again. Far better to start from ground level where mistakes are really hard to make and work up.

Do you have a jump command? You want Tevo to be checking the jump's height, so ensure that you point with your hand above the pole and not below it. Give Tevo space to take-off and land. Many inexperienced dogs often go under poles on turns because they arrive at the hurdle before they can gather themselves up and jump.

Jumps are always a problem. Dogs either refuse them outright, go around them, or go under them. When Tevo has turned into a speedo over the jumps, you might find that your next challenge is to stop him knocking them out of their cups.

Ducking The Issue

Q *My working sheepdog Diva is nearly two years old. I started training Diva when she was ten months and gradually brought the jumps up from the ground to full height. All was well until we started competing. She would rather do a piece of contact equipment than jump hurdles. She loves doing contacts and runs under most of the fences to get there. Should I train with the double poles? She doesn't have a problem with the lower height jumps so I can't see that there's much to gain from bringing the height down again.*

A When a dog starts competing, she starts making mistakes and exposes all the holes in a training programme. Your contact training must have been thorough, but lots of fun. Diva loves the contacts and she can't wait to get there. Did you invest as much time and thought into your jumping exercises? I'm not surprised she runs under the poles to get to an A-frame on the other side.

Don't let going under poles become a habit
If your dog insists on running underneath, make it

difficult for her to do so by using extra poles on each jump. Diva will start looking up to see how high she should jump and you can slowly fade the extra poles.

Use a jump command Back up your body signals with a verbal command. You should not only be facing the jump but giving the verbal command "Jump". You want Diva to check the jump's height, so point with your hand above the pole – not below it. When Diva gets the idea, body language may be all you need.

Reward Diva for going over If Diva goes under a fence, don't let her proceed to the next piece of equipment on the course. Recall her, set her up at the fence and re-command. For a dog that is struggling with agility, starting over again may be demotivating, but if your dog is running by fences with gusto you won't dampen her enthusiasm. Reward her for getting it right with lots of verbal praise and allowing her to go onto the next obstacle.

A-frame reward Set up a loop of fences that carries your dog past the A-frame. Start with them at midi height, as you know she can do this, and reward her for completing the sequence with a free trip up the A-frame. Raise the fences a few inches and do the same again. If she is sailing over the top of the fences, she wins another trip over the A-frame. Raise the fences till they are at full height. If at anytime Diva goes under, mark the refusal to jump with a "wrong" or "shame on you" and try again. No jump. No A-frame.

Teach Diva that hurdles are fun and rewarding too! Running under poles is a common fault with inexperienced agility dogs. Balance contacts in your training programme with jumping exercises and I'm sure it won't be long till Diva is going clear on the course.

Above: *You can certainly get where you want to go much faster if you duck under the poles, but it won't make your handler very happy!*

Demolition Dog

Q *Twister, the demolition dog, really makes the pole pickers work. They see my screaming collie on the start line and roll their eyes. I don't know how to teach her to stop knocking the poles. She is a young and inexperienced dog, but we can't go on like this. Please help me to help her.*

A Dogs knock poles for a variety of reasons and the first thing you must do is to look carefully at your dog and yourself. A video recording of Twister on the course would help you evaluate the problem. Is Twister knocking poles because she is so excited? Is she taking off too far away from the jump to clear it cleanly? Is it the spacing of the obstacles that causes the problems? Or does she drop a hind leg on the turns and catch the bar?

From your description of Twister on the start line, I guess that she is a green collie and keen to go as fast as she can on the course. I hope these tips will help you to help Twister keep the fences up.

It's not a race Let Twister work ahead. She is anxious to stay out in front so you pull the strings from behind. Keep up, but remember that she, not you, has to cross the finish line.

Don't dip and flap Keep your body upright. If you point to a fence, don't bend your knees or drop your outstretched arm. If you do, Twister will mimic your dip and the fence will come down. Keep all your body movements to the minimum. You'll look neater and Twister won't be distracted by a lot of extraneous and meaningless signals.

Keep quiet You don't need to tell Twister to jump

the fence in front of her. She has already worked that out. If you have been commanding her when to jump, you risk making her take off too early and knock a pole.

Jumping chute Set up a line of fences and give Twister the chance to establish clean jumping habits. Start with low hurdles and practise sendaways and recalls. And this is an opportunity for you to practise running from behind without flapping.

Respect for the poles Some trainers believe that dogs need to be taught to respect the poles. Poles are raised so that the dog has to jump higher than necessary or they are filled with sand to make them heavier and harder to dislodge. Other trainers attach tins to the poles so they rattle when they fall to the ground. And some trainers stretch elastic above the pole and between the wings to trip the dog that drops a leg. A few trainers even tell handlers to pick up dropped pole and threaten the dog with it. I disagree with this approach – I don't believe that lack of respect is the issue. These "solutions" could aggravate the problem and may be injurious to the dog.

Dogs knock poles on the course either because they don't know how to jump correctly or because they are handled badly.

The Last Hurdle

Q *This is my first season competing with my collie, Taggie. I've been told he has lots of potential and will go far if only he would jump the last fence. Instead of going over it, he turns back to me. Whatever I do, he won't take the last fence. It's the only thing stopping me from getting a clear round. Do you have any advice?*

A How very frustrating for you!

Why the last fence?

- Associations are made in a split second. Taggie may have knocked his toe on landing after the last fence – ouch! He hay have seen a helper throw a lead as he took off and assumed it was aimed at him – ouch! Is it a surprise that Taggie is suspicious of the last fence?
- All those dogs ringside are in a frenzy to get at the equipment. Taggie questions the wisdom of

Left and above: *Commit to the last fence just as you would to a fence somewhere in the middle of the course and so will Taggie.*

jumping the last fence and landing in the middle of them.
- It is possible that Taggie is anticipating the praise he receives at the end of a round and is pre-empting you. He turns back to his handler too early for congratulations on a job well done (but not finished).

Mental imagery You and Taggie are both apprehensive about the last fence and reinforce each other's anxiety. Picture another fence after the last one and continue to work Taggie over it. Pretend the finishing line is not where the judge has set it. This should help you avoid tensing up as you approach the final hurdle.

All fences are the same By becoming last-fence-obsessed, you may be unwittingly rubber-stamping Taggie's behaviour. Act at the last fence just like you do at fences number one, two and three. It's possible that your dog believes that all the extra attention he gets at the last fence is his reward for refusing it.

Lower the fence Make it as easy as possible for Taggie to jump the last fence so that you can praise him for his performance. Start with the fence at mini height. As the fence is raised, and your dog continues to jump it, both of you will relax and cease to think of the last hurdle as your biggest obstacle.

Go on Teach your dog the "Go on" command. Teach him to go over a fence to a target or toy. The reward and praise is delivered after the fence, not before it. And the spectators who cheer Tag to the end of his run will be shouting "Go on" too! Your command to send Tag down the home stretch will be reinforced by the crowd.

Have a break It's amazing. Some problems disappear as suddenly as they appear for no discernible reason. Have a week or two off and see what happens. You may be pleasantly surprised.

Don't let this problem dominate your dog's agility training. The last fence is only 1/20th of the course. Keep practising other agility exercises. If you get a hang-up about the last fence, so will your dog.

Double Trouble

Q *I have two terriers called Saffron and Waldo, sister and brother. They do everything together – hunting squirrels, ripping up their toys or re-making their bed. And they both compete in agility. My problem is that they are in separate classes on different nights of the week and I seem to spend all my time driving back and forth from training. Should I try to run them both in the same class?*

A We would all like to have more time at home to catch up on chores, but the more dogs we have, the more time we spend at agility classes. Although working Saffron and Waldo in the same class will be economical, there are a number of minuses.

Above: *They look alike but the similarity ends there. Treat them as individuals when you take them agility training.*

Catching your breath
Running two dogs in one class is tiring. As soon as you finish with Saffron, you will have to get Waldo ready for his turn. If class is a social occasion for you, you'll miss the chitchat with your friends but you will certainly get fit!

Two handling strategies Your dogs are both terriers, but they may be very different agility dogs. Perhaps Saffron is really motivated but Waldo is easily distracted. You will have to have two handling strategies at the ready and switching from one to the other may result in a few mistakes. How many times will you call Saffron when you want Waldo?

Separation If your dogs are accustomed to doing things in tandem, how will Saffron feel watching Waldo zip round the course with you? Will sibling love turn to rivalry? A little jealousy can fire up a dog, but it could also dampen his enthusiasm. "Let me have a go, I could do that!" may turn into "You do agility so well, I give up!"

Hitching post You have to decide what to do with the dog left out. Will you tie him up to a hitching post, get a friend to hold him, or rest him in a crate? Will you be bold and leave him in a sit stay?

Distracting Giving 100 per cent attention to the dog you are working while the other sits on the sideline is not easy. Will you be telling Saffron to stop barking when you should be telling Waldo to hit the contact? And what will you do if Waldo leaves the ring to join Saffron by her crate? Perhaps he prefers her company?

Homework It's a good idea to see how your dogs react to working in one another's company in advance. Put Waldo in his crate and have a game of tug with Saffron. What happens? If there is a problem, solve it at home. Don't bring it with you to training.

If you are short of time, you may decide that the advantages of working two dogs in one class more than outweigh the disadvantages. But, whether Saffron and Waldo are in the same class or not, you should certainly still try to reserve a portion of the day for spending quality time with each of them individually.

Playing With Matches

Q *Sally goes like the wind around the agility course. But only if my retired agility dog, Nellie, is ringside with her. If I leave Nellie at home, Sally walks around as if she has all the time in the world and is about to get out her knitting. How can I light Sally's fire without Nellie being the spark?*

A It's nice that your two dogs get along. They are probably good company for each other and have formed a special bond. Sally is taking her cue from Nellie, not you. Is it a question of security or jealousy and what are you going to do about it?

Security Sally feels secure when Nellie is around and so is able to give a top performance on the agility field. She is taking her lead from the older dog who is relaxed. Nellie has been to many venues and training fields. She knows there is nothing untoward to worry about and her confidence transmits itself to Sally.

Above: *The magic of agility is that it is just you and your dog on the course working together as a team.*

Jealousy Sally is a whiz kid on the agility field because she is having to work to earn your attention. She could be the one left on the sidelines instead of Nell. Jealousy can be a great motivator. When Nell is left at home, Sally doesn't have to make an effort. She has you all to herself.

Ignition Initially there is nothing wrong with using Nellie to light Sally's fire. In dog training, use whatever comes your way and works. If your dog likes playing with a cushion off the settee, bring it to class. But remember that these stimuli are only aids for ignition. Eventually, you must be the person that ignites Sally's flames and keeps the fire burning.

Independence Help Sally learn to stand up on her own four feet. Exercise and walk the two dogs separately. It will be extra work, but worth it. If you go to the supermarket, take Sal for the ride and leave Nellie at home. Sally will learn how to cope with new adventures in the outside world – and not just at agility shows – without Nell's back-up. What if Nellie had to spend the night at the vet's? Sally would have to go it alone.

Dependence Without Nell, Sally will look to you for guidance. Make sure you give it. She has to want brownie points from you, so earning them must be fun whether at home or at training. Reward effort, not just completed actions. Teach her the way to your heart and develop a partnership with Sally through doing things together.

Give it time You and Sally can't rely on Nellie all the time. The more agility you do together, the closer you will become and the harder Sally will work to please you.

Teaching By Example

Q *I wonder if you can tell me if it is normal for an agility instructor to work his own dog in the class that he is teaching? My instructor runs his dog at the end of every exercise. At first, I thought that it was going to be a one-off, but the same thing happens every week. Sometimes he takes more time trying to get the exercise right than attending to us paying pupils.*

A This is a tricky one. Many instructors are unpaid volunteers who help at their local training club, on the proviso that they may work their own dog in the class that they are teaching. Like most things, there are different ways of looking at it. Here are some scenarios:

Demo dog The instructor's dog can show and tell. "What do weaves look like?" ask the beginners. The instructor's dog can not only demonstrate the building blocks, but the finished product. Can't he? How embarrassing if the dog misses the entry or pops out half way through the poles. Demo dogs can do things the wrong way just as easily as the right way!

Words fail Not all instructors are blessed with the ability to explain things clearly. When the class is still puzzled by the term "blind cross" after a ten-minute verbal description, it can be easier for the instructor simply to show the manoeuvre with his own dog. All will become clear if the instructor is successful. If not, the class will be even more confused and muddled!

Making up the numbers The football is on and there's an outbreak of flu. The class is reduced to two. The instructor may decide to work his dog in order to give his students a rest so they may catch their breath between turns.

Role model If the instructor is one of the elite, his performance in front of his students will be breathtaking. The class will either imitate and aspire to be just like him or they will become disillusioned, give up hope and go home.

Focus If your instructor can give his class his full attention with his dog beside him in the ring, that's great. But if his dog is menacing the queue of students and takes ages to get the exercises right, you might start to question his agenda. The purpose of your class is not for your instructor to train his dog, but your dogs. You have reason to feel resentful and cause to complain.

If you do decide to voice your grievance to your club's committee, do so tactfully. They may be unaware of what is going on and you don't want anyone's feelings to be hurt. Worse, they may have no other instructors. It might be worth looking for another agility club and first observe other classes to see how things are run.

Above: *Agility classes are for you and your dog, so make sure that they are being run for your benefit and not for that of the instructor who should know better!*

Taking The Lead

Q *My dog Fergus is obsessed with his lead. He either tugs it noisily or masticates it silently. Last week, he chewed straight through it without me realizing what he was doing. My mind was on the course and when I reached down to take his lead off for his run, Fergus had half of it in his mouth and I had the other half in my hand!*

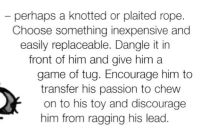

A You are very lucky that Fergus did not realize that he was unattached. He could have wandered off and got up to all kinds of mischief!

Dogs love their leads Pick up a dog's lead and it's the signal for a walk in the woods or a ride in the car to agility training. Many agility handlers make their dog's lead seem more desirable and powerful by treating it as if it were a toy. They play tug with their lead to wind and warm up their dog. They send their dog to a lead at the end of a run. Or they tie it in a knot and throw it for their dog to fetch. Don't treat Fergus's lead as if it is a toy; then he won't try to play with it.

A new toy If you don't allow Fergus to play with his lead, you must buy him a new toy. Something similar but different

Right: *It's my lead! NO! It's my lead! Who will win this test of strength?*

– perhaps a knotted or plaited rope. Choose something inexpensive and easily replaceable. Dangle it in front of him and give him a game of tug. Encourage him to transfer his passion to chew on to his toy and discourage him from ragging his lead.

Unchewable You could buy Fergus a metal chain lead. These aren't so nice to chew – Fergus would blunt his teeth on one of those. He will prefer gnawing his new tug toy.

Be vigilant When you are standing in the queue, keep your eye on Fergus. If he is resisting the temptation to chew his lead, praise him and give him a titbit. If he looks as if he is thinking about mouthing his lead, let him know that he has made the wrong choice. When you need to concentrate on the course, put Fergus in a down stay. Do your thinking. Return to Fergus and release him onto a toy and have a game. You could make this part of your warm-up routine.

Yanking, pulling and tugging If you try and get Fergus to let go of his lead by yanking, pulling or tugging, he will yank, pull and tug right back at you. It's so exciting and he will think you are having a game. Teach Fergus to "Leave" or "Drop", so that he will let go of his lead on command. If you exert all your strength to rip it out, you may end up damaging his teeth.

Of course, you could just let Fergus get on with it. Chewing his lead isn't such a bad habit. But it could cost you a fortune in replacements!

Quick-Release Collar

(Q) *My biggest problem at a show is getting the collar and lead off my sheltie, Taz. I get hold of her, but she is so keen to get into the ring she won't stay still. All the wiggling and straining to get started makes it impossible to find the buckle. She gets all snared up and her long coat doesn't help matters. I'm afraid the judge is going to fault me for delaying tactics.*

(A) I can picture you and Taz twisting together on the start line. Finding the collar is a common problem for handlers with long-haired dogs and by the time you have parted the fur and located it, the dog is agitated and restless. And then you lose it again! There are a number of options to help solve the problem.

Clip the dog This is a drastic solution and Taz wouldn't be able to face herself in the mirror.

Collar shopping Go shopping and test-drive a few collars. Look for one without a buckle. Try some quick-release collars. If you can't get the collar to open when the dog isn't wearing it, you don't stand a chance when it is around Taz's neck. Think about the width. Thin collars tend to embed themselves deeply in the fur. Something thicker might be easier to locate in Taz's coat. Consider slip leads. Would one of these be any easier for you to take off?

Touch my collar exercise Start this at home. Part Taz's coat so that her collar is exposed and sit her in front of you. Find her collar and gently slip a finger

Above: *Reward your dog for letting you touch her collar with a treat or, if you can fit a few fingers underneath it, massage her neck muscles until she turns to jelly.*

underneath. Praise and give her a treat. She gets the treat, not for sitting, but for letting you touch her collar. After a few repetitions, Taz will be begging you to put your hand on her collar. Keep your hand there a little longer. If Taz has been clicker-trained, she will learn this exercise very quickly. Touch her collar and click. When she is proficient, add a command like "Undress" or "Lead off". With practice, you should be able to transfer this exercise from your living room to an agility show.

Game of statues Staying still is very hard for wiggly worm puppies and even harder for excited agility dogs. Teach your dog to freeze with a game of statues. Get Taz to play with her tug toy or chase a treat. Interject a "Sit" command into the game. She must remain motionless until you release her. At first, release her quickly onto her toy. When she thoroughly understands the game's rules, wait a little bit longer. Build up slowly. Later still, introduce a distraction that she must sit through – clap your hands or take off her collar. She must sit still to get her reward. It might not help you to get Taz to stop squirming while you disrobe her at agility shows, but you will have had some fun together!

Eye On The Ball

Q *I have a little collie cross, Tetley. She's great at agility provided I have a ball in my hand. If I leave the ball at the side of the ring, or hide it in my pocket, she slows down or tries to find where I've hidden it. With her ball, she goes like greased lightning. Without it, she goes on strike. What can I do?*

A Tetley is a very, very good trainer. She has taught you to carry her beloved ball whenever the pair of you do any agility. No ball? No agility. Tetley needs to learn that her ball must be earned.

Small beginnings Start with one fence. Command Tetley to jump. After she jumps the hurdle, not before, she gets her reward. When the penny has dropped, you can build up to two, three or four fences. She will start thinking "What do I have to do to get my ball?"

Battle of wills The first few times will be difficult. Tetley may rather have her hair dyed pink than lose sight of her ball. She may have a tantrum. Be patient and work through it. Tetley may pout and be unenthusiastic to start with but when she realizes that she will be rewarded with her ball she will start making an effort. In the beginning, keep Tetley interested by rewarding her frequently. Later, you can adjust your expectations. She will have to do more work to justify getting her ball.

Keep guessing Continue to use Tetley's ball in training, but keep her guessing. Is it in your hand? Is it in your pocket? Is it under the A-frame? Does someone else have it? Tetley will really be surprised when you retrieve her ball from the top of the car. Sometimes Tetley can have a game with it after a few jumps, sometimes in the middle of your run, sometimes at the end. You decide where and when.

Other motivators Experiment with other motivators. Does Tetley like treats, tug toys, a Frisbee? The advantage of having a range of rewards to choose from lies in their differing value to the dog. So if Tetley was stunningly brilliant, she gets her cherished ball. If she was simply good, she gets a treat.

Out of sight Tetley will be learning that although she can't see her ball, it will be forthcoming. All she has to do is be keen. The faster she goes, the sooner she gets her ball…from somewhere.

Your ball Think about your feelings and Tetley's ball. How do you feel running without it in your hand? Is it a bit of a crutch for you? Do you feel naked and useless without it? Change your attitude to yourself to something more positive.

Stick with it and you will have a dog that is as motivated in the ring as she is in training. She will know that a reward is on its way and will be on her best behaviour to hurry it along.

Above: *Dogs can fall in love with a Frisbee as easily as a tennis ball. Take care not to substitute one obsession for another.*

Leaving His Mark

Q *It is so embarrassing. I have just started agility with Jake and he keeps cocking his leg. Although I've taught him to go on command, Jake doesn't care who or what he pees on. He has cocked his leg on other handlers in the class and the agility equipment. His favourite is the tunnel. How can I stop him from anointing everything in sight at class?*

Left: *Would you let your dog do this in your house? I doubt it.*

Castration Testosterone stimulates undesirable male behaviour like scent marking so it is possible that castration may help control the problem. This is something you may like to discuss in more detail with your vet.

A It is important to recognize that Jake is scent-marking as opposed to urinating. Dominant dogs will repeatedly mark their territory with small amounts of urine deposited in strategically chosen places to let other dogs know that they are around. In addition, insecure dogs will mark in order to surround themselves with their own smell. It reassures them and boosts their confidence.

I ask new agility students to think of the agility obstacles as they think of the furniture in their living room. They don't allow their dogs to cock their legs on the corner of the settee so they must not allow them to do so on the tunnel. I explain further that if one dog pees on a jump wing, all the boys in the class will want to lift their leg in the same spot. Male

dogs like to cover another dog's urine scent with their own. They will be so busy peeing that they won't have anytime to learn agility. And some dogs, like Jake, are very determined.

Watch your dog Be vigilant. Don't stand near anything vertical that Jake might find tempting. And that includes people. Look out for warning signals. Jake will probably sniff the area he wants to mark before he lifts his leg. This is your cue to move away.

Keep moving It is hard to pee while moving. As Jake becomes more proficient at the obstacles and starts stringing them together, he will have to run. He won't have the opportunities or time to mark.

Correction You can interrupt a dog that is cocking his legs by shouting "No" or clapping your hands; however, any harsh corrections may make an insecure dog worse. Jake will simply mark quickly when you are not looking.

Time If Jake is marking because he feels threatened or insecure, it will pass as he becomes more confident over the agility equipment and more comfortable with his classmates. Give it time.

Pee post I have put two "pee posts" at opposite ends of the exercise field at my agility venue. Any competitive scent-marking is done here rather than on the equipment. There may be a tree or gatepost in your exercise area where all the boys leave their calling cards and this is where Jake should be allowed to lift his leg before coming into the training area.

Caught On Film

Q *I have been competing for about a year with my dog Gabby. She is doing well and I am turning into an agility addict. I've received a nice bonus from work this month and want to use it to indulge my addiction. I'm thinking of buying a video camera, but they are so expensive. Do you think it would be a good purchase?*

A Videos are an invaluable tool in agility training. Punch the playback button and you can see over and over again your best moves as well as your worst. The video never lies and you can learn a lot about yourself and Gabby. Consider a few of these hypothetical examples.

Posture You are fed up with hearing your instructor tell you to stop bending over your dog and stand up. You are standing up. But look at the video. See. There you are running around as if you are a camel with a hump on your back.

Timing How good is it? You may think that you're spot on, but you are not. You've been recorded giving your contact command after your dog has jumped off the A-frame.

Spooky Why did your dog spook in that corner? She really lost the plot. Look closely at the video and perhaps you will see a cigarette packet blowing across the ground by the jump. That's the evidence you need.

Explanation Your dog finishes the course but is limping. What happened? Watch the video and you will see that she stubbed her toe going into the weaves.

Voice Do you sound as authoritative and commanding as you think? No. On the video you sound desperate and are pleading with your dog to enter the weaves.

Body signals Stop wondering why your dog went into the tunnel when you wanted her to turn onto the A-frame. There you are facing the tunnel. No wonder your dog was sucked in.

Training v. competition Your dog always gets her weave entries in training, but never in competition. What are you doing differently? The video will give you a clue.

Evaluate a problem Your dog is knocking poles. Is it because of over-excitement, taking off too early, or a poorly timed command? Analyze the dog's jumping style with a video recording.

Video recorders provide irrefutable feedback and allow you to stand back and look at yourself in the ring. The video is the friend who will always tell you the truth. You should have bought shorts in the next size up and you should have called your dog sooner. Your instructor can tell you, your friends can tell you and even your dog can try and tell you what you are doing wrong on the course, but you won't necessarily believe them. If it's on video, you can't deny it. If you want to invest in your agility, buy one!

Above: *Seeing is believing. If you are wondering how your dog uses his fluffy tail to balance through the weaves, look no further than what's on the screen.*

Vertigo

Q *My two-year-old bitch Apple has a problem on the A-frame. I think she is scared of heights because once she gets to the top, she stops dead and won't come down. When Apple does descend, she does so very slowly. Is it possible for dogs to have vertigo?*

A Dogs are rarely afraid of heights. They have no problem jumping off the kitchen table when caught cleaning the dinner plates. Reluctance to descend the A-frame happens for a number of reasons.

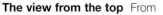

The view from the top From this vantage point Apple can see everything that is going on and can scan the horizon for biscuits. She is savouring the view.

Elevated position Apple relishes looking down on all the people trying to entice her off the A-frame. The harder they try, the more determined she is to remain aloof.

Toenails Apple's nails may be catching in the A-frame's slats. Descent is slow and painful. Trim them.

Cooing encouragement Try to tempt Apple down with sweet words and she may think you are praising her for staying on her perch. Don't pursue this option.

Two feet on/two feet off This position is fine for dogs with drive, but demotivating for those that lack confidence. Apple looks down and sees you standing at the bottom of the A-frame. She elects to stay on top rather than face any argy-bargy when she hit's the ground. It's safer for her to stick up top.

Retrain the A-frame

1 Lower the A-frame as far as it will go so it's easy to cross.

2 Give Apple a reason to get from one end to the other – a bowl of treats or a toy. Put it at the bottom of the A-frame.

3 With Apple on the lead, guide her over the A-frame to her prize. Let her clean up the bowl or give her a game with the toy.

4 When Apple knows the route to her goodies, try a recall. Ask someone to hold her, rev her up or tease her with toy and call her. She'll be eager to get to the other side.

5 If Apple is zooming over the A-frame as fast as she can to find her bowl or tug toy, it's time to try running along the right and left side. Leave Apple in a wait and, on your signal, make it a race between you to see who gets there first. If Apple lacks confidence or is a bit insecure, try letting her win by getting there first.

6 When you have the speed and drive that you want, it will be time to raise the A-frame gradually to its full height. Do this slowly over a period of time. If at any stage your dog loses her enthusiasm, lower the A-frame again.

7 Vary rewards. Sometimes instead of a treat, let Apple do her favourite piece of equipment or, if it's hot, enjoy an ice cream or a swim in the stream! With a little patience, Apple will quickly overcome her fear of heights.

Left: *From the top of the A-frame it looks a long way down, doesn't it? But remember that your dog has no trouble racing you down the stairs at home to catch the post as it drops through the letterbox. Try putting a few old letters at the bottom of the A-frame and see if you get the same result. Use whatever motivates your dog!*

Above: *Get your dog accustomed to your forward movement by running on both the left and right side of the A-frame. Who will get to the other side first?*

Chapter Four

BETTER HANDLING

You have taught your dog to do all the agility obstacles. He is no longer a couch potato but an action dog. He can climb the A-frame and wiggle between the weaving poles. Your dog does everything you tell him to do. Well, almost. Well, when he's in the mood. Sometimes he misses the first weave pole and sometimes he misses the last one. Sometimes he breaks his wait on the start line. Occasionally he goes right instead of left or he flies the seesaw. If only he hadn't jumped the contact on the A-frame you would have won the class. Your dog is good but, if you want him to be even better, you need to look at your handling skills on the course. There's room for improvement. Iron out all the little wrinkles in your training. What you do makes a difference to what your dog does as he runs over the obstacles.

I'm Lost!

Q *I get lost on the course. No matter how many times I walk it, I take a wrong turn somewhere. I've been blessed with Tilly because she does exactly what I tell her. It's me that gets her eliminated for sending her the wrong way. Are there any memory tricks that would help me?*

A It doesn't matter how many times you walk the course if you don't learn it as you go around. Concentrate! Are you looking for the Ladies toilets or are you looking for fence number three? Focus! Don't stop to chat with a friend who wants to tell you about her new puppy. Think! It's not enough to spot a trap on the course. Figure out what you are going to do when you get there.

By ear Talk yourself through the course. Practise your commands as you move from one obstacle to the next. You may want to say some louder than others. Does Tilly need encouragement at that corner? Remember to say "Touch" at the contacts, if that is what you say in training. Recite them in the correct order until you are word perfect. Listen to yourself on mental feedback. It will help you remember the course.

By eye Shut your eyes after you have walked the course. Visualize it. How many weave poles are there? What comes after the tunnel? What colour is the third jump? Can you see it all? Now add yourself and your dog. Imagine a perfect run. You will not only remember the course, but you will go clear!

By feet As you go walk around the course, rehearse your movements. Point, pull and pirouette. Refine your body language. Now run the course (but try not to crash into anyone) as if your dog is with you.

You can learn the course by just one of these methods or by a

Above: *Where the finger points, the nose will go. Practise pointing in the tunnel so your dog runs into it, rather than running around or jumping on top of it.*

combination of them. Whatever works for you. I usually walk the course at least three times. Once to get a feel for it. Again to learn it. And finally to test myself. Beware of over-walking a course. This is worse than not walking if at all. It's like staring at a page, seeing all the words but not reading it.

More than one course? If you have more than one course to walk at a show, walk the one you are going to run first, last. That way it will be freshest in your memory when the time comes to step up to the start line. You can always watch your second course from the sidelines later.

You are human and it's not easy to remember everything! We are all sometimes guilty of going the wrong way or getting lost. Watching your dog, giving commands and trying not to bump into the judge is just multitasking. And the good news is that the more courses you run, the easier it will be. Just keep flexing your memory cells.

Turning Right And Left

Q *Do I have to teach my Staffordshire Terrier Riva verbal directional commands? I usually shout "Left" and point to the right. No wonder the poor dog is confused. I tried painting "R" and "L" on Riva's paws but that didn't work!*

A Did you try painting "R" and "L" on your running shoes? You have to teach Riva directional commands, but it is up to you to decide if you will use them. One day you will walk a course and think to yourself how much easier a manoeuvre would be if Riva understood the commands "Right" and "Left". Keep your options open by teaching Riva what they mean. If you make training fun, you'll learn your rights from your lefts too.

Circles Start with Riva in a stand and use a treat to start to lure her in a circle to her right. As soon as she starts to twist to the right, click and let her have the treat. Ask her to twist a little further each time until she has completed a circle. With practice she will be circling

Below: Teaching your dog to twist to the right and the left is fun. She'll be doing a jive or boogie-woogie next!

to the right without a lure and you can put a command to the action, your command to turn her to the right. Repeat these steps to teach Riva to turn to the left.

Maypole Pretend you are a Maypole and teach Riva to dance around you to the right and then to the left. You can use a treat as a lure to start her off and click her as soon as she starts to go. Give her treat. Riva will soon get the idea and will circle you in both directions and on command. And this is something you can do in the queue at agility shows to remind your dog of the difference between left and right.

Apple tree I practise this around a little old apple tree in my garden, but a bollard, flower pot, or even your mother-in-law will do. Start close to the tree with Riva on your left-hand side. Send her away from you with your left hand towards the tree. As she goes behind it, lure her with your right hand around it and back to you. Click as she starts to turn right and give the titbit to her. When she becomes proficient, you can add your directional command and start standing further away from the tree. Send her away and command her to turn right around the tree and call her back to you. Do the same thing on the other side, starting with Riva on your right, but turning her left to circle the tree.

Ambidextrous Not all dogs or people are ambidextrous or comfortable on both the left and right side. Make sure you practise turning exercises in both directions. You and Riva will both benefit and your brains will become a little more elastic. You'll be happy to perform manoeuvres on either side.

Just make sure that you are saying "Right" when you want to turn right, not left!

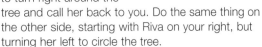

Agility Vocabulary

Q *My instructor insisted that when Tigre, my terrier, and I started agility we had a different command for each piece of agility equipment. But she never explained why and I hardly ever use them now when I am competing. Why did I bother to teach them to Tigre?*

A Your instructor wanted to make sure that you had as good a foundation in agility as possible. There are many good reasons to teach your dog the names of the different obstacles.

Above: *Help your dog to anticipate the different layout of the obstacles by using a separate command for each.*

Learning Names for the obstacles will make it easier for your dog to learn. If you say "over" for the long jump and "up" for a hurdle, Tigre will learn to jump low and long for one and high and short for the other. They need different actions and a verbal cue warns Tigre of what to expect.

Obstacle recognition When you say the name of an obstacle, Tigre should look for it and perform it. I bet that Tigre knows the word "tunnel" and you can send her into one from a distance. By saying "tunnel", Tigre goes into the tunnel while you take a short cut across the

course to position yourself ready for the next obstacle. Because she knows what a tunnel is, you can save seconds on the course time.

Obstacle discrimination Those nasty judges will place obstacles so close to each other. The A-frame is often placed over the tunnel and both are very tempting! If Tigre knows the names of the obstacles, she has a better chance of making the correct choice and she won't be eliminated for going in the tunnel when she should climb the A-frame.

Obstacle ambiguity A spread is easy to mistake for a hurdle in certain lights. Your dog is not able to walk the course and study the layout in advance like you. If you have a distinct command for the spread, Tigre will jump a little longer and the poles will stay up. If she mistook it for a hurdle, she could knock it and earn you five faults.

Not a shred of doubt Has this ever happened to you? You are running towards the seesaw. You run by it, assuming Tigre has done it. But no. She did not. Why should she? You didn't command her to do so. Maybe a "seesaw" would have helped her decide to walk up it rather than chase after you.

You might not use the names of the obstacles, but it does add another string to your bow. You may rely on your body language to direct Tigre, but one day you might walk a course and find a trap where a verbal obstacle command will get you out of trouble. And if you do, then thank your instructor for teaching them to you!

Getting It Wrong

Q *How should I correct my Labrador Retriever, Blaze? When he gets something right I give him a treat or throw his toy, but what do I do if he gets it wrong? If he breaks a wait, jumps off a contact or misses a weave entry, I don't want to yell at him or thump him.*

A I'm so glad to hear that! Blaze is a big dog and if you thumped him, he might thump you back! Mistakes are inevitable and an important part of the learning process. They'll happen even though you try to make it easy for Blaze to get things right. Mistakes also occur because our performance criteria change in different environments. A paw-perfect dog in training will break waits, miss weave entries and jump off contacts in competition.

Types of correction There are different types of correction. Not all mistakes are hanging offences. Use what is appropriate. Fit it to fix the error. Here are various options:
- Ignore it. It might never happen again.
- Look the other way and shrug your shoulders. Withdrawing your attention cuts a dog right to the heart.
- Mark the mistake with a phrase like "Oh dear" or "Wrong" so that Blaze will learn where he went wrong
- Withhold his praise and rewards. Don't give Blaze a treat or throw his toy if he goes wrong. Try again and if Blaze gets it right, he gets his goodies.
- Halt the game. If agility is his thing, go to the end of the queue in class. Or leave the building.

Above: *If your dog can't see your face, he won't be able to read your thoughts and feelings. Turn your back and you have hung up the phone. The line is dead.*

Right: *When you have a breakthrough, your dog needs a BIG reward. Tell him he's brilliant and get out the treats and toys. He will see how pleased you are by the BIG grin on your face.*

Get it right next time Mark the mistake and then show Blaze what you want. If he lies down when you left him in a sit-wait, put him back in the sit. If he pops off the contact, put him back on it. If he misses a weave pole, take him back to where he came out. You can do this at your local agility club or at simulated shows. But be aware that if you do this at a competition, the judge will eliminate you for training in the ring or touching your dog. He will ask you to leave his ring.

Balance If Blaze needs correction make sure that it is balanced with praise. Don't follow a strong "Wrong" with a weak, wishy washy "Good boy". And if Blaze is putting a lot of effort into trying to get something right, put a lot of effort into your praise. For example, if Blaze keeps missing his target at the bottom of the A-frame, he will need a big, big reward when he finally gives it a nose touch. You've had a breakthrough.

Drastic steps Don't let desperation lead you to desperate measures. Rattling a tin filled with pebbles or squirting water will certainly get Blaze's attention. A puff of vapour from a remote spray collar will stop him in his tracks. However, Blaze's misdeed must be pretty evil before you would want to take such drastic steps and resort to something so negative. You don't want him to be frightened of the agility equipment.

If Blaze makes a mistake, don't punish him. Correct him and show him how to win your love and approval next time.

Staying Put

Q *I am determined to teach my Boxer, Boris, a good start line stay. He always breaks the first time, but stays after I put him back. Sometimes he creeps forward but I'm so delighted that he is at least on the other side of the fence that I let him get away with it. Should I put superglue on his bottom?*

A Avoid the superglue. If Boris is really determined that won't hold him! There are three components to a good start line stay. Don't compromise on any of them.

- The stay. This means do not move. Do not change position from a sit to a down or a down to a stand. Do not creep forward. Do not twitch a single muscle. Freeze!
- The release. If it is a word, like "OK", the dog is dying to hear it. It means he can move again. He can get to jump those fences.
- The acceleration. You want your dog to drive over the first fence when you release him, not yawn and trot his way round the course.

Away from agility Train your sit-stays in as many different situations as possible, away from agility. Agility will be the final test. Will Boris sit-stay while you put your coat on to go out for a walk? Will Boris sit-stay while your other dogs play fetch? When he is 100 per cent reliable in these situations, he is ready to try it in front of a fence.

Say it once Don't keep repeating your stay command. Boris heard it the first time and saying it over and over again will only make you sound distrustful and desperate. Have confidence in your training.

Keep an eye open Walk away from Boris, but look over your shoulder. How else will you know if he moves? If there is one paw out of place, go back and reposition it. One paw is only a few short steps away from getting up before you signal.

When he breaks If Boris breaks his stay at agility class, take him to the end of the queue. Don't set him up again to start the exercise. He blew it. If Boris wants to get on the course, he has to do the sit-stay the first time.

And praise Boris has a stay problem, so he needs to know when he is getting it right. If he stays, tell him he is a good boy. Go back and give him a treat. He needs reassurance and rewards in order to continue doing what you want him to do.

It is worth mastering this exercise. If Boris can do a good sit-stay at the start, you will be able to leave him and position yourself on the course. You will be initiating your round in control and that will percolate through to the rest of the run. Remember that once your self-discipline slips for the start, it will probably start slipping for the contacts, the weaves and so on. Don't let your dog down. Have faith in your training.

Right: *Such a tease! What dog wouldn't be tempted to break a sit-stay if his favourite toy was placed on the floor just inches from his paws? Not this Boxer!*

But will he stay put when his toy is thrown up in the air?

Get Set, Go!

Q *I've watched handlers using different starting positions for their dogs. I can't decide whether to leave my dog in a stand, a down or a sit. Some handlers just break into a run and their dog follows. I have a keen Beardie cross called Purdy. Which one should I choose?*

A My position of choice is a sit-stay and that is what I would recommend. There are a number of reasons.

Ergonomic I think the sit is the best blast-off position. It's comfortable. The dog has his bottom on the ground, but is already halfway to stand. All he has to do is push and move his front paws so he doesn't fall on his nose.

Ambiguity The sit is a pretty unambiguous position. If your dog shuffles, creeps forward, or looks to the left or right, you'll be able to spot it. It is much harder to pinpoint changes or movement if the dog has been left in the down or the stand.

Wait and recall If your dog will wait, you have an advantage over the handler who drops and runs with his dog because you can pick the best place to position yourself on the course. And it's less likely that your dog will knock the first fence to beat you onto the course. With a wait you can take a few deep breaths to compose yourself before you signal "Go" to your dog.

Acceleration I like to motivate a dog to accelerate out of a sit-stay by making it an exciting game with the reward of a toy or a treat. The sit-stay shouldn't happen because the dog is bored and there is nothing else to do. The dog should be sitting

solidly but expecting good things to come. Handlers who run with their dog from the start can get into trouble if their dog loves to race. The dog runs so fast he overtakes, goes the wrong way and ends up with an elimination. In contrast, other dogs aren't so keen to get off their bottoms. They trot off and never catch up with their handlers. They get slower and slower and finally give up. Whether with a fast or slow dog, these handlers argue that their dog lacks enthusiasm and that a start line wait will shut them down. But not if they teach the dog to switch on with a sit and blast off with a release word!

The down Many of the dogs you see lying on the start line started their agility career in the sit. After the dog repeatedly broke the sit, their handlers downgraded in the belief that the down position would be easier to maintain. In reality, it takes a mere nanosecond for the dog to break and clear a fence from any position if he is keen. And many large dogs that are left in a down smash into or run under the pole of the first fence. They are so eager to get to the second obstacle, they don't see the first.

I nominate a sit-wait for Purdy. Practise till it's perfect!

Left: *A dog with a good sit-stay at the start line is both comfortable and alert. He is switched on and ready to blast off as soon as his handler gives the release command.*

Right On Target

Q *My first agility dog, a Schnauzer called Elvis, always missed his contacts. I have a new Schnauzer puppy, Poppy, and I don't want her to follow in Elvis's footsteps! I've been doing my homework – reading about different training methods and quizzing different agility handlers. She loves the clicker. What target behaviour on the contacts do you recommend?*

A There are a number of target behaviours that you can teach Poppy while she is a puppy. All you need is the lid from a tube of crisps or biscuits, your clicker and lots of treats. When Poppy is older and starts learning the agility obstacles, she will be a step ahead. She'll see her biscuit lid at the bottom of the A-frame and know exactly what she is supposed to do when she reaches it. These are my favourite target behaviours.

Peck and go Hold the biscuit lid in your hand and teach Poppy to touch it with her nose on a command like "Touch" or "Target". Slowly lower the target to the ground and continue to click and treat when she gives a nose touch. Practise pecking in different places. The kitchen, the garden, the car park at agility training. Will Poppy run to the biscuit lid and peck it? Brilliant. Try running on the left and right with Poppy to the target. She has to get accustomed to seeing you running by her side. What about if you run ahead of her? She still must peck and catch you up. No peck, no reward. Finally, if you command when the biscuit lid is in your pocket, will Poppy start pecking the ground like a chicken? Good! Quick click the pecking action and give her a treat.

Go to sleep You can also train Poppy to lie down and put her head on the biscuit lid. If she already has a nose touch, tell Poppy to lie down and place the target between her front legs. She will touch it with her chin as it is nearly impossible to touch it with her nose in that position, so click and treat. By withholding her click and reward, you can slowly

Above: *Teach your dog to "go to sleep" with a target. All he needs to do once his chin is on the ground is shut his eyes!*

extend the time she has her chin on her target. Teach Poppy a command like "Head" or "Chin" and get her to hold this position until she hears a release word. Dogs look so cute, as if they are about to say "night, night". Get her used to you running on either side and ahead. And fade her target. Will she put her chin to the ground when it's no longer there?

Teach Poppy both the "peck and go" and the "go to sleep". When you start agility training in earnest, you'll have a choice if you decide to ask for a target performance at the bottom of the contact. You'll never be able to take your biscuit lid into the competition ring, but if at any time you think Poppy is not performing up to scratch, you can reintroduce it to your training programme.

Creeping Contact

Q *Scully, my Tibetan Terrier, wastes loads of time on the A-frame. He creeps down at a snail's pace while I twiddle my thumbs. And worse, sometimes as he is just about to put his paw on the contact, he jumps off! What am I doing wrong?*

A There are many reasons why a dog will descend the A-frame slowly. The dog knows that something is supposed to happen on the contact, but not what, so he takes great pains to approach it cautiously or avoid it altogether. Perhaps the chosen training method has been incorrectly applied or too many training methods thrown at the dog in quick succession. Let's try something completely different with Scully so you stop twiddling your thumbs and put them to good use – a hand touch.

Hand target Teach your dog a hand touch with a clicker. Most dogs will sniff the palm of your hand if it is held out to them. Click and reward Scully for each nose touch. Most dogs just can't believe that all they have to do is touch your hand in order to receive a treat. Keep repeating the exercise to convince him it's true.

Above: *A dog that drives confidently down the dog walk into the contact will reward his handler with a good time.*

Work harder Hold your hand out a bit further so that Scully has to stretch his neck out to touch it. Click, reward and repeat. He is having to work harder for his treat. Increase the distance a bit at a time.

Movement Start moving your hand and have some fun. Will he zoom under a chair to touch your hand? Can he find your hand when it is held behind you? Will he jump over your cat to touch your hand? Look for drive.

Cue If you think Scully understands what he has to do to get a treat, add a cue like "touch" or "target". Your dog should be really keen to find and touch your hand with his nose.

Lure Now, you are ready to use your hand to lure your dog over a low A-frame. You will always have your hand in the ring – it's the sort of training aid that is impossible to leave in the car. No more creeping. Scully will be trying so hard to hit your hand that he will quickly descend the lowered A-frame to get to it.

Touch Gradually raise the A-frame, but don't lose your dog's momentum. Make sure you always use your hand to lure your dog right to the ground. If you take your hand away too soon, he will jump off the contact. Your hand must be moving all the time, but be just out of reach. When your dog gets to the bottom and has taken a few steps on the ground, stop moving your hand so your dog can catch it. He needs the opportunity to touch it and get his reward.

Stop twiddling your thumbs and try using your hand as a target instead. Good luck!

Making Contact

Q *My sheepdog, Clarrie, thinks contacts are a waste of time. I'm sure she thinks that they are put there to slow her down and she hates anything that slows her down! It's as if she thinks they are dangerous to touch.*

A Quite the opposite. They are perfectly safe to touch. It's jumping over them that is dangerous. If Clarrie flies off and lands badly, she risks hurting herself.

If you have a high-drive dog, I would suggest you train the two feet on, two feet off position at the bottom of the contacts. Start at home with a clicker and lots of treats.

1 Do you have stairs in your house? Place Clarrie with her bottom on last step and her front paws on the floor. Click and treat this position.
2 When she understands the position, use a command like "On it" or "Contact".
3 Don't forget to use a release command like "OK" or "Go". Clarrie must hold the position until you say it's all right to move. Get this part perfect before you move on to the next step.
4 When she is in the two feet on, two feet off position, put a treat about 60cm (24in) in front of her. If she is a good girl and holds her position, you can release her on to it. This will keep her looking forward. You don't want Clarrie looking up at you in expectation of her reward.
5 When you have become an expert on the stairs, place Clarrie on a lowered A-frame. Her back legs should rest on the bottom of the A-frame and her front two feet should rest on the ground. Click and treat. Clarrie is doing exactly what she was doing on the stairs so use the same command. Work through the progressions until she is being released on to a treat or toy on your command.
6 Back chain the A-frame. Make sure that each time you move Clarrie further up the A-frame that she drives into the two feet on, two feet off position.
7 Start the exercise from the other side of the lowered A-frame. And remember to run with

Clarrie on both the right and left. Sometimes run past the bottom of the A-frame. Look back to see if Clarrie is still staring at her toy and waiting to be released.

8 When you deem Clarrie's contact performance to be 100 per cent reliable, add other pieces of agility equipment like jumps and tunnels to make different sequences. You can dispense with your toy and use running on to an obstacle as a reward. She must still land at the bottom of the A-frame in a two feet on, two feet off position and wait for your release word before proceeding any further.
9 If Clarrie doesn't wait for her release word, place her back on the contact and praise her to reinforce the two feet on, two feet off position. Release her but do not allow her to continue over any other obstacles. Walk with her to a chair, sit down and count to ten. Now you are ready to start again.
10 You and Clarrie should be pretty good by now. Start to raise the A-frame until it is at full height and insist that Clarrie is paw perfect. You can always review your contact work or lower the A-frame if she looks confused or keeps jumping off.

If you make contact training rewarding and fun, Clarrie will learn that they are worth waiting on!

Last Link in the Chain

Q My dog walk contact is non-existent. Kaos, my bouncy Labrador, just bounces off the end every time. My instructor spent a whole lesson talking about back chaining. I didn't really understand what she was talking about, but was too embarrassed to interrupt her as the rest of the class nodded knowingly. What did she mean by back chaining?

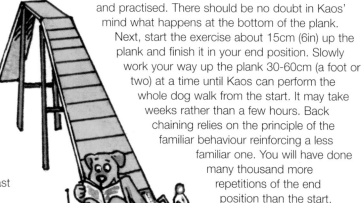

A Back chaining is training the last behaviour in a chain first, then training the next-to-last behaviour, then the behaviour before that, and so on. Working in reverse order may seem an upside-down way of doing things but it can be very effective.

If you are retraining your dog walk, start at the bottom of the plank. Place Kaos in his end position. This may be a two feet on, two feet off position, a sit or a down. All Kaos has to do is assume his end position. This is the place were he gets all his goodies and rewards when he is released from it.

Back chaining will be successful as long as this end position is familiar

Far left to right: *It is not enough to teach your dog to climb up and down the A-frame. He must also understand how to perform the contacts. Choose a training method that will persuade your dog to hit the contact confidently every time.*

and practised. There should be no doubt in Kaos' mind what happens at the bottom of the plank. Next, start the exercise about 15cm (6in) up the plank and finish it in your end position. Slowly work your way up the plank 30-60cm (a foot or two) at a time until Kaos can perform the whole dog walk from the start. It may take weeks rather than a few hours. Back chaining relies on the principle of the familiar behaviour reinforcing a less familiar one. You will have done many thousand more repetitions of the end position than the start. Remember these key points if you back chain the dog walk.

Be thorough Do not move Kaos up the dog walk until he is delighted and overjoyed to be on the contact in his position. This is a key stage. Everything depends on it so it's worth spending lots of time here. Don't worry. Subsequent stages will not take so long to teach him.

Don't let your standards slip If you want a certain attitude or a certain position, don't accept less. Make sure you have the drive and enthusiasm you are searching for at each stage. You don't want Kaos to stroll to the bottom of the dog walk and have a snooze. You want him driving to get there and get into position for a treat and your praise. If you have trained a two feet on, two feet off position, don't accept a toenail less.

Don't rush Do not add to the chain until the stage on which you are working is exactly as you want it – perfect. If you have a defective link, your chain will fall apart. Take the time to get things right.

I hope that makes the concept of back chaining a little clearer. And perhaps it helps explains why many handlers walk the course in reverse.

In A Fix With Contacts

Q *When I started agility with Diesel, my Springer Spaniel, he was really fast; too fast on the contacts and he kept missing them. My trainer told me to slow him down or he would hurt himself. He made me make sure Diesel hit the contact by grabbing his collar and guiding him down. Needless to say, Diesel has never shown the turn of speed he did in the beginning and I'm sure I was given bad advice. I'm in control but there's no oomph! Please help.*

A Students expect trainers to know all the answers and that's a big responsibility. It's easy to see how a method has failed in retrospect. I would guess that your instructor was a hands-on type of guy. Many dogs can cope with having their collar grabbed. They don't take it personally. Other dogs, especially the sensitive types, hate it. They react by jumping off too early to avoid being snatched or they proceed very, very warily … just in case someone lunges at them.

Your dog's established contact behaviour will be difficult to change and it may get worse before it gets better. Retraining is always an uphill struggle.

Above: If your dog is sensitive, grabbing him by the collar to hurry him up may, in fact, slow him down. Consider a hands-off method of teaching the contacts.

Ask anyone who has tried to give up smoking. But it's not impossible. Most retraining fails because the handler gives up too soon. So, don't be tempted to resurrect old handling habits if you do not see an immediate change in your dog.

Why? You seem sure that Diesel's lack of enthusiasm is due to your earlier instructor. It might be, but first rule out a physical problem that could be causing Diesel to slow down, before you start retraining.

Have a break The greater the distance between old patterns of behaviour and teaching new ones, the better. If Diesel thinks he is learning a brand new game rather than playing the old game with a few changes of rules, he will be easier to retrain and eager to learn.

Lighten up Turn your attention to games that will inspire and motivate Diesel. What turns him on – a toy or a treat? Keep training sessions short and reward him frequently. And don't forget that your smile is just as important as a squeaky plastic mouse or slice of frankfurter. Frown and training is hard work. Smile and it's fun.

Contact method Don't take a short cut. Although it may take longer, it is worth starting fresh rather than trying to doctor your existing contact performance. Pick a contact method that will allow you to continue to have fun together with your treats and toys. Diesel might find a two feet on, two feet off position depressing, but he might really like doing a hand touch and being lured down and through the contacts. Go back to the beginning and lower the contact equipment as far down as possible. You are not only rebuilding Diesel's confidence, but yours too.

Good luck with Diesel. I hope you succeed in energizing your contacts and putting the fun back into agility.

Running Contacts

Q *I have always taught my dogs a two feet on, two feet off position on the contacts and I have always been pleased by the results. However, I want to teach my new Staffy terrier, Pumpkin, running contacts as I think I'd be able to achieve better course times. How do I go about it?*

A A running contact is when the dog runs full pelt from the top of the contact equipment to the bottom and onto the ground. He doesn't jump off! There are a number of ways to train a running contact. Choose one that you can apply easily and it will give you the result you want.

Natural stride Some dogs have natural striding that turns into a running contact without any prompting from the handler. If this is what Pumpkin does, accept it as a gift from God and give thanks. Don't mess with it.

On the lead Put Pumpkin on the lead and run him over the contact equipment. The lead gives you the control to ensure that the dog maintains forward momentum but can't leap off into thin air. Repetition is the key. Pumpkin must achieve and maintain a good running contact performance without his lead.

Ball or toy Put a ball or toy at the bottom of the contact equipment to encourage Pumpkin to look earthwards and run to the bottom to collect it. You can allow him to carry his prize in his mouth over the course. This is a bonus for some dogs and ensures that drive is maintained. Fade out the toy slowly.

Physical barrier There are many strange contraptions fashioned by handlers – hoops, mesh tunnels and pipes – to shape their dog through the contact zone. Make one and practise running Pumpkin through it. When he is doing this happily, place it at the bottom of the contact equipment for him to race through. Don't let him jump over it. Eventually, Pumpkin will have to run to the bottom of the contact without the visible training aid that has been moulding his performance.

Target Instead of teaching Pumpkin to stop on a target, teach him to run over one. Introduce him to a 60cm (2ft) square piece of carpet and teach him what you want him to do. Then, place it at the bottom of a contact. Insist he continues to step on it as he runs, not jump over it. He will adjust his striding accordingly. You can fade the target out by cutting it into smaller pieces until it is out of sight.

Quick release Teach Pumpkin a two feet on, two feet off position as you have taught your other dogs. Timing is of the essence. A good, quick release will make the halt at the bottom of the contact imperceptible – a running contact.

Contact performance needs to be deeply embedded in the dog's muscle memory and must be independent of physical training aids to be effective in competition. Whichever training technique you choose, don't let your standards slip.

Below: *Some dogs have a natural running contact. Their stride lands them in the yellow before they exit the obstacle.*

Up Contacts

Q. *I have received a lot of help at club training with the down contacts, but no one has helped me teach my Brittany Spaniel Bounty how to hit the up contact. And this is where he keeps getting marked at shows. Do I just do what I did for the down contact?*

A. There are contact areas at both ends of the A-frame and dog walks so that these obstacles don't have to be lifted and turned around if the course is reversed. And having contacts at each end of the dog walk really makes the judge run!

Above: *Make sure that your dog does not leap onto the equipment and miss the up contact. Greyhound mixes and GSDs are the breeds most often faulted for this mistake.*

Shorten your dog's stride There are a number of ways you can do this, so experiment.

- You can place a pole on the ground in front of the obstacle so that Bounty has to step over it and adjust his pacing before he can mount it.
- Or you could teach Bounty a command like "Steady" which will cue him to decelerate. As he slows from a gallop to a trot, he will be less likely to leap the contact.
- Or you could say your dog's name as he is approaching the obstacle. He will momentarily take his eye off it and look at you. This is often enough to break his stride, but you must get the timing right – too early and it won't make any difference and too late and Bounty will have already leapt over the contact.

Teach your dog to step on a target with his paw. Place it just before or on the up contact so that Bounty will have to step on it before he mounts the obstacle. You will be able to find the best place for the target through trial and error. Some dogs are so intent on finding the target that they halt on it and then gather themselves up for a huge leap that takes them over the contact. Remember you do not want Bounty to stop, but to maintain forward momentum.

Shaping Teach Bounty to duck under a small arch or hoop. Place it in front of the obstacle so that he will have to hit the contact on his way up. This method can be very successful in training, but unless the behaviour is well established in the dog's muscle memory, it will disappear when the visible training aid is removed. Alternatively, you can teach Bounty to duck under your arm. Obviously for this to succeed you have to arrive at the contact at the same time as your dog. Not always possible. And some dogs see an arm stretched out across their path as an invitation to jump rather than duck.

Whatever method you choose, make sure Bounty still has the power to get onto the equipment. Otherwise you will get five faults not for missing the up contact, but for a refusal.

Flying Off The Seesaw

Q *Have you ever seen a dog fly? Then you should see Petra, my Irish Setter, launching herself into space from the seesaw. How can I stop her? I'm sure she will soon leave Earth entirely and find herself in orbit!*

A Seesaws are not launch pads! Dogs become airborne because they have not been taught how to do the obstacle properly. They fail to find the point of balance and tip the plank. Or, they are afraid of the seesaw. They try to get the obstacle over and done with as quickly as possible and end up scrabbling, airborne and scared silly. And some other dogs are so keen to complete the course, they dismount sooner rather than later.

Think of your ideal seesaw performance. It must touch the ground before Petra alights. She is a big dog so the seesaw will start tipping midway, near the fulcrum. You don't want her to creep up it, but to run, and work the tip. Then, run to the bottom of the contact and exit as soon as it hits the ground.

Above: *For a safe landing from the seesaw, this dog needs a parachute! His handler is too far behind to catch him in mid-air.*

The tip I like to see dogs finding the point of balance or the "tip" on the seesaw. The lighter the dogs, the higher up the seesaw they can go before it starts to move. Also, the tip will vary from one seesaw to the next, depending on the materials and manufacturer. Petra will notice a difference between the seesaw that she trains on at home and the ones she meets at shows. If you have played with Petra on a wobble board when she was a puppy, she shouldn't have too much trouble finding a seesaw's tip. She needs to locate it and shift her weight back for a split second so that gravity can take over. Start her on the lead. With a big and heavy dog like Petra, stop her in the middle of the seesaw. When it starts to move, use your treat to lure her into a play bow so she rides it while the seesaw finishes its journey to the ground. She gets a treat. Then she can follow another treat along the plank to the bottom. I have seen some dogs so keen to stop in the middle that they slide the rest of the way onto the contact. And, tempting though it is, don't teach Petra to balance both ends in the air!

The contact Teach the seesaw contact the same way as you would your other contacts. It is painted there for the same reason. Have you taught Petra nose-touch on a target? Look where the end of the seesaw is going to hit the ground. This is where you should place your target. Work through the same progression as you would do for the dog walk or the A-frame. If you use your hand to lure Petra to the bottom, make sure you move your hand downwards as the seesaw falls so she follows it right to the ground. If you make Petra wait for a release on the other contact obstacles, continue to use it on the seesaw.

When Petra shows proficiency on the seesaw, start adding a few other obstacles. She needs to practise entries and exits onto it at speed. If she starts leaping off again, review her basics.

Light As A Feather

Q *My Papillon, Tinkerbelle, is too light to tip the seesaw. She is a bold, speedy dog and runs up no problem. Besides putting her on a diet of fattening food or sewing lead weights in her collar, what can I do?*

A Little dogs often have a problem tipping the seesaw. They fail to make it to fall because they don't run right to the end of the plank. And when they have gone past the point of balance, it seems to take ages for the plank to hit the ground. Tinkerbelle doesn't need fattening but incentives to run to the very end.

Fear Did Tinkerbelle give herself a fright? Did the plank hit the ground with a bump and bounce her into the air? Or did a gust of wind make it wobble? It's no surprise that she avoids going right to the end of the seesaw.

Climb It's a steep climb up the seesaw from the perspective of a little dog. Did Tinkerbelle get three-quarters of the way to the end of the plank and then despair of being able to make it tip? No wonder she turned around and started back down. At least that end was still on the ground.

Squished treats Teach Tinkerbelle to run right to the end of the seesaw, not just the contact area. You want her front feet an inch or two from the edge so her weight is as far forward as possible. Give her an incentive to get there. Leave Tinkerbelle in a sit on the ground at the bottom of the seesaw and go to the other side. Squish a piece of cheese or sausage meat an inch or two from the end. Hold the end of the seesaw up in the air with your hand underneath so that it doesn't fall and recall Tinkerbelle to you. She will be keen to reach the top for her squished treat. As she bends down to eat, let the seesaw tip and gently guide it to the ground. Tinkerbelle will be too busy licking up squished cheese to notice she is travelling downwards.

More squished treats As Tinkerbelle grows confident on the seesaw, you can start to let it fall a little faster each time. Soon you will no longer need to control the fall with your hand – Tinkerbelle will do all the work without your aid. Keep squishing a treat so she still has a reason to climb the plank right to the end. And instead of recalling Tinkerbelle, try sending her on to the seesaw while you run along it on the right and left side.

Less squished treats Start to vary the size of the squished treats and sometimes don't use one at all. Tinkerbelle will still check out the end of the seesaw, just in case there is one there!

Tinkerbelle sounds a feisty girl. She won't get too fat from all the treats and she will soon be tipping the seesaw like an agility pro!

Above: *Cheese is a great treat to squish onto the seesaw. It stays put until your dogs licks it off!*

Wiggly Poles

Q) *I'm 12 years old and have a Cavalier King Charles Spaniel called Morgan. He's a year old and very smart. He can do lots of tricks like sit up and beg, roll over, and speak, but he will not weave. What should I do to make him weave?*

A) I'm so glad to hear that Morgan is your best friend. He must be very clever to learn so many tricks and agility is another thing you can have fun doing together. The weaves are one of the most difficult obstacles to teach. Wiggling in and out of poles can be really boring so you have to make it an enjoyable and rewarding experience for Morgan. Try luring Morgan through the poles. Most Cavies like their food and will follow a titbit anywhere.

1 Put two poles in the ground about 60cm (2ft) apart. The poles should be about 30cm (12in) taller than Morgan at his withers.

2 Face the poles and start with Morgan on your left. Have a treat in your left hand ready to attach to his nose. Step with your left foot across to the second pole and lure Morgan through the gap. Agility dogs must always enter the weaves with the first pole on their left.

3 Step forward with your right foot, throw the treat ahead of Morgan as he passes the second pole with his right shoulder.

4 When, after a few practice goes, Morgan has a wiggle, give the action a command like "weave" or "poles".

5 If Morgan thinks two poles are easy, try a row of four. Keep luring him in and out and throw his treat as he exits the fourth pole. He'll have to keep running ahead to find and eat it.

6 Add two more poles until you have a full set of 12. But if at any stage Morgan looks confused, make it easy for him to get it right by reducing the number of poles.

7 When Morgan is happily weaving, try keeping his treat in your right hand. Go through the motions with your left and at the end of the row throw his treat from your right hand. Did you fool him? Slowly wean him off your left hand. Move it a little less each time, but keep rewarding him at the end of the poles so that he runs forward to get his treat. He will begin to look forward to the end of the poles and not up at your hand.

It is important to keep it light and fun. Don't do too many repetitions. Even though Morgan is very smart, weaving may take months to learn.

Have you thought of teaching Morgan to weave between traffic cones or plant posts? There are many things you can set up in the garden and weave around. And don't forget to teach him to weave between your legs – you'll always have those handy!

Left: *A dog that is play-orientated is easy to lure with a toy between two poles. But don't hold the toy too high or your dog will look up rather than straight ahead. And don't bend down too much or you may poke your eye out on a pole!*

Weave Machine

Q *Where to start? I'm really having a problem with the weave poles with my poodle Sonic. I started training two poles at a time and eventually gave up and moved onto channel weaves. Sometimes I clicker-train. Sonic is so variable it's difficult to discover what's gone wrong. Sometimes she's fast and accurate. Sometimes she's too fast and does two at a time. Other times she's slow and unmotivated. And she's started entering at the fourth pole and jumping out at the sixth!*

A It sounds as if Sonic is keen to learn but doesn't understand what you are trying to teach her. That's why her performance is so variable and why she is losing confidence and motivation. Sonic has put all the things you have taught her in a mixing bowl, stirred well and shoved it in the oven. Sadly, what she has baked is not a delicious weave.

There are so many different ways that the weaves can be taught successfully. If you choose just one method, you must follow through even when the going gets tough. If you choose to combine different methods for teaching different aspects of weave behaviour, you must be thorough with each and teach your dog how to combine them. Here are some little pieces to consider:

Entry Using only two poles, click and reward the entry. Make sure Sonic is attacking them with gusto and from any angle before adding another two poles. Continue to click the entry but reward at the exit.

Speed Use channel weaves to build speed through the poles. It should be fast and furious with a favourite toy or treat at the end. And yes, channel weaves can teach accurate entries and exits, but if you are breaking things down, you will have selected this tool to teach one specific thing (speed) – anything else will be learned incidentally.

Accuracy Attach the lead or hold onto Sonic's collar. Thread her through the poles. Not my favourite method of training, but it's how they used to do it in the good old days. And you will be ensuring every pole is performed perfectly from beginning to end.

Below: *Poodle perfect weaving. This poodle has got a tick in all the boxes – entry, speed, accuracy and exit.*

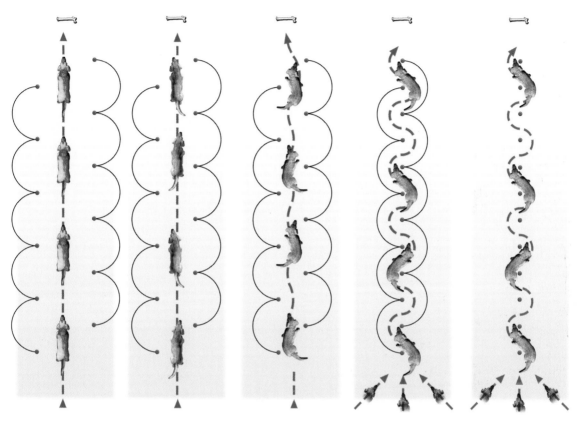

1 *A wide channel flanked by poles.*

2 *The two rows of poles move closer.*

3 *And then even closer together.*

4 *The poles are now in a straight line.*

5 *And finally the guide wires are removed.*

The weaves 1, 2 and 3 *When you introduce your dog to channel weaves, set them so that the channel is wider than his shoulders. At the start, he should be able to run straight to the end without touching the poles with his body. As the channel narrows, he will have to squeeze and bend.*

Exit Click and reward the last two poles. Start with four poles and gradually add two more until you have reached the maximum number of twelve. Continue to click and reward on your dog's exit, sometimes with a treat, toy or another obstacle.

Combining When you have broken the weaves down into little pieces, you have to think about what

The weaves 4 and 5: *When your dog masters the straight approach to channel weaves, try angled entries.*

order they will be taught and combined. For example, are you going to teach speed before entry? Entry before accuracy? Will you click both the entry to mark the beginning of weaving behaviour as well as clicking the exit to mark the end? Plan it. And don't be surprised if, when you add a new exercise to an old one, Sonic forgets what she learned before. As Sonic becomes more confident in the new exercise, her skill in the older one will re-surface. Have faith. It will all come together.

Perfect Entries

Q *Zero, my big Dalmatian, always misses his entry to the weaves. As soon as he misses it, I call him back and we start again. Second time round he gets his entry no problem and does the rest of the poles beautifully. How can I make sure he gets his entry on his first attempt?*

A By teaching him to get it at the first attempt! You are starting from a halt when you go for the second time and there is a big difference. Zero has not yet learned to nail his weave entry when he approaches the poles at speed. When he is running a course, Zero is accelerating from one obstacle to the next. He's a big dog and it isn't easy to squeeze himself between two poles when he is in top gear.

The first two poles Your first step should be to make sure that Zero understands weave entries. Set up two poles in your garden about 60cm (24in) apart. Position Zero so that the poles are in front of him – a big welcoming doorway. You can click as he goes through the gap but make sure he runs on to his toy or his treat bag to ensure that he continues moving forward. You don't want him looking back at you for his reward. Repeat until Zero is driving through confidently. Don't stand still. Accustom him to your movement. Run on his left and run on his right.

The squeeze Instead of starting the exercise with the two poles directly in front of Zero, begin by placing him a little to their left. The size of the gap between the poles remains the same, but it will look a little smaller from this angle.

Above: *The angle of approach determines the amount of squeeze needed to get a toy.*

Continue moving in an arc to the left. Zero will be squeezing between the poles as the entry becomes more oblique with each move. Eventually the two poles will appear to be in a straight line and the approach will finally look like the entry to the weaving poles that you see in competition. Remember that you are moving Zero, not the poles, and Zero should accelerate through each time. Keep him moving forward by continuing to throw a toy or treat bag ahead of him. Now do it all again with your dog on your right side.

More poles You should now have good entry to the weaves. Zero has learned to aim for the gap in the first two poles and to squeeze himself through. Add more poles a few at a time. Keep his rhythm going. Once he is in, there should be no problem. It's just one squeeze after another. Continue to run with Zero on the left and right.

More agility The weaves never stand alone in the middle of a course. It's time to practise them in combination with other pieces of agility equipment. Add a jump before the weaves. Does Zero still get his entry? Reward him with a jump after the

Above: *Put an obstacle like the tyre in front of the weaves to test the dog's entry.*

weaves if he wiggles through each and every pole.

Once you have re-taught and proofed your weave entries, Zero will be perfect first attempt.

Maverick Weaving

Q *I am training my rescue German Shepherd, Maverick, on V-weaves. I'm so pleased with the result. He picks up the entry really easily and has a good paddle action. The poles are almost at an upright, but not quite. Problem is, Mav loses it completely when he sees the poles are vertical!*

A There is nothing more spectacular than a big, muscular GSD paddling through the weaves! V-weaves are an adjustable channel of poles. The poles are fixed onto a base that allows the angle of the poles to be moved from nearly horizontal to the ground to completely vertical. You've come so far, but Maverick is losing it at the very last hurdle. Let's review.

1 Start with six poles and bend them alternately outward until they almost touch the ground on each side. The first pole is bent to the left so that Maverick will learn the correct entry. As a gentle introduction, walk Maverick on the lead down the middle of the poles. Now get someone to hold Maverick while you walk down the poles and call him through to you. Give him a treat or a game when he makes it through. When he is happily doing a recall, let him watch you place a toy or titbit about 1 metre (3ft) from the end of the channel. Send him away over the poles to collect his toy.

2 Raise the poles until they are about 25-30cm (10-12in) off the ground. Repeat the recall. And this time when you send Mav away to his toy or treat, run alongside on the right or the left. Continue to raise the poles in increments of about 5cm (2in).

3 When the poles are about 46cm (18in) off the ground, start Maverick off a little to one side of the entry to the poles instead of straight ahead. Practise angled entries from the left and right.

Instead of placing a toy, try throwing it ahead of Mav as he exits the poles.

4 When the poles are about 60cm (24in) off the ground, begin to combine the weaves with Maverick's favourite piece of agility equipment. Add a tunnel or a jump to the end of the weaves.

5 Continue raising the poles until they are vertical. Make sure that Maverick maintains speed and enthusiasm. Don't be afraid to lower the poles if you hit a problem. If Maverick slows down or ducks out of the poles, you have raised them too quickly. The last 15cm (6in) up to the true vertical will probably be the most difficult and this is where you are struggling. Don't rush. You may only be able to raise the poles in 1cm (0.4in) increments.

Remember that you can lower all or some of the poles if Mav looks confused. If he is having difficulty with the entry, raise the other poles but not the first two. All the poles will be vertical in the end, but it will take a little longer to get there with these poles.

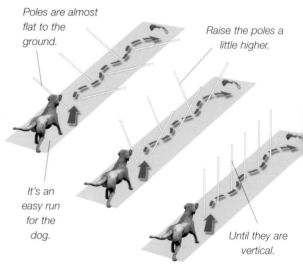

Poles are almost flat to the ground.

Raise the poles a little higher.

It's an easy run for the dog.

Until they are vertical.

The Last Pole

Q *Please can you tell me why my collie Kite always misses the last two poles? She usually shoots out and does the next obstacle before I can call her back. It never happens in training, but always at competitions which is really upsetting when the round has been faultless till then.*

A Take heart! Kite is making only one mistake instead of many for the judge to fault.

A question of time In class, you have all the time in the world but at a show you are trying to beat the clock. You push harder with your voice and your body. And out pops Kite. She is eager to get on and only too willing to miss the last two poles if it will help shave a few seconds off her time.

Voice If you are verbally encouraging Kite through the poles, listen to yourself. Are you repeating or holding onto one note that gets higher and more breathless as you approach the end of a line of weaves? Kite exits when you run out of air. In training, practise commanding Kite to "Weave" once and then say nothing.

Body language Make sure Kite has completed all the poles before you run on to the next obstacle. Stand still and upright. If you leave the weaves too quickly, so will Kite. And start training for independent weaves – recall, send away, left and right hand entries. When these exercises are solid, I would practise overrunning the weaves so that Kite will learn that even when her handler overtakes her, she must complete each and every pole.

Imaginary poles In order to help keep their voice normal and their body upright, some handlers visualize an extra pair of poles at the end of the weaves. Try this when you work Kite. It will stop you congratulating yourself for completing the poles too early.

Dogs can count If you only practise on six weave poles in training, Kite will be stupefied when she finds a set of 12 on the course. Teach your dog to weave right to the end no matter how many poles are in a line. Sometime six, sometimes ten and sometimes 12. If you want to be a contender for the Guinness Book of Records, you'll have to work your way up to 60!

Correction What do you do if Kite pops out of the weaves? If she is missing the last two poles because she is so driven to perform the next obstacle, you must stop her before she gets there. Not easy with a fast dog, I know. But if you mark the error with an "Oops" or "Wrong" the second she pops out, she will know where the mistake occurred. Call her back and guide her through the last two poles. Now she can reward herself with the next obstacle on the course. Soon that longed-for clear round won't be far away.

Where Mistakes Happen

Q *I'm fairly new to agility and will soon be entering my first show. Spud, my collie cross sheltie, is really good but sometimes makes a mistake in the weaves. I don't know how to correct him when this happens. Should I take him back and start all over again from the beginning or should I take him back to where he made the mistake?*

A Handler and dog can learn from mistakes provided they know where they made them. Think about the different kinds of mistakes that Spud makes in the weaves to determine a plan of action.

Random mistakes Is it impossible to predict where Spud will make a mistake? Sometimes he pops out in the middle, sometimes at the end, and sometimes he misses the entry? Spud's mistakes are random and it's not a case of correcting errors, but retraining the weaves. He doesn't understand what he is supposed to do when confronted by poles.

Last two poles Many dogs miss the last two poles because they are so eager to get on and complete the course. If this is where Spud is making mistakes, I would mark the error with an "Oops", call him back before he did any more obstacles and guide him through the last two poles. I would also do some remedial training to correct the problem. If you have clicker-trained Spud, click as he goes through the gap between the final poles to get a treat. And think about your body position. Don't be in such a hurry to move on to the next fence that you pull Spud out of the weaves.

In the middle If Spud is fast and excitable, he might be getting a hiccup in his weaving rhythm. Putting Spud back is problematic because it's difficult to tell exactly where he popped out. Moreover, it is unlikely that you would have been able to stop him carrying on after his error. When you can't mark exactly where the error occurred, go back to the beginning to start again and make sure that your dog does each and every pole.

Above: *A mistake in the poles can be difficult to spot, especially if your dog is a fast weaver.*

Metal feet Does Spud have twitchy toes? A dog with sensitive feet may be reluctant to step on the metal feet on the base and so may pop out of the weaves. An extra command at these points will encourage Spud to weave. Take out the poles and, as a separate exercise, work to accustom Spud to walking over and stepping on the metal base.

Motivation If Spud is a careful worker and only makes an occasional mistake, taking him back to redo a section of the weaves will demotivate him and erode his confidence. If the mistakes are one-offs, it will pay you to overlook them and do nothing.

But you must decide if it is a case of learning from a mistake or a case of needing to retrain the entire apparatus, or just a matter of going back a step.

Bending In The Poles

Q *My Whippet Parsley is really fast over the course until he hits the weaves. We have had some good places at shows, but they could have been higher if Parsley could speed up in the weaving poles. We lose so much time when we hit this obstacle. How can I get him to wiggle faster?*

A Whippets, Greyhounds and their crosses all seem to have trouble bending in the middle! Parsley already knows how to weave, so try this game.

Below: *Whippets are born to run, not bend in the middle.*

1 Set up four weaves in the garden.
2 Leave Parsley in a "Sit" at the start and walk to the end.
3 Recall him through the weave poles and give him a treat when he reaches you. Most dogs move faster towards their handler. Especially if their handler is smiling. But remember, Parsley must do all four weaves to get his reward.
4 Do this enough times so that Parsley is keen to break out of his sit and wiggle his way down the weave poles to you and his reward.
5 Sit Parsley in front of the weaves and move to the next stage. Recall him as before, but just as he reaches you, turn away from the poles and throw his treat so that he has to continue running past you to catch up with it. The game now has a chase dimension that many dogs find irresistible. Make sure your treat will be easy to find in the grass and is something that Parsley can eat quickly.

6 Continue at this stage until Parsley is exploding out of the last two poles.
7 Is Parsley ready for a new twist to the game? While he is bounding after his treat, you run to the opposite end of the poles. As soon as Parsley finishes eating his treat and looks up at you, recall him through the weaves again for another titbit.
8 You can do this back and forth as many times as you like as long as your dog remains enthusiastic. You will both end up tired, but fit.

The difficulty can be increased in three ways:

Distance The further you throw the treat, the more ground your dog will have to cover to get back to the poles and the greater his speed of approach will be. Parsley will be more likely to miss the entry.

Number of poles The more poles, the more likely your dog is to slow down. Make sure he is travelling through four with energy before adding any more.

Angled entries If you throw the treat off to the right or the left of the weaves, your dog will have to perform an angled entry to return to you through the poles for his treat. Only try this if your dog has a good weave entry straight on.

This game has not only turned my dogs into fast wigglers, but it's made the weave poles their favourite agility obstacle.

Speeding Up

Q *My young German Shepherd Flash is steady but slow. We have been competing in agility for a few months now and always get a clear round or lower placing. I've taught him to go on. I can send him into a tunnel or direct him over a fan of fences from five metres. But he is reluctant to move too far away from me at shows. How can I help him live up to his name and speed him up?*

A German Shepherds are versatile and enthusiastic workers and much valued as guard dogs. They are on the look out for danger, intruders and titbits forgotten in your pocket. It's important for a German Shepherd to know what is

Above: *German Shepherds love to work. Their boldness allows them to attack agility obstacles with confidence.*

going on around them in order to protect their mistress or master. The farther you are away from them, the harder you are to guard. This can make German Shepherds less willing than other breeds to work at a distance from their handlers in agility. There are a number of things you can try.

Confidence breeds speed You have a young dog with potential. As Flash grows more confident running agility courses, he will speed up. Give him time.

Independent worker Flash is able to perform distance work in training. Build on this and teach him to negotiate the contacts and weaves regardless of where you are on the course.

Run faster The tendency for many handlers is to hang back when they want a dog to work ahead. Yes, Flash will do it without you, but he would do it ten times faster with you by his side. Turn it into a race. That's much more exciting.

Experiment Does Flash speed up if you cheer or clap? Does he get excited if you run with little busy steps or long strides? Does he like you to be in his face all the time (front cross) or does he prefer you in the background (rear crosses)?

Don't whine Don't nag Flash to go faster. He'll know you are annoyed with him and slow down.

Encouragement Don't put Flash in the position where he could mistake encouragement to go faster as praise for going slowly. Be discerning.

Praise speed Make sure you are praising Flash for accelerating up a gear. Praise speed wherever you find it – when Flash is chasing a toy, running to you for a biscuit or simply having a case of the zoomies. Don't miss opportunities to let him know that it's not just a question of getting the job done, but getting it done fast.

Strengths If Flash likes working close to you, I suspect your turns are nice and tight. He will be less likely to miss body signals or commands. Off courses and eliminations will be fewer. Speed will come.

Speed is not everything, but attitude is. If Flash is enthusiastic and motivated, he will give you 100 per cent in training and at shows. Who can ask for more?

Tunnel Trouble

Q *My Brittany spaniel cross hates the collapsible tunnel. Beanie always pops out. I get all excited because he goes in and I rush to the other end to greet him only to find he's come out and is running up the side. Most dogs love the tunnel. Why doesn't Beanie?*

A Beanie loves you more than he loves the tunnel! When a dog goes into any kind of tunnel, he loses sight of his beloved handler. He figures that the quickest way out is to exit the way he went in. There are a number of things you can do to make sure you meet Beanie at the right exit.

Go back to basics Ask your instructor to hold Beanie at one end of the tunnel entrance while you go to the other end and hold up the chute. Bend down and when you have eye contact with Beanie, recall him through the tunnel. He needs to see your face at the other end, not your ankles. Praise and reward his efforts. Beanie gets treats and your reassurance at the tunnel exit – he'll want more of the same, so do it a few more times. Gradually allow the chute to lie flat. Beanie will no longer be able to see you and he will have to push through to get to you. It is worse for small dogs as it's such a long,

dark way to go, but if you progress slowly, Beanie will surprise you with his bravery.

Quick exit As above, but if Beanie likes to chase a ball, throw one as he comes out of the end of the chute. This will increase his speed and acceleration out of the tunnel. You don't want him to sit at the end of the tunnel anticipating a biscuit, but to drive on to the next obstacle.

Go it alone You won't always have your instructor handy to hold Beanie at the tunnel entrance. It's time to try running alongside the tunnel. Beanie will be keen to go through. Continue to throw a toy or treat at the end or send him over a fence. Practise running on the left and the right. If you make a bit of noise – clapping or cheering – Beanie will know that you are right outside, travelling the length of the tunnel with him.

Body language Make sure that when you send Beanie into the tunnel that you are pointing into it, not above it. You don't want him to jump it! But don't point with a treat in your hand or Beanie will stick with you rather than abandon his titbit. Your arm is not long enough to stretch from one end of the tunnel to the other.

Don't rush If Beanie thinks he can't catch you up, he will take a short cut around the tunnel rather than going through it. Make sure he is committed before you run by.

Left: *It's no good running around the course hoping your dog will take whatever obstacle is in front of him. He won't target the tunnel until he has learned to perform it confidently.*

Tunnel entries When Beanie is happy going straight in and through the tunnel, practise some angled entries. When you approach the tunnel from the side, it will look different to Beanie. He won't be able to see the entrance and baulk. Give him the opportunity to discover that the large dark entry hole is round the corner.

Tunnels are fun! Enjoy them and you'll have trouble keeping Beanie out of them, especially if it's dry inside and raining outside!

Body Language

Q *My instructor keeps telling me that my body language is ambiguous. Shouldn't my collie, Billy, just do what I tell him? He's very fast and I'm sure he doesn't have time to see what I'm doing with my arms.*

A You'd be surprised how well Billy can read your body language. When you get up off the settee, Billy knows if you are going to make a cup of tea, if you are going to fetch your coat for a walk or if you are going to switch off the television. Dogs are very good observers and they practise reading their owner's every move. It's their preferred channel of communication most of the time. Think of all the occasions that you may have shouted tyre and pointed at the tunnel (your dog did the tunnel) or yelled right and turned left (your dog turned left with you).

Expedient Many handlers with fast dogs just don't have time to spit out a long list of commands when they are running a course. Can you say "Billy left jump" before he has turned right and climbed the A-frame? These handlers act rather than speak. Especially those that don't know their left from their right. It's much simpler to use their dog's name combined with a body signal.

Body language You can cue Billy in a number of ways. You can make physical signs very obvious or very subtle to suit your dog and the course.

- Arms – an outstretched hand directs the dog to an obstacle.
- Face – your dog will look at whatever obstacle you are looking at.
- Shoulder roll – bring your arm across your body and roll your shoulder in and your dog will be pulled towards you.

- Feet – your dog runs in the same direction that your feet are moving.
- Movement – slow down or halt and your dog will slow down and stop. Change sides before your dog takes a fence and your dog will turn that way when he lands.
- Position – where you place yourself on the course will affect your dog's performance. Stand too close to the contacts and you might push your dog off them.

Above: *Can there be any doubt? The handler raises her arms in the air to call the dog up over, not down under, the jumps and straight to her.*

These are just a few examples, but they are enough to get you round a course. Body signals will help you traverse a box or snake down a line of fences. Don't think that because you are working Billy from behind that he will miss them. Dogs have great peripheral vision and he will pick them up and respond.

Experiment Try running a course without saying a word to Billy. Pretend you have laryngitis. It will make you work hard to sharpen your body language and make it meaningful. And, if Billy is the type of dog that barks his way round the course or gets very excited, keeping quiet will encourage him to focus on you and concentrate on your signals. Make sure those signals are clear and readable.

Some things like contact performance should be independent of body language, but as a means of directing your dog over the course, it's hard to beat the natural movement of your arms and legs.

Sending Ahead

Q *Silva sticks to me like glue. She is a Staffordshire Terrier and I always know where she is. The faster I run, the faster she runs. But I know she can run even faster. I would like her to work more independently and further away from me. How do I go about it?*

A Silva is a joy, but every now and again you wish she wasn't right at your feet? If you can't run any faster, you will have to teach Silva to work ahead of you.

Send aways Send aways are the foundations of distance work and are often overlooked. Handlers

Below: *Disappearing into a tunnel won't shake off this handler! She's doing all the chasing to try and catch up!*

practise recalls and working their dogs on the right and left. But send aways get left at the bottom of the barrel.

• Start at home. Sit Silva about 60cm (2ft) in front of her dinner bowl. Is she looking hungry? She'll be keen to get there so send her to it. After a couple of meal times, you can start commanding her with a "Go on" or "Away". Gradually increase the distance. Can she run from the living room into the kitchen to her bowl?

• Food bowls aren't just for meal times. You can use her food bowl as a target for send aways anywhere, anytime. Instead of putting her breakfast in it, use a single favourite treat. Send her to it from the top to the bottom of the garden or from one end of the drive to the other.

• Set up a line of three low jumps. Stand behind the last jump and send Silva over it to her bowl. Now stand behind the second jump and send her over two jumps to her bowl. If she goes on without any hesitation, try standing behind the first jump and sending her over all three. You can also throw a toy after the last jump but make sure she is committed to taking it before you chuck it. Be creative. You don't always have to use three jumps. What about trying jump, tunnel, jump? Your aim should be to get Silva to work the line of obstacles independently. It's you that varies your position.

Circles Stand in the middle of a circle of fences. Send Silva around to the left. You can make the circle bigger as she starts to flow and learns to work around you. Again, you can use different obstacles in your circle, but make sure they are things that Silva can execute competently. There is no point in putting weaves in the loop if she has a problem with her entry. Send her round from the right, too.

Lines and circles of obstacles will help Silva to work ahead with confidence. Initially, these exercises demand minimum movement from you. When you are competing, you will be running. So I would gradually introduce more movement when you have established some distance and Silva is driving away from you. She has to get used to you sending her ahead while you chase her from behind.

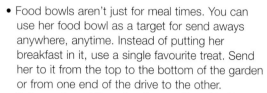

Changing Sides

Q *I have tried to tighten my Springer Spaniel's turns by doing front crosses. Yes, the turns are tighter, but Sassy ends up knocking the pole. Where am I going wrong?*

A Knocked poles are a sign of a badly timed manoeuvre or incorrectly positioned handler. Moreover, it indicates that the manoeuvre chosen was not necessarily the best one for the job. There are three types of crosses that enable a handler to change sides and turn his dog. Practise them so that you can execute all with equal comfort but, more importantly, learn to recognize which cross will be most effective in specific handling situations.

Above: *Agility is not all straight lines. The handler who can turn his dog tightly and keep the poles up will have a faster course time.*

Front cross A front cross is just what it says. The handler changes sides by crossing in front of his dog – dancing face to face. A front cross will focus a dog on the handler and cause it to decelerate in order to make a tighter turn. But you must ask yourself if the loss of speed will be worth any seconds gained. And you must make sure that you give your dog enough space to land and take off. Stand too close to the fence and you will be too much of a physical barrier – your dog will knock the pole.

Rear cross The handler crosses behind the dog and the dog's bottom is always in view. To be effective the dog must work in front confidently. The dog is focused on the equipment and speed will not be compromised. However, turns may be wide and control can be a problem if the dog is too far ahead, misses the cross and then picks his own route. And position and timing is everything. You need to cross on the dog's take-off side of the fence, not his landing side. And, if you cross before the dog commits to the fence, you risk pulling him off it.

Blind cross The handler crosses in front of his dog but instead of turning to face the dog, the handler changes sides with his back to the dog. As the dog finishes the turn, he is chasing his handler's bottom. Forward momentum is maintained. The dog must be comfortable with the handler ahead of him. If the handler is unable to get far enough ahead of his dog for the cross, he risks colliding with him when he tries to switch sides. Instead of allowing the dog to keep driving forward to the obstacles, everything comes to a halt while the First Aiders are called to the scene. Don't assume that a blind cross means that you don't have to turn your head to look where your dog is. The result can be an elimination or worse if you don't.

Decision time When you are deciding which cross to use, consider where you dog is coming from and where he is going to next on the course. Your handling of the first obstacle will have implications for the one that follows it. Also, think about the distance between the obstacles and the shortest path between them. Work not just the obstacles, but the spaces between them.

Select the right tool for the job. Practise all the crosses and use them where you think they will benefit you most on the course.

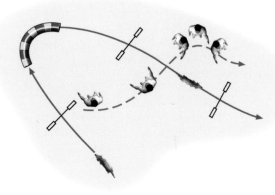

Above left: *The handler stays on the same side of the dog throughout. If he sends his dog into the tunnel from a distance, he hardly needs to move.*

Above: *This is a front cross. The handler sends the dog into the tunnel from his left side. He moves across the gap and faces the dog as he exits from the tunnel and collects him on his right side. Cut it too fine and he risks interfering with his dog's landing after the fence.*

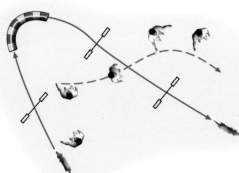

Above: *A blind cross. Sending the dog into the tunnel from his left, the handler turns his back on him during the cross and needs to look over his right shoulder to see the dog.*

Right: *A rear cross. Sending his dog into the tunnel, the handler waits for him to exit and jump the fence before crossing behind and collecting him on his right to send him on.*

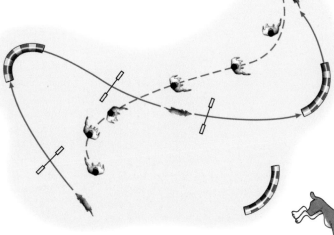

Dreaded Pull-Throughs

Q *Whenever I walk a course and see three fences in a line, my heart sinks – pull-throughs. When it comes to my turn, sure enough, instead of running through the gap, my sheepdog cross Winnie back-jumps the second fence. I'm eliminated. Do you have any tips?*

A Handlers usually miss pull-throughs on a course because they start with a negative attitude. Inwardly, they sigh "I can't do this" and it turns out that they're right! Don't avoid pull-throughs. Practise them in training. Make them fast and fun and you will find that your heart will be soaring when you next see them on a course. You'll want to shout. "I can do this!" And you will!

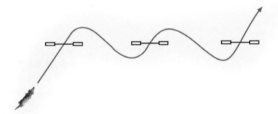

Above: *Pull-throughs are tricky if you don't practise them. Pretend your dog is a threaded needle and you are pulling him in and out of the material to make a hem.*

Above: *Ooops! It's all unravelling. If you don't give your dog a signal to run through the gap between the hurdle wings, he'll back-jump the second fence and you will be eliminated.*

Pull-throughs A judge can set a pull-through between two fences in a line or through the corner of a box. There are three parts to the manoeuvre. You begin by sending your dog away from you over the first fence. Next, you turn your dog back towards you so that he comes toward you between the wings of the first and second fence. Lastly, you turn your dog away from you to send him over the second fence. Done well, a pull-through looks effortless. Done badly and it looks like you are trying to turn your dog into a pretzel.

Threadle A threadle is a series of pull-throughs on a straight line of jumps. It's a bit like sewing. You thread your dog in and out and hope your cotton doesn't break!

Through the gap Your dog needs to decelerate and change direction quickly in order to pull off a pull-through. And you need to learn to give Winnie the commands she needs to target the gap as well as the space to run through it. Reasons for failure are many.

Commit to the gap Treat the gap between the wings just like you would a fence. Make sure that Winnie has committed to it before you move across to turn her back into the second fence. Hold your position. If you move too soon she will back-jump the second fence rather than running between the wings towards you. In competition, you will be tempted to move too soon and hurry her, but resist it! There are three ways to commit and bring Winnie through the gap.

Directional commands The earlier Winnie is warned that a pull-through is coming the better. She needs a clear signal that she needs to come through the gap. You can use your directional

Above: *If your body starts to turn, so will your dog. Twist from the waist, use your shoulders and keep moving. Try putting your hands together in the shape of an arrowhead!*

commands to turn Winnie towards you between the wings and then to turn her away from you over the second fence.

Body signals Send Winnie over the first fence with your nearest arm. Then pull your outside arm into your chest which will turn your leading shoulder away from the second fence – a dummy turn.

As Winnie comes through the gap, turn, face the second fence and point to it with your opposite arm.

Hand touch If Winnie knows a hand touch, reach through the gap with your hand. She should come between the wings to try and touch it.

You can work commands and signals in combination to reinforce each other. But even if you use magic spells and potions, Winnie will back-jump fence number two if you fail to hold your position and allow her to commit to the gap.

Tunnel Traps

Q *If there is a tunnel trap on the course you can bet money that Vadar my Petit Basset will succumb. I can shout and threaten, but in he goes into the wrong end regardless. My trainer says to use my body and keeps telling me to do a "dummy" turn. Is he calling me dumb?*

A In agility, a "dummy turn" is also known as a "false turn" or "reverse flow pivot". The handler pulls his dog in towards him with his outside arm. But the poor dog is fooled; he's not going that way. The handler completes the manoeuvre by turning away from his dog and pushing him out towards an obstacle with his opposite arm. To be successful, the dog must be good at reading his handler's body language.

Turn tighteners Dummy turns will tighten turns. They are well suited to threadles when the handler wants his dog to be both tight and fast. The dog is sent over the first jump with the nearest arm, then called between the wings of the first and second fence as the handler pulls his outside arm into his chest, turning his shoulder inward. The dog is then sent back over the second fence as the handler straightens up, turns, and points with his nearest arm.

Discrimination aids Dummy turns can also be used as discrimination aids when there are obstacle choices on the course. If you use a dummy turn, it will be easier for Vadar to pick the right tunnel entrance rather than the wrong one. Shouting will not be enough! A dummy turn will direct Vadar to the entrance closest to you. Without the dummy turn, Vadar will run into the entrance closest to him.

Timing As in all agility handling, timing is important. If Vadar sees the dummy turn too soon, he is in danger of being pulled off the obstacle and missing it altogether. If he sees it too late, he will already be committed to whatever lies in front of him. Rather than being pulled in, Vadar will just keep going and be eliminated.

Above: *Nasty judges count on tunnel-happy dogs being sucked into the wrong end of the obstacle on their courses.*

Position Dummy turns can be very bold or very subtle. The longer you hold still as you pull your dog into you, the more you will get out of your dummy turn. The louder it will scream to Vadar to turn towards you and away from other tempting obstacles. Hold your position for a mere split second and Vadar will be better able to maintain speed and forward momentum. It's up to you to decide what is needed in any given situation on the course.

Dummy turns are a valuable handling tool. Practise them so that you can do them in your sleep. Vadar will be on the look out for your signals. But don't be a dummy! Learn to recognize when dummy turns are the most appropriate handling manoeuvre to apply on the course, and when to give them a miss. And you won't be the class dummy!

Turning A Corner

Q *My boy Ockley is a large greyhound cross and I wonder if it's his size that makes it hard for him to tighten up his turns. He really drives down the straights but on the turns sweeps round in a wide arc. He looks as if he is about to come to a standstill. How can I help him?*

Above: *The handler performs a subtle dummy turn to call his dog over the middle fence in the snake. If he made the turn more pronounced, the dog would come through the gap as in a threadle.*

A It is always easier to run in a straight line than to turn the corner. Many agility handlers complain that their dogs slow down on the turns. And they are right.

- Dogs have to shift down a gear to negotiate a corner safely just like you do when you are driving a car. The trick is not to exchange safety for speed.
- Handlers have to wait for their dogs to turn corners. They perceive their dog as losing speed because they themselves are standing still.
- Dogs that dawdle on the turns fall prey to ringside distractions and actually slow down and widen their turns to get a better view of whatever has caught their eye.

Clear and consistent commands Does Ockley understand what you want him to do? If you variously shout, "Left!, "Back!" and "To me!", instead choose just one and he will respond more quickly.

Ever decreasing circles Set up a big circle of about six to eight fences. Run Ockley over these. Gradually remove fences and make your circle smaller and smaller until you have a tiny pinwheel of four fences with enough room for you to pivot in the middle. You must maintain your dog's enthusiasm throughout each decreasing circle while the turns get tighter and tighter. Repeat in the opposite direction.

Dummy turns The convention is to turn in the same direction as you want to turn your dog. By feinting a turn in the opposite direction, the turn sharpens. The dog is momentarily pulled towards you and then straightened up to continue on his way. This is called a dummy or false turn. Set up three jumps side by side and snake or threadle Ockley through them.

Front crosses If used correctly and at the right place on the course, a front cross will tighten Ockley's turns. Set up two jumps side by side. Send Ockley over fence one and recall him over fence two and redirect him back over fence one – a 360 degree circle. Don't get in his way or Ockley could refuse the jump or drop a pole. Make each front cross a little closer to the fences. How close can you get? Repeat in the opposite direction.

Above: *Long-striding dogs can find it difficult to turn tight to the fences.*

These exercises will help you. Use the appropriate tool to turn Ockley and he will tighten up. But remember that shortening the distance that your dog will have to travel to turn will not necessarily result in a faster time. Don't sacrifice speed for tightness. You may find your time is better when you allow your dog to flow between fences.

Chapter Five

COMPETITION CRAFT

Don't let the fear of elimination put you off strutting your stuff in front of the judge. Fill out an entry form. Make some sandwiches and pack the car for the journey. Did you remember to stow a folding chair? Step up to the start line knowing that you have done your best to train your dog for this moment but don't be surprised if it all goes wrong. Your own nerves may turn your dog into a canine delinquent and there's a lot to think about. What if a loose dog runs into the ring? Who spilt all those treats by the dog walk? Not you! And why are you the only person with a wolfhound in a queue of poodles and papillons? Instead of your friendly instructor, a judge is standing in the middle of the obstacles waving his arms at the competitors. What does it all mean? The best way to find out is by volunteering your help at the ring. It's a good way to make friends, and you'll get a T-shirt too.

Turning Into A Canine Delinquent

Q *I have a problem with Hudson, my Springer Spaniel. He's great in training but at shows he runs by jumps, loops past tunnels and, if we are competing outdoors, he takes off over the fields. It's no surprise when we are eliminated. My well-behaved Springer turns into a delinquent. It's like he's a different dog.*

A It's not Hudson that's changed but his surroundings. And Hudson is indeed a different dog when he lacks confidence or is confused. His training venue is familiar and welcoming. There is his smiling instructor and fellow students. There are lots of treats and toys in the ring and you are relaxed. In contrast, an agility show has many new smells and sights. There are queues of nervous and noisy competitors. There are no treats or toys in the ring. And you are stressed and anxious! No wonder Hudson acts like a different dog.

You are not alone Sit by the side of the ring at a show and watch. Yes, some dogs are born agility stars, but others looked completely untrained. They run up to the judge or do a lap of honour before heading for the hills. Just like Hudson.

Relax Competition is stressful. The more you dread going into the ring, the more likely your spaniel is going to find an excuse to leave.

Right: *De-stress yourself and your dog with a tug game. It may help you to forget your nerves.*

Have fun Don't aim for perfection. Ignore mistakes. Teach Hudson that the agility ring is not where he gets into trouble, but the best place in the world to have fun.

Togetherness Try to leave the ring together. If Hudson leaves the ring and you chase after him, he will think that you, too, have found a good reason to say good-bye to the judge.

Check-in Teach Hudson to check in with you at training. Stuff your pockets with treats or a portion of his dinner. Call him to you after the first obstacle, third obstacle, maybe the fourth and so on and give him a treat for giving you attention. He will acquire the habit of looking back to you – just in case you are going to ask him to check-in.

Different places, changing faces Give Hudson a chance to get used to different distractions. Train him in new locations and introduce him to new people. You should be the constant he can count on.

Thoroughness Make sure you have thoroughly taught the agility obstacles. If Hudson is a teeny bit unsure of how to make a seesaw tip in training, that flaw in his training may overwhelm him at a show. He would rather run by it than try and attempt to mount it. And your disappointment will just make it worse next time.

I believe that once the competition environment becomes familiar to him, Hudson will gain confidence and start enjoying himself (provided you, too, relax and have some fun). You don't want running out of the ring to become Hudson's way of coping with the unfamiliar or something stressful. Work now to show him what he'll be missing if he leaves the agility party early.

Are You Ready?

Q *I have been training Buddy in agility for about a year and I think the time has come to take the plunge and enter a show. My trainer says to wait a bit. How do you know when your dog is ready to compete?*

A I will never forget my first agility show! I didn't win anything, but I was so proud of how I handled myself and my dog on the courses. Your first time in the ring with Buddy will be a lasting memory. Make sure it is a good one.

Is your dog prepared?

Assess your dog's performance in class honestly. Buddy must be able to tackle all the agility obstacles and string them together on a course. Competition introduces new variables into the agility equation – different equipment, a strange venue, and a nervous handler. Don't be hasty to fill in your entry form.

- Proof your performance. Try running a course at a higher level than you will enter at a show. Can Buddy cope with increased difficulty? If he sails over the finish line with no faults and a fast time, you have nothing to worry about. If he struggles, it's back to the drawing board.
- Introduce Buddy to some of the things he will meet at his first show. Get a friend to stand in the middle of the ring as a judge and find someone else to stand at the side eating ice cream. Is Buddy still focused on his agility?
- Take advantage of practice rings and progress tests. Put your name down for interclub matches. Look out for simulated shows. These are the

Left: *Before you enter your dog for competition, prepare yourself by visiting an agility show as a spectator.*

closest you can get to the real thing and you can still correct Buddy if he goes wrong.

Are you prepared? Even the most seasoned agility handler will get nervous at a show. You and Buddy are a team and your dog will pick up on any negative thoughts racing through your mind as you stand on the start line. Can you cope with the extra pressure of competition?

- Offer to help at a show. It's a good way to learn the ropes and meet fellow competitors. You'll get an idea of what to expect when it's your turn to strut your stuff in the ring.
- Practise running different courses. There are an infinite number of equipment combinations and you should know where to go without reading the numbers on the jumps. Work the spaces between the obstacles.
- Learn to think positively. If you stand in the queue wishing you had done more contact training, your dog will sense your doubts.

You can do Buddy more harm than good if you put him in the ring too early. If you have not adequately prepared yourself and your dog to meet the challenges set by the judge, you will leave your first show disappointed and frustrated. Buddy will wonder how he has let you down and the agility game won't be much fun anymore.

What To Take?

Q *I have entered my kelpie, Kez, in his first agility show next month. I'm not expecting too much from Kez as we haven't been training for very long. But I want to have a good day out even if we don't take home a rosette. What should I take with me besides Kez.*

A The more self-sufficient you are the better! Agility shows are held anywhere there is enough space for rings – playing fields, leisure parks, equestrian centres or country houses. The amenities will vary so be prepared.

The dog Take everything with you that you would take to class – lead, treats, toys, water and a bowl. Check that everything is in your training bag – clicker and targets and diary. You'll need a stash of poo bags. And, if you don't know what time you will be getting home, pack a meal for him too.

Important documents These include the show schedule, running orders, directions to the venue and your Kennel Club Record Book.

Catering There may be a posh restaurant, a tea room or only an ice cream van. So, rather than finding yourself with no lunch, pack a few sandwiches and fill a flask. Don't be stingy. Shove in some cakes and biscuits to eat on the way home. You might be stuck in traffic and need something on which to snack.

Toilets There are never enough of them and they always run out of soap and toilet paper. Pack tissues and stock up on hand-wipes to clean your fingers.

Weather The weather may well be unpredictable. You can get goose bumps, sunburned and soaked all on the same day. Pack an umbrella, hat and gloves. Add waterproofs and sun screen. Along

with a spare set of clothes for you, don't forget Kez. Have you dog towels, his reflective coat and a cage fan with spare batteries?

Shoes Don't leave your running shoes at home. And if you have a favourite pair of socks to wear with them, they'll not do you any good at home in your bedroom drawer.

Time Most of us kill time between runs chatting with friends. Some knit. Why don't you take the opportunity to fill in your training diary – don't forget to bring it!

Money Don't leave your purse at home or you won't be able to buy anything at the stalls. How can you resist the giant tennis balls? But will you have room for them in your car to take them home?

Chair No one likes to be on their feet all day. Pack a folding chair and kennel so you and Kez can sit by the ring in comfort and cheer your friends when they run.

Agility equipment Can you fit a few practice jumps in your car? You'd be surprised what you can squeeze in with a little determination.

Start with the bare necessities for your first agility show. You'll find the list of essentials will grow the more shows you enter!

Stand To Be Measured

Q *I have been told that my dog has to be measured before he competes. Is this true? Gnat is a little Chihuahua cross and I think he will freak out if someone tries to measure him. It's so obvious that he is small!*

A All dogs competing under Kennel Club rules and regulations in the UK must be measured before their first show. Even if Gnat was the size of an elephant, he needs to have an official measurement noted in his Kennel Club Record Book. It is the same for all dogs whatever their size.

Height is not always clear cut, especially if a dog is borderline. How would you feel if Gnat was fluffy and looked larger than he really is? If size is questioned, the competitor has his record book as proof that he is entered in the correct class.

Measuring also ensures that dogs always jump in the same height category over the same height fences. Once upon a time, a medium dog could compete as "midi" one day and as a "standard" the next. And, there was nothing stopping a "mini" dog competing as a "standard".

Sizes Gnat will not be measured for a specific height but for inclusion in a specific height category.
• Large Dogs – over 430mm
  (1ft 5in) at the withers.
• Medium Dogs – over 350mm
  (1ft 1.75in) and measuring
  430mm (1ft 5in) or under at
  the withers.
• Small Dogs – 350mm (1ft
  1.75in) or under at the
  withers.

Measuring There are two measures shaped like croquet hoops with feet at the bottom – a small and a medium size. The hoop is positioned above the highest point of the dog's withers. If the feet of the hoop do not touch the floor, the dog is too big for that height category. There are a number of things that you can do to prepare Gnat for his first measuring session.

Table Gnat can have his first measurement at 15 months but you can start getting him ready when he is a puppy. Teach Gnat to stand squarely and quietly on the table. It is much easier to measure a dog that is still than one that is a wiggly worm. You can click and treat him for a good stand. He should have all four paws on the ground and be neither stretched out or scrunched up. Gnat's head should be in a natural position, not tucked between his legs.

Gentle introduction If Gnat has never been measured before, he might think the person passing the hoop over his back is trying to staple him to the floor. However, if you have practised with your own hoop at home and have asked your friends and family to do it too, Gnat will recognize a familiar procedure. He won't be frightened.

All you have to do now is buy a Kennel Club Record Book, fill in the details and find a measuring session. Unless Gnat is crossed with a Bernese Mountain Dog, you shouldn't be in for any nasty surprises!

The withers are the highest point above the shoulders, behind the dog's neck.

Large

Medium

Small

A dog must be standing upright with the head held naturally when measured.

Volunteering To Help

Q *I want to put something back into agility and have put my name down to help at my next show. What sort of things will they ask me to do? They won't ask me to judge, will they? I've only ever been to two shows before!*

A They won't ask you to judge, but they might give you a packed lunch or a T-shirt as thanks for helping! Without volunteers like yourself, many shows would come to a standstill. There are a number of jobs that need to be done around a ring and many hands make light work. Here are some examples:

Pole pickers/Tunnel straighteners
This is a great job because you can watch each dog run. Volunteers are placed around the edge of a ring. If a pole falls, you pick it up. If the collapsible tunnel twists, you straighten it up. Moreover, you need to keep an eye on any equipment that is pegged down. It might become loose and need to be hammered back into place.

Callers My favourite. The caller controls the length of the queue into the ring. Calling up to one hundred and ten! As the handlers book in to run, you can wish them luck and put faces to the names on your list.

Scrimers The scrimer keeps one eye on the judge who signals faults. It is quite a responsible job and many judges like to nominate their own scrimer who is accustomed to working with them and familiar with their signalling system. The scrimer keeps the other eye on the timing equipment and notes this with the score. And, in case you are wondering, "scrimer" is a new word that describes a person who is part scribe and part timer.

Lead runners Not a job for you if you have bad knees as there may be quite a lot of walking involved. You will be in charge of collecting the competitor's lead from the start and placing it at the finish.

Pad runners Pad runners check the information on the score sheet before the competitor goes into the ring. Is it the right handler's name, dog's name and so on? No one wants their score to be recorded on the wrong pad, especially if they go clear. The score pads are then given to the scrimer who will note the judge's marks. Then the runner will collect it and take it to the score tent. Often this job is done by two people.

Scorers Not for you if you have forgotten your glasses or hate maths. You will be asked to record the results as they come in – time faults, eliminations, clears. You're guaranteed a chair and table and, best of all, shelter. Scorers usually have their own tent.

Ring managers The ring manager is usually appointed well in advance. He deploys the volunteers and makes sure all the jobs are done. If there aren't enough helpers, the ring manager does them himself!

Movers and shakers Everyone in the ring party will help to set up a new course or break up the equipment at the end of the day. Not for anyone who has recently had surgery for a hernia as it can be heavy work.

I hope you enjoy your day helping on a ring. I'm sure your ring manager will look after you. He'll probably want you to come back next year and help!

Judging Signals

Q *I took my daughter and her Cocker Spaniel, Tootsie, to their first show. I had a lovely time watching the dogs run and I was fascinated by the judge who appeared to be working very hard running around the ring and flapping his hands. What was he doing?*

A It's great that you were there to support your daughter and Tootsie at their first show. I'm sure they did you proud.

Keeping an eye on the dog An agility judge does have to work hard. He must not take his eyes off the dog that is competing in the ring. How active the judge is depends on the type of class, the design of his course and the judge. He needs to have a clear view of each piece of equipment and may have to move around a lot to see or he may be able to clock everything that happens from one spot. Also, he mustn't get in the competitor's way. Not always easy if the dog is very fast or the handler's manoeuvre is unexpected.

Signals If a dog is making a lot of mistakes, the judge's arms will spin like windmills as he raises one arm for a knocked fence and the other arm for a run-by. Yes, sometimes the judge looks as if he is bringing in a plane for landing rather than marking faults. Judging signals are pretty universal. Faults are in units of five.

Left: *The judge is signalling five faults for a knocked pole, not waving hello to the competitor.*

- Raised hand with open palm – one fault (for example, knocked fence, missed contact, popping out of the weaves).
- Raised hand with closed fist – refusal.
- Touching one hand on the other – handler touching the dog.
- Drawing a hand across the throat or crossing the arms over the chest – elimination
- Head nod – indicates to scribe that the judge is ready to start marking the next competitor.

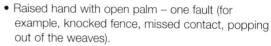

The judge will brief his scrimer on his signals before the competition begins. Some judges have embellished existing signals or added their own creations. When I judge, I have a signal to indicate to my scrimer that I need a break and to ask the ring manager not to take any more dogs in the queue. That way I get five minutes to visit the Ladies' loos!

Scribe's signals You might see the scrimer signalling to the judge. If she raises her hand with three fingers up, the competitor has had three refusals and the judge needs to eliminate the dog. It's easy to forget how many times you have put your hand in the air if a dog and handler are struggling on your course.

It is always a good game if you are sitting outside the ring to try and mark each dog along with the judge. Would you have put your arm up for a refusal at that fence? Would you have marked the dog walk contact as missed? And what would you have done when the dog pirouetted on the seesaw before dismounting? It's a good way to learn how to judge and it can make you a better agility competitor.

Walking The Course

Q *I haven't entered a show yet, but I went to one with my friend and watched the handlers walking the course without their dogs. Some were gesturing and running around while others stood around talking. What were they all up to?*

A Time is set aside before each competition class starts to walk the course set by the judge. It can be anything from 15 minutes to the whole lunch hour. During that time, competitors must learn the route and plan their handling strategies. Once the class has started, they won't be allowed back into the ring unless it is their turn to run. And that might be some time. It is not unusual to walk a course at eight in the morning and run it at four in the afternoon.

Planning The people you saw on the course were not only learning the order of the obstacles but they were practising their runs without their dogs. They

Above: *When the course is being walked, it's best to catch up with your friends later outside the ring rather than in it.*

were trying out different body signals and positions and they may well have been muttering commands under their breath, too. It does look silly without a dog, but it is an effective way to remember where you are going and what you are supposed to do when you get there. And they will be walking it several times, not only to memorize it, but to come up with an emergency plan if things don't go as expected.

A social occasion The other people you saw on the course were just chatting. Agility people come from all corners of the country and it's great to meet up with old friends. It's inevitable that when you are walking the course you bump into old friends and stop to catch up on the latest news – who has a new puppy or who's had a baby. Traffic jams result and usually occur at the trickiest point of the course where another group of competitors have stopped to talk about handling strategies!

The crowd There can be hundreds of competitors walking a course all at once. Often you can't see the obstacles for the bodies. And it's made worse by competitors who push prams round the course as they walk it. Cunning competitors wait until the crowds have died down a bit. There won't be as much time on the course before the class starts, but at least they'll avoid other people's elbows and be able to see where they're going. They will be lingering when the ring manager bellows "Clear the course please!" so that judging can begin.

No dogs or food Competitors must leave their dogs behind when they walk the course. It's crowded enough as it is. And I hope you didn't see anyone eating their breakfast as they walked the course. Think of all the crumbs they would leave behind.

I love watching competitors walk a course – swaying and swirling and peeling off into groups here and there. If I have time to watch the class later in the day, I like to see if these handlers run the course exactly as they have walked it!

Disputing The Judge

Q *I came out the ring last week ecstatic. What a round! I came back to earth when I checked the score sheet and learned from my friends that I had been given five faults for missing the A-frame contact. My wife has the round on video and you can clearly see Timmy's paw on the contact. What should I do?*

Above: *Photographic evidence may clearly show that your dog hit the contact with a paw, but it's what the judge sees on the day that gets marked on your score sheet.*

A There is nothing you can do about this round. The judge can only mark what he sees at the time. On the day, a judge will have hundreds of dogs to work through and it's unlikely

he will remember you even an hour or so after your run. He certainly won't thank you if you try and stop his ring to talk to him. And, once he has hung up his judging hat, he'll want to concentrate on his own dogs. My advice would be to think of your next round. Teach Timmy the type of contact performance that will leave no room for doubt. Then, whether Timmy actually hit the bottom of the A-frame or not will not be up for discussion.

A match? What you see will not necessarily be the same as what the judge sees. Remember that you are working your dog against the clock, but the judge has all the time in the world to watch you perform. In addition, you may be right on top of your dog whereas the judge may be standing on the other side of the ring. Your perspectives are bound to be different and that can be reflected in the marks you receive.

Coming out ahead So this time you got five faults, but you may not next time. If you saw on your video that Timmy had missed the contact but had not been marked, would you have complained to the judge? It works both ways.

But, but, but ... Contact marking can be controversial but a pole is either up or knocked down. Nevertheless, if the judge didn't see it, he won't mark it. He is not going to change the score sheet on a spectator's say so. He won't be smiling if you march into the middle of his ring, halt the class and start arguing the toss. And neither will the competitors waiting their turn in the queue.

Decision The judge's decision is final. Your judge will do the best he can to mark accurately and fairly. If he is unsure, he will give you and your dog the benefit of the doubt and not mark you. But he is human.

I'm sure that Timmy's round was not a fluke. You did it once so you can do it again. Forget about what happened last week and concentrate on preparing for next time.

Running Surfaces

Q *I know that my Hungarian Vizsla Gladys is going to encounter all sorts of new sights and sounds at shows. It has just occurred to me that the flooring will be different too! What should I expect to find under foot?*

A A soft landing can make a big difference to the health and performance a dog. Ring surface is yet another variable that needs to be taken into account when walking the judge's course. The transition from one kind of flooring to another is not always easy as both dog and handler will have to make adjustments to work the surface. This is why handlers who are accustomed to working on grass and have qualified to compete at Crufts include carpet work in their pre-event training programme. Here are some of the surfaces that Gladys's feet will meet.

Above: *Long grass and flowers are perfect for studying the birds and bees but not so good for agility class.*

Grass field Nothing like it on a dry, sunny day. Unfortunately, the weather can be capricious and a nice patch of green can turn into a mud pool in a matter of seconds. Playing fields are carefully manicured and the ground is flat. But if the rings are located on Farmer Jones's farm, you'll find long grass and a few molehills. Pity the small dog handlers who lose sight of their mini dogs and make sure that you steer Gladys clear of the sheep droppings.

Mats, carpets and astro-turf These are usually laid over concrete or wooden floors. Thickness varies – sometimes the coverings are very cushioned and sometimes very thin. Be aware that carpet can be slippery and dogs might spend more time on their bottoms than on their feet. By contrast, astro-turf can provide a good grip, so much so that some handlers complain that it gives their dogs too much traction and takes the skin off their pads.

Dirt arena Horse arenas can be covered in anything from a clay and sand mixture to common garden soil. They may have a top dressing of shredded rubber or a filler of ground wood chips. Some dogs react to walking over a top dressing as if they are walking over broken glass. The bits get stuck between their toes and they hate it. A good surface should be moist enough so that it doesn't get dusty and it should be raked and turned so that it does not become packed. Arenas that are well maintained are a pleasure. But beware if you run behind Gladys. You could get a cloud of sand kicked in your eyes. Also, if Gladys is a particularly light-coloured dog, she could finish an evening's training the same colour as the floor.

Whatever surface you encounter, make sure that you choose the right shoes and handling strategy. For example, if Gladys is a big, fast dog that is likely to slide on carpet, don't rush her through her turns. Hold your position a little longer to make sure she has her balance and footing before moving onto the next obstacle. The more shows you attend, the more experience you and Gladys will gain of working different surfaces. It always pays to look beneath your feet.

A Pocketful Of Treats!

Q *My Cairn Terrier, Elsa, would never come back to me at the end of a round in class so I have started to carry a few treats in my pocket to give to her. She nibbles them while I attach her lead. This works, but will I be able to continue doing this at a show?*

A The Kennel Club rules and regulations say that food should not be carried in the competitor's hand or be fed to their dog while it is in the ring. It says nothing about food being in pockets or being given to the dog when it is outside the ring.

Pockets Whenever I unload the washing machine and fold the laundry, I find cleansed and sanitized dog treats in the linings of my jackets and trouser pockets. It's a fact of life for dog owners. I dare say many handlers unwittingly compete with bits of biscuit stuck in their seams. Or simply forget that they are there nestled amongst poo bags and tissues in pockets.

Body search Competing in agility is not like going through security at an airport. The caller is not going to give you a body search when you join the queue. But he might query you if you reek of garlic sausage, you squeak with each step or your pockets bulge unnaturally.

Litter bug Think how embarrassing it would be to bend over Elsa at the bottom of the contact and see all of her treats tumble out of your breast pocket. The queue would curse you. Their own food-orientated dogs would make a beeline to the contact instead of jumping the first fence. It's not a good idea to rely on zippers, snaps or buttons!

Alternative plan To avoid embarrassment and eliminations, leave your treats in a pot outside the ring with your bum bag or jacket. Or ask a friend to hold it for you. As soon as you finish your round you can leave the ring and go to the treat pot. Elsa won't be far behind you. But do be careful. If the treat pot is in plain sight, another dog in the queue might get there first or Elsa might leave the course to find it before she has finished running it.

Keep rewarding Elsa with a titbit in training. You may find that by the time you enter your first show that Elsa returns to you each and every time you call her whether she gets a treat or not.

It is so obvious to the dog. I sit. You treat.

Left: *There is an unwritten contract between handler and dog that if the dog works hard, he gets a treat. Build anticipation and your dog will be able to wait for his pay off at the end of the round.*

Multi-Dog Handling

Q *I have two dogs. A small Jack Russell called George and large Labrador Retriever called Gwennie. They both compete in agility in different classes – one is a novice and the other is a senior. Sometimes I feel like a headless chicken running from one ring to another. Is there a trick or two that would help me manage the situation better?*

Above: *Even if your dogs are best friends, they will almost certainly need different handling strategies depending on their size and ring experience.*

A You have doubled your work load, not to mention the amount of dog hair on the settee. You have two classes to walk, two courses to remember and two different handling strategies to apply. How to simplify?

Parking Park as near to the rings as you can. That reduces the amount of walking you'll have to do back and forth, fetching George from your vehicle, putting George back in your vehicle and then starting all over again with Gwennie.

Friends They can be roped into saving places in the queue for you at one ring while you walk the course in another. But don't abuse them. They'll probably have their own dogs to run too!

Every dog has its day Look out for shows that cater only for small or novice dogs. Enter those and George will receive all your fuss and treats that day.

Right: *Some shows restrict entry to a specific height category. If you enter your Jack Russell at a Small/Medium Show, your large retriever will have to have a day off.*

Look for shows that accept only large novice plus dogs on another day. Fill in your entry form and you can focus all your attention on Gwennie. If you do this, you will never warm up George and take him to the ring only to discover that you are trying to book into Gwennie's class. Didn't the size of the dogs in the queue give it away?

Consistency Aim for consistency with both your Jack and your Lab. Don't use different commands for each dog. If you say "target" for George's contact, but "touch" for Gwennie's, you'll find yourself at the bottom of the A-frame tongue-tied and saying neither. If an independent weave performance is your aim with your Lab, it should be your aim with your terrier too. Make sure both dogs are familiar with all your available handling skills. If you go on autopilot and suddenly whip out a blind turn, Gwennie will oblige since you've been practising with her. But George will put his paws in the air in horror – he's never seen you do that before.

Multi dogs Some handlers are really good at running lots of dogs. They switch effortlessly from one dog to another with relish. They never forget the course they walked five hours ago, even though they have already run three bafflingly similar ones earlier that day. You'll find out that the more you do, the easier it will become and the better you will be at it. It comes with practice. Really!

Are you considering getting a third dog – a medium-sized one? Then you'd be a real all-rounder!

A Friend In Need!

Q *Help! My best friend Cathy has broken her leg and has asked me to run her Cocker Spaniel, Murray, while her leg is in plaster. I already have a Cocker, Twister, that I compete with so I'm hoping running one more won't make too much difference. Any tips?*

A I'm sorry to hear that Cathy has hurt herself. She must have a great deal of faith in your handling abilities to entrust Murray to you and I know you'll do your best not to let her down.

Will he? Some dogs love agility so much that they will run for anyone. They really don't care who is shouting directions as long as they are allowed to have fun. They are happy to pass on the buzz they get from agility to any lucky handler holding their lead.

Won't he? Some dogs won't run for anyone else for love, money or frankfurter. They are real Mummy's boys. For them, agility is something special and they only do it with the person they love and trust the most. If Murray doesn't want to run with you, don't take it personally. You don't live with him and it is Cathy, not you, who has fed, walked and cuddled him since puppyhood. Decide if it is worthwhile working through this or if it is better just to wait till Cathy's cast comes off.

Training I hope that you are not just going to run Murray at competitions. If you attend training classes together it will help you bond and give you better results at shows. You'll learn a lot about his personality and will be able to build a working relationship with him. Don't assume that just because he is the same breed as Twister that he has the same strengths and weaknesses. And he will learn a lot about you too. In addition, if he does run back to Cathy, it's better that you find out here and not at your first show.

Communicate Although Cathy is going to sit on the sidelines, she needs to be involved in Murray's training. Don't introduce new commands or attempt different contact strategies without consultation. When Cathy is back on her feet, she needs to be able to pick up where you left off so discuss with her how you are going to handle problems on the course. You could learn a lot from one another.

Stay friends Decide in advance who sends in show entries, who keeps the rosettes and who pays for training. Disagreements can escalate and you don't want your friendship to suffer on points of technicality. Don't blame any of Murray's errors on the course on Cathy's training and she won't blame your handling for Murray's eliminations.

Above: *How will your friend feel if your trainer says that her dog runs better for you than he does for her?*

Loose Dog In The Ring

Q *My cross breed, Yettie, is a real babe magnet. I don't know why other dogs find him so attractive but they flirt with him in the queue and, once at training, a dog that really loves him ran into the ring while he was working. What should I do if this happens at a show?*

A Just keep working Yettie unless the judge asks you to stop.

Distractions Yettie should be so focused on you and his agility that he doesn't notice any canine interlopers in the ring. Dogs visiting are viewed in the same way as cigarette packs that blow across the ground in front of jumps – just another distraction to be ignored. And I know that's unfair. But it is also unfair when half the competitors run their dogs in the sun in the morning and the other half have to run in the rain in the afternoon. As a rule of thumb, keep working your dog unless the judge tells you to stop because he'll keep marking you.

Calling a halt Yettie's visitor in the ring might follow Yettie as he makes his way round the course or she might settle down by the tunnel to adore her hero. Yettie might not even be aware that he has a visitor. However, the judge will call a halt if he thinks that the interloper is going to actively interfere, impede your dog or pose a potential danger. For example, if the other dog takes up residence in front of the weaves, you haven't a chance of making the entry. Or if the visiting dog is raising her lips and her fur is standing straight up on her back, it's not love but a fight in the offing. Someone will collect the loose dog and you will probably be awarded a re-run.

Above: *I know I'm irresistible, but I'm meant to be jumping fences not kissing you. Get to the back of the queue!*

Your call You know your dog best. If Yettie is a shy dog, easily frightened and lacking in confidence, you might decide to quit the course before the judge calls a halt. You might decide that it's not worth risking Yettie colliding with the other dog or getting involved in a fight. It's your call, but you will be eliminated for leaving the ring and not finishing the course. No re-run will be offered but you know that there will always be another show tomorrow.

Loose dogs The only time a dog should be off-lead at an agility show is when he is in the exercise area or working in a ring. But accidents do happen. It is not uncommon for a handler's second dog to escape and join him with his first dog – at least he knows they will get along but it is so embarrassing! Yettie shouldn't be bothered by a loose dog, but if he is, the owner will be terribly apologetic and will take steps to make sure it doesn't happen again.

Staying On Your Feet

Q *I'm a bit of a clumsy type and always tripping over my big feet or running into pieces of agility kit. What happens if I fall over in the ring when I compete? Will I be marked if I knock the pole instead of my Jack Russell, Spud?*

A Oh dear! You need to watch where you are going. Keeping one eye on Spud, the other eye other on the course and standing up at the same time is not always easy.

Falling over You will not be marked for falling over, but it will cost you time on the course. Unless you have hurt yourself, get up as quickly as you can and keep going. Spud may come over to investigate your prostrate body out of curiosity or concern. On the other hand, Spud may take no notice of you writhing on the ground in agony and he'll keep driving forward over fences. If so, you'll have no trouble picking up where you left off. It depends on the type of dog.

Shoes Make sure that you are wearing the best running shoe for the ground and weather conditions. If you step into the ring in a pair of Wellington boots, I'm not surprised to hear that you sometimes end up on your bottom.

Knocking over the equipment You will be penalized for caressing, hitting or beating the equipment. Don't touch it! It doesn't matter if it is an intentional or an accidental touch. If a pole hits the ground, it's still five faults regardless of whether you or Spud knocked it out of its cups.

Handling When you walk the course, look at the equipment and the surrounding space. Are you too big to fit through a narrow gap? Will you be dangerously close to fence ten if you do a reverse turn after fence nine? If you step back after fence eight, will your foot hit the tunnel behind you? If you do a pivot turn after the A-frame, will you become dizzy and collapse in a heap on the ground? These are valid handling considerations. Take them into account when you plan your route.

Everyone falls over at some time – some more gracefully than others. And everyone has been in the middle of at least one winning round until they knocked over the wing of the last fence. Happily, there is always the next time to get it right!

Left: *Avoid reaching across the agility equipment. If you lose your balance and accidentally touch it, the judge will mark you down!*

Contact Failure

Q *My poodle Travis loves agility. At training, he is fantastic and never makes a mistake. But the minute he puts a foot into the ring he steps up a gear and forgets everything I've ever taught him, especially the contacts. I invested a lot of time teaching these and Trav is usually really reliable. Maybe he's a jumping-only dog? Why doesn't he do his contacts?*

A The ultimate test of any training is competition. You will never get the same rush of adrenalin at your local agility club as you will standing under starter's orders at a show. When you are running under the watchful eye of a judge, nerves usually combine with anxiety to produce a performance that isn't as good as it is when you are being assessed by your instructor. Contacts are a prime example of good training that flies out the window the minute there is a possibility of a rosette. Consider the following points:

Was Trav's contact performance trained as static exercises? It's easy to hit the contact when nothing follows it, but there can be up to 20 obstacles on an agility course. Dogs pick up speed and excitement as they travel from start to finish. Their striding as well as their entries and exits on equipment is bound to be less exact, sometimes non-existent. Start practising your contacts in sequences of equipment.

Perhaps Travis has not generalized his contact training? The dog doesn't understand that he is expected to tackle the A-frame at a show in exactly the same way as he tackles the A-frame at his local agility ground. The A-frame may be in a different part of the country, painted a different colour and embedded in a different sequence of obstacles, but it is still an A-frame. Help him to learn that an A-frame is still an A-frame by taking him to different venues and by always maintaining your performance criteria. Be confident in your chosen training method and remember to apply it. Don't rely on luck.

Do you get nervous and lose confidence in yourself? Nerves can make a handler forget his own protocols. Do you plan to pause at the foot of the contact, but keep running? Do you always say "On it" in training but shout "Stop" at the show? Does your voice sound pleading instead of commanding? No wonder Travis jumps off the contact.

You need to develop your training programme to include competition work. Your dog is not the only one that forgets everything when stepping up a gear at a show. In addition to learning the judge's course, you need to master your own nerves. Give Travis 100 per cent wherever and whenever you work him. Be consistent and Trav will know what you expect and produce the goods. If you don't accept one toenail on the contact in training, don't be tempted to accept it in competition.

Above: *All four feet in the contact zone. Any handler would be pleased with this performance in training. The next challenge is to get the same result in the adrenalin-charged atmosphere of a show.*

Catch A Falling Dog

Q *My terrier cross Daisy fell off the seesaw sideways at a show the other day. She caught sight of a bird overhead and was looking at that instead of where she was putting her feet. It frightened her a bit when she fell off so I took her to the front of the seesaw and did it again with lots of praise and encouragement. I finished the course but was so surprised to learn that I had been eliminated. But she fell off! How can this be?*

Left: *A confident seesaw performance is the result of careful training. If your dog has a fright on this obstacle, you will have to work hard to convince him that the seesaw is great fun and not an instrument of torture.*

A I think you were right to reassure Daisy and repeat the obstacle despite being eliminated for doing so. You have to learn to live with the judge's call.

Seesaw marking The seesaw is divided in two equal halves at its pivot point. If a dog jumps, falls or slides off the seesaw after passing the pivot point that dog will be faulted for missing the contact on the down side. If the seesaw is not touching the ground before the dog dismounts, that dog will be faulted for exiting too early. And further, if the dog jumps, falls or slides off the seesaw before reaching the pivot point that dog will be marked with a refusal. The dog will have to try the seesaw again and

complete it correctly before moving on to the next obstacle. If he doesn't or refuses twice more, the dog will be eliminated.

Performance The judge is only interested in marking performance. He is not interested in the whys or wherefores of your dog's behaviour. On the other hand, you are. It is your responsibility to make sure that Daisy executes each obstacle competently and happily. If she is worried or fearful, do something about it.

Elimination I didn't see your run but I think Daisy probably fell off the seesaw after she had gone past the pivot point but before the contact in which case you would have been faulted. Even if a flying saucer had flown by, the judge's mark would be the same. Having completed the seesaw, albeit badly, the expectation would be to proceed to the next obstacle. When you repeated the seesaw, you were eliminated for taking the wrong course (doing seesaw and then the seesaw again instead of seesaw and then jump).

Thinking forward So, you may have been eliminated on the course but you took steps to ensure that Daisy won't spook next time she gets on the seesaw. That's an investment for future agility. And, although they don't give out rosettes at shows for considerate handling, you would certainly get a pat on the back from me!

Jumping Out Of The Ring

Q *At a show today my dog Clover jumped out of the ring. She is a big, long-striding cross-breed. She cleared a hurdle, landed and found herself directly in front of the ring rope – so she jumped it! She immediately turned and we were back on track on the judge's course. How should I have been marked? Should I have lost points?*

A I wish I had seen Clover in action! I'm sure your judge was as surprised as you were and was scratching his head. The Kennel Club rules and regulations are very clear in most instances; for example, if a dog pees in the ring, it's an elimination. But there is no specific ruling on jumping ring ropes. It doesn't happen as often as peeing in the ring!

Course design and safety A good course will be fun and testing for the competitors. It should also be safe for the dogs to run. Jumps positioned too close to the ropes are asking for trouble. What if Clover had caught her leg in the ring rope, fallen and hurt herself? Poor Clover had no alternative but to jump it. It was either that or garrotting herself. The ropes should not be another obstacle for the competitor to negotiate and a considerate course designer will steer clear of them. I suspect that when Clover did her leap, the judge kicked himself for putting equipment too near the edge of his ring and will give more thought to his course design next time.

Marking The price you paid for Clover's leap was time wasted and extra seconds on the clock. Depending on your dog's speed elsewhere on the course, you may have incurred time faults.

Elimination Clover would not have been eliminated. Despite the hiccup of jumping the ring rope, Clover picked up where she left off immediately. She worked the course and responded to your commands. On the other hand, dogs that jump barriers and leave the ring to heckle the queue, chase rabbits in the adjoining field, or beg at the burger van **will** be eliminated. These dogs have something other than agility on their mind and their handlers have lost their grip on the situation. Unlike Clover, the dogs are out of control and they will be eliminated.

Walking the course Jumping the ring rope is probably a one-off incident and Clover will never do it again. However, it's a good idea to check how near the ring ropes are to the jumps when you are walking your next course. If you think Clover is going to land on top of them, mention it to your judge before his briefing. He may not realize that there is a potentially dangerous trouble spot and will in all likelihood adjust his course or move the ropes before the class starts.

Below: *A jumping dog needs room on both sides of the hurdle.*

We have lift off!

And a safe landing!

Double Handling

Q My German Shepherd, Fudge, loves my boyfriend Steve. In class, I get Steve to stand at the finish line with Fudge's toy and Fudge beats it down the home stretch to see him. If Steve encourages him, Fudge really steps up a gear! I'm hoping Steve will be able to come to the shows with me when I start competing, but he likes to play golf at the weekends. What should I do?

A It's good to hear that Steve comes to training class with you and lends a hand, but he won't be able to do that at an agility show. When you are competing, it's up to you and Fudge to run clear and within the course time all on your own.

Double-handling Getting outside assistance when you are in the ring is known as double-handling. It can be hard to spot, but if the judge notices, he will reprimand or penalize you. Double-handling is frowned upon and some people would simply call it cheating. I'll give you two examples.

Start line You set your dog up on the start line and tell Fudge to stay. Steve is just outside the ring, but only a few feet behind Fudge. You move away from your dog to position yourself past the second fence for a recall. Fudge shuffles and your boyfriend tells him to sit and then commands him to stay. Who is working the dog? The person in the ring or the person outside the ring?

Finish line Steve stands at the finish line playing with Fudge's toy to encourage him over the last fence. He says, "Ready, steady, get it!". Fudge runs to him for a game of tug. Would Fudge have been so fast if he had not received this incentive from the wrong side of the ring ropes? Did he jump the last fence because you sent him over it or because your boyfriend called him?

Training Two people working together can accomplish a great deal, especially in the early stages of learning, for example, by practising restrained recalls. Indeed, double-handling may be the safest way to proceed in some instances. A person either side of the dog walk when your dog trots along its length for the first time is a good safety measure. It means that if he falls off, there's someone to catch him. But if you enter a competition, your training should have advanced to the point where you alone are enough.

So, let Steve go to the golf course! But if he does come to watch you run Fudge, explain that you could be eliminated for double-handling. Do be careful and keep your fingers crossed that Fudge won't run out of the ring to your boyfriend in the middle of the course instead of finishing it!

Below: *A game of tug with your boyfriend after the last fence could get your dog eliminated.*

Grooming For Success

Q *This may sound silly, but my husband is coming to an agility show with me this weekend. I worry that he will be bored unless I can think of a way to involve him. He doesn't want to run one of my two Collies and he doesn't want to help on a ring. Any suggestions?*

A A good wife never lets a good husband get bored! They only wander off and get into mischief. Employ your husband as your groom – there'll be plenty for him to do.

Above: *Your husband can walk the dogs while you queue to collect your ring numbers and running orders.*

Queuing This is such a Godsend. If you have forgotten the course, your husband can hold the dog in the queue while you walk around the ring and study the equipment from different angles to refresh your memory. How is it running? Are all the eliminations in the same place? Where is the judge standing? You can do all this and never lose your place in the queue. And the reverse works. If your dog is easily hyped, he can take the dog away from all the excitement of the ring while you stand in line. When he returns the dog to you near the start, the dog will be cool and calm.

Above: *Minding two agility dogs at a show will never be boring! They will need exercising, toileting and brushing.*

Driving He can chauffeur you to and from the show. This allows you to catnap in the passenger seat and you will arrive fresh and ready to compete.

Exercising the dogs While you are walking the course, he can take the dogs for a walk and toilet them. He may not want to run a dog in competition, but if he loves the dogs as much as you do he'll be happy to warm them up by jogging up and down the field a few times or playing a game of ball with them.

Timing It is not always possible to be in two places at once. He can keep an eye on how classes are running and alert you if you should be at a ring rather than standing in a queue for hamburgers.

Above: *Your dog is your best friend – so is your husband so share the highs and lows of the day with him!*

Coat stand He can hold your coat, your bum bag, your dog's toy and so on when you go into the ring and give it all back to you when you come out. You'll never have to dig your jacket out of a pile of competitors' clothes thrown on the ground again.

Shopping If there are stalls at the show, take your husband shopping. Stare longingly at the pair of poodle earrings. Try on a waterproof. He might take the hint and buy something for you.

Being a groom is an important but undervalued job. Your husband will be supporting you and your dogs and, if you work together, you can become an indomitable team. Talk to him about your successes, your difficulties and your failures. He can give you an objective view and offer valuable advice. Even if he only listens and nods his head in the right places, he will be helping to keep you sane.

Chapter Six

FIT FOR THE RING

Once hooked on agility, neither you nor your dog will want to miss a single training night or show. But when should you take a break and for how long? Can you run with your dog with the same style and panache when you are nine months pregnant? Can you handle your dog from a wheelchair? How long should you wait after your dog is neutered to return to class? Will your dog ever be able to jump again if he has been lame? Don't be impatient! There are some things you just need to learn to work around. Deafness and old age won't stop your dog from enjoying the obstacles. Keep yourself and your dog in tip-top condition and you will have a long-lasting working relationship. Remember, when it comes to your pet's health, it's more important to play safe than jump hurdles. Always ask your vet for his opinion.

Canine Callisthenics

Q *My friends at agility class keep calling my terrier "Toby the Tub". They love to tease me and Toby isn't tubby, he's just big boned! Nonetheless, I want Toby to be in top condition, a real canine athlete. What exercises and fitness routines do you recommend?*

A Many handlers think that their dog is fit because he does agility. Running over jumps is good exercise, right? But think how much faster and better the dog could jump if fitness was a prerequisite for his agility training. If Toby's exercise regime is varied and fun, he will relish working out with you and you will see an improvement in his performance over courses.

Above: *Time for a wet kiss? Turn your pet into an aqua-doggy. A session in the pool is a great way to maintain fitness or regain condition after injury.*

Is your dog out of shape? Have your vet check Toby's general health before embarking on a new fitness regime for agility. Is Toby a bit overweight? Does he suffer from any medical conditions. Does he have an old injury. Is he getting on in years? All these factors should be taken into account before you start exercising your dog.

Left: *A vet can help you determine your pet's health and fitness and suggest appropriate exercise levels.*

Strength and stamina When you take Toby to the park, alternate between walking, jogging and running. You'll lose weight too. Throw a ball low to the ground for him to chase. Check out your local hydro-therapy pool and arrange a swimming session for your dog. They might let you join him in the water!

Don't be too ambitious Do not attempt to jog ten miles with Toby on your first day. Build up gradually and remember that exercise is not just for Saturdays. Doing a little bit every day is what will get you results. Increase duration and intensity slowly.

Flexibility Toby needs to be agile to be an agility dog. Just watch him wiggle through the weaves. Find activities that will keep him supple. Put on the radio and teach him to do the twist!

Static exercises Static exercises don't take up much space. Teach Toby some tricks. Can he walk backwards? Do a bow? Sit up and beg? Tricks are valuable tools that teach your dog spatial awareness, strengthen muscles and enhance flexibility.

Warm up and cool down When Toby is in prime condition, make sure he can make the most of it. Always give him a warm-up before you step into the ring. A quick jog or game with a tug toy will kick-start his heart and get his blood pumping. He'll be

Above: *Jumping through your arms is a trick that will impress your friends and keep your dog strong and supple. Start with your arms low and gradually raise them higher.*

ready for action. A gentle massage after a run will help Toby to cool down and give you the opportunity to check areas for tenderness. Treat to compete.

Keeping Toby fit to meet the requirements of competition takes time and effort, but the results will be worth it. Be creative in designing an exercise plan so that Toby enjoys keeping in shape and make it relevant to the demands of agility. In addition there are a growing number of canine fitness specialists ranging from chiropractors to physiotherapists. Toby has no excuse for being tubby. He soon will become Toby the Tiger!

Performance Diet

Q *I don't know if you can help, but my Boxer Sidney has just started agility training. He had colitis as a youngster and has been on a special diet available only from the vet ever since. His stools are fine and he bounces around happily, but I'm wondering whether, now that he is an agility dog, he needs a diet for active dogs. Any advice?*

A The only way that you can tell if the food you are putting into your dog's mouth is the right stuff is by what comes out the other end. If Sid is bouncing with good health and producing stools of an acceptable smell, colour and consistency, then the diet your vet has prescribed is doing what it is intended to do. It is a successful feeding regime. I would be loath to mess with what your vet has prescribed without discussing it with him. Changing

Above: *Good quality food will taste yummy and provide the nutrients and calories your dog needs to be fit and active.*

a dog's diet suddenly or introducing a new food is not without consequences. Some dog's tummies are so sensitive that even a minuscule titbit of something different can spark a bout of diarrhoea or sickness.

Agility is a high energy sport and there are a number of dog food manufacturers that cater especially for active or sporting dogs. The food is not only well-balanced but a calorie- and nutrient-dense product that the manufacturers claim can make your dog a champion. Price and availability varies. Some brands are found at the supermarket and others are available only through special outlets.

It is not only the choice of food that is important for the agility dog but when it is fed. To benefit fully from a calorie- and nutrient-dense food, a dog should find it in his food bowl for about two months before starting a busy, competition-filled season. A single meal of the stuff the night before the show won't make much difference. Moreover, off-peak energy demands will be lower. An agility dog that is rested over the winter does not need food that is packed with calories as he is likely to return to training in the Spring carrying some extra weight.

Your dog is just starting his agility career and is still a long way away from entering his first show or a hectic season on the circuit. Discuss your diet concerns with your vet. It is as important for you to enjoy peace of mind as it is for your pet to have good bowel movements.

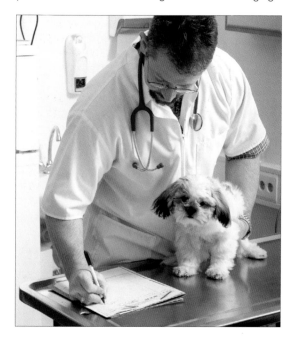

Above: *If your vet has prescribed your pet a special diet, please don't change it without consulting him first.*

Bitch In Season – Hey Boys!

Q *My little bitch, Flash, has just started her first season. Does this mean I have to stop taking her to agility training? We are halfway through a course of eight classes and I paid in advance.*

A Unless you want puppies, stop taking Flash to agility classes until her season is finished. Her presence will be disruptive and it will be unfair to the other dogs in the class who are there to work.

When Flash is in season (on heat), she is fertile and may become pregnant if mated. You can start looking out for a bitch's first season when she is six months to a year old; larger breeds of dogs tend to have their first season later than smaller breeds. During her season, Flash will have a bloody discharge and her vulva will swell. A season will last for approximately three weeks and occur every six months or so. You will need to give Flash extra care and be extra vigilant when other dogs are around.

Left: It's not fair to the other participants to take an in-season bitch to agility class. The male dogs will probably be distracted and chaos may ensue!

odour as a signal that love is in the air. They become even more determined to find a mount. And you may discover that Flash is only too willing to oblige.

The dogs in your agility class will turn into canine Romeos who only have one thing on their minds They will no longer think of the thrill of jumping hurdles but the excitement of fulfilling their sexual desires. And worse, they may start to behave aggressively in the hope of seeing off any rivals for Flash's affections. Macho males with one-track minds will be a real handful.

A bitch in season will leave a delicious olfactory trail for dogs to track Flash will leave her mark all over the agility ring. Even though she trained in the morning, the dogs in the afternoon classes will be looking for her. "Hurrah! a bitch in season has gone through the tunnel. Is she still in there!" It will be difficult for their handlers to convince them that they are in class for agility, not speed dating.

Three weeks is not too long a time to miss your agility classes and if you explain the situation to your instructor, he may reimburse you or put your fees towards the next course. There are plenty of agility exercises you can practise in the privacy of your own garden to keep Flash ticking over. And if you are thinking of entering shows, study the conditions outlined on your entry form. Bitches in seasons are not allowed to compete at Kennel Club shows in Great Britain. Is it time to think about having Flash spayed?

A bitch in season will attract the attention of every male dog in your agility class Leave Flash at home, rather than risk an accidental mating that will result in unwanted puppies. There are a number of sprays on the market that claim to mask the scent of a bitch in season, but many dogs recognize the

To Spay Or Not To Spay

Q *I'm thinking about spaying Ellie, my three year old Golden Retriever. She loves agility and is getting a lot faster. However, unfortunately her seasons usually arrive in August/September and we have to miss the summer shows. Also, I'm worried that spaying may affect her confidence in the ring. If I decide to have her spayed, how long until we can do agility again?*

Left: *If you have your dog spayed, give her time to recover from her surgery before you return to agility.*

Sometimes spaying can help a dog settle down and stay on an even keel. If Ellie is getting more and more confident in the ring and producing faster and faster course times, there is no reason why this trend should not continue after she is spayed.

A Such a nuisance! You can't take a bitch in season to training or shows without risking a big male dog jumping on her. And worse, you have to stay at home to keep her company.

Talk to your vet Your vet will be happy to discuss the pros and cons of spaying with you. If you are certain that you will never want puppies from Ellie and she is fit and healthy, there is no reason not to have her neutered. Some vets will spay a bitch as young as six months before the animal's first season. Older animals are usually spayed when they are mid-cycle, halfway between seasons. The advantages of early spaying include a reduced risk of mammary cancer, uterine ovarian cancer, false pregnancies and pyometra (infection of the womb). On the down side, a few bitches develop urinary incontinence as a result of spaying but this is easily treated with daily medication. Also, the coats of some dogs get a little more fluffy after neutering.

Will my dog's personality change?
Personality is difficult to measure objectively, but you may find your dog becomes less moody. Bitches can be so hormonal – up one minute and down the next. They go broody or they pout to get their own way.

How long before returning to agility? This will depend on the surgery and your dog. Most vets will recommend lead walks and no jumping up on the settee or climbing the stairs for the first two weeks followed by a gradual reintroduction of normal exercise. Take your time. Just because your dog looks fit doesn't mean that she is 100 per cent. Start with mini-jumps and slowly work up to full height. Don't rush. Your dog may be sore. If she feels an odd pinch when she is jumping a hurdle during her recovery, she will approach the next one with some trepidation.

I am always surprised by how quickly many dogs return to competition. The fur has barely had time to re-grow. Get out your calendar and have a chat with your vet.

Motherhood And Puppies

Q *My bitch Teasel is a gorgeous Border Collie and a star agility dog. Whenever I come out of the ring, people ask me if I am going to let her have puppies. I don't think I would have trouble finding good homes for her offspring, but I am worried about my agility. Would I have to stop agility training and for how long?*

A Agility is like riding a bicycle. It will not be something that Teasel forgets because she has taken a break to have puppies. Give her time off during her pregnancy and while she is nursing her pups. Don't rush her recovery to return to agility training.

To be absolutely safe, halt agility training as soon as Teasel is mated. Some handlers carry on for a little while longer. Your dog's size, condition and changing shape will be deciding factors. Agility is a high energy, high impact exercise. The longer you continue training, the greater the risk of compromising the pregnancy or injuring your dog. Exercise is still important, but choose something less stressful and more gentle than jumping hurdles. Walking is ideal. Let Teasel pick the pace. As she becomes big and heavy with pups, she'll tire easily and will probably be happy with a saunter around the garden.

Although you have stopped agility training with Teasel, there is no reason why you can't do a few less demanding exercises. She will need to continue to feel special and have quality time with you. If she is up for less strenuous static training, go ahead. Review your target work and hand touches.

Don't hurry back to agility training. Let Teasel guide you. She may not want to leave her babies and they need lots and lots of feeds. When the pups have been weaned and gone to their new homes, you can start to build up Teasel's fitness. But do it gradually. Start by training over mini height jumps. Nothing too demanding to start with – keep it short and simple. Every dog is different, so read your dog. You know her better than anyone else. Some bitches make a quick comeback and others take a little more time to regain condition. I know of some dogs that are back at agility competitions by the time the puppies are 12 weeks old.

If you are going to breed from Teasel you need to have a chat with your vet about her care during pregnancy as well as whelping and weaning the puppies. Motherhood can be an expensive and time-consuming business. There's more to it than a simple act of nature. Agility should take a back seat. After her time off, Teasel will return to the circuit the gorgeous agility star that she was before.

Above: *Make the transition from motherhood back to agility gradual. Build fitness and start small with mini jumps.*

Deaf Not Dumb

Q *I already do agility with my Golden Retriever, Ace, and I have just rescued a three-year-old deaf Border Collie, Kermit. I would like to do agility with Kermit, too. He needs to let off steam. Will I be attempting the impossible?*

A Kermit's deafness will be a problem only if you let it be. There are a number of deaf dogs that do very well in agility. Watching them race around the ring, you would never suspect that they can't hear a thing their handlers are saying to them. This can be a good thing, especially if the handler gets the verbal commands for right and left mixed up or calls the tunnel the tyre by mistake! A deaf dog relies on visual communication. Body, hand and facial signals are important in agility, but they are even more important for the deaf dog.

Make sure your signals are consistent Don't sign to your dog to stay still with an outstretched hand and open palm one day and then change it to an outstretched hand and pointed finger the next. He'll see the difference.

Make sure your signals are clear and visible Remember your dog will have to see you in order to react to your commands. Don't sign to him to come to you unless he is looking at you. Make your body signals as clear as possible. If your dog is behind you, he will not be able to see you point across your body to a jump.

Treat your signals as a language You will be able to amplify some signals to make then louder or urgent. If smiling at your dog means "good boy"

Above: *Stay – The handler holds the flat of his hand in front of his dog's nose. Don't move until you are released! It's an important exercise if a dog can't hear traffic.*

Above: *Sit – The handler stretches out his hand to his dog and then bends it with an upward motion to his shoulder. It means put your bottom on the ground!*

172

Above left: *Down – Start in the sit position and the dog is already half way into a down.*

Above centre: *Now point to the ground and your dog's nose and body will follow your finger downward.*

Above right: *The dog is securely in the down position. Now it's time for thumbs up for "good boy"!*

then smiling at your dog till your cheeks hurt and the sun comes out of your eyes means "what a superstar!". If you want to turn your dog to the right, drop your right shoulder and twist your left one to the right. If you want to really tighten the turn, twist it even more bringing your arm across your body.

Try different training methods on for size It is your responsibility to tailor the training method to fit your dog's abilities – take in the cuffs or let out the hem. Kermit can't hear a clicker, but he will be able to sniff out a frankfurter. Find a way of giving your dog the thumbs up and marking good behaviour that isn't dependent on sound.

Don't stop talking People who stop talking to their dogs can look insincere or wooden. Your facial expressions and body movements will flow more freely if you continue to speak to Kermit, even though he can't hear you.

Don't use your dog's deafness as an excuse Your dog can do anything that you decide to teach him … except hear. Provided his training is fun, Kermit will want to learn.

Training a deaf dog in agility is not impossible, but it can be a challenge. One day Kermit will thank you for your efforts by going clear on the course.

Left: *Come – First make sure the dog is looking at you. Give your dog a big smile and open your arms. This is an irresistibly warm welcome!*

Getting The Snip

Q *I have a lively, two-year-old male Border Collie called Blue and have been having agility lessons for the past couple of months. He is getting really good and we are enjoying it. The problem is he loves the ladies! I am considering having him neutered as I will not be breeding from him. Would castration calm him down too much for agility?*

A You can't blame Blue for looking at the ladies, but you would be upset if, instead of going through the tunnel, he left the ring to introduce himself to a pretty poodle in the queue. Your boy has just grown up.

Above: *Male dogs cock their legs on just about anything – trees, posts or even you.*

As a dog matures, the male hormone testosterone starts to be released in his body. The testicles are the main source of this hormone and they are responsible for stimulating the development of macho male characteristics. A male dog may start roaming the countryside looking for bitches to have his puppies. He may start cocking his leg on the gate post thus marking his territory with a big sign that says "MINE". And he may begin to show aggression to other dogs and proclaim himself king of the castle. Woe betide any dog that comes near his gate post.

Castration halts the production of testosterone and it may eliminate some of the more undesirable male behaviours in your dog. The hormone is only the trigger and if Blue now spends every night out chasing bitches, losing his testicles won't stop him trying to spread his favours. He is already in the habit of eyeing up the ladies and habits are hard to break. For the best chance of castration changing a dog's outlook on life, the earlier he is neutered the better. But there are no guarantees.

Although castration may not change Blue, it will probably affect how other dogs react to him. Your dog may strut around like he is the king of the castle, but no one is going to take his bluster seriously. The dogs on the exercise field will give him a sniff in greeting but no longer see him as a threat or rival.

Some people argue that castration makes dogs fat and lazy. They insist it takes the edge off an agility dog. Clowning rather than jumping become the business of the day. But perhaps the day would be like that anyway? It is impossible to tell as so many other factors play an important part influencing a dog's behaviour. Next time you are at an agility show, check the dogs in the queue at the ring. You will find that many of the dogs have lost their manhood but not their lust for agility. They will be fit and lively and because they have been castrated they will be less likely to develop prostatic disease or testicular cancer in the future.

Castration may make no difference to your dog at all, but it will certainly do him no harm and could do him a lot of good.

Below: *The message is clear. You are nothing and I am king of the castle.*

Eye Care

Q *A few weeks ago I discovered that my poodle Yogi had an eye infection. He is receiving treatment from our vet but I'm so worried that Yogi will lose his sight in the infected eye. Yogi loves his agility. Would he be able to continue training if he is partially sighted?*

A There are many causes of eye infections ranging from the simple to the complex and you should discuss your worries with the vet who is treating Yogi. He will be able to give you the full picture and allay your fears.

Eye disorders will present in a number of ways. Signs of a problem include excessive tearing or discharge. A dog that squints in bright light or continually rubs his eye with his paw is trying to tell you it hurts. The sooner the dog is under the vet's care, the sooner he can be diagnosed and his symptoms treated.

If your vet gives you the OK to return to agility, remember that dogs do not see or understand the world in the same way that we do. Agility dogs will never be able to read the numbers on the course or tell the difference between a green hurdle and a red one. They aren't very good at judging distance but they have great peripheral vision and are very sensitive to movement. It is these visual characteristics that enable the dogs to read a handler's body signals and to work ahead. And they often override the verbal commands.

Medication If Yogi has drops or creams for his eye, his vision may be blurred for a while after you administer them so hold off training until they have been fully absorbed and he can see clearly again. Also, some topical ointments leave a sticky residue around the eye so avoid working Yogi in dusty environments or sand riding schools.

Bumps Take extra care when you return to training as Yogi's eye may still be sensitive. Leave out any equipment that comes into close contact with Yogi's face like the weaving poles and collapsible tunnel in case he accidentally knocks his eye.

Light and dark Yogi's eye may not be able to respond to changes of light as quickly. He might find the bright sunlight that hits him as he exits the dark rigid tunnel temporarily blinding. Give him help to get his bearings if he looks unsure.

I hope that Yogi's vision is not permanently affected by his eye infection. If it is, whether he continues in agility will depend on how significant the loss of sight proves to be for him and how well he adapts. I know of a one-eyed dog that runs for fun in Veteran classes over mini-jumps and there are many partially sighted dogs competing on the circuit. The dogs have adjusted and their owners have modified their handling techniques to take this into account. Remain confident in your vet and follow his advice. Worry about agility later.

Below: *Eyes are delicate windows on the world. An eye check by your vet will make sure they stay open.*

Three-Legged Agility

Q *My collie, Gem, was hit by a car and we are lucky still to have her. But Gem had to have her right foreleg amputated to save her life. She is managing amazingly well on three legs and I would like to continue training and competing in agility. I realize that some of the equipment may be out of the question, but what about working her over mini-jumps? Any reason why I should not take her to a class and see how she copes?*

A I am sorry to hear that Gem has had such a horrible accident but glad that she has made a good recovery. You have a responsibility to Gem to ensure that she continues to enjoy life on three legs. Much of what an amputee dog would like to do and should be allowed to do will clash. It's up to you to have the last word.

Above: *Some dogs are so active and boisterous that it is hard to believe that they are amputees. But agility?*

and motor skills to keep them on their feet. Gem's remaining legs are already compensating for the loss of her foreleg and I think agility would put added stress on her joints and accelerate deterioration in their condition.

Is agility necessary to Gem's happiness or yours? I suspect that you both miss the partnership you gained through agility training and the exhilaration of working as a team in competition. You both love agility and, even on three legs, Gem would give it her best shot. However, I think this is one of those occasions when your head should rule your heart (and hers) and you should say no to more agility training. Try other activities that you and Gem could do together that are less demanding and more achievable. And, if you want to continue in agility think about getting a puppy.

Future risks When considering a three-legged dog's future training, there are a number of things to take into account including the dog's build, weight, muscle tone and the amount of time passed since surgery. But the most important thing to consider is how would you feel if disaster struck again. Fit and healthy four-legged dogs have accidents in agility. They tumble off A-frames, trip in the weaves, or crash into jumps. What if one of her remaining good legs was injured? The consequences for a three-legged dog would be dire.

Confusing confidence with ability Gem may be very confident and self-assured on three legs. She can manage to climb stairs and to jump on and off the living room chairs, but this is not agility. Agility asks a dog to perform these actions repeatedly and at high speed. Agility dogs need good co-ordination

Old Age Pensioner

Q *I got the taste for agility with my first dog, a Belgian Shepherd named Taz. He got me hooked on the sport and I have added two more dogs to my agility pack. Taz will have his ninth birthday next September and still barks on the start line in anticipation of the jumps. When should I retire him?*

A It sounds as if Taz is still up for a round of agility. If he is fit and healthy, there is no reason why he should not continue to compete for a little longer. It's good exercise and although Taz may be a little grey around the muzzle, you don't want him to lose his waist line.

Dogs age at different rates. The older they become, the more likely they are to suffer age-related ailments like arthritis. They don't see or hear as well and they sleep more. It takes a little longer to walk to the park in the morning. Many of the signs of ageing are symptomatic of other medical conditions so have Taz checked by a vet who will prescribe the appropriate treatment. Be vigilant and look out for:

Slower course times As Taz gets older, he will get slower. His turns will be looser and his course times won't be as fast. He might incur the odd time fault. You can help him by giving him a little longer to warm up before a round.

Did you say "go" or "no"? Many older dogs suffer a degree of hearing loss. Taz was not being naughty when he went into the tunnel instead of turning towards you when you called his name. Work on your body signals and make sure your verbal commands are well timed and clear.

Measuring the jumps Older dogs knock more poles. They measure their strides approaching a fence and often rock back forth when they get there. Taz may have trouble seeing the hurdle, finding his take off spot and gathering the strength to clear the pole. If Taz knocks a pole, don't rush him. Run with him. Don't get ahead of him.

What will you find acceptable on the course?
A few time faults and knocked poles is one thing. A dog that trots instead of runs, looks disorientated and trips over every hurdle is another. Extra help on the course and sensitive handling, won't make any difference to performance. The dog may love agility, but it's time to retire before he is injured.

In England, there are Veteran classes that cater especially for the older competitor. The courses are simple and flowing – no tight turns – and course times are generous. Jumps are set at the minimum height and contact equipment and weaves are removed. The accent is giving the older dog a blast. Taz would love it!

Compete with your other two dogs, but run for fun with Taz while he is still enthusiastic and fit enough to enjoy agility with you.

Above: *Old dogs can continue a love affair with agility, if they are fit and their handlers don't expect miracles.*

Big Boys!

Q *Do Rottweilers and agility mix? My boy Ronnie weighs 45kg (100lb) and is quite lean but that's still a lot of Rottweiler to manoeuvre through the weaves. The earth shakes when he lands after a jump and he hits the A-frame like a sledge hammer. Are his joints going to hold out if I continue training?*

A The short answer is if your dog is sound and loves agility, there is no reason to stop doing a sport you both enjoy. But I would take sensible measures to ensure that Ronnie can continue training for as long as possible. Keep your eyes peeled for any signs that might indicate that agility isn't as much fun as it used to be.

Weight Everything works better when your dog is the correct weight – heart, lungs and muscles can operate at full capacity. Ronnie is nice and lean and that's good. He will be able to give you his optimum performance and he'll live longer.

Equipment Ensure that the agility equipment at your training venue and at competitions is strong enough to withstand the force of a turbocharged Rottie. Look out for poles that may splinter or planks that could give way under Ronnie's weight. Most equipment is reinforced, but it can lose flexibility and strength if not adequately maintained.

Noise factor The sound of a dog hitting a pole or the upside of the A-frame can be extraordinarily loud. Listen to the featherweights, like the terriers or shelties, when they are running. Is the noise just as thunderous?

Pain threshold Many dogs have high pain thresholds and will train through an injury without raising a single objection. The thrill and excitement

of agility keeps them going. Would Ronnie keep jumping for the sake of it or would he be sensible and ask for his lead? Watch him carefully so you don't miss the signs of an injury.

Reduce the stresses and strains of agility, not the fun
- Lower the jumps and lower the A-frame. You don't need to train at competition height all the time. If you are going to retrain your A-frame so that Ronnie runs up it rather than jumping through it, you want to lower this obstacle anyway. You can bring everything back to full height before a show.
- Keep Ronnie fit by doing work on the flat – practise turns, send aways and recalls. Play games of fetch and work on your obedience basics.
- Train one night a week instead of two or three. This will cut down on the number of repetitions that you do with Ronnie over the equipment. Aim for quality of performance rather than quantity.

If you and Ronnie are sensible, there is no reason why you shouldn't jump around to your heart's content for a long time yet.

Vertical Take-Offs

Q *My dog Luka is a terrier cross and has an unusual jumping style. I have never seen another terrier jump like he does so I guess his method is not a breed specific. Luka takes off vertically with all four feet pointing straight downwards. Is there something wrong with him? Although he never knocks a pole, I'm sure that his jumping method costs me time on the course and I worry that if he persists, he could injure himself.*

A Luka must be something to see on the agility course. Have you explained to Luka that the judge does not award bonus points for innovative

Bounce jumps Set up a line of low fences quite close together. If Luka is unable to take a stride between fences, he will have to bounce between them. As soon as he lands, Luka will have to lift his front feet to jump the next hurdle in the line.

Arc of the jumper Luka needs to learn to arc over the hurdles. Going vertically up in the air means that he will come straight back down again. There's little margin for error. Set up some gentle spreads to jump over so that he has to lengthen and arc his body. The shape of his jump will improve.

You can't say to a dog, "You have to stop jumping off all four legs to clear a jump. You need to raise your front paws and push off your back legs and arc in the air." He won't understand. But he will learn through experience so give him the opportunity to improve his jumping style and he will reward you with improved times on the course.

technique? Unfortunately a dog's natural jumping action may not always be the most economical one. It is your responsibility as Luka's handler to take steps to change and improve it.

Peace of mind Before attempting to correct Luka's jumping style, visit your vet for a check-up. Rule out any physical reasons for his vertical take-offs.

Defensive jumping You often see young or inexperienced dogs jumping like this. They want to make sure that their take-offs and landings are perfect. They want to jump straight over the middle of the pole, not the sides. And they may have lost confidence because the jumps have been raised too quickly. They are afraid of knocking a pole. It sounds as if Luka is jumping defensively. He wants to do it right, but he doesn't want to hurt himself.

Lower jumps Set up lines or circles of low jumps – the lower the better, just a few inches off the ground. Race Luka over these and cheer him on. He will gain confidence with speed and it is really difficult to knock a jump that is almost on the ground already! The faster you go, the harder it will be for Luka to pause for a vertical take-off.

Above: *What goes up, must come down. Examine your dog's jumping style, especially take-offs and landings. Study his mid-air body shape. Could it be improved?*

Limping Now And Again

Q *Sheba woke up one morning after agility training and was lame. I took her to the vet who gave me some tablets and told me to rest her. He said it was a soft tissue injury and nothing to worry about. Ever since, Sheba has had brief spells of lameness. She will get off her bed, limp a few steps and then all is well. Months will pass before she has another episode. Is agility the cause of her problem? What can I do to help her?*

A I would make an appointment with your vet so that he can have another look at Sheba. Tell him about her occasional episodes of lameness. He is the best person to diagnose and treat your dog.

Put your vet in the picture As well as Sheba's symptoms, you must tell your vet that Sheba is a competing agility dog. He needs the full picture of your activities with your pet. You might not be representing your country at the World Agility Championships this year, but that doesn't mean your training is any less intensive or dedicated. Explain your expectations as an agility handler and be honest about how many hours a week you spend training contacts. Your vet probably thinks that after dinner Sheba curls up with you on the settee to watch TV. Not likely! You're off to your agility club.

Return to training When Sheba's treatment is complete and your vet has given you permission to return to agility training, don't rush. Build up Sheba's general fitness before you start training more specific agility skills. Take it slow and steady. Put the jumps down. Lower the A-frame. Avoid twists and turns. Don't overdo it. Five minutes can be a long time for a dog that is returning from injury. You are back in the agility saddle so make sure you stay there by working one step at a time – otherwise you could find that Sheba's old injury flares up again or, worse, she incurs a new one.

Minimize the risk of injury Like any sport, agility is not without risk of injury. Minimize it by making sure that Sheba is always physically fit and healthy. Regular exercise, like walking or jogging combined with games of fetch or tug, will keep her in peak condition and she will be able to meet the rigours of challenging agility courses that demand speed and flexibility. And, always give Sheba a warm-up before you go into the ring. She needs to prime her muscles for a burst of activity. Walk her briskly or trot her around. Do some tricks that will stretch her back and legs. A dog that is in good physical condition and is adequately warmed-up before it goes into the ring is less likely to have an injury than the dog that is overweight, unfit and has just woken up from a nap.

Below: A controlled game of tug will help a dog keep in shape, maintain fitness and minimize the risk of future injury.

Poorly Pads

Q *My dog, Quiz, keeps getting contact burns on his pads. He is a very fast collie and when I get home after training, his pads are grazed from the surface material of the contacts. How can I stop him from getting sore feet?*

A Check Quiz's pads regularly. They should feel rough and look like fine sandpaper. Worn pads feel smooth and they may have little dots on them. Cracked, swollen or bleeding pads can lead to prolonged pain or lameness. Does Quiz lick or chew his feet? It's worthwhile having a vet check Quiz's feet to make sure there is no medical reason why they are suffering from wear and tear.

Above: *Cracked or grazed pads can make walking painful. Get a vet to give your pet's feet a full examination.*

Salves and lotions There are a number of commercial products available on the market claiming to help toughen and protect pads if applied routinely. Some agility handlers smear a thin coat of Vaseline before the pads are worn badly. However, care must be taken to remove this coating once training has finished. It does form a protective layer on the pads, but it will also inhibit a dog's ability to sweat through his feet.

Boots Boots can help stop trouble developing in the first place and will guard pads while they are healing. They are designed for sled dogs or hunting dogs that work over tough terrain, especially snow and ice. However, I think booties would impede an agility dog during training – a bit like asking a ballet dancer to pirouette in clogs.

Agility equipment Has your training club recently overhauled its agility equipment? Usually sand is mixed with paint to roughen the surface of the contact areas and give the dogs some traction. It could be that the grade of sand chosen is too abrasive for Quiz's feet. I know of one agility club that opted for a softer alternative and mixed bird seed in the paint for the contact areas. This worked fine and, despite expectations, the sparrows did not roost on the dog walk.

Training method If you are using a training method that results in Quiz screeching to a halt in a two feet on, two feet off position at the bottom of the contacts, perhaps it is time to consider something different? You could teach an alternative contact behaviour that won't be so harsh on his paws. Many people are now advocating running contacts because they are faster and kinder to a dog's shoulder joints. And kinder to your dog's feet!

You can always take a break from agility to give Quiz's pads time to heal and when you return, limit your contact training.

Finding The Itch

Q *Last week, I stood in the queue next to a handler with a little crossbreed hound that was bald in patches and kept scratching (until it got on the course and then the dog went on to win the class). Do you think it had fleas? My dog Clarrie is scratching now and I'm worried she might have caught something nasty. And what should I do to make sure it doesn't happen again?*

A Dogs will scratch because they itch and they could itch for any number of reasons. Itching may be because the dog has fleas or other parasites, or an allergy to something in his environment. It could be the result of a fungal or other infection. A dog may scratch his ear once, or his scratching my be chronic and persistent. He may itch in just one spot or he may itch all over. It can be simply irritating or extremely painful. Scratching can be the sign of a problem that your vet should know about or it may be something completely innocent. For example, if your dog is not groomed regularly, he could have a knot of hair behind his ear and he is trying to dig it out.

You could have asked the handler what was wrong with his dog instead of speculating. If his dog had something contagious and he is a responsible owner, he would not have attended the show. Most people love to talk about their pet's health and medical histories. It is this exchange of information that makes all dog owners amateur vets. You may discover that his dog does indeed have problems, but that they are nothing for you worry about.

It is your responsibility to make sure that Clarrie doesn't itch and is parasite-free. She should regularly receive worm and flea treatment. Choose a product that suits your pocket and is easy for you to apply. Read the label. You will find that most products will not only get rid of parasites but will give your pet protection against future infestation for some weeks. So, if Clarrie has been treated she won't catch fleas from mixing with other dogs that are carrying a few "friends".

If Clarrie is itching despite recent de-fleaing, a trip to the vet is in order. He will examine Clarrie and advise you on whether her scratching is flea-related or is indicative of some other problem that may require further medical attention.

Above: *The more a dog nibbles and scratches, the more he itches. Persistent scratchers can do a lot of damage. The skin breaks leaving the wound open to secondary infections.*

Poo Picking

Q *I have a ten-month-old crossbreed called Ted. His only interest in life is eating poo. When I let him out in the garden he poo-picks after my five other dogs. I have just started agility training and he is more interested in poo than in me! I never had this trouble training my other dogs. Help!*

A The scientific word for your dog's behaviour is "coprophagia", the consumption of faeces by animals. "Autocoprophagia" is when an animal eats his own poo. Puppies often do this, but usually grow out of it. "Intraspecific coprophagia" is when an animal eats the faeces of animals of the same species. This is what Ted is doing when he cleans up after your other dogs in the garden. "Interspecific coprophagia" is when an animal eats poo indiscriminately – sheep droppings, horse manure, bunny balls. It's all good stuff.

Why do dogs eat faeces?

- Coprophagia may be a result of a medical problem. Discuss Ted's eating habits with your vet to rule out any conditions that may make your pet unusually ravenous.
- Dogs are scavengers and eat the most disgusting things, including poo, to survive in the wild. If they had insisted on a sanitized diet the canine race would have died out years ago.
- Many of the things we feed our dogs still smell appetizing after being digested and excreted. Feeding your dog a bland diet that won't smell at all attractive the second time around can help.
- Poo-eating gets your attention. Your dog lowers his head to sniff some droppings and you race to stop him. Good game!
- Your dog likes the taste and can't help himself. When was the last time you left the last chocolate in the box for someone else?

What you can do

- Pick up after your other dogs have toileted. Ted will stop looking for the stuff if he never finds any.
- Teach your dog a "Leave" command. Ted's reward for withdrawing from the faeces should be of greater value than the poo itself. Would you leave a five pound note on the pavement if someone offered you a one pound coin? No.
- Remote punishment can be effective. Rattling a tin or squirting water can interrupt poo snacking. Time it so that Ted thinks the interruption comes from heaven above or the surrounding environment, not from you.
- Ted won't be able to eat faeces if he is wearing a muzzle *(below)*, but he will try. Beware. When his muzzle is coated with the stuff, he'll try to rub his nose on your trousers.

- Forget agility training in a field where horses, cows or sheep have been grazing. Build a relationship with your dog in a poo-free environment.
- Switch your dog onto a toy. If Ted becomes obsessed with a tennis ball, he will lose his interest in faeces.

You must accept that eating poo is something that dogs do. If your dog gets excited by a pile of horse manure, my final advice is to quickly look the other way!

Bringing It Up Again

Q *My two-year-old Sheltie, Vanya, gets so excited about going to agility class that she throws up. It's either a bit of bile or a treat that I've just fed her. I don't know if it's because of standing with the other dogs waiting for her turn. She doesn't do it any other place and it hasn't put her off, but it's not nice for the other people in our class. It's unpleasant to clean it up and I'm worried about her health. What should I do?*

A The excitement of agility affects dogs in different ways. Vomiting is a rather anti-social habit, especially when you are standing with a group of friends waiting for your turn in the ring. Here are some things to think about.

Have Vanya checked by a vet Rule out any medical reasons for her behaviour before you try other remedies.

Vanya may be vomiting because she is excited The prospect of a few agility jumps and her stomach

Above: *Your dog may vomit because he has an intestinal blockage, has been poisoned or has worms. Perhaps he is suffering from a metabolic disease? Consult your vet.*

starts doing back flips – which means she empties it at your feet. Try to be cool as a cucumber at agility class. If you remain calm, your dog might too.

Many dogs like to make sure that their stomachs are emptied before taking part in any activity that requires total concentration Nerves affect us all in different ways. Vanya may feel she performs better when her digestive system is on standby – not finishing off the remnants of a biscuit or sloshing with water. And there are a few agility competitors who have lost their breakfast before an important run.

Keep Vanya on empty I would reward Vanya with play, toys, and her favourite agility obstacle instead of treats. She is probably too excited or stressed to eat and digest titbits and they won't stay down her very long. If she is training in the evening, feed her in the morning so that there is nothing left in her stomach when she goes to class.

Stop worrying If there is no medical reason for Vanya vomiting, learn to ignore it and start concentrating on your agility. Stop giving her attention for bringing her treats back up. It may be that your concern has reinforced the behaviour rather than helped eliminate it. The words "Oh no! Vanya has been sick AGAIN" may well be music to her ears.

Vanya may grow out of it Puppies are prone to travel sickness, but it becomes a thing of the past as they become big enough to keep their balance and dinner. They become accustomed to car journeys. Vanya will probably always be excited by agility, but her initial enthusiasm will lose its edge the more she does and she could stop being sick.

Consider a few private lessons Vanya would be more comfortable and so would you. No other dogs and not too long to wait between turns, so less reason to throw up.

Too Hot For Agility

Q *If I go to a show and the sun is shining, my heart sinks. My dog Silva hates the heat. She slows right down to a walk and potters round the course. She's black and her coat absorbs the sun. What can I do to keep her cool? Should I give up competing in the summer?*

A There's no way round it. If you stand out in the sun with your dog, you'll be hot. We perspire to cool down. Dogs have a few sweat glands on their feet but rely on panting to regulate

Above: *Waving his big, pink tongue in the wind will help your dog cool down on a hot summer's day.*

their body temperatures. It can be a pretty inefficient system especially for dogs that are overweight, have big double coats or short muzzles like Boxers. Don't let Silva overheat.

Find shade Keep Silva out of the direct sun as much as possible. Look for shade under the trees or behind the marquee. Make a tent out of reflective sheets where she can shelter.

Provide fresh water Keep Silva's water bowl full so she can cool down with a drink and avoid dehydrating. Add a few ice cubes. Freeze a bowl of water the night before to take with you to agility shows.

Wet, wet, wet Is there a clean stream near the show ground where you can let Silva have a quick swim? If you are going to be away for the weekend, consider packing a paddling pool. Many show grounds have stand pipes that are perfect for doggy showers. What about a water pistol? Some dogs enjoy having their tongue, toes and tummy misted, but not those who have been squirted in the past for being naughty!

Summer accessories
You can buy bonnets, bandanas and sun glasses. Would Silva shake her head in disgust until they came off? Try keeping her body temperature down by dressing her in a reflective coat or wet towelling jacket (these dry quickly, but the wet dog smell lingers on). For Silva's travelling kennel you can buy a cool bed and pillow to keep her chilled as well as a battery-operated fan. Don't forget the sun block for areas of exposed skin.

A hair cut There are a number of agility dogs sporting summer hair cuts. Who needs a furry coat on a July day? Be aware that Silva may look hot, but her fur is there to insulate her (keeping her cooler) and to protect her skin. And, remember that although Silva's coat can be taken off in minutes, it will take months to grow back. She'll stay pretty with a simple tidy up and trim. Avoid shaving to the skin.

I keep my cool on hot days by lowering my expectations. I know my dogs will perform a bit slower. I do, too. We run slower, think slower and pant more. I try and arrange my runs for early morning or evening. And if it's unbearably hot, I forego the runs and join my dogs in the paddling pool.

Warming Up

Q *I have started entering my collie Storm at agility shows. I'm an athletic type, in good physical condition and use my gym membership! How can I warm up inconspicuously at an agility show? I don't want to cut my competition season short with a sprained muscle, but I don't want to draw attention to myself either.*

A Never fear, if you have to spend the rest of the season with your leg in plaster, your agility club will find some work for you to do in the score tent at shows!

The majority of the injuries in agility happen through a single accident, like tripping over the dog walk, or they are the result of an inefficient action over time, like repeatedly bending to pull a dog down the contacts. You can avoid injury by making sure that you are in good physical condition, but you need a warm-up routine too. It will not only reduce the risk of injury but it will help you give Storm 100 per cent on the course. You'll perform better and so will he. Develop a warm-up routine that will start your heart pumping. All your body's systems should be warm and ticking over, ready for ignition. It will only take five minutes or so.

Make warming up a joint enterprise If you tend to feel self-conscious when you do exercises in public, try warming up with your dog for company. Can you beat Storm to his ball? If you run away, can Storm catch you? Don't do heelwork – do runwork. Who can jump up in the air higher? You'll both end up out of breath.

Above: *A little jogging on the spot and few simple muscle stretches may be enough to protect you from injury when you are running in the ring.*

Disguise your warm-up exercises so you can do them in the queue
- Touch your toes, but pretend you are bending down to tie your shoe laces. Remember to keep your legs straight and exhale as you bend.
- Reach to the sky. Stretch your arms as high in the air as you can till you are pulled onto tiptoes. Then give a big yawn. It will make your work-out look like you are merely stretching after a mid-morning nap.
- Place your hands on your hips. Keep your hips facing forward but twist to your left and chat to your neighbour in the queue. Now, don't be rude. Twist to the right and chat to your other neighbour.
- Take off your hat and do a few head or shoulder rolls. It will look like you are flicking the sweat off your forehead.

Look cool and you'll get away with it No one will ever know. Tighten and relax your tummy muscles. How about some pelvic floor exercises? And flexing your bum muscles. All while standing still in the queue.

Take a look at your fellow competitors. They'll be warming up, too. Completely oblivious to anyone that may be watching. Over time, you'll lose your shyness and be just as bold. You'll feel as comfortable stretching your quadriceps with your agility buddies as you do with the guys at the gym and you'll be able to warm up less covertly.

Casting Doubt

Q *You will probably think this is a really stupid question. I fell off the kerb and broke my arm. I'm absolutely fine but the cast will have to stay on for at least four weeks. My dog Otley has been doing really well and I don't want to miss any training sessions or shows. Will the cast be a problem?*

A There are many that would argue that if the cast is too much of a hindrance for ordinary household chores like the washing up, it's bound to stop you from agility training. But the bottom line is do whatever you can manage without hurting yourself or confusing your dog. Remember that the cast is there to stabilize and protect your arm so that the bones will knit satisfactorily. Don't let your zeal for agility jeopardize the healing process.

Balance You will find it more difficult to balance with only one working arm. Walking is easy, but running and pivoting over rough ground will give you a few problems. If you fall over, please don't break the other arm or a leg!

Above: *You can run with a cast on your arm, but can you do agility? You won't know till you try, but, if it hurts, stop before you do yourself more damage.*

Cues You will not be able to give Otley the visual cues that he has learned. If your arm is tender and your cast is heavy, you will probably be clutching it close to your chest to stop it jiggling up and down. Vibration can be painful. Now you know why your doctor told you to take it easy. Otley wonders what he is supposed to do when you clasp your arm to yourself. In fact the lop-sided way that you are running is a mystery to him. No wonder he looks confused.

Training aid It might seems like good idea, but do refrain from teaching Otley that your cast is a tug toy. Think how embarrassing it will be at the doctor's explaining all those teeth marks. And no matter how tempting, don't hit Otley over the head with it if he misses a contact! That's not good training. As for competitions, I don't think a judge would eliminate you for competing with a cast – it's not a training aid and it's not something you can remove at a moment's notice.

The cast could be a big problem initially. However, the longer you wear it, the more comfortable it will become and Otley will find it less distracting as the days go by. You will both adapt. Be honest with your doctor and follow his advice. If he thinks that agility is a gentle stroll with your pet, he will give you the OK to continue. But he would be horrified if he saw you tear around the course and fall over the finish line in an exhausted heap!

Agility Bump

Q *I have just had it confirmed by my doctor – I'm pregnant! My husband and I are delighted and our families and friends are helping us celebrate our good news. The only one who seems a bit down is our agility dog, Kimmy. I've reassured her that she and I will still go to agility classes and competitions. I won't have to quit agility because I'm pregnant, will I?*

A Congratulations! You will be able to continue training and competing with Kimmy as long as you feel able to do so. But don't be surprised if your child's first word is "dog". When you decide to halt is up to you.

You may suspend training immediately I have friends who gave up agility in their third month and passed their dogs to their husbands to take to training and competitions. This meant that life didn't change very much. Although taking a back seat, they were still involved in the social whirl of agility. At shows they could help in the score tent when they weren't grooming for their other halves. Just make sure that if you decide to sit on the side lines, you make your coaching positive and don't sound like a nag. Do not wail, "Why did you let Kimmy take the tunnel instead of jump number ten?" Instead, say "let's work together on why Kimmy was eliminated so we can avoid traps like that in the future".

You may continue to the bitter end of your pregnancy I have watched a lady who was in her ninth month work her dog at an agility show. She had the judge and spectators in the palm of her hand because we all thought the baby would present at any moment. She waddled a few steps here and there and managed a top ten place. The

Above: *Pregnancy is a very special time for your family and pet. Let caution be your watchword. Don't risk it by falling on the agility field and harming your baby.*

dog was superbly trained and worked at a distance while responding quickly to directional commands. She gave birth the following week. The woman is exceptional. She is amazing and so are her dogs.

Comfort and safety should be your prime considerations As you grow larger and your shape changes, you probably won't be able to move around the agility course so easily and you will tire more quickly. And remember that if you slip on wet grass, you could hurt not only yourself but your growing baby.

Listen to your instructor If your instructor thinks that the continued training of your dog during your pregnancy is doing you no favours, he will say so. During pregnancy your timing will be off and your body language will be gravid. Kimmy will wonder what's up. You will start making errors on the course that you normally would not make and become frustrated. Kimmy won't thank you. And neither will your instructor if you give birth or fall over in his class. When he starts keeping a first aid box by his side and covering his eyes when it is your turn, it's time to stop.

More Women's Troubles

Q *I am a lady agility handler and I'm a slave to my hormones. I suffer painful period cramps and really don't feel like running my dog, Luger. If I go to training, I can't remember the course and I blame Luger for taking the wrong turn. PMT is a nightmare! Can you help?*

A It's all too easy to blame five faults or an elimination on raging hormones. Without a doubt, many of us ladies do not feel ourselves when we are premenstrual. We become short-tempered and moody. Our bodies seem to have a life of their own. No wonder our friends, family and dogs try to stay out of our way! Try and remember that although your body, mind and emotions may change when you are premenstrual, your dog remains constant in his affection and loyalty.

Damage control Preventative measures go a long way towards reducing the symptoms of PMT. Make sure your diet is healthy and you eat regular meals.

Below: *Try yoga to relax. Your dog will want to go with you to the spot in your mind where you find inner peace.*

Get a good night's sleep. Avoid stress and learn to relax. Yoga teaches you how to breathe as well as how to relieve tension. I have a friend who swears by it ... And so does her dog.

Change your expectations If it is that time of the month, work on something light and fun rather than training exercises that require concentration and precision. Leave refining your contacts to another time. Forget about weave entries. Concentrate on motivation exercises or general conditioning. This is not the time to try and teach Luger something new. If you are not totally with it, he's bound to make mistakes.

Have a break Practice does make perfect, but give yourself a break for holidays and saints' days – and PMT days. If you think you will not be able to accomplish anything positive, have a rest. Give agility a miss. You and Luger will return to the training ground refreshed and eager to get stuck in.

Grin and bear it Sometimes working your dog is unavoidable. Show organizers are not going to rearrange the competition calendar just because you are premenstrual. So get on with it. There are plenty of other ladies out there who feel bloated and irritable. For the few minutes that you are running in the ring, try to be a human being and agility handler. Remind yourself that a little exercise is good for cramps!

Dogs are wonderful, forgiving creatures. They love us even when we haven't brushed our teeth or combed our hair. And they still think we are the best person in the whole world despite PMT.

Agility Wheels

Q *I am a wheelchair user and bought my Golden Retriever, Reekie, as a companion. She has opened the doors to a whole new world. I take her to obedience classes and have met a group of fellow dog lovers who are now my best friends. We now enter heelwork to music competitions and have done very well. If we try agility, do you think we will be biting off more than we can chew?*

A I think you are already a very able dog trainer who will be able to go far in whatever canine sport you choose. If you want to do something, have a go. Adapt the task to your abilities. You won't be alone and you're ahead of the game. Reekie is already au fait with obedience basics and is clicker trained.

Growing number There are a growing number of agility competitors who work their dogs from a wheelchair with excellent results. Choose an instructor who shares your ambitions and has an accessible venue.

Training strategies The strategies you use to train Reekie may be a little different from those used by the rest of the class. You will have to develop your own ideas for teaching agility basics like the contacts or the weaves. Don't be afraid to double handle the initial stages. And your training focus may be a little different, too. Wheelchair handlers need their dogs to work independently from their position on the course. Your instructor will help you find a way to teach Reekie distance control and obstacle discrimination as these skills will be especially useful to you.

Wheelchair power Start training Reekie with what you've got. You will be accustomed to its operation and there will be enough new things to learn in class. Later on, you may decide to upgrade to something more powerful and

manoeuvrable. Look at chairs that respond quickly and can cope with different terrain, especially muddy, bumpy fields.

Invaluable resource Consult the Disabled Handlers Association. It is an invaluable resource and will help you find out how other people have met training and mobility challenges on the agility field.

If you do decide to try agility, you will make even more friends who are dog lovers. Make agility a game that's fun to play and Reekie will love learning how to jump hurdles and climb the A-frame with you. If you live in Britain, you can register with the Disabled Handlers League and submit your places for the points table. And why stop there? If you are feeling adventurous, consider entering the ParAgility World Cup (PAWC).

Wheelchair users and their dogs love agility, too!

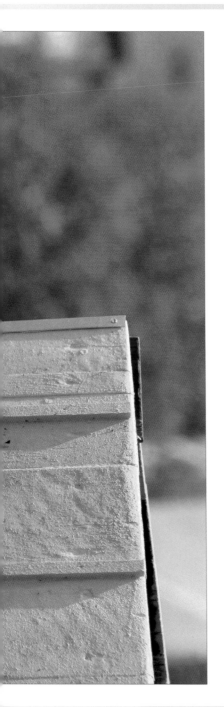

RESOURCES
& INDEX

Don't you hate it when someone gives you advice but not the resources to act on it. "Go find your local agility club", they tell you. Where do you start looking? Do they expect you to drive around looking for a field of hurdles? If you are lucky enough to find a field full of agility equipment, do you have to camp by the gate waiting to meet someone to ask about memberships and classes? There has to be an easier way! There is. The Resource section is intended to give you a starting point in your hunt for further agility information. Where can you buy a clicker? How do you find a canine massage therapist? What agility shows are held in July? The more answers you find, the more questions you'll want to ask. And the more resources you'll discover. Good luck and have fun learning new things!

Resources

Entering a show

There will be more than one organization sanctioning agility shows in your country of residence. Each is governed by its own set of rules and regulations regarding registration, competition and progression through classes. Some organizations are large national bodies covering a number of canine disciplines in addition to agility and others are regional groups that are purely focused on agility. Any additional services that they offer will vary but may include newsletters, lists of training clubs, or discussion forums. In the United Kingdom the main organizations are:

The Kennel Club

1 Clarges Street, London W1J 8AB
Telephone: 0870 606 6750
www.the-kennel-club.org.uk

UKAgility

Langdale, Church Street, Offenham, Evesham, Worcestershire, WR11 8RW
Telephone: 01386 424218
info@ukagility.com
www.ukagility.com

Agility Addicts

Contact via website
www.agilityaddicts.freeuk.com

EMDAC (East Midlands Dog Agility Club)

June Bass
54 Ferneley Crescent,
Melton Mowbray,
Leicestershire, LE13 1RZ
Telephone: 01664 500327
www.emdac.co.uk

BAA (British Agility Association)

June Bass
54 Ferneley Crescent, Melton Mowbray,
Leicestershire, LE13 1RZ
Telephone: 01664 500327
www.baa.uk.net

International

International competition is growing and there are a number of organizations, each with its own rules and regulations, hosting world championship competitions. The **FCI** (Fédération Cynologique Internationale) is the oldest and best known. To participate, your Kennel Club must be a member or associate of the FCI and your dog must be a pure breed recognized by your home Kennel Club. By contrast, the **IMCA** (International Mix and Breed Championship Agility) is open to both pedigree and mixed breed dogs. This competition is held in conjunction with **PAWC** (ParAgility World Cup) for disabled handlers. The **IFCS** (International Federation of Cynological Sports) also welcomes pedigrees and their crosses. It holds a biennial event and countries must be IFCS members or associate organizations in order to be represented. And, not to be overlooked, the **European Open** has a growing number of competitors of both pedigrees and crosses each year. The introduction of pet passports has meant that many people are combining a holiday abroad with agility competition. And Britain is likewise receiving her share of overseas visitors to events like the Kennel Club International Festival.

Looking for a training club

Your Kennel Club will have a list of affiliated agility clubs, but don't let that prevent you from looking around further. There are probably a number of unaffiliated or independent training clubs near you. You can find them on:

Agilitynet

Agilitynet has the most inclusive list of clubs in the UK plus advice and helpful hints on finding a club that is best for you and your dog. You can search by club name, county or region.

Ellen Rocco
38 Northolme Road, London N5 2UU
Telephone: 020 7359 6461
Fax: 020 7704 1906
www.agilitynet.com and www.agilitynet.co.uk

Are you a disabled handler looking for help and support?

The Disabled Handlers Association was set up in 2005 and is run by disabled handlers for disabled handlers. There's a league table too!

The Disabled Handlers Association

Co-founded by Anne Gill
63 Fairfax Road, Farnborough, Hants, GU14 8JR
Telephone: 01252 661442
Email: annegill48@hotmail.com
and
Philippa Armstrong
Telephone: 01803 867074
Email: philippa.armstrong@lineone.net
www.disabledhandlersassociation.co.uk

Becoming an instructor

Put something back into agility and teach. There are a number of routes you can take. Each organizations will have specific criteria for certifying trainers and courses will vary in length and assessment methods.

APDT (Association for Pet Dog Trainers)

PO Box 17,
Kempsford, GL7 4WZ
Telephone:
01285 810811
apdtoffice@aol.com
www.apdt.co.uk

The Agility Club

Bobby Rowling
15 Links Road, Ashtead, Surrey KT21 2HB
Telephone: 01372 276391
www.agilityclub.co.uk

BIPDT (The British Institute of Professional Dog Trainers)

Bowstone Gate,
Nr Disley, Cheshire SK12 2AW
Telephone: 01663 762772
www.bipdt.com

Something to read in bed

Clean Run Magazine

LLC 35 North Chicopee Street,
Chicopee, MA 01020, USA
Telephone: (413) 532 1389
www.cleanrun.com

Agility Eye Magazine

Margaret Pennington
74 Coastal Road, Hest Bank,
Lancaster LA2 6HQ
www.agilityeye.co.uk

Agility Voice Magazine

Virginia Harry
6 Fane Way, Maidenhead,
Berkshire SL6 2TL
Telephone: 01628 680823
editor@agilityclub.co.uk
www.agilityclub.co.uk

Getting the latest news

If your want an internet magazine to open with your morning cup of coffee, click onto Agilitynet. It is the largest dog agility site in the UK with essential information about shows, training and special features. It also has a flea market, message board and club listing.

Agilitynet

Ellen Rocco
38 Northolme Road,
London N5 2UU
Telephone: 020 7359 6461
Fax: 020 7704 1906
www.agilitynet.com and www.agilitynet.co.uk

Hands-on therapies

A massage for you or your dog can be a luxurious bit of pampering, perfect after a hard day's training. Or it may be part of a programme of remedial therapy after an injury. However, it is advisable to consult with your doctor or vet before booking an appointment for any hands-on treatment.

AMA (Animal Massage Association)

This association offers a national register of qualified animal massage practitioners.
Telephone: 01626 852485
www.animalmassageassociation.com
info@animalmassageassociation.com

Galen Therapy Centre

The Centre offers canine massage therapy to treat injuries or improve performance. It also offers workshops and a Canine Massage Diploma for those who would like to study the subject in more detail or become professional practitioners.
Julia Robertson
Telephone: 01403 740189
Mobile: 07810 600329
Email - Julia@caninetherapy.co.uk
www.galentherapycentre

ICAT – The Institute of Complementary Animal Therapies

The Institute offers a diploma course in Canine Remedial Massage. This course is intended for anyone wishing to become a professional practitioner or for those who just want to practise these skills on their own pet.
Julie Boxall, Principal
PO Box 299, Chudleigh,
Devon, TQ13 0ZQ
Telephone: 01626 852485
www.theicat.co.uk
info@theicat.co.uk

McTimoney Chiropractic Association

Mctimoney chiropractors are qualified to treat both humans and animals. They seek to promote good health and alleviate the causes of aches and pains through the realignment of the spine. They use their hands to adjust the bones in the body.
Marisa Pinnock DC AMC FMCA,
Chair, Animals Group
McTimoney Chiropractic Association
Crowmarsh Gifford, Wallingford OX10 8DJ

Telephone: 01883 743355
E-mail : marisap@enterprise.net
www.mctimoney-chiropractic.org

Tellington Ttouch

The Tellington TTouch uses massage
and ground exercises to help animals improve
overall athletic ability while at the same time
enriching the bond between the animal and owner.
   Sarah Fisher,
   UK Tteam Centre, Tilley Farm, Timsbury Road,
   Farmborough, Nr. Bath, Somerset, BA2 0AB
   Telephone: 01761 471182
   www.ttouchtteam.co.uk
   www.tilleyfarm.co.uk

Getting fit for agility

Improve fitness and performance with **SAQ®**
(Speed Agility Quickness) and **DAQ®** (Dog Agility
Quickness) continuums. Each continuum is a
progressive sequence of movements and physical
training phases that can be applied to the sport of
agility. You and your dog will benefit, so don't delay.
Courses can be booked at PACE-Agility.

PACE-Agility (Performance Agility Coaching & Evaluation)

   Steve and Yvonne Croxford
   Shade Cottage, Coventry Road, Wigston Parva,
   Leicestershire, LE10 3AP
   Telephone: 01455 220245
   www.pace-agility.org
   www.daqinternational.com

See you and your dog in lights!

You may already be on film – your best and your
worst runs! Check out this website to find out if you
or your friends have been caught on video.

Agility Movies

   Contact: Amanda Brophy
   Email: amanda@agilitymovies.com
   www.agilitymovies.com

Learn to click!

If you want to buy a clicker, polish your clicker
training skills or participate in a clicker challenge,
visit these sites.

Crosskeys Training and Behaviour Centre

   Collier Row Road, Romford, Essex, RM5 2BH
   Telephone: 020 8590 3604
   www.clickerzoneuk.co.uk

Learning About Dogs

   PO Box 13, Chipping Campden, GL55 6WX
   Telephone: 01386 430189
   www.learningaboutdogs.com

How to find the perfect present for you and your dog

Not everyone wants flowers and chocolate. And not
everyone wants to pound the pavement looking for
the perfect present. Explore these online shopping
sites instead. You will find everything you will ever
need to compete, train and love your dog. There is
camping equipment, clothes, toys and hundreds of
other things you have never even thought of...
Why not treat yourself to an A-frame!

The Agility Warehouse

   www.agilitywarehouse.com and
   www.agilitywarehouse.co.uk

The Clean Run Online Store

   www.cleanrun.com

Crosskeys Select Books at Discover Pets

   www.discoverpets.co.uk

Thanks For Their Help

Acknowledgements

This book must mention my ninth grade teacher, Mrs. Lucas, who told me, "You must write!". Mrs. Lucas tried to commit suicide under a train a week later and was subsequently committed so I never really took her threat seriously. That is until Ellen Rocco of www.agilitynet.co.uk asked me to write a book review for her internet magazine. Ellen has encouraged me to put fingers to keyboard and supported me for many years. She gave me the job of "Agility Auntie" for Agilitynet and it is that body of work that forms the foundations of this book. I would also like to thank my friend Melanie Raymond who not only shared my excitement for the project but has continued to be enthusiastic to the very last page, all my colleagues at VetsNow Emergency Service (Northampton) who held my hand when I was flagging and Anthony Medcalfe who loaned me Ridducks Agility School to help in the book's production and photoshoot. Thanks also to Philippa Armstrong for her input on "agility wheels". Moreover, it is impossible to forget the many people who have helped me problem-solve in my own agility career. Thank you Mary Ray for showing me how to "smush" cheese! And where would I be without my Mom who allowed me to have a variety of pets eventually leading to my first agility dog, Aslan? Aslan got me hooked on agility and I've been an addict ever since.

My thanks also to everyone who agreed to take part in the photoshoot (and their dogs). What naturals you all are in front of the camera – true agility stars! Step forward each of you and take a bow…

Peter Alliot and Ember and Sunny

Harriet Anthony and Bella

Sarah Arnold and Toody

Maureen Goodchild and Woody and Lou

James Greenhow and Marley

Lisa Greenhow and Tyler and Bailey

Amy Lightfoot and Basil

Lynn Marlow and Shandy

Jill Pipe and Marco

Toni Slater and Peggy

Lynet Smith and Sara

Marion Watkinson and Jenny

Jo Bidgood and Henry

Lorraine Chappell and Meg and Deefa

Maggie Cheek and Rupert and Pascal

Christine Cowling and Conker

Carolyn Errington and Murphy

Jo-Ann Essex and Sumi-e, Suggs and Bacon

Gillian Griffiths and Bryn

Clare Griffiths and Lucy

Tim Griffiths and Travis

Bridget Hardy and Archie

Bridget Jamieson and Rupert, Brodie and Bailey

Ken Jeffery and Suki III

David Piper and Barclay and Jack

Soraya Porter and Ernie

Maxine Pymer and Bob

Christine Ripley and Rufus and Robbie

Alma Ryman and Tilly and Starr

Tony Ryman and Bluey

Lesley Wells and Barney and Bonnie

Index

Picture Credits

Unless otherwise credited below, all the photographs that appear in this book were taken by **Mark Burch** especially for Interpet Publishing.

The credits for the inset pictures that appear on pages 1-3 number the images from left to right on their appropriate pages.

Jane Burton, Warren Photographic: 95 bottom, 114, 160, 170 bottom, 174 bottom.

Interpet Archive (Neil Sutherland): 50, 51, 54 both, 57 bottom, 58, 62 bottom, 64 top, 66, 67, 68 top, 69, 72 top, 78, 79 bottom, 81 bottom, 97, 98, 110 both, 112, 146 left, 149, 153 left, 161, 168 top, 183 top left, 190.

iStockphoto.com:
Ana Abejon: 165.
Scott Anderson: 189.
Galina Barskaya: 57 top left.
Tamara Bauer: 131.
Dagmar Bensberg: 70 top.
Hagit Berkovich: 188.
David Brimm: 64 bottom.
Captured Nuance: 184.
Andraz Cerar: 22 top, 22 bottom, 71, 75.
Robert Churchill: 72 bottom.
Anne Clark: 96.
James Cote: 1 (inset 2 and inset 4).
Barry Crossley: 174 top.
Jaimie Duplass: 175 top, 175 bottom.
Lee Feldstein: 76, 83 top, 171.
Joy Fera: 81 top.
Peter Finnie: 1 (inset 3).
Bill Hanson: 163.
Mandy Hartfree-bright: 183 right.
Andrew Hill: 36.
Rick Hyman: 99 bottom.
Eric Isselée: 1 (inset 5), 2-3 (inset 3), 47 top right, 178.
Suzann Julien: 185.
Renee Lee: 99 top.
Sue McDonald: 34, 74, 84 bottom.
Dennis Minix: 182.
Peter Mlekuz: 123.
Iztok Nok: 15 top, 17, 23, 24 top, 31 top right, 47 bottom, 77, 109.

Leif Norman: 146 right.
Photopix: 2-3 (inset 9).
Thomas Polen: 83.
Glenda Powers: 186.
Tina Rencelj: 80.
Ashok Rodrigues: 187 right.
David Scheuber: 28 top.
Leigh Schindler: 169.
Tomislav Stajduhar: 111 bottom.
Jolanta Stozek: 152.
Willie B Thomas: 166 left, 168 bottom left, 181.
Jan Tyler: 25, 59 bottom, 166 top right.
Craig Veltri: 153 right.
André Weyer: 32.
Roger Whiteway: 154 left.
Annette Wiechmann: 27, 59 top, 167.

Shutterstock Inc:
Laura Aqui: 61.
Andraz Cerar: 8, 26-7, 33, 192-3.
J Crihfield: 42.
Waldemar Dabrowski: 87 top left.
Slobodan Djajic: 38.
Dewayne Flowers: 85.
Sergey Ivanov: 204.
JD: 40 top.
JoLin: 30, 89.
Erik Lam: 47 top left.
Michael Ledray: 53 top.
George Lee: 2-3 (inset 10), 200.
Litwin Photography: 73 top.
Cristi Matei: 62 centre.
Tammy McAllister: 39.
Iztok Nok: 1 (inset 1), 2-3 (inset 1, inset 2, inset 4, inset 5, inset 7, inset 11, inset 12), 20, 44, 45, 60-1, 73 bottom, 87 right, 88, 90, 104-5, 105, 115, 124, 126, 127, 164-5, 128, 129, 136, 139, 141, 142-3, 154 top right, 158, 162 left, 176, 177 top, 177 bottom, 179, 193, 195, 196, 203, 206, 207.
Jason X Pacheco: 100.
SI: 84 top, 95 top, 143, 170 top, 191.
Fernando Jose Vasconcelos Soares: 55.
Claudia Steininger: 53 bottom.
Magdalena Szachowska: 82.
Jeffrey Van Daele: 37.